*"We, the jury, find the
defendant guilty of murder
in the first degree."*

PERRY MASON
HAD LOST HIS FIRST CASE!

Paul Drake, his voice sympathetic, said,
"Gosh, Perry, it's. . . . I can imagine how you
feel. It's the first time you've ever had a client
convicted of murder."

Mason turned to Drake, his eyes cold and
hard. "No client of mine is ever convicted of
anything until I stop trying. Now get the
address of that girl and let's get going!"

THE CASE OF THE TERRIFIED TYPIST and
THE CASE OF THE GILDED LILY
were originally published by
William Morrow & Company, Inc.

Two Complete Novels by
ERLE STANLEY GARDNER

PERRY MASON

2 in 1

The Case of
the Terrified Typist

The Case of
the Gilded Lily

PUBLISHED BY POCKET BOOKS NEW YORK

PERRY MASON 2 IN 1

POCKET BOOK edition published October, 1975

The Case of the Terrified Typist

William Morrow edition published 1956

POCKET BOOK edition published October, 1958

7th printing......................August, 1975

The Case of the Gilded Lily

William Morrow edition published 1956

POCKET BOOK edition published June, 1959

7th printing......................August, 1975

L

Standard Book Number: 671-78780-2.
Front cover photograph by Fred Samperi.

Printed in the U.S.A.

The Case of
the Terrified Typist

FOREWORD

IT IS SO TRITE to say that truth is stranger than fiction that one dislikes to use the expression, yet there is absolutely no other way of describing the strange situation that took place in Texas, where within the framework of the law a principality was created that was completely foreign to all of our American traditions.

All of this started out innocently enough. A large section of Texas was peopled by Spanish-speaking citizens and an American acquired a position of leadership and started advising these people how to mark their ballots. Apparently he had their best interests at heart and received their virtually unanimous support.

The community became known as the Principality of Duval and the man who gave the instructions to the voters was known as the "Duke of Duval."

Later on this situation developed to a point where successors to the Duke of Duval used their power to establish what was in effect a principality within a state. That principality became steeped in hatreds and ruled by fear, and fear ruled with an iron hand.

The state seemed powerless. The whole machinery of government in Duval was in the hands of one person.

Then my friend the Honorable John Ben Shepperd became the attorney general of the State of Texas.

Shepperd went into Duval and started fighting.

It was a knockdown drag-out fight. The story of what happened is so lurid, so utterly inconceivable that it staggers the imagination.

John Ben Shepperd won that fight. It took courage, honesty, competence, resourcefulness and guts.

When I first knew John Ben Shepperd, he was the attorney general of Texas. I am honored that he made me an honorary special assistant attorney general of Texas, and my commission as such hangs in my office today.

Texans don't do things the way other people do. If a Texan likes you, he is for you a hundred per cent. If he doesn't like you, he may or may not be polite, but his formal politeness will be as frigid as a blizzard wind in the Texas Panhandle.

Texas is a big, raw, blustering state with a highly developed sense of the dramatic, a spirit of the Old West still rampant, and is peopled by citizens who think only in terms of the superlative. This causes many people to doubt the sincerity of the Texan. The trouble is some of these critics simply don't understand the Texan language and the Texan thought. When a Texan uses superlatives, he is completely sincere. He thinks in superlatives. He expresses himself in superlatives.

On one of my recent trips to Texas, I was the speaker at a noonday banquet. My big plate tried in vain to hold a Texas-size steak which overflowed it at the edges.

As soon as that banquet was over, the chief of police rushed me out to his automobile and with red light and screaming siren, we started for the airport.

At the airport my friend the late Jim West, one of Texas' rugged multimillionaires, had his plane waiting and as soon as he heard the siren screaming in the distance, he started warming up the motors. By the time the police car speeded onto the airport's runway and stopped within a few feet of the airplane, the motors were warmed up and ready for a take-off.

I was rushed up into the interior of the plane, the door slammed, the motors roared and the plane was in the air.

An hour and a half later, almost an hour of which had been spent in flying over Jim West's ranch, we came down at the ranch house. A servant put a gallon flagon in my hand. It was filled with cold, frothy beer. It was a hot summer day and I drank copiously of the beer. As fast as I lowered the flagon an inch or so, someone would reach over my shoulder with a couple more cans of ice-cold beer and keep it up to the brim.

Shortly afterward we had a "little old barbecue." I was given a steak that was so big it had to be served on a platter.

When we had finished that repast, Jim West announced that his nearest neighbor, who lived thirty-odd miles away, wanted to meet our group and we were transferred in specially made Jeeps to the ranch of Dolph Briscoe.

Briscoe greeted us with typical Texas hospitality. He invited us in for a "snack."

The snack consisted of—you guessed it. And Dolph Briscoe was properly apologetic.

"That steer," he said in his Texas drawl, "played me false. I tried to make him weigh a ton, but after he got up to nineteen hundred and sixty pounds he just wouldn't put on any more fat, and in order to have the meat properly aged for you folks when you got here, I had to kill him when he was just forty pounds short of a ton. I'm not going to lie to you folks, that there's a Texas steer but he's forty pounds short of a ton."

Now that's Texas. If you don't understand it, it seems weird and bizarre. If you understand it, you love it and you love the Texans, and your understanding has to be based on the fact that the underlying keynote of the Texan is sincerity. If he likes you, he wants to do everything he can for you.

There is the old story of the Texan who went out to lunch with his friend. After lunch the friend stopped in at a Cadillac agency to look over a new car he was thinking of buying.

When he finally made up his mind to buy the car, the Texan whipped out his checkbook. "Here," he said, "this one is on me. You paid for the lunch."

That story is probably an exaggeration, but it is nevertheless typical.

My friend John Ben Shepperd is a Texan. When he embarked upon a career of law enforcement as attorney general of Texas, he went all the way. Entirely at his own expense he published a newsletter roundup of crime and justice for the Lone Star State. He tried to see that all law enforcement officers knew what the law was.

As my friend the Honorable Park Street, a prominent trial attorney of San Antonio and for years an associate of mine on the Court of Last Resort, expressed it, "Many a criminal is caught in Texas by a cowboy-booted constable or sheriff whose standard equipment includes a .45 revolver and a blue-backed *Peace Officer's Handbook,* written by John Ben Shepperd."

"Crime," drawls John Ben Shepperd, "is not sluggish or unintelligent. It plays infinite variations on its own theme, developing new forms and methods. Like the hare and the tortoise, it outruns us unless we plod relentlessly along carrying the law forward on our backs."

From time to time, I made talks on law enforcement in Texas while John Ben Shepperd was the attorney general of the state.

From the time my group arrived at the borders of Texas, we would be met by assistant attorneys general, airplanes and prominent citizens. We would be whisked from place to place at breath-taking schedule, yet the whole itinerary would be carefully planned to the last detail: Planes would be waiting for us at dawn, would take off on schedule and arrive on schedule for breakfast appointments and conferences. Lunches would be at points several hundred miles distant and we would be back in Austin for dinner. The pace was relentless and terrific. Yet the assistants assured me that this was the tempo at which John Ben Shepperd conducted his office.

Heaven knows how many honors were conferred upon him. I do know that he was the deserving recipient of three honorary Doctor of Laws degrees, and I also know that one of the honors he valued at the top of the list was a simple plaque presented to him by United Mothers and Wives of Duval County. It says, "To John Ben Shepperd, who purchased with courage and Christian integrity the right of our children to grow up uncorrupted and unafraid."

And so I dedicate this book to my friend—

THE HONORABLE JOHN BEN SHEPPERD

—Erle Stanley Gardner

Temecula, 1955

CAST OF CHARACTERS

1

PERRY MASON EYED THE BRIEF WHICH JACKSON, HIS LAW clerk, had submitted for his approval.

Della Street, sitting across the desk from the lawyer, correctly interpreted the expression on Mason's face.

"What was wrong with it?" she asked.

"Quite a few things," Mason said. "In the first place, I've had to shorten it from ninety-six pages to thirty-two."

"Good heavens," Della said. "Jackson told me he had already shortened it twice and he couldn't take out another word."

Mason grinned. "How are we fixed for typists, Della?"

"Stella is down with the flu and Annie is simply snowed under an avalanche of work."

"Then we'll have to get an outside typist," Mason told her. "This brief has to be ready for the printer tomorrow."

"All right. I'll call the agency and have a typist sent up right away," Della Street promised.

"In the meantime," Mason told her, "I'm going over this thing once again and see if I can't take out another four or five pages. Briefs shouldn't be written to impress the client. They should be concise, and above all, the writer should see that the Court has a clear grasp of the *facts* in the case before there is any argument about the *law*. The judges know the law. If they don't, they have clerks who can look it up."

Mason picked up a thick blue pencil, held it poised in his hand, and once more started reading through the sheaf of pages, which already showed signs of heavy editing. Della Street went to the outer office to telephone for a typist.

When she returned Mason looked up. "Get one?"

"The agency doesn't have one at the moment. That is, those they have are rather mediocre. I told them you wanted one who is fast, accurate and willing; that you didn't want to have to read this thing through again and find a lot of typographical errors."

Mason nodded, went on with his editing. "When can we expect one, Della?"

"They promised to have someone who would finish it by two-thirty tomorrow afternoon. But they said it might be a while before they could locate just the girl they wanted. I told them there were thirty-two pages."

"Twenty-nine and a half," Mason corrected, smilingly. "I've just cut out another two and a half pages."

Mason was just finishing his final editing half an hour later when Gertie, the office receptionist, opened the door and said, "The typist is here, Mr. Mason."

Mason nodded and stretched back in his chair. Della started to pick up the brief, but hesitated as Gertie came in and carefully closed the door behind her.

"What's the trouble, Gertie?"

"What did you say to frighten her, Mr. Mason?"

Mason glanced at Della Street.

"Heavens," Della said, "I didn't talk with *her* at all. We just rang up Miss Mosher at the agency."

"Well," Gertie said, lowering her voice, "this girl's scared to death."

Mason flashed a quick smile at Della Street. Gertie's tendency to romanticize and dramatize every situation was so well known that it was something of an office joke.

"What did *you* do to frighten her, Gertie?"

"*Me!* What did *I* do? Nothing! I was answering a call at the switchboard. When I turned around, this girl was standing there by the reception desk. I hadn't heard her come in. She tried to say something, but she could hardly talk. She just stood there. I didn't think so much of it at the time, but afterward, when I got to thinking it over, I

2

realized that she was sort of holding on to the desk. I'll bet her knees were weak and she—"

"Never mind what you thought," Mason interrupted, puzzled. "Let's find out what happened, Gertie. What did you tell her?"

"I just said, 'I guess you're the new typist,' and she nodded. I said, 'Well, you sit over at that desk and I'll get the work for you.'"

"And what did she do?"

"She went over to the chair and sat down at the desk."

Mason said, "All right, Gertie. Thanks for telling us."

"She's absolutely terrified," Gertie insisted.

"Well, that's fine," Mason said. "Some girls are that way when they're starting on a new job. As I remember, Gertie, *you* had *your* troubles when you first came here, didn't you?"

"Troubles!" Gertie exclaimed. "Mr. Mason, after I got in the office and realized I'd forgotten to take the gum out of my mouth, I was just absolutely gone. I turned to jelly. I didn't know what to do. I—"

"Well, get back to the board," Mason told her. "I think I can hear it buzzing from here."

"Oh Lord, yes," Gertie said. "I can hear it now myself."

She jerked open the door and made a dash for the switchboard in the outer office.

Mason handed Della Street the brief and said, "Go out and get her started, Della."

When Della Street came back at the end of ten minutes Mason asked, "How's our terrified typist, Della?"

Della Street said, "If that's a terrified typist, let's call Miss Mosher and tell her to frighten all of them before sending them out."

"Good?" Mason asked.

"Listen," Della Street said.

She eased open the door to the outer office. The sound of clattering typewriter keys came through in a steady staccato.

"Sounds like hail on a tin roof," Mason said.

Della Street closed the door. "I've never seen anything like it. That girl pulled the typewriter over to her, ratcheted in the paper, looked at the copy, put her hands over the keyboard and that typewriter literally exploded into action. And yet, somehow, Chief, I think Gertie *was* right. I think she became frightened at the idea of coming up here. It may be that she knows something about you, or your fame has caused her to become self-conscious. After all," Della Street added dryly, "you're not entirely unknown, you know."

"Well," Mason said, "let's get at that pile of mail and skim off a few of the important letters. At that rate the brief will be done in plenty of time."

Della Street nodded.

"You have her at the desk by the door to the law library?"

"That seemed to be the only place to put her, Chief. I fixed up the desk there when I knew we were going to need an extra typist. You know how Stella is about anyone using *her* typewriter. She thinks a strange typist throws it all out of kilter."

Mason nodded, said, "If this girl is good, Della, you might arrange to keep her on for a week or two. We can keep her busy, can't we?"

"I'll say."

"Better ring up Miss Mosher and tell her."

Della Street hesitated. "Would it be all right if we waited until we've had a chance to study her work? She's fast, all right, but we'd better be sure she's accurate."

Mason nodded, said, "Good idea, Della. Let's wait and see."

2

DELLA STREET PLACED A SHEAF OF PAGES ON MASON'S desk. "Those are the first ten pages of the brief, Chief."

Mason looked at the typewritten sheets, gave a low whistle and said, "Now *that's* what I call typing!"

Della Street picked up one of the pages, tilted it so that the light reflected from the smooth surface. "I've tried this with two or three sheets," she said, "and I can't see where there's been a single erasure. She has a wonderful touch and she certainly is hammering it out."

Mason said, "Ring up Miss Mosher. Find out something about this girl. What's her name, Della?"

"Mae Wallis."

"Get Miss Mosher on the line."

Della Street picked up the telephone, said to Gertie at the switchboard, "Mr. Mason wants Miss Mosher at the secretarial agency, Gertie. . . . Never mind, I'll hold the line."

A moment later Della Street said, "Hello, Miss Mosher? . . . Oh, she is? . . . Well, I'm calling about the typist she sent up to Mr. Mason's office. This is Della Street, Mr. Mason's secretary. . . . Are you sure? . . . Well, she must have left a note somewhere. . . . Yes, yes . . . well, I'm sorry. . . . No, we don't want *two* girls. . . . No, no. Miss Mosher sent one up—a Mae Wallis. I'm trying to find out whether she'll be available for steady work during the next week. . . . Please ask Miss Mosher to call when she comes in."

Della Street hung up the phone, turned to Perry Mason. "Miss Mosher is out. The girl she left in charge doesn't know about anyone having been sent up. She found a note on the desk to get us a typist. It was a memo Miss Mosher had left before she went out. The names of three girls were on it, and this assistant has been trying to locate the girls. One of them was laid up with flu, another one was on a job, and she was trying to locate the third when I called in."

"That's not like Miss Mosher," Mason said. "She's usually very efficient. When she sent this girl up, she should have destroyed the memo. Oh, well, it doesn't make any difference."

"Miss Mosher's due back in about an hour," Della Street said. "I left word for her to call when she comes in."

Again Mason tackled the work on his desk, stopping to see a client who had a three-thirty appointment, then returning to dictation.

At four-thirty Della Street went out to the outer office, came back and said, "She's still going like a house afire, Chief. She's really pounding them out."

Mason said, "That copy had been pretty badly hashed up and blue-penciled with strike-outs and interlineations."

"It doesn't seem to bother her a bit," Della Street said. "There's lightning in that girl's finger tips. She—"

The telephone on Della Street's desk shrilled insistently. Della Street, with her hand on the receiver, finished the sentence, ". . . certainly knows how to play a tune on a keyboard."

She picked up the receiver, said, "Hello. . . . Oh, yes, Miss Mosher. We were calling about the typist you sent up. . . . What? . . . You didn't? . . . Mae Wallis? . . . She *said* she came from your agency. She said you sent her. . . . Why, yes, that's what I understood she said. . . . Well, I'm sorry, Miss Mosher. There's been some mistake—but this girl's certainly competent. . . . Why, yes, she's got the work almost finished. I'm terribly sorry, I'll speak with her and— Are you going to be there for a while? . . . Well, I'll speak with her and call you back. But that's what she said . . . yes, from your agency. . . . All right, let me call you back."

Della Street dropped the phone into its cradle.

"Mystery?" Mason asked.

"I'll say. Miss Mosher says *she* hasn't sent anyone up. She's had a hard time getting girls lined up, particularly ones with qualifications to suit you."

"Well, she got one this time," Mason said, fingering through the brief. "Or at least *someone* got her."

"So what do we do?" Della Street asked.

"By all means, find out where she came from. Are you sure she said Miss Mosher sent her?"

"That's what Gertie said."

"Are you," Mason asked, "going *entirely* on what Gertie said?"

Della Street nodded.

"You didn't talk it over with Miss Wallis?"

"No. She was out there waiting to go to work. While I was talking with you, she found where the paper and carbons were kept in the desk. She'd ratcheted them into the machine, and just held out her hand for the copy. She asked if I wanted an original and three carbons. I said that we only used an original and two for stuff that was going to the printer. She said she had one extra carbon in the machine, but that she wouldn't bother to take it out. She said that she'd only make an original and two on the next. Then she put the papers down on the desk, held her fingers poised over the keyboard for a second, then started banging out copy."

"Permit me," Mason said, "to call your attention to something which clearly demonstrates the fallacy of human testimony. You were doubtless sincere in telling Miss Mosher that Mae Wallis said she had been sent up from her agency, but if you will recall Gertie's exact words, you will remember that she said the girl seemed frightened and self-conscious, so Gertie asked her if she was the new typist. The girl nodded, and Gertie showed her to the desk. At no time did Gertie say to us that she asked her if Miss Mosher had sent her."

"Well," Della Street said, "I had the distinct impression—"

"Certainly you did," Mason said. "So did I. Only long years of cross-examining witnesses have trained me to listen carefully to what a person actually says. I am quite certain that Gertie never told us she had specifically asked this girl if she came from Miss Mosher's agency."

"Well, where *could* she have come from?"

"Let's get her in and ask her," Mason said. "And let's not let her get away, Della. I'd like to catch up on some of this back work tomorrow, and this girl is really a wonder."

Della Street nodded, left her desk, went to the outer office, returned in a moment and made motions of powdering her nose.

"Did you leave word?" Mason asked.

"Yes, I told Gertie to send her in as soon as she came back."

"How's the brief coming?"

Della Street said, "She's well along with it. The work's on her desk. It hasn't been separated yet. The originals and carbons are together. She certainly does neat work, doesn't she?"

Mason nodded, tilted back in his swivel chair, lit a cigarette and said, "Well, we'll wait until she shows up and see what she has to say for herself, Della. When you stop to think about this, it presents an intriguing problem."

After Mason had smoked a leisurely cigarette Della Street once more went to the outer office and again returned.

Mason frowned, said, "She's probably one of those high-strung girls who use up a lot of nervous energy banging away at the typewriter and then go for a complete rest, smoking a cigarette or . . ."

"Or?" Della Street asked, as Mason paused.

". . . or taking a drink. Now, wait a minute, Della. Although there's nothing particularly confidential about that brief, if we keep her on here for four or five days, she's going to be doing some stuff that *is* confidential. Suppose you slip down to the powder room, Della, and see if perhaps our demon typist has a little flask in her purse and is now engaged in chewing on a clove."

"Also," Della Street said, "I'll take a whiff to see if I smell marijuana smoke."

"Know it when you smell it?" Mason asked, smiling.

"Of course," she retorted. "I wouldn't be working for one of the greatest trial attorneys in the country without having learned at least to recognize some of the more common forms of law violation."

"All right," Mason said. "Go on down and tell her that we want to see her, Della. Try and chat with her informally for a minute and size her up a bit. You didn't talk with her very much, did you?"

"Just got her name, and that's about all. I remember asking her how she spelled her first name, and she told me M-A-E."

Mason nodded. Della Street left the room and was back within a couple of minutes.

"She isn't there, Chief."

"Well, where the devil *is* she?" Mason asked.

Della Street shrugged her shoulders. "She just got up and went out."

"Say anything to Gertie about where she was going?"

"Not a word. She just got up and walked out, and Gertie assumed she was going to the washroom."

"Now that's strange," Mason said. "Isn't that room kept locked?"

Della Street nodded.

"She should have asked for a key," Mason said. "Even if she didn't know it was locked, she'd have asked Gertie how to find it. How about her hat and coat?"

"Apparently she wasn't wearing any. She has her purse with her."

"Run out and pick up the last of the work she was doing, will you, Della? Let's take a look at it."

Della Street went out and returned with the typed pages. Mason looked them over.

"She has a few pages to go," Della Street said.

Mason pursed his lips, said, "It shouldn't take her long, Della, I certainly cut the insides out of those last few pages. That's where Jackson was waxing eloquent, bombarding the Court with a peroration on liberties, constitutional rights and due process of law."

"He was so proud of that," Della Street said. "You didn't take it *all* out, did you?"

"I took out most of it," Mason said. "An appellate court isn't interested in eloquence. It's interested in the law and the facts to which it is going to apply the law.

"Good Lord, Della, do you realize that if the appellate judges tried to read every line of all of the briefs that are submitted to them, they could work for twelve hours each day without doing one other thing, and still couldn't read the briefs?"

"Good heavens, no! Aren't they supposed to read them?"

"Theoretically, yes," Mason said. "But actually, it's a practical impossibility."

"So what do they do?"

"Most of them look through the briefs, get the law points, skip the impassioned pleas, then turn the briefs over to their law clerks.

"It's my experience that a man does a lot better when he sets forth an absolutely impartial, thoroughly honest statement of facts, including those that are unfavorable to his side as well as those that are favorable, thus giving the appellate court the courtesy of assuming the judge knows the law.

"The attorney can be of help in letting the judge know

the case to which the law is to be applied and the facts in the case. But if the judge didn't know what the law was, he wouldn't have been placed on the appellate bench in the first place. Della, what the devil *do* you suppose happened to that girl?"

"She must be in the building somewhere."

"What makes you think so?"

"Well, there again—well, it's just one of those presumptions. She certainly is coming back for her money. She put in a whale of an afternoon's work."

"She should have stayed to finish the brief," Mason said. "It wouldn't have taken her over another forty or fifty minutes, at the rate she was working."

"Chief," Della Street said, "you seem to be acting on the assumption that she's walked out and left us."

"It's a feeling I have."

Della Street said, "She probably went down to the cigar counter to buy some cigarettes."

"In which event, she'd have been back long before this."

"Yes, I suppose so. But . . . but, Chief, she's bound to collect the money for the work she's done."

Mason carefully arranged the pages of the brief. "Well, she's helped us out of quite a hole." He broke off as a series of peculiarly spaced knocks sounded on the corridor door of his private office.

"That will be Paul Drake," Mason said. "I wonder what brings *him* around. Let him in, Della."

Della Street opened the door. Paul Drake, head of the Drake Detective Agency, with offices down the corridor by the elevator, grinned at them and said, "What were *you* people doing during all of the excitement?"

"Excitement?" Mason asked.

"Cops crawling all over the building," Drake said. "And you two sitting here engaged in the prosaic activities of running a humdrum law office."

"Darned if we weren't," Mason said. "Sit down, Paul.

Have a cigarette. Tell us what it's all about. We've been putting in our time writing briefs."

"You would," Drake told him, sliding down into the big overstuffed chair reserved for clients, and lighting a cigarette.

"What's the trouble?" Mason asked.

"Police chasing some dame up here on this floor," Drake said. "Didn't they search your office?"

Mason flashed a swift, warning glance at Della Street.

"Not that I know of."

"They must have."

Mason said to Della Street, "See if Gertie's gone home, Della."

Della Street opened the door to the outer office, said, "She's just going home, Chief."

"Can you catch her?"

"Sure. She's just at the door." Della Street raised her voice, "Oh, Gertie! Can you look in here for a minute?"

Gertie, ready to leave for the evening, came to stand in the doorway of the office. "What is it, Mr. Mason?"

"Any officers in here this afternoon?" Mason asked.

"Oh, yes," Gertie said. "There was some sort of a burglary down the corridor."

Again Mason caught Della's eye.

"What did they want?" Mason asked.

"Wanted to know if everyone in the office was accounted for, whether you had anyone in with you, and whether we had seen anything of a girl burglar."

"And what did you tell them?" Mason asked, keeping his voice entirely without expression.

"I told them you were alone, except for Miss Street, your confidential secretary. That we only had the regular employees here in the office and a relief typist from our regular agency who was working on a brief."

"And then what?"

"Then they left. Why?"

12

"Oh, nothing," Mason said. "I was just wondering, that's all."

"Should I have notified you? I know you don't like to be disturbed when you're working on correspondence."

"No, it's all right," Mason said. "I just wanted to get it straight, Gertie. That's all. Good night, and have a good time."

"How did you know I have a date?" Gertie asked.

"I saw it in your eyes," Mason said, grinning. "Good night, Gertie."

"Good night," she said.

"Well," Drake said, "there you are. If you'd happened to have had some woman client in your private office, the police would have insisted on talking to you and on getting a look at the client."

"You mean they searched the floor?" Mason asked.

"They really went through the joint," Drake told him. "You see, the office where the trouble occurred is right across from the women's restroom. One of the stenographers, opening the restroom door, saw this young woman whose back was toward her fumbling with the lock on the office door, trying first one key then another.

"The stenographer became suspicious. She stood there watching. About the fourth or fifth key, the girl managed to get into the office."

"What office was it?" Mason asked.

"The South African Gem Importing and Exploration Company."

"Go on, Paul."

"Well, this stenographer was a pretty smart babe. She telephoned the manager of the building and then she went out to stand by the elevators to see if this girl would come out and take an elevator. If she did that, the stenographer had made up her mind she'd try to follow."

"That could have been dangerous," Mason said.

"I know, but this is one very spunky gal."

"She could have recognized the woman?"

"Not the woman. But she knew the way the woman was dressed. You know the way women are, Perry. She hadn't seen the woman's face, but she knew the exact color and cut of her skirt and jacket, the shade of her stockings and shoes; the way she had her hair done, the color of her hair, and all that."

"I see," Mason said, glancing surreptitiously at Della Street. "That description was, of course, given to the police?"

"Oh, yes."

"And they didn't find her?"

"No, they didn't find a thing. But the manager of the building gave them a passkey to get into the office of the gem importing company. The place looked as if a cyclone had struck it. Evidently, this girl had made a very hurried search. Drawers had been pulled out, papers dumped out on the floor, a chair had been overturned, a typewriter stand upset, with the typewriter lying on its side on the floor."

"No sign of the girl?"

"No sign of anyone. The two partners who own the business, chaps named Jefferson and Irving, came in right on the heels of the police. They had been out to lunch, and they were amazed to find how much destruction had taken place during their brief absence."

Mason said, "The girl probably ran down the stairs to another floor and took the elevator from there."

Drake shook his head. "The building manager got this stenographer who had given the description, and they went down to stand at the elevators. They watched everyone who went out. When the police showed up—and believe me, that was only a matter of a minute or two; these radio cars are right on the job—well, when the police showed up, the manager of the building briefed them on what had happened. So the police went up and the girl and the manager continued to stand at the elevators. The police weren't conspicuous about it, but they dropped in at every office on the floor, just checking up."

"And I suppose the restrooms," Mason said.

"Oh, sure. They sent a couple of girls into the restrooms right away. That was the first place they looked."

"Well," Mason said, "we seem to be doing all right, Paul. If I don't go out and get tangled up in crime, crime comes to me—at least indirectly. So Jefferson and Irving came in right after the police arrived, is that right?"

"That's right."

"And the manager of the building was down there at the elevators, waiting for this girl to come out?"

"That's right."

Mason said, "He knew, of course, the office that the girl was burglarizing?"

"Of course. He told the police what office it was and all about it. He even gave them a passkey so they could get in."

"And then he waited down there at the elevators with the stenographer who had seen this woman burglarizing the office?"

"That's right."

"A lot of elaborate precautions to catch a sneak thief."

"Well, I'm not supposed to talk about clients, Perry, and I wouldn't to anyone else, but as you know, I represent the owners of the building. It seems this gem importing company is expecting half a million dollars' worth of diamonds before long."

"The deuce!"

"That's right. You know the way they do things these days—insure 'em and ship 'em by mail."

"The strange thing," Mason said thoughtfully, "is that if Irving and Jefferson came in right on the heels of the police, with the manager of the building standing down there at the elevators, he didn't stop them and tell them that they'd find police in their office and—

"What's the matter?" Mason asked, as Drake suddenly sat bolt upright.

Drake made the motion of hitting himself on the head.

"What are you trying to do?" Mason asked.

"Knock some brains into my thick skull," Drake said. "Good Lord, Perry! The manager of the building was telling me all about this, and that point never occurred to me. Let me use the phone."

Drake moved over to the phone, called the office of the manager and said, "Paul Drake talking. I was thinking about this trouble down at the gem importing company. According to police, Irving and Jefferson, the two partners who run the place, came in while they were searching."

The receiver made squawking noises.

"Well," Drake said, *"you* were standing down at the foot of the elevators with this stenographer. Why didn't you tell them that police were in their office—" Drake was interrupted by another series of squawking noises from the receiver. After a moment the detective said, "Want me to look into it, or do you want to? . . . Okay. Call me back, will you? I'm up here in Perry Mason's office at the moment. . . . Well, wait a minute. The switchboard is disconnected for the night, I guess. I'll catch that call at my—"

"Hold it, Paul," Della Street interrupted. "I'll connect this line with the switchboard, so you can get a call back on this number."

"Okay," Drake said into the telephone. "Mason's secretary will fix the line, so this telephone will be connected on the main trunk line. Just give me a buzz when you find out about it, will you?"

Drake hung up the telephone, went back to the client's chair, grinned at Mason and said, "You'll pardon me for taking all the credit for your idea, Perry, but this is my bread and butter. I couldn't tell him the idea never occurred to me until I got to talking with you, could I?"

"No credit," Mason said. "The thing is obvious."

"Of course it's obvious," Drake said. "That's why I'm kicking myself for not thinking of it right at the start. The trouble was, we were so interested in finding out how this girl vanished into thin air that I for one completely over-looked wondering how it happened that the manager didn't stop Jefferson and his partner and tell them what was happening."

"The manager was probably excited," Mason said.

"I'll tell the world he was excited. Do you know him?"

"Not the new one. I've talked with him on the phone, and Della Street's talked with him. I haven't met him."

"He's an excitable chap. One of those hair-triggered guys who does everything right now. At that, he did a pretty good job of sewing up the building."

Mason nodded. "They certainly went to a lot of trouble trying to catch one lone female prowler."

The telephone rang.

"That's probably for you," Della Street said, nodding to Paul Drake.

Drake picked up the telephone, said, "Hello. . . . Yes, this is Paul Drake. . . . Oh, I see. Well, of course, that could have happened, all right. Funny you didn't see them. . . . I see. Well, thanks a lot. I just thought we ought to check on that angle. . . . Oh, that's all right. There's no reason why that *should* have occurred to you. . . . Not at all. I'd been intending to ask you about it, but it slipped my mind. I thought I'd better check up on it before knocking off for the night. . . . Okay. Thanks. We'll see what we can find out."

Drake hung up, grinned at Mason and said, "Now the guy thinks I was working overtime, cudgeling my brain on his problem."

"What about the two partners?" Mason asked. "What's the answer?"

"Why, they evidently walked right by him and got in the elevator. Of course, the manager and the stenographer were watching the people who were getting *out* of the elevators. At that time, right after lunch, there's quite a bit of traffic in the elevators.

"The manager just finished talking with Jefferson on the phone. Jefferson said *he* saw the manager and this girl standing there and started to ask him a question about something pertaining to the building. Then he saw from the way the man was standing that he was evidently waiting for someone, so the two partners just went on past and got in the elevator just as it was starting up."

Mason said, "That sounds plausible, all right. What do you know about Jefferson and Irving? Anything?"

"Not too much. The South African Gem Importing and Exploration Company decided to open an office here. Their business is mostly wholesale diamonds. They have their main office in Johannesburg, but there's a branch office in Paris.

"This deal was made through the Paris office. They wrote the manager of the building, received a floor plan and rental schedules, signed a lease and paid six months' rent in advance.

"They sent Duane Jefferson out from South Africa. He's to be in charge. Walter Irving came from the Paris office. He's the assistant."

"Are they doing business?"

"Not yet. They're just getting started. I understand they're waiting for a high-class burglarproof safe to be installed. They've advertised for office help and have purchased some office furniture."

"Did those two chaps bring any stock of diamonds with them?" Mason asked.

"Nope. Unfortunately, things aren't done that way any more, which has cost us private detectives a lot of business. Gems are sent by insured mail now. A half a million dollars' worth of stones are sent just as you'd send a package of soiled clothes. The shipper pays a fee for adequate insurance and deducts it as a business cost. If gems

18

are lost, the insurance company writes out its check. It's an infallible, foolproof system."

"I see," Mason said thoughtfully. "In that case, what the devil was this girl after?"

"That's the sixty-four dollar question."

"It was an empty office—as far as gems go?"

"That's right. Later on, when the first shipment of gems arrives, they'll have burglar alarms all over the place, an impregnable safe and all the trimmings. Right now it's an empty shell.

"Gosh, Perry, it used to be that a messenger would carry a shipment of jewels, and private detective agencies would be given jobs as bodyguards, special watchmen and all of that. Now, some postal employee who doesn't even carry a gun comes down the corridor with a package worth half a million, says, 'Sign here,' and the birds sign their name, toss the package in the safe and that's all there is to it.

"It's all done on a basis of percentages. The insurance business is tough competition. How'd you like it if an insurance company would insure your clients against any loss from any type of litigation? Then your clients would pay premiums, deduct them as a business cost, and—"

"The trouble with that, Paul," Mason said, "is that when they come to lock a guy in the gas chamber it would take an awful big insurance check to make him feel indifferent."

Drake grinned. "Damned if it wouldn't," he agreed.

3

WHEN PAUL DRAKE HAD LEFT THE OFFICE MASON turned to Della Street.

"Well, what do *you* think, Della?"

Della Street said, "I'm afraid it could be—it was about the same time and . . . well, sometimes I think we don't pay enough attention to Gertie because she *does* exaggerate. Perhaps this girl really was frightened, just as Gertie said, and . . . well, it could have been."

"Then she must have come in here," Mason said, "because she knew her escape was cut off. There was no other place for her to go. She had to enter some office. So she came in here blind and was trying to think of some problem that would enable her to ask for a consultation with me, when Gertie let the cat out of the bag that we were expecting a typist."

Della Street nodded.

"Go out and look around," Mason said. "I'm going out and do a little scouting myself."

"What do you want me to do?" Della Street asked.

"Look over the typewriter she was using. Look over the typewriter desk. Then go down to the restroom and look around. See if you can find anything."

"Heavens, the police have been all through the restroom."

"Look around, anyhow, Della. See if she hid anything. There's always the chance she might have had something in her possession that was pretty hot and she decided to cache it someplace and come back for it later. I'll go down and get some cigarettes."

Mason walked down the corridor and rang for an elevator, went down to the foyer and over to the cigar stand. The girl behind the counter, a tall blonde with frosty blue eyes, smiled impersonally.

"Hello," Mason said.

At the personal approach the eyes became even more coldly cautious. "Good afternoon," the girl said.

"I am looking for a little information," Mason said.

"We sell cigars and cigarettes, chewing gum, candy, newspapers and magazines."

Mason laughed. "Well, don't get me wrong."

"And don't get *me* wrong."

"I'm a tenant in the building," Mason said, "and have been for some time. You're new here, aren't you?"

"Yes, I bought the cigar stand from Mr. Carson. I—Oh, I place you now! You're Perry Mason, the famous lawyer! Excuse me, Mr. Mason. I thought you were . . . well, you know a lot of people think that just because a girl is running a cigar counter she wraps herself up with every package of cigarettes she sells."

Mason smiled. "Pardon *me*. I should have introduced myself first."

"What can I do for you, Mr. Mason?"

"Probably nothing," Mason said. "I wanted a little information, but if you're new here, I'm afraid you won't know the tenants in the building well enough to help me."

"I'm afraid that's right, Mr. Mason. I don't have too good a memory for names and faces. I'm trying to get to know the regular customers. It's quite a job."

Mason said, "There are a couple of relative newcomers here in the building. One of them is named Jefferson, the other Irving."

"Oh, you mean the ones that have that gem importing company?"

"Those are the ones. Know them?"

"I do *now*. We had a lot of excitement here this afternoon, although I didn't know anything about it. It seems their office was broken into and—"

21

"They were pointed out to you?"

"Yes. One of them—Mr. Jefferson, I believe it was—stopped here for a package of cigarettes and was telling me all about it."

"But you didn't know them before?"

"You mean by sight?"

Mason nodded.

She shook her head. "I'm sorry, I can't help you, Mr. Mason."

"Well, that's all right," Mason told her.

"Why do you ask, Mr. Mason? Are you interested in the case?"

Mason smiled. "Indirectly," he said.

"You're *so* mysterious. I may not have recognized you when you walked up, but I have heard so much about you that I feel I know you very well indeed. What's an indirect interest, Mr. Mason?"

"Nothing worth talking about."

"Well, remember that I'm rather centrally located down here. If I can ever pick up any information for you, all you have to do is to let me know. I'll be glad to co-operate in any way that I can. Perhaps I can't be so efficient now, since I am relatively new here, but I'll get people spotted and . . . well, just remember, if there's *anything* I can do, I'll be glad to."

"Thanks," Mason told her.

"Did you want me to talk with Mr. Jefferson some more? He was quite friendly and chatted away with me while I was waiting on him. I didn't encourage him, but I have a feeling . . . well, you know how those things are, Mr. Mason."

Mason grinned. "You mean that he's lonely and he likes your looks?"

Her laugh showed that she was flustered. "Well, I didn't exactly say that."

"But you feel he could be encouraged?"

"Do you want me to try?"

"Would you like to?"

"Whatever you say, Mr. Mason."

The lawyer handed her a folded twenty dollar bill. "Try and find out just where the manager of the building was when Jefferson and Irving came back from lunch."

"Thank *you*, Mr. Mason. I feel guilty taking this money, because now that you mention the manager of the building I know the answer."

"What is it?"

"They came in while the manager and a young woman were standing watching the elevators. One of the men started to approach the manager as though he wanted to ask him a question, but he saw the manager was pre-occupied watching the elevators, so he veered off.

"I didn't think anything about it at the time, but it comes back to me now that those were the two men who were pointed out to me later. I hope that's the information you wanted, Mr. Mason."

"It is, thanks."

"Thank *you*, Mr. Mason. If there's ever anything I can do for you I'd be glad to, and it isn't going to cost you a twenty every time either."

"Thanks," Mason said, "but I never want something for nothing."

"*You* wouldn't," she said, giving him her most dazzling smile.

Mason rode back up in the elevator.

Della Street, in a state of subdued excitement, was waiting to pounce on him as soon as he opened the door of his private office.

"Good heavens!" she said. "We're mixed in it up to our eyebrows."

"Go on," Mason said. "What are we mixed in?"

Della Street produced a small, square tin box.

"What," Mason asked, "do you have there?"

"A great big hunk of semi-dried chewing gum."

"And where did you get it?"

"It was plastered on the underside of the desk where Mae Wallis had been working."

"Let's take a look, Della."

Della Street slid open the lid of the box and showed Mason the chewing gum. "This is just the way it was plastered to the underside of the desk," she said.

"And what did you do?"

"Took an old safety razor blade and cut it off. You can see there is an impression of fingers where she pushed the gum up against the desk."

Mason looked at Della Street somewhat quizzically. "Well," he said, "you *are* becoming the demon detective, Della. So now we have a couple of fingerprints?"

"Exactly."

"Well," Mason told her, "we're hardly going to the police with them, Della."

"No, I suppose not."

"So in that case, since we aren't particularly anxious to co-operate with the police, it would have been just as well if you had destroyed the fingerprints in removing the gum, Della."

"Wait," she told him. "You haven't seen anything yet. You observe that that's a terrific wad of gum, Chief. A girl could hardly have had all that in her mouth at one time."

"You think it was put there in installments?" Mason asked.

"I think it was put there for a purpose," Della Street said. "I thought so as soon as I saw it."

"What purpose?" Mason asked.

Della Street turned the box over on Mason's desk so that the wad of gum fell out on the blotter. "This," she said, "is the side that was against the desk."

Mason looked at the coruscations which gleamed through a few places in the chewing gum. "Good Lord, Della!" he said. "How many are there?"

"I don't know," Della said. "I didn't want to touch it.

This is just the way it came from the desk. You can see parts of two really large-sized diamonds there."

Mason studied the wad of chewing gum.

"Now then," he said thoughtfully, "this becomes evidence, Della. We're going to have to be careful that nothing happens to it."

She nodded.

"I take it the gum is hard enough so it will keep all right?" Mason asked.

"It's a little soft on the inside, but now that the air's getting to the top, the gum is hardening rapidly."

Mason took the small tin box, replaced the gum and studied it, tilting the box backwards and forwards so as to get a good view of both the top and bottom sides of the chewing gum. "Two of those fingerprints are remarkably good latents, Della," he said. "The third one isn't so good. It looks more like the side of the finger. But those two impressions are perfect."

Della Street nodded.

"Probably the thumb and the forefinger. Which side of the desk was it on, Della?"

"Over on the right-hand side of the desk."

"Then those are probably the impressions of the right thumb and forefinger."

"So what do we do?" Della Street asked. "Do we now call in the police?"

Mason hesitated a moment, said, "I want to know a little more about what's cooking, Della. You didn't find anything in the restroom?"

Della Street said, "I became a scavenger. I dug down into the container that they use for soiled paper towels—you know, they have a big metal box with a wedge-shaped cover on top that swings back and forth and you can shove towels in from each side."

Mason nodded. "Find anything, Della?"

"Someone had used the receptacle to dispose of a lot of love letters, and the disposal must either have been very, very hasty, or else the girl certainly took no precautions to keep anyone who might be interested from getting quite an eyeful. The letters hadn't even been torn through."

"Let's take a look at them," Mason said.

Della Street said, "They were all in one bunch, and I salvaged the whole outfit. Gosh, I'm glad the rush hour is over. I would have felt pretty self-conscious if someone had come in and caught me digging down in that used towel container!"

Mason's nod showed that he was preoccupied as he examined the letters.

"What do you make of them?" Della Street asked.

"Well," Mason said thoughtfully, "either, as you suggested, the person who left them there was in very much of a hurry, or this was a plant and the person wanted to be certain that the letters would be noticed and could be read without any difficulty. In other words, it's almost too good. A girl trying to dispose of letters would hardly have been so careless about dropping them into the used-towel receptacle in one piece—unless it was a plant of some kind."

"But how about a man?" Della Street asked. "Apparently, the letters were sent to a man and—"

"And they were found in the *ladies'* restroom."

"Yes, that's so."

Mason studied one of the letters. "Now, these are rather peculiar, Della. They are written in a whimsical vein. Listen to this:

" 'My dearest Prince Charming,

" 'When you rode up on your charger the other night, there were a lot of things I wanted to say to you, but I couldn't think of them until after you had left.

" 'Somehow the glittering armor and that formidable helmet made you seem so virtuous and righteous that I felt a distant creature from another and more sordid world. . . . You perhaps don't know it, Prince Charming, but you made quite a handsome spectacle, sitting there with the visor of your helmet raised, your horse with his head down, his flanks heaving and sweating from the exertion of carrying you on that last mission to rescue the damsel in distress, the setting sun reflecting from your polished armor . . .' "

Mason paused, glanced up at Della Street, and said, "What the devil!"

"Take a look at the signature," Della Street said.

Mason turned over two pages and looked at the signature—"Your faithful and devoted Mae."

"You will notice the spelling," Della Street said. "It's M-A-E."

Mason pursed his lips thoughtfully, said, "Now, all we need, Della, is a murder to put us in a thoroughly untenable position."

"What position?"

"That of withholding important evidence from the police."

"You're not going to tell them anything about Mae Wallis?"

Mason shook his head. "I don't dare to, Della. They wouldn't make even the slightest effort to believe me. You can see the position I'd be in. I'd be trying to explain that while the police were making a search of the building in order to find the woman who had broken into the offices of the South African Gem Importing and Exploration Company, I was sitting innocently in my office; that I had no idea that I should have mentioned the typist who dropped in from nowhere at exactly the right time, who seemed completely terrified, who was supposed to have been sent from Miss Mosher's agency, even though, at the time, I *knew* that she hadn't been sent from Miss Mosher's agency."

"Yes," Della Street said, smiling. "With your connections and reputation, I can see that the police would be at least skeptical."

"Very, very skeptical," Mason said. "And since it's bad for the police to develop habits of skepticism, Della, we'll see that they aren't placed in an embarrassing position."

4

It was three days later when Perry Mason unlocked the door of his private office and found Della Street waiting for him, his desk carefully cleaned and for once the pile of mail far to one side.

"Chief," Della Street said in a voice of low urgency, "I've been trying to get you. Sit down and let me talk with you before anyone knows you're in."

Mason hung up his hat in the hat closet, seated himself at the desk, glanced at Della Street quizzically and said, "You're certainly worked up. What gives?"

"We have our murder case."

"What do you mean 'our murder case'?"

"Remember what you said about the diamonds? That we only needed a murder case to make the thing perfect?"

Mason came bolt upright in his chair. "What is it, Della? Give me the low-down."

"No one seems to know what it's all about, but Duane Jefferson of the South African Gem Importing and Exploration Company has been arrested for murder. Walter

Irving, the other member of the company, is out there in the outer office waiting for you. There's a cablegram from the South African Gem Importing and Exploration Company sent from South Africa, advising you that they are instructing their local representative to pay you two thousand American dollars as a retainer. They want you to represent Duane Jefferson."

"Murder?" Mason said. "Who the devil is the corpse, Della?"

"I don't know. I don't know very much about it. All I know is about the cablegram that came and the fact that Walter Irving has been in three times to see you. He asked that I notify him just as soon as you arrived, and this last time he decided that he wouldn't even take chances on the delay incident to a telephone call but was going to wait. He wants to see you the minute you come in."

"Send him in, Della. Let's find out what this is all about. Where's that tin box?"

"In the safe."

Mason said, "Where's the desk Mae Wallis was using when she was here?"

"I moved it back into the far corner of the law library."

"Who moved it?"

"I had the janitor and one of his assistants take it in for us."

"How are you on chewing gum, Della?"

"Pretty good. Why?"

Mason said, "Chew some gum, then use it to plaster that wad with the diamonds in it back on the desk in exactly the same place you found it."

"But there'll be a difference in freshness, Chief. That other gum is dry and hard now, and the new gum that I chew will be moist and—"

"And it will dry out if there's a long enough interval," Mason interrupted.

"How long will the interval be?"

"That," Mason told her, "will depend entirely on luck. Send Walter Irving in, Della, and let's see what this is all about."

Della Street nodded and started for the outer office.

"And fix that gum up *right away*," Mason reminded her.

"While Irving is in here?"

Mason nodded.

Della Street went to the outer office and returned with Walter Irving, a well-dressed, heavy-set man who had evidently prepared for the interview by visiting a barber shop. His hair was freshly trimmed, his nails were polished, his face had the smooth pink-and-white appearance which comes from a shave and a massage.

He was about forty-five years old, with reddish-brown, expressionless eyes, and the manner of a man who would show no surprise or emotion if half of the building should suddenly cave in.

"Good morning, Mr. Mason. I guess you don't know me. I've seen you in the elevator and you've been pointed out to me as being the smartest criminal lawyer in the state."

"Thank you," Mason said, shaking hands, and then added dryly, " 'Criminal lawyer' is a popular expression. I prefer to regard myself as a 'trial lawyer.' "

"Well, that's fine," Irving said. "You received a cablegram from my company in South Africa, didn't you?"

"That's right."

"They've authorized me to pay you a retainer for representing my associate, Duane Jefferson."

"That cablegram is a complete mystery to me," Mason said. "What's it all about?"

"I'll come to that in a moment," Irving told him. "I want to get first things first."

"What do you mean?"

"Your fees."

"What about them?"

30

Irving raised steady eyes to Mason. "Things are different in South Africa."

"Just what are you getting at?"

"Just this," Irving said. "I'm here to protect the interests of my employers, the South African Gem Importing and Exploration Company. It's a big, wealthy company. They want me to turn over a two-thousand-dollar retainer to you. They'd leave it to your discretion as to the balance of the fee. I won't do business that way. On this side of the water, criminal attorneys are inclined to grab all they can get. They— Oh, hell, Mr. Mason, what's the use of beating around the bush? My company has an idea that it's dealing with a barrister in a wig and gown. It doesn't have the faintest idea of how to deal with a criminal lawyer."

"Do you?" Mason asked.

"If I don't I'm sure as hell going to try and find out. I'm protecting my company. How much is it going to cost?"

"You mean the total fee?"

"The total fee."

Mason said, "Tell me about the case, just the general facts and I'll answer your question."

"The facts are utterly cockeyed. Police raided our office. Why, I don't know. They found some diamonds. Those diamonds had been planted. Neither Jefferson nor I had ever seen them before. Our company is just opening up its office here. Some people don't like that."

"What were the diamonds worth?"

"Something like a hundred thousand dollars retail."

"How does murder enter into it?"

"That I don't know."

"Don't you even know who was murdered?"

"A man named Baxter. He's a smuggler."

"Were these his diamonds—the ones the police found in your office?"

"How the hell would *I* know?"

Mason regarded the man for a few seconds, then said, "How the hell would *I* know?"

Irving grinned. "I'm a little touchy this morning."

"So am I. Suppose you start talking."

"All I can tell you for sure is that there's some kind of a frame-up involved. Jefferson never killed anyone. I've known him for years. My gosh, Mr. Mason, look at it this way. Here's a large, exceedingly reputable, ultraconservative company in South Africa. This company has known Duane Jefferson for years. As soon as they hear that he's been arrested, they're willing to put up whatever amount is required in order to secure the very best available representation.

"Mind you, they don't suggest they'll advance Jefferson money to retain counsel. The company itself instructed me to retain the best available counsel for Jefferson."

"And you suggested me?" Mason asked.

"No. I would have, but somebody beat me to it. I got a cablegram authorizing me to draw a check on our local account in an amount of two thousand dollars and turn that money over to you so you could start taking the necessary legal steps immediately. Now if my company pays your fees, who will your client be?"

"Duane Jefferson."

"Suppose Jefferson tries to get you to do something that isn't in his best interests. What would you do—follow his instructions, or do what was best for him?"

"Why do you ask that question?"

"Duane is trying to protect some woman. He'd let himself get convicted before he'd expose her. He thinks she's wonderful. *I* think she's a clever, two-timing schemer who is out to frame him."

"Who is she?"

"I wish I knew. If I did, I'd have detectives on her trail within the next hour. The trouble is I don't know. I only know there *is* such a woman. She lost her head over Duahe. He'll protect her."

32

"Married?"

"I don't think so. I don't know."

"What about the murder case?"

"It ties in with smuggling. Duane Jefferson sold a batch of diamonds to Munroe Baxter. That was through the South African office. Baxter asked Jefferson to arrange to have the diamonds cut, polished and delivered to our Paris office. Our Paris office didn't know the history of the transaction. It simply made delivery to Baxter on instructions of the South African office. Usually we try to know something about the people with whom we are dealing. Baxter juggled the deal between our two offices in such a way that each office thought the other one had done the investigating.

"Baxter had worked out one hell of a slick scheme. He had faked a perfect background of respectability."

"How did you find out about the smuggling?" Mason asked.

"His female accomplice broke down and confessed."

"Who is she?"

"A girl named Yvonne Manco."

"Tell me about it," Mason said.

"Didn't you read the account about a fellow jumping overboard from a cruise ship and committing suicide a while back?"

"Yes, I did," Mason said. "Wasn't *that* man's name Munroe Baxter?"

"Exactly."

"I knew I'd heard the name somewhere as soon as you mentioned it. How does the murder angle enter into it?"

Irving said, "Here's the general sketch. Yvonne Manco is a very beautiful young woman who sailed on a cruise ship around the world. She was the queen of the cruise. The ship touched at Naples, and when Yvonne started down the gangplank, she was met by Munroe Baxter, a man who had the appearance of a Frenchman, but the name, citizenship and passport of a United States citizen.

You must understand all of these things fully in order to appreciate the sequence of events."

"Go ahead," Mason said.

"Apparently, Munroe Baxter had at one time been in love with Yvonne Manco. According to the story that was given to the passengers, they had been going together and then the affair had broken up through a misunderstanding.

"Whoever wrote that script did a beautiful job, Mr. Mason."

"It was a script?" Mason asked.

"Hell, yes. It was as phony as a three dollar bill."

"What happened?"

"The passengers naturally were interested. They saw this man burst through the crowd. They saw him embrace Yvonne Manco. They saw her faint in his arms. There was a beautiful romance, the spice of scandal, a page out of this beautiful young woman's past. It was touching; it was pathetic—and, naturally, it caused an enormous amount of gossip."

Mason nodded.

"The ship was in Naples for two days. It sailed, and when it sailed Munroe Baxter was pleading with Yvonne Manco to marry him. He was the last man off the ship; then he stood on the pier and wept copiously, shedding crocodile tears."

"Go on," Mason said, interested.

"The ship sailed out into the Mediterranean. It stopped in Genoa. Munroe Baxter met the ship at the dock. Again Yvonne Manco swooned in his arms, again she refused to marry him, again the ship sailed.

"Then came the pay-off. As the ship was off Gibraltar a helicopter hovered overhead. A man descended a rope ladder, dangled precariously from the last rung. The helicopter hovered over the deck of the ship, and Munroe Baxter dropped to the deck by the swimming pool, where Yvonne Manco was disporting herself in the sunlight in a seductive bathing suit."

"Romantic," Mason said.

"And opportune," Irving said dryly. "No one could resist such an impetuous, dramatic courtship. The passengers virtually forced Yvonne to give her consent. The captain married them on the high seas that night. The passengers turned the ship upside down in celebration. It was wonderful stuff."

"Yes, I can imagine," Mason said.

"And, of course," Irving went on, "since Baxter boarded the ship in that dramatic manner, without so much as a toothbrush or an extra handkerchief, how would the customs people suspect that Munroe Baxter was smuggling three hundred thousand dollars' worth of diamonds in a chamois-skin belt around his waist?

"In the face of all that beautiful romance, who would have thought that Yvonne Manco had been Munroe Baxter's mistress for a couple of years, that she was his accomplice in a smuggling plot and that this courtship was all a dramatic hoax?"

"I see," Mason said.

Irving went on, "The stage was all set. Munroe Baxter, in the eyes of the passengers, was a crazy Frenchman, a United States citizen, of course, but one who had acquired all the excitability of the French.

"So, when the ship approached port and Yvonne Manco, dressed to the hilt, danced three times with the good-looking assistant purser, it was only natural that Munroe Baxter should stage a violent scene, threaten to kill himself, break into tears, dash to his stateroom and subsequently leap overboard after a frenzied scene in which Yvonne Manco threatened to divorce him."

"Yes," Mason said, "I remember the newspapers made quite a play of the story."

"It was made to order for press coverage," Irving said. "And who would have thought that the excitable Munroe Baxter carried with him three hundred thousand dollars in diamonds when he jumped overboard, that he was a powerful swimmer who could easily swim to a launch which was opportunely waiting at a pre-arranged spot, and that later on he and the lovely Yvonne were to share the proceeds of a carefully written, superbly directed scenario, performed very cleverly for the sole purpose of fooling the customs men?"

"And it didn't?" Mason asked.

"Oh, but it did! Everything went like clockwork, except for one thing—Munroe Baxter didn't reappear to join Yvonne Manco. She went to the secluded motel which was to be their rendezvous. She waited and waited and waited and waited."

"Perhaps Baxter decided that a whole loaf was better than half a loaf," Mason said.

Irving shook his head. "It seems the lovely Yvonne Manco went to the accomplice who was waiting in the launch. At first, the accomplice told her that Baxter had never showed up. He told her that Baxter must have been seized by cramps while he was swimming underwater."

"Did this take place within the territorial waters of the United States?" Mason asked.

"Right at the approach to Los Angeles Harbor."

"In daylight?"

"No, just before daylight. You see, it was a cruise ship and it was gliding in at the earliest possible hour so the passengers could have a maximum time ashore for sightseeing."

"All right, Baxter was supposed to have drowned," Mason said. "What happened?"

"Well, Yvonne Manco had a horrible suspicion. She thought that the accomplice in the launch might have held Baxter's head underwater and might have taken the money belt.

"Probably, she wouldn't have said anything at all, if it hadn't been for the fact that customs agents were also putting two and two together. They called on the lovely Yvonne Manco to question her about her 'husband' after it appeared that she and her 'husband' had sailed on another cruise ship as man and wife some eighteen months earlier."

"And Yvonne Manco broke down and told them the whole story?" Mason asked.

"Told them the whole story, including the part that it had been Duane Jefferson who had been involved in the sale of the jewels. So police became very much interested in Duane Jefferson, and yesterday afternoon, on an affidavit of Yvonne Manco, a search warrant was issued and police searched the office."

"And recovered a hundred thousand dollars in gems?" Mason asked.

"Recovered a goodly assortment of diamonds," Irving said. "Let us say, perhaps a third of the value of the smuggled shipment."

"And the remaining two-thirds?"

Irving shrugged his shoulders.

"And the identification?" Mason asked.

Again Irving shrugged his shoulders.

"And where were these gems found?"

"Where someone had very cleverly planted them. You may remember the little flurry of excitement when an intruder was discovered in the office—the police asked us to check and see if anything had been taken. It never occurred to us to check *and see if anything had been planted.*"

"Where were the diamonds found?"

"In a package fastened to the back of a desk drawer with adhesive tape."

"And what does Duane Jefferson have to say about this?"

"What could he say?" Irving asked. "It was all news to him, just as it was to me."

"You can vouch for these facts?" Mason asked.

"I'll vouch for them. But I can't vouch for Duane's romantic, crazy notions of protecting this girl."

"She was the same girl who entered the office?"

"I think she was. Duane would have a fit and never speak to me again if he knew I ever entertained such a thought. You have to handle him with kid gloves where women are concerned. But if it comes to a showdown, *you're* going to have to drag this girl into it, and Duane Jefferson will cease to co-operate with you as soon as you mention her very existence."

Mason thought the matter over.

"Well?" Irving asked.

"Make out your check for two thousand dollars," Mason told him. "That will be on account of a five-thousand-dollar fee."

"What do you mean—a five-thousand-dollar fee?"

"It won't be more than that."

"Including detectives?"

"No. You will have to pay expenses. I'm fixing fees."

"Damn it," Irving exploded. "If that bunch in the home office hadn't mentioned a two-thousand-dollar retainer, I could have got you to handle the whole case for two thousand."

Mason sat quietly facing Irving.

"Well, it's done now, and there's nothing I can do about it," Irving said, taking from his wallet a check already made out to the lawyer. He slid the check across the desk to Perry Mason.

Mason said to Della Street, "Make a receipt, Della, and put on the receipt that this is a retainer on behalf of Duane Jefferson."

"What's the idea?" Irving asked.

"Simply to show that I'm not responsible to you or your company but only to my client."

Irving thought that over.

"Any objections?" Mason asked.

"No. I presume you're intimating that you'd even turn against me if it suited Duane's interests for you to do so."

38

"I'm more than intimating. I'm telling you."

Irving grinned. "That's okay by me. I'll go further. If at any time things start getting hot, you can count on me to do anything needed to back your play. I'd even consent to play the part of a missing witness."

Mason shook his head. "Don't try to call the plays. Let me do that."

Irving extended his hand. "I just want you to understand my position, Mason."

"And be sure *you* understand *mine,*" Mason said.

5

MASON LOOKED AT DELLA STREET AS WALTER IRVING left the office.

"Well?" Della Street asked.

Mason said, "I just about had to take the case in self-defense, Della."

"Why?"

"Otherwise, we'd be sitting on top of information in a murder case, we wouldn't have any client whom we would be protecting, and the situation could become rather rugged."

"And as it is now?" she asked.

"Now," he told her, "we have a client whom we can be protecting. An attorney representing a client in a murder case is under no obligation to go to the police and set forth his surmises, suspicions, and conclusions, particularly if he has reason to believe that such a course would be against the best interests of his client."

"But how about the positive evidence?" Della Street asked.

"Evidence of what?"

"Evidence that we harbored a young woman who had gone into that office and planted diamonds."

"We don't *know* she planted diamonds."

"Who had gone into the office then."

"We don't *know* she was the same woman."

"It's a reasonable assumption."

"Suppose she was merely a typist who happened to be in the building. We go to the police with a lot of suspicions, and the police give the story to the newspapers, then she sues for defamation of character."

"I see," Della Street said demurely. "I'm afraid it's hopeless to try and convince you."

"It is."

"And now may I ask you a question, Counselor?"

"What?"

"Do you suppose that it was pure coincidence that you are the attorney retained to represent the interests of Duane Jefferson?"

Mason stroked his chin thoughtfully.

"Well?" she prompted.

"I've thought of that," Mason admitted. "Of course, the fact that I am known as a trial attorney, that I have offices on the same floor of the same building would mean that Irving had had a chance to hear about me and, by the same token, a chance to notify his home office that I would be available."

"But he said he didn't do that. He said somebody beat him to it and he got the cable to turn over the two thousand dollars to you."

Mason nodded.

"Well?" Della Street asked.

"No comment," Mason said.

"So what do we do now?"

"Now," Mason said, "our position is very, very clear, Della. I suggest that you go down to the camera store, tell them that I want to buy a fingerprint camera, and you also might get a studio camera with a ground-glass focusing arrangement. Pick up some lights and we'll see if we can get a photograph of those latent fingerprints on the gum."

"And then?" she asked.

"Then," Mason said, "we'll enlarge the film so that it shows only the fingerprints and not the gum."

"And then?"

"By that time," Mason said, "I hope we have managed to locate the girl who made the fingerprints and find out about things for ourselves. While you're getting the cameras I'll go down to Paul Drake's office and have a chat with him."

"Chief," Della Street asked somewhat apprehensively, "isn't this rather risky?"

Mason's grin was infectious. "Sure it is."

"Hadn't you better forget about other things and protect yourself?"

Mason shook his head. "We're protecting a client, Della. Give me a description of that girl—the best one you can give."

"Well," Della Street said, "I'd place her age at twenty-six or twenty-seven, her height at five feet three inches, her weight at about a hundred and sixteen pounds. She had reddish-brown hair and her eyes were also a reddish-brown—about the same color as her hair, very expressive. She was good-looking, trim and well proportioned."

"Good figure?" Mason asked.

"Perfect."

"How was she dressed?"

"I can remember that quite well, Chief, because she looked stunning. I remember thinking at the time that she looked more like a client than a gal from an employment agency.

"She wore a beautifully tailored gray flannel suit, navy blue kid shoes. Umm, let me see . . . yes, I remember now. There was fine white stitching across the toes of the shoes. She carried a matching envelope purse and white gloves. Now let me think. I am quite sure she didn't wear a hat. As I recall, she had a tortoise-shell band on, and there wasn't a hair out of place.

"She didn't take her jacket off while she was working, so I can't be certain, but I think she had on a pale blue cashmere sweater. She opened just the top button of her jacket, so I can't say for sure about this."

Mason smiled. "You women never miss a thing about another woman, do you, Della? I would say that was remembering *very* well. Would you type it out for me—the description? Use a plain sheet of paper, not my letterhead."

Mason waited until Della Street had finished typing the description, then said, "Okay, Della, go down and get the cameras. Get lots of film, lights, a tripod, and anything we may need. Don't let on what we want to use them for."

"The fingerprint camera—isn't that a giveaway?"

"Tell the proprietor I'm going to have to cross-examine a witness and I want to find out all about how a fingerprint camera works."

Della Street nodded.

Mason took the typed description and walked down the hall to Paul Drake's office. He nodded to the girl at the switchboard. "Paul Drake in?"

"Yes, Mr. Mason. Shall I say you're here?"

"Anybody with him?"

"No."

"Tell him I'm on my way," Mason said, opening the gate in the partition and walking down the long glassed-in runway off which there were numerous cubbyhole offices. He came to the slightly more commodious office marked "Paul Drake, Private," pushed open the door and entered.

"Hi," Drake said. "I was waiting to hear from you."

Mason raised his eyebrows.

"Don't look so innocent," Drake said. "The officials of the South African Gem Importing and Exploration Company have been checking up on you by long-distance telephone. They called the manager of the building and asked him about you."

"Did they ask him about me by name," Mason asked, "or did they ask him to recommend some attorney?"

"No, they had your name. They wanted to know all about you."

"What did he tell them?"

Drake grinned and said, "Your rent's paid up, isn't it?"

"What the devil is this all about, do you know, Paul?"

"All I know is it's a murder rap," Drake said, "and the way the police are acting, someone must have caved in with a confession."

"Sure," Mason said, "a confession that would pass the buck to someone else and take the heat off the person making the so-called confession."

"Could be," Drake said. "What do we do?"

"We get busy."

"On what?"

"First," Mason told him, "I want to find a girl."

"Okay, what do I have to go on?"

Mason handed him Della Street's typewritten description.

"Fine," Drake said. "I can go downstairs, stand on the street corner during the lunch hour and pick you out a hundred girls of this description in ten minutes."

"Take another look," Mason invited. "She's a lot better than average."

"If it was average, I could make it a thousand," Drake said.

"All right," Mason said. "We're going to have to narrow it down."

"How?"

"This girl," Mason said, "is an expert typist. She probably holds down a very good secretarial job somewhere."

43

"Unless, of course, she *was* an exceedingly fine secretary and then got married," Drake said.

Mason nodded, conceding the point without changing his position. "She also has legal experience," he said.

"How do you know?"

"That's something I'm not at liberty to tell you."

"All right, what do I do?"

Mason said, "Paul you're going to have to open up a dummy office. You're going to telephone the Association of Legal Secretaries; you're going to put an ad in the bar journal and the newspapers; you're going to ask for a young, attractive typist. Now, I don't *know* that this girl takes shorthand. Therefore, you're going to have to state that a knowledge of shorthand is desirable but not necessary. You're going to offer a salary of two hundred dollars a week—"

"My Lord!" Drake said. "You'll be deluged, Perry. You might just as well ask the whole city to come trooping into your office."

"Wait a minute," Mason told him. "You don't have the sketch yet."

"Well, I certainly hope I don't!"

"Your ad will provide that the girl must pass a typing test in order to get the job. She must be able to copy rapidly and perfectly and at a very high rate of speed —fix a top rate of words per minute.

"Now, the type of girl we want will already have a job somewhere. We've got to get a job that sounds sufficiently attractive so she'll come in to take a look. Therefore, we can't expect her in during office hours. So mention that the office will be open noons and until seven o'clock in the evening."

"And you want me to rent a furnished office?" Drake asked.

"That's right."

Drake said lugubriously, "You'd better make arrangements to replace the carpet when you leave. The one

44

that's there will be worn threadbare by the horde of applicants— How the devil will I know if the right girl comes in?"

"That's what I'm coming to," Mason said. "You're going to start looking these applicants over. You won't find many that can type at the rate specified. Be absolutely hard-boiled with the qualifications. Have a good secretary sitting there, weeding them out. Don't pay any attention to anyone who has to reach for an eraser. The girl I want can make that keyboard sound like a machine gun."

"Okay, then what?"

"When you get girls who qualify on the typing end of the job," Mason said, "give them a personal interview. Look them over carefully to see how they check with this description and tell them you want to see their driving licenses. A girl like that is bound to have a car. That's where the catch comes in."

"How come?"

Mason said, "Sometime this afternoon I'm going to send you over a right thumbprint—that is, a photograph of a thumbprint—perhaps not the best fingerprinting in the world but at least you'll be able to identify it. When you look at their driving licenses, make it a point to be called into another room for something. Get up and excuse yourself. You can say that there's another applicant in there that you have to talk to briefly, or that you have to answer a phone or something. Carry the girl's driving license in there with you, give the thumbprint a quick check. You can eliminate most of them at a glance. Some of them you may have to study a little bit. But if you get the right one, you'll be able to recognize the thumbprint pretty quickly."

"What do I do then?"

"Make a note of the name and address on the driving license. In that way, she won't be able to give you a phony name. And call me at once."

"Anything else?" Drake asked.

45

"This is what I think," Mason said, "but it's just a hunch. I *think* the girl's first name will be Mae. When you find a girl who answers that general description and can type like a house afire, whose first name is Mae, start checking carefully."

"When will you have that thumbprint?"

"Sometime this afternoon. Her driving license will have the imprint of her right thumb on it."

"Can you tell me what this is all about?" Drake asked.

Mason grinned and shook his head. "It's better if you don't know, Paul."

"One of those things, eh?" Drake asked, his voice showing a singular lack of enthusiasm.

"No," Mason told him, "it isn't. It's just that I'm taking an ounce of prevention."

"With you," Drake told him, "I prefer a *pound* of prevention. If things go wrong, I know there won't be more than an ounce of cure."

6

■

MASON SAT IN THE VISITORS' ROOM AT THE JAIL AND looked across at Duane Jefferson.

His client was a tall, composed individual who seemed reserved, unexcited, and somehow very British.

Mason tried to jar the man out of his extraordinary complacency.

"You're charged with murder," he said.

Duane Jefferson observed him coolly. "I would hardly be here otherwise, would I?"

"What do you know about this thing?"

"Virtually nothing. I knew the man, Baxter, in his lifetime—that is, I assume it was the same one."

"How did you know him?"

"He represented himself as a big wholesale dealer. He showed up at the South African office and wanted to buy diamonds. It is against the policy of the company to sell diamonds in the rough, unless, of course, they are industrial diamonds."

"Baxter wanted them in the rough?"

"That's right."

"And he was advised he couldn't have them?"

"Well, of course, we were tactful about it, Mr. Mason. Mr. Baxter gave promise of being an excellent customer, and he was dealing on a cash basis."

"So what was done?"

"We showed him some diamonds that were cut and polished. He didn't want those. He said that the deal he was putting across called for buying diamonds in the rough and carrying them through each step of cutting and polishing. He said he wanted to be able to tell his customers he had personally selected the diamonds just as they came from the fields."

"Why?"

"He didn't say."

"And he wasn't asked?"

"In a British-managed company," Jefferson said, "we try to keep personal questions to a minimum. We don't pry, Mr. Mason."

"So what was done finally?"

"It was arranged that he would select the diamonds, that we would send them to our Paris office, that there they would be cut and polished, and, after they were cut and polished, delivery would be made to Mr. Baxter."

"What were the diamonds worth?"

"Wholesale or retail?"

"Wholesale."

"Very much less than their retail price."

47

"How much less?"

"I can't tell you."

"Why not?"

"That information is a very closely guarded trade secret, Mr. Mason."

"But I'm your attorney."

"Quite."

"Look here," Mason said, "are you British?"

"No."

"American?"

"Yes."

"How long have you been working for a British company?"

"Five or six years."

"You have become quite British."

"There are certain mannerisms, Mr. Mason, which the trade comes to expect of the representatives of a company such as ours."

"And there are certain mannerisms which an American jury expects to find in an American citizen," Mason told him.

"If a jury should feel you'd cultivated a British manner, you might have reason to regret your accent and cool, impersonal detachment."

Jefferson's lip seemed to curl slightly. "I would have nothing but contempt for a jury that would let personal considerations such as those influence its judgment."

"That would break the jurors' hearts," Mason told him.

Jefferson said, "We may as well understand each other at the outset, Mr. Mason. I govern my actions according to principle. I would rather die than yield in a matter of principle."

"All right," Mason said. "Have it your own way. It's your funeral. Did you see Baxter again?"

"No, sir, I didn't. After that, arrangements were completed through the Paris office."

"Irving?" Mason asked.

"I don't think it was Irving, Mr. Mason. I think it was one of the other representatives."

"You read about the arrival of the cruise ship and Baxter's supposed suicide?"

"I did, indeed, Mr. Mason."

"And did you make any comment to the authorities?"

"Certainly not."

"You knew he was carrying a small fortune in diamonds?"

"I assumed that a small fortune in diamonds had been delivered to him through our Paris office. I had no means, of course, of knowing what he had done with them."

"You didn't make any suggestions to the authorities?"

"Certainly not. Our business dealings are highly confidential."

"But you did discuss his death with your partner, Irving?"

"Not a partner, Mr. Mason. A representative of the company, a personal friend but—"

"All right, your associate," Mason corrected.

"Yes, I discussed it with him."

"Did he have any ideas?"

"None. Except that there were certain suspicious circumstances in connection with the entire situation."

"It occurred to you that the whole thing might have been part of a smuggling plot?"

"I prefer not to amplify that statement, Mr. Mason. I can simply say that there were certain suspicious circumstances in connection with the entire transaction."

"And you discussed those with Irving?"

"As a representative of the company talking to an associate, I did. I would prefer, however, not to go into detail as to what I said. You must remember, Mr. Mason, that I am here not in an individual but a representative capacity."

"You may be in this country in a representative capacity," Mason said, "but don't ever forget that you're here in this jail in a purely individual capacity."

"Oh, quite," Jefferson said.

"I understand police found diamonds in your office," Mason went on.

Jefferson nodded.

"Where did those diamonds come from?"

"Mr. Mason, I haven't the faintest idea. I am in my office approximately six hours out of the twenty-four. I believe the building provides a scrubwoman with a master key. The janitor also has a master key. People come and go through that office. Police even told me that there was someone trying to break into the office, or that someone had broken into the office."

"A girl," Mason said.

"I understand it was a young woman, yes."

"Do you have any idea who this woman was?"

"No. Certainly not!"

"Do you know any young women here in the city?"

Jefferson hesitated.

"Do you?" Mason prodded.

Jefferson met his eyes. "No."

"You're acquainted with *no* young woman?"

"No."

"Would you perhaps be trying to shield someone?"

"Why should I try to shield someone?"

"I am not asking you why at the moment. I am asking you if you are."

"No."

"You understand it could be a very serious matter if you should try to falsify any of the facts?"

"Isn't it a rule of law in this country," Jefferson countered, "that the prosecution must prove the defendant guilty beyond all reasonable doubt?"

Mason nodded.

"They can't do it," Jefferson said confidently.

"You may not have another chance to tell me your story," Mason warned.

"I've told it."

"There is no girl?"

"No."

"Weren't you writing to some young woman here before you left South Africa?"

Again there was a perceptible hesitancy, then Jefferson looked him in the eyes and said, "No."

"Police told you there was some young woman who broke into your office?"

"Someone who opened the door with a key."

"Had you given your key to any woman?"

"No. Certainly not."

Mason said, "Look here, if there's anyone you want protected, tell me the whole story. I'll try to protect that person as far as possible. After all, I'm representing you. I'm trying to do what is for your best interests. Now, don't put yourself in such a position that you're going to have to try to deceive your attorney. Do you understand what that can lead to?"

"I understand."

"And you are protecting no one?"

"No one."

"The district attorney's office feels that it has some evidence against you, otherwise it wouldn't be proceeding in a case of this kind."

"I suppose a district attorney can be mistaken as well as anyone else."

"Better sometimes," Mason said. "You're not being very helpful."

"What help can I give, Mr. Mason? Suppose *you* should walk into your office tomorrow morning and find the police there. Suppose they told you that they had uncovered stolen property in your office. Suppose I should ask you to tell me the entire story. What could you tell me?"

"I'd try to answer your questions."

"I have answered your questions, Mr. Mason."

"I have reason to believe there's some young woman here in the city whom you know."

"There is no one."

Mason got to his feet. "Well," he told the young man, "it's up to you."

"On the contrary, Mr. Mason. I think you'll find that it's up to *you*."

"You're probably right, at that," Mason told him, and signaled the guard that the interview was over.

7

∎

MASON UNLOCKED THE DOOR OF HIS PRIVATE OFFICE. Della Street looked up from her work. "How did it go, Chief?"

Mason made a gesture of throwing something away.

"Not talking?" Della Street asked.

"Talking," Mason said, "but it doesn't make sense. He's protecting some woman."

"Why?"

"That," Mason said, "is something we're going to have to find out. Get the cameras, Della?"

"Yes. Cameras, lights, films, tripod—everything."

"We're going into the photographic business," Mason said. "Tell Gertie we don't want to be disturbed, no matter what happens."

Della Street started to pick up the connecting telephone to the outer office, then hesitated. "Gertie is going to make something out of *this!*" she said.

Mason frowned thoughtfully. "You have a point there," he said.

"With her romantic disposition, she will get ideas in her head that you'll never get out with a club."

"All right," Mason decided. "Don't let her know I'm in. We'll just go into the law library and—do you think you could help me tilt that desk over on its side, Della?"

"I can try."

"Good. We'll just go into the library, close and lock the door."

"Suppose Gertie should want me for something? Can't we tell her what we're doing so she can—"

Mason shook his head. "I don't want *anyone* to know about this, Della."

Della went through the motions of throwing something in the wastebasket. "There goes my good name," she said.

"You'll need to stay only to help me get the desk over on its side, and you can fix up the lighting. We'll lock the door from the law library to the outer office and leave the door to this office open. You can hear the phone if Gertie rings."

"That's all right," Della Street said, "but suppose she comes in for something?"

"Well, if the door's open," Mason said, "she'll see that we're photographing something."

"Her curiosity is as bad as her romanticism," Della said.

"Does she talk?" Mason asked.

"I wish I knew the answer to that one, Chief. She must talk to that boy friend of hers. You couldn't keep Gertie quiet with a muzzle. I doubt that she talks to anyone else."

"Okay," Mason said, "we'll take a chance. Come on, Della. Let's get that desk on its side and get the floodlights rigged up."

"Here's a chart," Della Street said, "giving all the exposure factors. I told the man at the camera store we wanted to copy some documents. You have to change your exposure factor when you do real close-up photography. He suggested that we use film packs with the camera where you focus on the ground glass. The fingerprint camera is supposed to be a self-contained unit, with lights and every—"

"I understand," Mason interrupted. "I want to get the wad of chewing gum photographed in place on the bottom of the desk, then I want to get close-ups showing the fingerprints. We can get the photographer to enlarge the fingerprints from these photographs in case the fingerprint camera doesn't do a good job."

"The fingerprint camera seems to be pretty near—" She paused suddenly.

Mason laughed. "Foolproof?"

"Well," Della Street said, "that's what the man at the camera store said."

"All right," Mason told her, "let's go. We'll take photographs at different exposures. You have plenty of film packs?"

"Heavens, yes! I figured you'd want to be sure you had the job done, and I got enough film so you can take all the pictures you want at all kinds of different exposures."

"That's fine," Mason told her.

Della Street took one end of the typewriter desk, Mason the other. "We'll have to move it out from the wall," Mason said. "Now tilt it back, Della. It'll be heavy just before it gets to the floor. You think you can—?"

"Good heavens, yes, Chief. It's not heavy."

"The drawers are full of stationery, and that typewriter — We could take some of the things out and lighten it."

"No, no, let's go. It's all right."

They eased the desk back to the floor.

"All right," Mason said, "give me a hand with the lights and the tripod. We'll get this camera set up and focused."

"I have a magnifying glass," Della Street said. "They seem to think that on the critical focusing necessary for close-ups it will help."

"Good girl," Mason told her. "Let's see what we can do. We'll want an unbalanced cross-lighting, and since light varies inversely as the square of the distance, we'll space these lights accordingly."

Mason first took a series of pictures with the fingerprint camera, then got the lights plugged in and adjusted, the studio camera placed on the tripod and properly focused. He used a tape measure to determine the position of the lights, then slipped a film pack into the camera, regarded the wad of chewing gum thoughtfully.

"That's going to be fine," Della Street said. "How did you know about using unbalanced cross-lighting to bring out the ridges?"

"Cross-examining photographers," Mason said, "plus a study of books on photography. A lawyer has to know a little something about everything. Don't you notice *Photographic Evidence* by Scott over there?" Mason indicated the book bound in red leather.

"That's right," she said. "I remember seeing you studying that from time to time. You used some of his stuff in that automobile case, didn't you?"

"Uh huh," Mason said. "It's surprising how much there is to know about photography. Now, Della, I'm going to start with this lens at *f11,* taking a photograph at a twenty-fifth of a second. Then we'll take one at a tenth of a second, then one at a second. Then I'll use the cable release and we'll take one at two seconds. Then we'll try *f16,* run through the exposures all over again, then take another batch at *f22.*"

"All right," Della Street said. "I'll keep notes of the different exposures."

Mason started taking the pictures, pulling the tabs out of the film pack, tearing them off, dropping them into the wastebasket.

"Oh oh," Della Street said. "There's the phone. That's Gertie calling."

She made a dash for Mason's private office. Mason continued taking pictures.

Della Street was back after a moment. "Walter Irving wants you to call just as soon as you come in."

Mason nodded.

"Gertie asked if you were in yet, and I lied like a trooper," Della Street said.

"Okay, Della. Walter Irving didn't say what he wanted, did he?"

"He said he wanted to know if you'd been able to get any information out of Duane Jefferson about the woman in the case."

Mason said, "As soon as we get finished here, Della, tell Paul Drake I want to put a shadow on Irving."

"You suspect him?"

"Not exactly. The policy of this office is to protect our client and to hell with the rest of them."

"What's the client doing?"

"Sitting tight. Says he knows nothing about the girl who broke into the office, that he doesn't know any girl here, hasn't been corresponding with anyone, and all that."

"You think he has?"

"That wasn't just a casual visit that Mae Wallis paid to their office."

"You've decided she was the girl?"

"Oh, not officially. I'd deny it to the police. But where did the diamonds in the chewing gum come from?"

"Chief, why would *she* plant a hundred thousand dollars' worth of diamonds and then keep a couple of diamonds with her and conceal them in a wad of chewing gum?"

"I can give you *an* answer," Mason said, "but it may not be *the* answer."

"What is it?"

"Suppose she had been given some gems to plant. She must have had them wrapped in tissue paper in her purse. She had to work in a hurry and probably became somewhat alarmed. Something happened to make her suspicious. She realized that she had been detected."

56

"What makes you say that?"

"Because she roughed up the office, making it appear she was looking *for* something. Otherwise she'd have slipped in, planted the diamonds and left."

"Then you think the diamonds that she put in the chewing gum were ones she had overlooked when she was making the plant?"

"I said it was *an* answer. After she got established as a typist in our office, she had a breathing spell. She opened her purse to make sure she hadn't overlooked anything, and found several of the diamonds. She knew that police were on the job and that there was a good chance she might be picked up, questioned, and perhaps searched. So she fastened the diamonds to the underside of the desk."

"I keep thinking those 'Prince Charming' letters have something to do with it, Chief."

Mason nodded. "So do I. Perhaps she planted the diamonds in the office and at the same time deliberately planted the letters in the restroom."

"She could have done that, all right," Della Street admitted. "There's the phone again."

She gathered her skirts and again sprinted for Mason's private office. Mason continued to take photographs while she answered the phone and returned.

"What is it?" Mason asked.

"I have to announce," she said, "that Gertie is just a little suspicious."

"Yes?" Mason asked.

"Yes. She wants to know why it's taking me so long to answer the phone."

"What did you tell her?"

"Told her I was doing some copy work and I didn't want to stop in the middle of a sentence."

Mason snapped out the floodlights. "All right, Della. We'll quit. We have enough pictures. Tell Paul Drake I want shadows put on Walter Irving."

■

8

A FEW MORNINGS LATER MASON WAS SCANNING THE papers on his desk. "Well, I see that the grand jury has now filed an indictment, charging Duane Jefferson with first-degree murder."

"Why the indictment?" Della Street asked.

"The district attorney can proceed against a defendant in either of two ways. He can file a complaint or have someone swear to a complaint. Then the Court holds a preliminary hearing. At that time the defendant can cross-examine the witnesses. If the Court makes an order binding the defendant over, the district attorney then files an information and the case is brought on to trial before a jury.

"However, the district attorney can, if he wishes, present witnesses to the grand jury. The grand jury then returns an indictment, and the transcript of the testimony of the witnesses is delivered to the defendant. In that case, there is no opportunity for counsel for the defense to cross-examine the witnesses until they get to court.

"Now, in this case against Duane Jefferson, the main witness before the grand jury seems to have been Yvonne Manco, who tells a great story about how her lover-boy, Munroe Baxter, was rubbed out by some nasty people who wanted to steal the diamonds he was smuggling. Then there is the testimony of a police officer that a large portion of those diamonds was found in the office occupied by Duane Jefferson."

"Is that testimony sufficient to support an indictment?" Della Street asked.

Mason grinned and said, "It certainly wouldn't be sufficient standing by itself to bring about a conviction in a court of law."

"Do you intend to question the sufficiency of the evidence?"

"Lord, no," Mason said. "For some reason the district attorney is breaking his neck to get a prompt trial, and I'm going to co-operate by every means in my power."

"Wouldn't it be better to stall the thing along a bit until—?"

Mason shook his head.

"Why not, Chief?"

"Well, the rumor is that the district attorney has a surprise witness he's going to throw at us. He's so intent on that he may overlook the fact that there isn't any real *corpus delicti.*"

"What do you mean?"

"The body of Munroe Baxter has never been found," Mason said.

"Does it have to be?"

"Not necessarily. The words *corpus delicti,* contrary to popular belief, don't mean the 'body of the victim.' They mean the 'body of the crime.' But it *is* necessary to show that a murder was committed. That can be shown by independent evidence, but of course the *best* evidence is the body of the victim."

"So you're going to have an immediate trial?"

"Just as soon as we can get an open date on the calendar," Mason said. "And with the district attorney and the defense both trying to get the earliest possible trial date, that shouldn't be too difficult. How's Paul Drake coming with his office setup?"

"Chief, you should see that. It's wonderful! There's this ad in all of the papers, advertising for a legally trained secretary who can type like a house afire. The salary to start—to start, mind you—is two hundred dollars a week. It is intimated that the attorney is engaged in cases of international importance and that there may be an opportunity to travel, to meet important personalities. It's a secretary's dream."

"And the office where he's screening applicants?" Mason asked.

"All fitted out with desks, typewriters, law books, plush carpets and an air of quiet dignity which makes it seem that even the janitor must be drawing a salary about equal to that of the ordinary corporation president."

"I hope he hasn't overdone it," Mason said. "I'd better take a look."

"No, it isn't overdone. I can assure you of that. The air of conservatism and respectability envelops the place like a curtain of smog, permeating every nook and cranny of the office. You should see them—stenographers who are applicants come in chewing gum, giggling and willing to take a chance that lightning may strike despite their lack of qualifications. They stand for a few seconds in that office, then quietly remove their gum, look around at the furniture and start talking in whispers."

"How does he weed out the incompetents?" Mason asked.

"There's a battery of typewriters; girls are asked to sit at the typewriters, write out their names and addresses and list their qualifications.

"Of course, a good typist can tell the minute a girl's hands touch the keyboard whether she is really skillful, fairly competent, or just mediocre. Only the girls who can really play a tune on the keyboard get past the first receptionist."

"Well," Mason said, "it's—"

The private, unlisted phone jangled sharply.

"Good Lord," Della Street said, "that must be Paul now. He's the only other one who has that number."

Mason grabbed for the phone. "That means he's got information so hot he doesn't dare to go through the outer switchboard. Hello . . . hello, Paul."

Drake's voice came over the wire. He was talking rapidly but in the hushed tones of one who is trying to keep his voice from being heard in an adjoining room.

"Hello, Perry. Hello, Perry. This is Paul."

"Yes, Paul, go ahead."

"I have your girl."

"You're certain?"

"Yes."

"Who is she?"

"Her name is Mae W. Jordan. She lives at Seven-Nine-Two Cabachon Street. She's employed at the present time in a law office. She doesn't want to give the name. She would have to give two weeks' notice. She wants the job very badly, and, boy, can that girl tickle the typewriter! And it's wonderful typing."

"What does the *W* stand for?" Mason asked. "Wallis?"

"I don't know yet. I'm just giving you a quick flash that we have the girl."

"You know it's the same one?"

"Yes. The thumbprints match. I'm holding her driving license right at the moment."

"How about the address?" Mason asked.

"And the address is okay. It's Seven-Nine-Two Cabachon Street, the same address that's given on her driving license."

"Okay," Mason said. "Now here's what you do, Paul. Tell her that you *think* she can do the job; that you'll have to arrange an appointment with Mr. Big himself for six o'clock tonight. Tell her to return then. Got that?"

"I've got it," Drake said. "Shall I tell her anything else about the job?"

"No," Mason said. "Try and find out what you can. Be interested but not *too* curious."

"You want me to put a shadow on her?"

"Not if you're certain of the address," Mason said.

"Think we should try to find out about the law office where she's working?"

"No," Mason said. "With her name and address we can

get everything we need. This girl is smart and sharp, and she may be mixed up in a murder, Paul. She's undoubtedly connected in some way with a diamond-smuggling operation. Too many questions will—"

"I get it," Drake interrupted. "Okay, Perry, I'll fix an appointment for six o'clock and call you back in fifteen or twenty minutes."

"Do better than that," Mason said. "As soon as you've finished with this girl, jump in your car and come up here. There's no use waiting around there any longer. We've found what we were looking for. You can close the office tomorrow. Take your ads out of the papers and tell all other applicants that the job has been filled. Let's start cutting down the expense."

"Okay," Drake said.

Mason hung up the phone and grinned at Della Street. "Well, we have our typist, Della. She's Mae W. Jordan of Seven-Nine-Two Cabachon Street. Make a note of that— and keep the note where no one else can find it."

9

◾

PAUL DRAKE WAS GRINNING WITH THE SATISFACTION OF a job well done as he eased himself into the big overstuffed chair in Perry Mason's office.

"Well, we did it, Perry, but it certainly was starting from scratch and working on slender clues."

Mason flashed Della Street a glance. "It was a nice job, Paul."

"What gave you your lead in the first place?" Drake asked.

"Oh," Mason said with a gesture of dismissal, "it was just a hunch."

"But you had a damn good thumbprint," Drake said.

"Purely fortuitous," Mason observed.

"Well, if you don't want to tell me, I don't suppose you will," Drake said. "I see they've indicted Jefferson."

"That's right."

"The district attorney says there are certain factors in the situation which demand a speedy trial in order to keep evidence from being dissipated."

"Uh huh," Mason said noncommittally.

"You going to stall around and try for delay?"

"Why should I?"

"Well, ordinarily when the D.A. wants something, the attorney for the defense has different ideas."

"This isn't an ordinary case, Paul."

"No, I suppose not."

"What have you found out about Irving?" Mason asked.

Drake pulled a notebook from his pocket. "Full name, Walter Stockton Irving. Been with the Paris branch of the South African Gem Importing and Exploration Company for about seven years. Likes life on the Continent, the broader standards of morality, the more leisurely pace of life. Quite a race horse fan."

"The deuce he is!"

"That's right. Of course, over there it isn't quite the way it is here."

"A gambler?"

"Well, not exactly. He'll get down to Monte Carlo once in a while and do a little plunging, but mostly he likes to get out with a pair of binoculars and a babe on his arm, swinging a cane, enjoying the prerogatives of being a quote gentleman unquote."

"Now that," Mason said, "interests me a lot, Paul."

"I thought it would."

"What's he doing with his time here?"

"Simply waiting for the branch to get ready for business. He's leading a subdued life. Doubtless the murder charge pending against Jefferson is holding him back slightly. He seems to have made one contact."

"Who?" Mason asked.

"A French babe. Marline Chaumont."

"Where?"

"A bungalow out on Ponce de Leon Drive. The number is 8257."

"Does Marline Chaumont live there alone?"

"No. She has a brother she's taking care of."

"What's wrong with the brother?"

"Apparently he's a mental case. He was released from a hospital, so that his sister could take care of him. However, elaborate precautions are being taken to keep the neighbors from knowing anything about it. One of the neighbors suspects, but that's as far as it goes at the present time."

"Violent?" Mason asked.

"No, not at this time. Just harmless. You've heard of prefrontal lobotomy?"

"Yes, sure. That's the treatment they formerly used on the hopelessly violent insane and on criminals. I understand they've more or less discontinued it."

"Turns a man into a vegetable more or less, doesn't it?"

"Well, you can't get doctors to agree on it," Mason said. "But I think it now has generally been discontinued."

"That's the operation this chap had. He's sort of a zombie. I can't find out too much about him. Anyhow, Marline knew your man Irving over in Paris. Probably when Marline is freed of responsibilities and gets dolled up in glad rags she's quite a number."

"How about now?" Mason asked.

"Now she's the devoted sister. That's one thing about those French, Perry. They go to town when they're on the loose, but when they assume responsibilities they *really* assume them."

"How long has she been here?" Mason asked.

"She's been in this country for a year, according to her statements to tradesmen. But we haven't been able to check up. She's new in the neighborhood. She moved into her house there when she knew that her brother was coming home. She was living in an apartment up to that time. An apartment house would be a poor place to have a mental case. Marline knew it, so she got this bungalow."

"Living there alone with her brother?"

"A housekeeper comes in part of the day."

"And Irving has been going there?"

"Uh huh. Twice to my knowledge."

"Trying to get Marline to go out?"

"What he's *trying* to get is a question. Marline seems to be very devoted to her brother and very domesticated. The first time my operative shadowed Irving to the place it was in the afternoon. When Marline came to the door there was an affectionate greeting. Irving went inside, stayed for about an hour, and when he left, seemed to be trying to persuade Marline to come with him. He stood in the doorway talking to her. She smiled but kept shaking her head.

"So Irving went away. He was back that night, went inside the house, and apparently Marline sold him on the idea of brother sitting because Marline went out and was gone for an hour or two."

"How did she go?"

"By bus."

"She doesn't have a car?"

"Apparently not."

"Where did she go?"

"Gosh, Perry! You didn't tell me you wanted me to shadow *her*. Do you want me to?"

"No," Mason said, "I guess not, Paul. But the thing interests me. What's happened since?"

"Well, apparently Irving recognized the futility of trying to woo Marline away from her responsibilities, or else the trouble Jefferson is in is weighing heavily on his shoulders. He's keeping pretty much to himself in his apartment now."

"What apartment?" Mason asked.

"The Alta Loma Apartments."

"Pick up anything about the case, Paul?"

"The D.A. is supposed to be loaded for bear on this one. He's so darned anxious to get at you, he's running around in circles. He's told a couple of friendly reporters that this is the sort of case he's been looking for and waiting for. Perry, are you all right on this case?"

"What do you mean, 'all right'?"

"Are *you* in the clear?"

"Sure."

"You haven't been cutting any corners?"

Mason shook his head.

"The D.A. is acting as though he had you where he wanted you. He's like a kid with a new toy for Christmas —a whole Christmas tree full of new toys."

"I'm glad he's happy," Mason said. "What about this Mae Jordan, Paul?"

"I didn't get a lot more than I told you over the phone, except that she's promised to be there at six tonight."

"She's working?"

"That's right."

"What kind of an impression does she make, Paul?"

"Clean-cut and competent," Drake said. "She has a nice voice, nice personality, very neat in her appearance, knows what she's doing every minute of the time, and she certainly can type. Her shorthand is just about as fast as you'd find anywhere."

"She's happy in her job?"

"Apparently not. I don't know what it's all about, but she wants to get away from her present environment."

"Perhaps a thwarted love affair?"

"Could be."

"Sounds like it," Mason said.

"Well, you can find out tonight," Drake told him.

"When we get her into that office tonight, Paul," Mason said, "don't mention my name. Don't make *any* introductions. Simply state that I am the man for whom she will be working."

"Will she recognize you?" Drake asked.

"I don't think I've ever seen her," Mason said, glancing at Della Street.

"That doesn't necessarily mean anything. Your pictures get in the paper a lot."

"Well, if she recognizes me it won't make any difference," Mason said, "because outside of the first few questions, Paul, I'm not going to be talking to her about a job."

"You mean that she'll know the thing was a plant as soon as you walk in?"

"Well, I hope not quite *that* soon," Mason said. "But she'll know it shortly after I start questioning her. As long as she talks I'm going to let her talk."

"That won't be long," Drake said. "She answers questions, but she doesn't volunteer any information."

"All right," Mason said. "I'll see you a little before six tonight, Paul."

"Now remember," Drake warned, "there may be a little trouble."

"How come?"

"This girl has got her mind all set on a job where she can travel. She wants to get away from everything. The minute you let her know that you were simply locating her as a witness, she's going to resent it."

"What do you think she'll do?" Mason asked.

"She may do anything."

"I'd like that, Paul."

"You would?"

"Yes," Mason said. "I'd like to know just what she does

67

when she's good and angry. Don't kid yourself about this girl, Paul. She's mixed up in something pretty sinister."

"How deep is she mixed up in it?"

"Probably up to her eyebrows," Mason said. "This Marline Chaumont knew Walter Irving in Paris?"

"Apparently so. She was sure glad to see him. When he rang the bell and she came to the door, she took one look, then made a flying leap into his arms. She was all French."

"And Irving doesn't go there any more?"

Drake shook his head.

"What would she do if I went out to talk with her this afternoon?"

"She might talk. She might not."

"Would she tell Irving I'd been there?"

"Probably."

"Well, I'll have to take that chance, Paul. I'm going to call on Marline Chaumont."

"May I suggest that you take me?" Della Street asked.

"As a chaperon or for the purpose of keeping notes on what is said?" Mason asked.

"I can be very effective in both capacities," Della Street observed demurely.

"It's that French background," Drake said, grinning. "It scares the devil out of them, Perry."

10

PERRY MASON DROVE SLOWLY ALONG PONCE DE LEON Drive.

"That's it," Della Street said. "The one on the left, the white bungalow with the green trim."

Mason drove the car past the house, sizing it up, went to the next intersection, made a *U* turn, and drove back.

"What are you going to tell her?" Della Street asked.

"It'll depend on how she impresses me."

"And on how we impress her?"

"I suppose so."

"Isn't this somewhat dangerous, Chief?"

"In what way?"

"She'll be almost certain to tell Irving."

"Tell him what?"

"That you were out checking up on him."

"I'll tell him that myself."

"And then he'll know that you've had people shadowing him."

"If he's known Miss Chaumont in Paris, he won't know just *how* we checked up. I'd like to throw a scare into Mr. Walter Irving. He's too damned sure of himself."

Mason walked up the three steps to the front porch and pushed the bell button.

After a moment the door was opened a cautious three inches. A brass guard chain stretched taut across the opening.

Mason smiled at the pair of bright black eyes which surveyed him from the interior of the house. "We're looking for a Miss Chaumont."

"I am Miss Chaumont."

"Of Paris?"

"*Mai oui.* I have lived in Paris, yes. Now I live here."

"Would you mind if I asked you a few questions?"

"About what?"

"About Paris?"

"I would love to have you ask me questions about Paris."

"It's rather awkward, standing out here and talking through the door," Mason said.

"Monsieur can hear me?"

"Oh, yes."

"And I can hear you."

Mason smiled at her. Now that his eyes were becoming accustomed to the half-light he could see the oval of the face and a portion of a trim figure.

"Were you familiar with the South African Gem Importing and Exploration Company in Paris?"

"Why do you ask me that question?"

"Because I am interested."

"And who are you?"

"My name is Perry Mason. I am a lawyer."

"Oh, *you* are Perry Mason?"

"That's right."

"I have read about you."

"That's interesting."

"What do you want, Mr. Mason?"

"To know if you knew of the company in Paris."

"I have known of the company, yes."

"And you knew some of the people who worked for that company?"

"But of course, Monsieur. One does not become, as you say, familiar with a company, *non*. One can only become familiar with people, with some of the people, yes? With the company, *non*."

"Did you know Walter Irving while you were in Paris?"

"Of course. He was my friend. He is here now."

"You went out with him occasionally in Paris?"

"But yes. Is that wrong?"

"No, no," Mason said. "I am simply trying to get the background. Did you know Duane Jefferson?"

"Duane Jefferson is from the South African office. Him I do not know."

"Did you know anyone from the South African office?"

"Twice, when people would come to visit in Paris, they asked me to help . . . well, what you call, entertain. I put on a daring dress. I act wicked with the eyes. I make of them . . . what you call the visiting fireman, *non?*"

"And who introduced you to these men?"

"My friend, Walter."

"Walter Irving?"

"That is right."

"I would like to find out something about Mr. Irving."

"He is nice. Did he tell you I am here?"

"No. I located you through people who work for me. They have an office in Paris."

"And the Paris office locates me here? Monsieur, it is impossible!"

Mason smiled. "I am here."

"And *I* am here. But . . . well, a man of your position, Monsieur Mason, one does not—how you call it?—contradict."

"What sort of a fellow is Walter Irving?"

"Walter Irving has many friends. He is very nice. He has—how you say?—the too big heart. That big heart, she is always getting him in trouble. He gives you too much . . . the shirt off his back. When he trusts, he trusts, that one. Sometime people, they take advantage of him. You are his friend, Monsieur Mason?"

"I would like to know about him."

"This woman with you is your wife?"

"My secretary."

"Oh, a thousand pardons. You seem . . . well, you seem as one."

"We have worked together for a long time."

"I see. Could I say something to you as the friend of Walter Irving?"

"Why not?"

"This Duane Jefferson," she said. "Watch him."

"What do you mean?"

"I mean he is the one to watch. He is sharp. He is very smooth. He . . . he is filled with crazy ideas in his head."

"What do you know about him?"

"*Know,* Monsieur? I *know* but little. But a woman has intuition. A woman can tell. Walter, I know very well.

He is big. He is honest. He is like a dog. He trusts. But Walter likes what you call the show-off, the grandstand. He likes many clothes and to show off the good-looking woman on his arm. He likes crowds. He likes—"

She broke off and laughed. "He is simple, that one, for one who is so smart otherwise. He cares about a girl, that she should make people turn to look when he walks with her. So when I go out with Walter I put on a dress that . . . well, your secretary will know. The curves, yes?"

Della Street nodded.

She laughed very lightly. "Then Walter is very happy. I think, Monsieur Mason, that this Jefferson—"

"But I thought you didn't know Jefferson?"

"I hear people talk, and I listen. At times I have very big ears. And now, Monsieur Mason, you will pardon me, no? I have a brother who is sick in his upstairs. He will get better if he can be kept very quiet and have no excitement. You are nice people, and I would invite you in, but the excitement, no."

"Thank you very much," Mason said. "Does Walter Irving know you are here in the city?"

"Know I am here? Of course, he knows. He has located me. He is very eager, that Walter Irving. And he is nice company. If I did not have my brother, I would put on clothes that show the curves and go with him to the night clubs. That he would love. That also I would like. However, I have responsibilities. I have to stay home. But, Monsieur Mason, please . . . you listen to Marline Chaumont. This Duane Jefferson, he is very cold, very polished, and treacherous like a snake."

"And if you see Walter Irving, you will tell him we were here?"

"You wish me not to?"

"I don't know," Mason said. "I am simply checking."

"I will make you the bargain, Monsieur Mason. You do not tell Walter Irving what I have said about Duane

Jefferson, and I do not say to Walter Irving anything that you are here. We keep this a little secret between us, no?

"But, Monsieur Mason, please, if this Duane Jefferson has done things that are wrong, you see that he does not pull my friend Walter down with him?"

"You think Jefferson did something wrong?"

"I have heard people talk."

"But his company gives him an excellent reputation. His company feels the utmost confidence in his honor and his integrity."

"I have told you, Monsieur Mason, that companies cannot feel; only the people in the companies. And later on, when the case comes to trial, Monsieur Mason, I shall read the papers with much interest. But you watch closely this Duane Jefferson. Perhaps he will tell you a story that is very fine as stories go when you do not question, but when he gets on the witness stand and finds that he cannot use the cold English manner to hide behind, then perhaps he gets mad, and when he gets mad, poof! Look out!"

"He has a temper?" Mason asked.

"That, Monsieur Mason, I do not know, but I have heard what others say. He is bad when he gets mad. His manner is a mask."

"I thank you," Mason said.

She hesitated a moment, then archly blew him a kiss with the tips of her fingers. The door closed gently but firmly.

11

PERRY MASON AND PAUL DRAKE LEFT THE ELEVATORS, walked down the corridor of the big office building.

"Here's the suite," Drake said, pausing in front of a door which had on its frosted glass only the single word "Enter" and the number 555.

Drake opened the door.

"Well," Mason said, looking around, "you certainly fixed up a place here, Paul."

"Rental of desks and chairs," Drake said. "Rental of typewriters. The rest of it all came with the furnished office."

"I didn't know you could rent places like this," Mason said.

"This building caters to an international clientele," Drake explained. "Occasionally they need a large furnished office for directors' meetings, conferences, and things of that sort. The last time this was rented, which was last week, a big Mexican company had it for a trade conference.

"They expect to lose money on this office, of course, but the international goodwill and the convenience to tenants in the building who have big meetings from time to time are supposed to more than offset the loss. Come on in here, Perry."

Drake led the way into a private office.

"This where the interviews take place?" Mason asked.

"That's right."

"This girl will be here at six o'clock?"

"Right on the dot. I have an idea that girl prides herself on being prompt and efficient."

"That's the way I had her sized up," Mason said.

"You aren't ready to tell me yet how you got a line on her?"

"No."

"Or what she has to do with the case?"

Mason said, "She *may* be the girl who made the surreptitious entry into the offices of the South African Gem Importing and Exploration Company."

"I surmised that," Drake said. "It's almost the same description that the police had."

"You have a tape recorder connected?" Mason asked.

"This room is bugged with three microphones," Drake told him. "There's a tape recorder in that closet."

"And what about a receptionist?" Mason asked.

"My receptionist is coming in to—" He broke off as a buzzer sounded. "That means someone's coming in."

Drake got up, went out into the big reception room, came back in a moment with a very attractive young woman.

"Meet Nora Pitts, Perry. She's one of my operatives, working as a receptionist here, and she really knows the ropes."

Miss Pitts, blushing and somewhat flustered, came forward to give Perry Mason her hand.

"I'd been hoping I'd meet you on one of these jobs, Mr. Mason," she said. "Mr. Drake keeps me for the office type of work. Usually I'm on stake-outs. I was beginning to be afraid I was just *never* going to meet you."

"You shouldn't hold out on me like this, Paul," Mason said to the detective.

Drake grinned, looked at his wrist watch, said, "You understand the setup, Nora?"

She nodded.

"Do you know Della Street, my secretary?" Mason asked.

"I know her by sight, yes."

"Well," Mason said, "after this girl has been in here

for a few minutes, Miss Street is going to come in. I told her to be here promptly at fifteen minutes past six."

Nora was listening now, her personal reaction at meeting Mason completely subdued by professional concentration.

"What do I do?" she asked.

"I think that this girl will be here by six o'clock, or at least a couple of minutes past six," Mason said. "You send her in as soon as she arrives. I'll start talking with her and questioning her. Della Street will be in at six-fifteen on the dot. We'll hear the buzzer in the office when the door opens and know that she's here, so there'll be no need for you to notify us. Just have Della sit down and wait. I'll buzz for her when I want her sent in."

"Okay," she said.

"You got it, Nora?" Drake asked.

She nodded. "Of course."

Drake looked at his watch. "Well, it's seven minutes to six. She may come in early. Let's go."

Nora Pitts, with a quick smile at Mason, went back to the reception room.

In the office Drake settled down for a smoke, and Mason joined him with a cigarette.

"The newspapers indicate your client is a cold fish," Drake said.

Mason said irritably, "The guy is trying to protect some girl, and we're not going to get his story out of him until after we've got the story out of this girl."

"And you think Mae Jordan is the girl?"

"I don't know. Could be."

"Suppose she is?"

"Then we'll break her down and get her story."

"What do you propose to do then?"

"We'll get a tape recording," Mason said. "Then I'll go down to the jail, tell Jefferson what I have, and tell him to come clean."

"Then what?"

"Then I'll have his story."

"How's the district attorney going to identify those diamonds, Perry?"

"I don't know much about the case, Paul, but I do know a lot about the district attorney. He's been laying for me for years.

"This time he thinks he has me. He must have a pretty good case. But I'm gambling there's a legal point he's overlooked."

"What's the point?"

"The *corpus delicti.*"

"You think he can't prove it?"

"How's he going to prove a murder?" Mason asked. "They've never found Munroe Baxter's body. Now then, I can show the jury, by Hamilton Burger's own witnesses, that Munroe Baxter was a clever actor who planned to fake a suicide in order to smuggle in gems. Why wouldn't he fake a murder in order to keep from splitting the profit with his female accomplice?

"I'll tell the jury that it's almost certain Baxter has some new babe he's stuck on, some oo-la-la dish who is ready, able and willing to take Yvonne Manco's place as his female accomplice.

"What would be more likely than that Baxter would pretend he had been murdered, so that Yvonne Manco wouldn't be looking for him with fire in her eye?"

"Well, of course, when you put it that way," Drake said, "I can see the possibilities."

"All right," Mason grinned, "that's the way I'm going to put it to the jury. Hamilton Burger isn't going to have the smooth, easy sailing he's anticipating. He'll surprise me. I'll concede he must have something that will hit me hard, but after that, we're going to get down to fundamentals. He can hurt me, but I don't think he can do any more than that. I can blast his case out of court."

They smoked in silence for a few minutes, then Mason said, "What time have you got, Paul? I have five minutes *past* six."

"I have six minutes past, myself," Drake said. "What do you suppose has happened?"

"Do you think she's changed her mind?" Mason asked.

"Hell, no! She was too eager."

Mason began to pace the floor, looking from time to time at his watch.

Promptly at six-fifteen the buzzer sounded.

Mason opened the door to the reception room, said, "Hello, Della. Come in."

Della Street entered the private office. "No typist?" she asked.

"No typist," Mason said.

"Suppose it's simply a case of her being delayed or—"

Mason shook his head. "That girl wasn't delayed. She has become suspicious."

"Not while she was here," Drake said positively. "When she left the place, her eyes were shining. She—"

"Sure," Mason said. "But she's smart. She went to the Better Business Bureau or a credit agency and got somebody to call up the office of this building and find out who was renting this office."

"Oh-oh!" Drake exclaimed.

"You mean you left a back trail?" Mason asked.

"I had to, Perry. If she went at it that way, she could have found out this office was being rented by the Drake Detective Agency."

Mason grabbed for his hat. "Come on, Paul. Let's go."

"Want me?" Della Street asked.

Mason hesitated, then said, "You may as well come on, and we'll buy you a dinner afterward."

Mason paused in the big reception office only long enough to tell Nora Pitts to stay on the job until Drake phoned.

"If that girl comes in, hold her," Drake said. "Keep her here and phone the office."

They got in Mason's car. Mason drove to the address on Cabachon Street, which was a narrow-fronted, two-story apartment house.

"Apartment two-eighteen," Drake said.

Mason repeatedly jabbed the button. When there was no answer he rang the bell for the manager.

The door latch clicked open. Drake held the door open. They went in. The manager, a big-boned woman in her sixties, came out to look them over. She studied the group with a cold, practiced eye. "We have no short-term rentals," she said.

Drake said, "I'm an investigator. We're looking for information. We're trying to locate Mae Jordan."

"Oh, yes," the woman said. "Well, Miss Jordan left."

"What do you mean she left?"

"Well, she told me she'd be away for a while and asked me if I'd feed her canary."

"She was going somewhere?"

"I guess so. She seemed in a terrific hurry. She dashed into the apartment and packed a couple of suitcases."

"Was she alone?" Mason asked.

"No. Two men were with her."

"Two men?"

"That's right."

"Did she introduce them?"

"No."

"They went up to the apartment with her?"

"Yes."

"And came down with her?"

"Yes. Each one of them was carrying a suitcase."

"And Miss Jordan didn't tell you how long she'd be gone?"

"No."

"How did she come here? Was it in a car or a taxi-cab?"

"I didn't see her come, but she left in a private car with these two men. Why? Is there anything wrong?"

Mason exchanged glances with Paul Drake.

"What time was this?" Mason asked.

"About . . . oh, let's see . . . It's been a little over an hour and a half, I guess."

"Thank you," Mason said, and led the way back to the car.

"Well?" Drake asked.

"Start your men going, Paul," Mason said. "Find out where Mae Jordan worked. Get the dope on her. Dig up everything you can. I want that girl."

"What are you going to do with her when you get her?" Drake asked.

"I'm going to slap her with a subpoena, put her on the witness stand, and tear her insides out," Mason said grimly. "How long will it take you to find out where Walter Irving is right now?"

"I'll know as soon as my operatives phone in the next report. I've got two men on the job. Generally, they phone in about once an hour."

"When you locate him, let me know," Mason said. "I'll be in my office."

Della Street smiled at Paul Drake. "Dinner," she said, "has been postponed."

12

MASON HAD BEEN IN HIS OFFICE LESS THAN TEN MIN-utes when the unlisted phone rang. Della Street glanced inquiringly at Mason. The lawyer said, "I'll take it, Della," and picked up the phone.

"Hello, Paul. What is it?"

Drake said, "One of my operatives reported Irving is on his way to this building, and he's hopping mad."

"To *this* building?"

"That's right."

"That leaves three objectives," Mason said. "His office, your office, or mine. If he comes to your office send him in here."

"If he comes to your office, will you want help?"

"I'll handle it," Mason said.

"My operative says he's really breathing fire. He got a phone call when he was right in the middle of dinner. He never even went back to his table. Just dashed out, grabbed a cab, and gave the address of this building."

"Okay," Mason said. "We'll see what develops."

Mason hung up the telephone and said to Della Street, "Irving is on his way here."

"To see you?"

"Probably."

"So what do we do?"

"Wait for him. The party may be rough."

Five minutes later angry knuckles banged on the door of Mason's private office. "That will be Irving," Mason said. "I'll let him in myself, Della."

Mason got up, strode across the office and jerked the door open.

"Good evening," he said coldly, his face granite hard.

"What the hell are you trying to do?" Irving asked furiously. "Upset the apple cart?"

Mason said, "There are ladies present. Watch your language unless you want to get thrown out."

"Who's going to throw me out?"

"I am."

"You and who else?"

"Just me."

Irving sized him up for a moment. "You're one hell of a lawyer, I'll say that for you."

"All right," Mason told him. "Come in. Sit down. Tell

me what's on your mind. And the next time you try to hold out anything on me, you'll be a lot sorrier than you are right now."

"I wasn't holding out on you. I—"

"All right," Mason told him. "Tell me *your* troubles, and then *I'll* tell *you* something."

"You went out to call on Marline Chaumont."

"Of course I did."

"You shouldn't have done it."

"Then why didn't you tell me so?"

"To tell you the truth, I didn't think you could possibly find out anything about her. I still don't know how you did it."

"Well, what's wrong with going to see her?" Mason asked.

"You've kicked your case out of the window, that's all that's wrong with it."

"Go on. Tell me the rest of it."

"I'd been nursing that angle of the case until I could get the evidence we needed. She was pulling this gag of having an invalid brother on her hands so she—"

"That's a gag?" Mason interrupted.

"Don't be any simpler than you have to be," Irving snapped.

"What about her brother?" Mason asked.

"Her brother!" Irving stormed. "Her brother! You poor, simple-minded boob! Her so-called brother is Munroe Baxter."

"Go on," Mason said. "Keep talking."

"Isn't that fact enough to show you what you've done?"

"The fact would be. Your statement isn't."

"Well, I'm telling you."

"You've told me. I don't want your guesses or surmises. I want facts."

"Marline is a smart little babe. She's French. She's chic, and she's a fast thinker. She's been playing around with

Munroe Baxter. He likes her better than Yvonne Manco. He was beginning to get tired of Yvonne.

"So when Munroe Baxter took the nose dive, he just kept on diving and came up into the arms of Marline Chaumont. She had a home all prepared for him as the invalid brother who was weak in the upper story."

"Any proof?" Mason asked.

"I was getting proof."

"You've seen Marline?"

"Of course I've seen her. After I got to thinking things over, I made it a point to see her."

"And did you see her brother?"

"I tried to," Irving said, "but she was too smart for me. She had him locked in a back bedroom, and she had the only key. She wanted to go to the all-night bank and transact some business. I told her I'd stay with her brother. She took me up on it.

"After she was gone, I prowled the house. The back bedroom was locked. I think she'd given him a sedative or something. I could hear him gently snoring. I knocked on the door and tried to wake him up. I wanted to look at him."

"You think he's Munroe Baxter?"

"I know he's Munroe Baxter."

"How do you know it?"

"I don't have to go into that with you."

"The hell you don't!"

Irving shrugged his shoulders. "You've started messing the case up now. Go ahead and finish it."

"All right, I will," Mason said. "I'll put that house under surveillance. I'll—"

"You and your house under surveillance!" Irving exclaimed scornfully. "Marline and her 'brother' got out of there within thirty minutes after you left the place. That house is as cold and dead as a last-year's bird's nest. In case you want to bet, I'll give you ten to one you can't find a fingerprint in the whole damn place."

"Where did they go?" Mason asked.

Irving shrugged his shoulders. "Search me. I went out there. The place was empty. I became suspicious and got a private detective agency to get on the job and find out what had happened. I was eating dinner tonight when the detective phoned. Neighbors had seen a car drive up. A man and a woman got out. A neighbor was looking through the curtains. She recognized you from your pictures. The description of the girl with you checked with that of your secretary here, Miss Street.

"Half an hour after you left, a taxi drove up. Marline sent out four big suitcases and a handbag. Then she and the taxi driver helped a man out to the car. The man was stumbling around as though he was drunk or drugged or both."

"And then?" Mason asked.

"The cab drove away."

"All right," Mason said. "We'll trace that cab."

Irving laughed scornfully. "You must think you're dealing with a bunch of dumb bunnies, Mason."

"Perhaps I am," Mason said.

"Go on and try to trace that couple," he said. "Then you'll find out what a mess you've made of things."

Irving got to his feet.

"How long had you known all this?" Mason asked, his voice ominously calm.

"Not long. I looked Marline up when I came here. She knows everyone in the Paris office. She was our party girl. She always helped in entertaining buyers.

"She's smart. She got wise to the Baxter deal and she put the heat on Baxter.

"As soon as I went out to Marline's place to call on her, I knew something was wrong. She went into a panic at the sight of me. She tried to cover up by being all honey and syrup, but she overdid it. She had to invite me in, but she told me this story about her brother. Then she kept me waiting while she locked him up and knocked him out with a hypo. That evening she left me alone, so I could prowl the house. Baxter was dead to the world. She's a smart one, that girl.

"I was getting ready to really bust this case wide open, and then you had to stick your clumsy hand right in the middle of all the machinery."

Irving started for the door.

"Wait a minute," Mason said. "You're not finished yet. You know something more about all—"

"Sure I do," Irving said. "And make no mistake, Mason. What I know I keep to myself from now on. In case you're interested, I'm cabling the company to kiss their two-thousand-dollar retainer good-by and to hire a lawyer who at least has *some* sense."

Irving strode out into the corridor.

Della Street watched the closing door. When it had clicked shut she started for the telephone.

Mason motioned her away. "Remember, it's all taken care of, Della," he said. "Paul Drake has two men shadowing him. We'll know where he goes when he leaves here."

"That's fine," she said. "In that case, you can take me to dinner now."

13

DELLA STREET LAID THE DECODED CABLEGRAM ON MASON's desk as the lawyer entered the office.

"What's this, Della?" Mason asked, hanging up his hat.

"Cablegram from the South African Gem Importing and Exploration Company."

"Am I fired?"

"Definitely not."

"What does it say?" Mason asked.

"It says you are to continue with the case and to protect the interests of Duane Jefferson, that the company investigated you before you were retained, that it has confidence in you, and that its official representative in this area, and the only one in a position to give orders representing the company, is Duane Jefferson."

"Well," Mason said, "that's something." He took the decoded cablegram and studied it. "It sounds as though they didn't have too much confidence in Walter Irving."

"Of course," she told him, "we don't know what Irving cabled the company."

"We know what he told us he was cabling the company."

"Where does all this leave him?" Della Street asked.

"Out on a limb," Mason said, grinning, and then added, "It also leaves us out on a limb. If we don't get some line on Mae Jordan and Marline Chaumont, we're behind the eight ball."

"Couldn't you get a continuance under the circumstances until—"

Mason shook his head.

"Why not, Chief?"

"For several reasons," Mason said. "One of them is that I assured the district attorney I'd go to trial on the first date we could squeeze in on the trial calendar. The other is that I still think we have more to gain than to lose by getting to trial before the district attorney has had an opportunity to think over the real problem."

"Do you suppose this so-called brother of Marline Chaumont is really Munroe Baxter?"

Mason looked at his watch, said, "Paul Drake should have the answer to that by this time. Get him on the phone, Della. Ask him to come in."

Ten minutes later Paul Drake was laying it on the line.

"This guy Irving is all wet, Perry. Marline Chaumont

showed up at the state hospital. She identified herself as the sister of Pierre Chaumont. Pierre had been there for a year. He'd become violent. They'd operated on his brain. After that, he was like a pet dog. He was there because there was no other place for him to be. Authorities were very glad to release Pierre to his sister, Marline. The chance that he is Munroe Baxter is so negligible you can dismiss it.

"In the first place, Marline showed up and got him out of the state hospital more than a month before Baxter's boat was due. At the time Marline was getting him out of the hospital, Munroe Baxter was in Paris."

"Is his real name Pierre Chaumont?"

"The authorities are satisfied it is."

"Who satisfied them?"

"I don't know; Marline, I guess. The guy was going under another name. He'd been a vicious criminal, a psychopath. He consented to having this lobotomy performed, and they did it. It apparently cured him of his homicidal tendencies, but it left him like a zombie. As I understand it, he's in sort of a hypnotic trance. Tell the guy anything, and he does it."

"You checked with the hospital?"

"With everyone. The doctor isn't very happy about the outcome. He said he had hoped for better results, but the guy was a total loss the way he was and anything is an improvement. They were damn glad to get rid of him at the hospital."

"Yes, I can imagine. What else, Paul?"

"Now here's some news that's going to jolt you, Perry."

"Go ahead and jolt."

"Mae Jordan was picked up by investigators from the district attorney's office."

"The hell!" Mason exclaimed.

Drake nodded.

"What are they trying to do? Get a confession of some sort out of her?"

"Nobody knows. Two men showed up at the law office where she works yesterday afternoon. It took me a while to get the name of that law office, but I finally got it. It's one of the most substantial, conservative firms in town, and it created quite a furor when these two men walked in, identified themselves and said they wanted Mae Jordan.

"They had a talk with her in a private office, then came out and hunted up old man Honcut, who's the senior member of the firm Honcut, Gridley and Billings. They told him that for Mae's own safety they were going to have to keep her out of circulation for a while. She had about three weeks for vacation coming, and they told Honcut she could come back right after the trial."

"She went willingly?" Mason asked.

"Apparently so."

Mason thought that over. "How did they find her, Paul?"

"Simplest thing in the world. They searched Jefferson when they booked him. There was a name and address book. It was all in code. They cracked the code and ran down the names. When they came to this Jordan girl she talked."

"She tried to talk herself out by talking Duane Jefferson in," Mason said grimly. "When that young woman gets on the stand she's going to have a cross-examination she'll remember for a long, long time. What about Irving, Paul? Where did he go after he left here?"

"Now there," Drake said, "I have some more bad news for you."

Mason's face darkened. "That was damn important, Paul. I told you—"

"I know what you *told* me, Perry. Now *I'm* going to tell *you* something about the shadowing business that I've told you a dozen times before and I'll probably tell you a dozen times again. If a smart man knows he's being tailed and doesn't want to be shadowed, there's not much

88

you can do about it. If he's smart, he can give you the slip every time, unless you have four or five operatives all equipped with some means of intercommunication."

"But Irving didn't *know* he was being tailed."

"What makes you think he didn't?"

"Well," Mason said, "he didn't act like it when he came up here to the office."

"He sure acted like it when he left," Drake said. "What did you tell him?"

"Nothing to arouse his suspicions. Specifically, what did he do, Paul?"

"He proceeded to ditch the shadows."

"How?"

"To begin with, he got a taxi. He must have told the taxi driver there was a car following him that he wanted to ditch. The cab driver played it smart. He'd slide up to the traffic signals just as they were changing, then go on through. My man naturally tried to keep up with him, relying on making an explanation to any traffic cop who might stop him.

"Well, a traffic cop stopped him and it happened he was a cop who didn't feel kindly toward private detectives. He got tough, held my man, and gave him a ticket. By that time, Irving was long since gone.

"Usually a cop will give you a break on a deal like that if you have your credentials right handy, show them to him and tell him you're shadowing the car ahead. This chap deliberately held my man up until Irving got away. Not that I think it would have made any difference. Irving knew that he was being tailed, and he'd made up his mind he was going to ditch the tail. When a smart man gets an idea like that in his head, there's nothing you can do about it except roll with the punch and take it."

"So what did you do, Paul?"

"Did the usual things. Put men on his apartment house to pick him up when he got back. Did everything."

"And he hasn't been back?"

Drake shook his head.

"All right. What about the others?"

"Marline Chaumont," Drake said. "You thought it would be easy to locate her."

"You mean you've drawn a blank all the way along the line?" Mason interposed impatiently.

"I found out about Mae Jordan," Drake said.

"And that's all?"

"That's all."

"All right. What about Marline Chaumont? Give me the bad news in bunches."

"It took me a devil of a time to find the taxicab driver who went out to the house," Drake said. "I finally located him. He remembered the occasion well. He took the woman, the man, four suitcases and a handbag to the airport."

"And then what?" Mason asked.

"Then we draw a blank. We can't find where she left the airport."

"You mean a woman with a man who is hardly able to navigate by himself, with four big suitcases and a handbag, can vanish from the airport?" Mason asked.

"That's right," Drake said. "Just try it sometime, Perry."

"Try what?"

"Covering all of the taxicab drivers who go to the air terminal. Try and get them to tell you whether they picked up a man, a woman, four suitcases and a handbag. People are coming in by plane every few minutes. The place is a regular madhouse."

Mason thought that over. "All right, Paul," he said. "Irving told me we'd get no place, but I thought the four suitcases would do it."

"So did I when you first told me about it," Drake said.

"They went directly to the airport?"

"That's right."

"Paul, they must have gone *somewhere.*"

"Sure, they went somewhere," Drake said. "I can tell you where they *didn't* go."

"All right. Where didn't they go?"

"They didn't take any plane that left at about that time of day."

"How do you know?"

"I checked it by the excess baggage. The taxi driver says the suitcases were heavy. They must have weighed forty pounds each. I checked the departures on the planes."

"You checked them by name, of course?"

Drake's look was withering. "Don't be silly, Perry. That was the first thing. That was simple. Then I checked with the ticket sellers to see if there was a record of tickets sold at that time of day with that amount of excess baggage. There wasn't. Then I checked with the gate men to see if they remembered some woman going through the gate who would need help in getting a man aboard the plane. There was none. I also checked on wheel chairs. No dice. So then I concluded she'd gone to the airport, unloaded, paid off the cab, and had picked up another cab at the airport to come back."

"And you couldn't find that cab?"

"My men are still working on it. But that's like going to some babe wearing a skirt reaching to her knees, a tight sweater, and asking her if she remembered anybody whistling at her yesterday as she walked down the street."

After a moment Mason grinned. "All right, Paul. We're drawing a blank. Now why the devil would the district attorney have Mae Jordan picked up?"

"Because he wanted to question her."

"Then why wouldn't he have let her go after he questioned her?"

"Because he hasn't finished questioning her."

Mason shook his head. "You overlook what happened. She went up to her room, packed—got two suitcases. The district attorney is keeping her in what amounts to custody."

"Why?"

Mason grinned. "Now wait a minute, Paul. That's the question that I asked you. Of course, the only answer is that he wants her as a material witness. But if he does that, it means she must have told a story that has pulled the wool completely over his eyes, and he fell for it hook, line, and sinker."

"You don't think she's a material witness?" Drake asked.

Mason thought the situation over for a minute, then a slow smile spread over his features. "She would be, if she told the truth. I don't think there's any better news that I could have had."

"Why?"

"Because if the district attorney doesn't put her on the stand as a witness, I'll claim that he sabotaged my case by spiriting away *my* witnesses. If he does put her on the stand, I'll make him the sickest district attorney west of Chicago."

"You're going to play into his hands by going to an immediate trial?" Drake asked.

Mason grinned. "Paul, did you ever see a good tug of war?"

Drake thought for a moment, then said, "They used to put them on in the country towns on the Fourth of July."

"And did you ever see the firemen having a tug of war with the police department?"

"I may have. I can't remember. Why?"

"And," Mason went on, "about the time the fire department was all dug in and huffing and puffing, there would be a secret signal from the police department and everybody would give the firemen a lot of slack and they'd go over backwards, and then the police department would give a big yo-heave-ho and pull the whole aggregation right over the dividing line on the seat of their pants."

Drake grinned. "Seems to me I remember something like that, now that you speak of it."

"Well," Mason said, "that is what is known as playing into the hands of the district attorney, Paul. We're going to give him lots of slack. Now, answering your question more specifically—yes, I'm going to an immediate trial. I'm going to go to trial while the D.A. is hypnotized by Mae Jordan's story and before he finds out I know some of the things I know and that he doesn't know."

14

■

THE SELECTION OF THE JURY WAS COMPLETED AT TEN-thirty on the second day of the trial. Judge Hartley settled back on the bench, anticipating a long, bitterly contested trial.

"Gentlemen," he said, "the jury has been selected and sworn. The prosecution will proceed with its opening statement."

At that moment, Hamilton Burger, the district attorney, who had left the selection of the jury to subordinates, dramatically strode into the courtroom to take charge of the trial personally.

The district attorney bowed to the judge and, almost without pausing, passed the counsel table to stand facing the jury.

"Good morning, ladies and gentlemen of the jury," he said. "I am the district attorney of this county. We expect to show you that the defendant in this case is an employee of the South African Gem Importing and Exploration Company; that through his employment he had reason to know that a man named Munroe Baxter had in his possession a large number of diamonds valued at more than three hundred thousand dollars on the retail market; that the defendant knew Munroe Baxter intended to smuggle those diamonds into this country, and that the defendant murdered Munroe Baxter and took possession of those diamonds. We will introduce witnesses to show premeditation, deliberation and the cunning execution of a diabolical scheme of murder. We will show that a goodly proportion of the diamonds smuggled into the country by Munroe Baxter were found in the possession of the defendant. On the strength of that evidence we shall ask for a verdict of first-degree murder."

And Hamilton Burger, bowing to the jury, turned and stalked back to the counsel table.

Court attachés looked at each other in surprise. It was the shortest opening statement Hamilton Burger had ever made, and no one missed its significance. Hamilton Burger had carefully refrained from disclosing his hand or giving the defense the faintest inkling of how he intended to prove his case.

"My first witness," Hamilton Burger said, "will be Yvonne Manco."

"Come forward, Yvonne Manco," the bailiff called.

Yvonne Manco had evidently been carefully instructed. She came forward, trying her best to look demure. Her neckline was high and her skirt was fully as long as the current styles dictated, but the attempt to make her look at all conservative was as unsuccessful as would have been an attempt to disguise a racing sports car as a family sedan.

Yvonne gave her name and address to the court reporter, then looked innocently at the district attorney—after having flashed a sidelong glance of appraisal at the men of the jury.

Under questioning of the district attorney, Yvonne told the story of her relationship with Munroe Baxter, of the carefully laid plot to smuggle the gems, of the tour aboard the cruise ship, the spurious "whirlwind courtship."

She told of the plot to arrange the fake suicide, her deliberate flirtation with the assistant purser, the scene on the ship, and then finally that early morning plunge into the waters of the bay. She disclosed that she had carried a small compressed air tank in her baggage and that when Baxter went overboard, he was prepared to swim for a long distance underwater.

Hamilton Burger brought out a series of maps and photographs of the cruise ship. He had the witness identify the approximate place where the leap had taken place, both from the deck of the steamer and from its location in the bay.

"You may cross-examine," he said to Perry Mason.

Mason smiled at the witness, who promptly returned his smile, shifted her position slightly and crossed her legs, so that two of the masculine members of the jury hitched forward in their chairs for a better look, while the chins of two of the less attractive women on the jury were conspicuously elevated.

"You go by the name of Yvonne Manco?" Mason asked.

"Yes."

"You have another name?"

"No."

"You were really married to Munroe Baxter, were you not?"

"Yes, but now that I am a widow I choose to keep my maiden name of Yvonne Manco."

"I see," Mason said. "You don't want to bear the name of your husband?"

"It is not that," she said. "Yvonne Manco is my professional name."

"What profession?" Mason asked.

There was a moment's silence, then Hamilton Burger was on his feet. "Your Honor, I object. I object to the manner in which the question is asked. I object to the question. Incompetent, irrelevant, and immaterial."

Judge Hartley stroked his chin thoughtfully. "Well," he said, "under the circumstances I'm going to sustain the objection. However, in view of the answer of the witness— However, the objection is sustained."

"You were, however, married to Munroe Baxter?"

"Yes."

"On shipboard?"

"Yes."

"Before that?"

"No."

"There had been no previous ceremony?"

"No."

"Are you familiar with what is referred to as a common law marriage?"

"Yes."

"Had you ever gone by the name of Mrs. Baxter?"

"Yes."

"Prior to this cruise?"

"Yes."

"As a part of this plot which you and Munroe Baxter hatched up, he was to pretend to be dead. Is that right?"

"Yes."

"With whom did the idea originate? You or Munroe Baxter?"

"With him."

"He was to pretend to jump overboard and be dead, so he could smuggle in some diamonds?"

"Yes. I have told you this."

"In other words," Mason said, "if at any time it should be to his advantage, he was quite willing to pretend to be dead."

"Objected to as calling for the conclusion of the witness as already asked and answered," Hamilton Burger said.

"Sustained," Judge Hartley said.

Mason, having made his point, smiled at the jury. "You

knew that you were engaging in a smuggling transaction?" he asked the witness.

"But of course. I am not stupid."

"Exactly," Mason said. "And after this investigation started, you had some contact with the district attorney?"

"Naturally."

"And was it not through the offices of the district attorney that arrangements were made so you could testify in this case, yet be held harmless and not be prosecuted for smuggling?"

"Well, of course—"

"Just a minute, just a minute," Hamilton Burger interrupted. "I want to interpose an objection to that question, Your Honor."

"Go ahead," Judge Hartley ruled.

"It is incompetent, irrelevant and immaterial. It is not proper cross-examination."

"Overruled," Judge Hartley said. "Answer the question."

"Well, of course there was no definite agreement. That would have been . . . unwise."

"Who told you it would be unwise?"

"It was agreed by all that it would be unwise."

"By all, whom do you mean? Whom do you include?"

"Well, the customs people, the district attorney, the detectives, the police, my own lawyer."

"I see," Mason said. "They told you that it would be unwise to have a definite agreement to this effect, but nevertheless they gave you every assurance that if you testified as they wished, you would not be prosecuted on a smuggling charge?"

"Your Honor, I object to the words 'as they wished,'" Hamilton Burger said. "That calls for a conclusion of the witness."

Judge Hartley looked down at the witness.

Mason said, "I'll put it this way, was there any conversation as to what you were to testify to?"

"The truth."

"Who told you that?"

"Mr. Burger, the district attorney." '

"And was there some assurance given you that if you so testified, you would be given immunity from the smuggling?"

"If I testified to the *truth?* Yes."

"Before this assurance was given you, you had told these people what the truth was?"

"Yes."

"And that was the same story you have told on the witness stand here?"

"Certainly."

"So that when the district attorney told you to tell the truth, you understood that he meant the same story you have just told here?"

"Yes."

"So then, the assurance that was given you was that if you would tell the story you have now told on the witness stand, you would be given immunity from smuggling."

"That was my understanding."

"So," Mason said, "simply by telling this story you are given immunity from smuggling?"

"Well, not— It was not that . . . not that crude," she said.

The courtroom broke into laughter.

"That," Mason said, "is all."

Hamilton Burger was plainly irritated as the witness left the stand. "My next witness will be Jack Gilly," he said.

Jack Gilly was a slender, shifty-eyed man with high cheekbones, a long, sharp nose, a high forehead, and a pointed chin. He moved with a silence that was almost furtive as he glided up to the witness stand, held up his hand, was sworn, gave his name and address to the court reporter, seated himself, and looked expectantly at the district attorney.

"What's your occupation?" Hamilton Burger asked.

"At the moment?" he asked.

"Well, do you have the same occupation now you had six months ago?"

"Yes."

"What is it?"

"I rent fishing boats."

"Where?"

"At the harbor here."

"Were you acquainted with Munroe Baxter during his lifetime?"

"Just a moment before you answer that question," Mason said to the witness. He turned to Judge Hartley. "I object, Your Honor, on the ground that the question assumes a fact not in evidence. As far as the evidence before this court at the present time is concerned, Munroe Baxter is still alive."

"May I be heard on that, Your Honor?" Hamilton Burger asked.

"Well," Judge Hartley said, hesitating, "it would certainly seem that the logical way to present this case would be first to— However, I'll hear you, Mr. District Attorney."

"If the Court please," Hamilton Burger said, "Munroe Baxter jumped overboard in deep water. He was never seen alive afterward. I have witnesses from the passengers and the crew who will testify that Munroe Baxter ran to the rear of the ship, jumped overboard and vanished in the water. The ship called for a launch to come alongside, the waters were searched and searched carefully. Munroe Baxter never came up."

"Well," Judge Hartley said, "you can't expect this Court to rule on evidence predicated upon an assumption as to what you intend to prove by other witnesses. Moreover, your own witness has testified that this was all part of a scheme on the part of Munroe Baxter to—"

"Yes, yes, I know," Hamilton Burger interrupted. "But

schemes can go astray. Many unforeseen things can enter into the picture. Jumping from the deck of a ship is a perilous procedure."

Judge Hartley said, "Counsel will kindly refrain from interrupting the Court. I was about to say, Mr. District Attorney, that the testimony of your own witness indicates this was all part of a planned scheme by which Munroe Baxter intended to appear to commit suicide. In view of the fact that there is a presumption that a man remains alive until he is shown to be dead, the Court feels the objection is well taken."

"Very well, Your Honor, I will reframe the question," Hamilton Burger said. "Mr. Gilly, did you know Munroe Baxter?"

"Yes."

"How well did you know him?"

"I had met him several times."

"Were you acquainted with Yvonne Manco, who has just testified?"

"Yes."

"Directing your attention to the sixth day of June of this year, what was your occupation at that time?"

"I was renting boats."

"And to the fifth day of June, what was your occupation?"

"I was renting boats."

"Did you rent a boat on the fifth of June at an hour nearing seven o'clock in the evening?"

"Yes, sir."

"To whom did you rent that boat?"

"Frankly, I don't know."

"It was to some man you had never seen before?"

"Yes."

"Did the man tell you what he wanted?"

"He said that he had been directed to me because I was—"

"Just a moment," Mason interrupted. "I object to any

conversation which did not take place in the presence of the defendant and which is not connected up with the defendant."

"I propose to connect this up with the defendant," Hamilton Burger said.

"Then the connection should be shown before the conversation," Mason said.

Judge Hartley nodded. "The objection is sustained."

"Very well. You rented a boat to this man who was a stranger to you?"

"Yes, sir."

"From what this man said, however, you had reason to rent him the boat?"

"Yes."

"Was money paid you for the boat?"

"Yes."

"And when did the man start out in the boat, that is, when did he take delivery of it?"

"At about five o'clock the next morning."

"What were the circumstances surrounding the delivery of the boat?"

"He stood on the dock with me. I had a pair of powerful night glasses. When I saw the cruise ship coming in the harbor, I said to this man that I could see the cruise ship, and he jumped in the boat and took off."

"Did he start the motor?"

"The motor had been started an hour previously so it would be warm and so everything would be in readiness."

"And what did the man do?"

"He guided the boat away from my dock and out into the channel."

"Just a moment," Mason said. "Your Honor, I move to strike all of this evidence out on the ground that it has not been connected with the defendant in any way."

"I am going to connect it up," Hamilton Burger said, "within the next few questions."

"The Court will reserve a ruling," Judge Hartley said.

"It seems to me that these questions are largely preliminary."

"What did *you* do after the boat was rented?" Hamilton Burger asked the witness.

"Well," Gilly said, "I was curious. I wanted to see—"

"Never mind your thoughts or emotions," Hamilton Burger said. "What did you *do?*"

"I walked back to where my car was parked, got in the car and drove out to a place I knew on the waterfront where I could get out on the dock and watch what was going on."

"What do you mean by your words, 'what was going on'?"

"Watch the boat I had rented."

"And what did you see?"

"I saw the cruise ship coming slowly into the harbor."

"And what else did you see?"

"I saw Munroe Baxter jump overboard."

"You know it was Munroe Baxter?"

"Well, I— Of course, I knew it from what happened."

"But did you recognize him?"

"Well . . . it looked like Baxter, but at that distance and in that light I couldn't *swear* to it."

"*Don't* swear to it then," Hamilton Burger snapped. "You saw a man jump overboard?"

"Yes."

"Did that man look like anyone you knew?"

"Yes."

"Who?"

"Munroe Baxter."

"That is, as I understand your testimony, he looked like Munroe Baxter, but you can't definitely swear that it *was* Munroe Baxter. Is that right?"

"That's right."

"Then what happened?"

"I saw people running around on the deck of the cruise

ship. I heard voices evidently hailing a launch, and a launch came and cruised around the ship."

"What else happened?"

"I kept my binoculars trained on the boat I rented."

"What did you see?"

"There were two men in the boat."

"*Two* men?" Hamilton Burger asked.

"Yes, sir."

"Where did the other man come from, do you know?"

"No, sir. I don't. But I am assuming that he was picked up on one of the docks while I was getting my car."

"That may go out," Hamilton Burger said. "You don't know of your own knowledge where this man came from?"

"No, sir."

"You know only that by the time you reached the point of vantage from which you could see the boat, there were two men in the boat?"

"Yes, sir."

"All right, then what happened?"

"The boat sat there for some time. The second man appeared to be fishing. He was holding a heavy bamboo rod and a line over the side of the boat."

"And then what happened?"

"After quite a while I saw the fishing pole suddenly jerk, as though something very heavy had taken hold of the line."

"And then what?"

"Then I could see a black body partially submerged in the water, apparently hanging onto the fish line."

"And then what did you see?"

"One of the men leaned over the side of the boat. He appeared to be talking—"

"Never mind what he appeared to be doing. What did he do?"

"He leaned over the side of the boat."

"Then what?"

"Then he reached down to the dark object in the water."

"Then what?"

"Then I saw him raise his right arm and lower it rapidly several times. There was a knife in his hand. He was plunging the knife down into the dark thing in the water."

"Then what?"

"Then both men fumbled around with the thing that was in the water; then one of the men lifted a heavy weight of some kind over the side of the boat and tied it to the thing that was in the water."

"Then what?"

"Then they started the motor in the boat, slowly towing the weighted object in the water. I ran back to my automobile, got into it and drove back to my boat pier."

"And what happened then?"

"Then after a couple of hours the man who had rented the boat brought it back."

"Was anyone with him at the time?"

"No, sir, he was alone."

"What did you do?"

"I asked him if he had picked anyone up and he—"

"I object to any conversation which was not in the presence of the defendant," Mason said.

"Just a moment," Hamilton Burger said. "I will withdraw the question until I connect it up. Now, Mr. Gilly, did you recognize the other man who was in the boat with this stranger?"

"Not at the time. I had never seen him before."

"Did you see him subsequently?"

"Yes, sir."

"Who was that man?"

"The defendant."

"You are referring now to Duane Jefferson, the defendant who is seated here in the courtroom?"

"Yes, sir."

"Are you positive of your identification?"

"Just a moment," Mason said. "That's objected to as an attempt on the part of counsel to cross-examine his own witness."

"Overruled," Judge Hartley said. "Answer the question."

"Yes, sir, I am positive."

"You were watching through binoculars?"

"Yes, sir."

"What is the power of those binoculars?"

"Seven by fifty."

"Are they a good pair of binoculars?"

"Yes, sir."

"With coated lenses?"

"Yes, sir."

"You could see the boat clearly enough to distinguish the features of the people who were in the boat?"

"Yes, sir."

"Now then, after the boat was returned to you, did you notice any stains on the boat?"

"Yes, sir."

"What were those stains?"

"Bloodstains that—"

"No, no," Hamilton Burger said. "Just describe the stains. You don't know whether they were blood."

"I know they *looked* like blood."

"Just describe the stains, please," Hamilton Burger insisted, striving to appear virtuous and impartial.

"They were reddish stains, dark reddish stains."

"Where were they?"

"On the outside of the boat, just below the gunwale, and over on the inside of the boat where there had been a spattering or spurting."

"When did you first notice those stains?"

"Just after the boat had been returned to me."

"Were they fresh at that time?"

"Objected to as calling for a conclusion of the witness and no proper foundation laid," Mason said.

"The objection is sustained," Judge Hartley ruled.

"Well, how did they appear to you?"

"Same objection."

"Same ruling."

"Look here," Hamilton Burger said, "you have been engaged in the fishing business and in fishing for recreation for some time?"

"Yes, sir."

"During that time you have had occasion to see a lot of blood on boats?"

"Yes, sir."

"And have you been able to judge the relative freshness of the stains by the color of that blood?"

"Yes, sir."

"That's fish blood the witness is being asked about?" Mason interposed.

"Well . . . yes," Hamilton Burger conceded.

"And may I ask the prosecutor if it is his contention that these stains on the boat the witness has described were fish blood?"

"Those were stains of human blood!" Hamilton Burger snapped.

"I submit," Mason said, "that a witness cannot be qualified as an expert on human bloodstains by showing that he has had experience with fish blood."

"The principle is the same," Hamilton Burger said. "The blood assumes the same different shades of color in drying."

"Do I understand the district attorney is now testifying as an expert?" Mason asked.

Judge Hartley smiled. "I think the Court will have to agree with defense counsel, Mr. District Attorney. There must first be a showing as to whether there is a similarity in the appearance of fish blood and human blood *if* you are now trying to qualify this witness as an expert."

"Oh, well," Hamilton Burger said, "I'll get at it in another way by another witness. You are positive as to your identification of this defendant, Mr. Gilly?"

"Yes, sir."

"And he was in the boat at the time you saw this thing—whatever it was—stabbed with a knife?"

"Yes, sir."

"Were these stains you have mentioned on the boat when you rented it?"

"No."

"They were there when the boat was returned?"

"Yes."

"Where is this boat now?" Hamilton Burger asked.

"In the possession of the police."

"When was it taken by the police?"

"About ten days later."

"You mean the sixteenth of June?"

"I believe it was the fifteenth."

"Did you find anything else in the boat, Mr. Gilly?"

"Yes, sir."

"What?"

"A sheath knife with the name 'Duane' engraved on the hilt on one side and the initials 'M.J.' on the other side."

"Where is that knife?"

"The police took it."

"When?"

"At the time they took the boat."

"Would you know that knife if you saw it again?"

"Yes."

Hamilton Burger unwrapped some tissue paper, produced a keen-bladed hunting knife, took it to the witness. "Have you ever seen this knife before?"

"Yes. That's the knife I found in the boat."

"Is it now in the same condition it was then?"

"No, sir. It was blood—I mean, it was stained with something red then, more than it is now."

"Yes, yes, some of those stains were removed at the

crime laboratory for analysis," Hamilton Burger said suavely. "You may cross-examine the witness, Mr. Mason. And I now ask the clerk to mark this knife for identification."

Mason smiled at Gilly. "Ever been convicted of a felony, Mr. Gilly?" Mason asked, his voice radiating good feeling.

Hamilton Burger jumped to his feet, apparently preparing to make an objection, then slowly settled back in his chair.

Gilly shifted his watery eyes from Mason's face to the floor.

"Yes, sir."

"How many times?" Mason asked.

"Twice."

"For what?"

"Once for larceny."

"And what was it for the second time?" Mason asked.

"Perjury," Gilly said.

Mason's smile was affable. "How far were you from the boat when you were watching it through your binoculars?"

"About . . . oh, a couple of good city blocks."

"How was the light?"

"It was just after daylight."

"There was fog?"

"Not fog. A sort of mist."

"A cold mist?"

"Yes. It was chilly."

"What did you use to wipe off the lenses of the binoculars—or did you wipe them?"

"I don't think I wiped them."

"And you saw one of these men fishing?"

"Yes, sir. The defendant held the fishing rod."

"And apparently he caught something?"

"A big body caught hold of the line."

"Have you seen people catch big fish before?"

"Yes, sir."

"And sometimes when they have caught sharks you have seen them cut the sharks loose from the line or stab them to death before taking them off the hook?"

"This wasn't a shark."

"I'm asking you a question," Mason said. "Have you seen that?"

"Yes."

"Now, did this thing that was on the fishing line ever come entirely out of the water?"

"No, sir."

"Enough out of the water so you could see what it was?"

"It was almost all underwater all the time."

"You had never seen this man who rented the boat from you before he showed up to rent the boat?"

"No, sir."

"And you never saw him again?"

"No, sir."

"Do you know this knife wasn't in the boat when you rented it?"

"Yes."

"When did you first see it?"

"The afternoon of the sixth of June."

"Where?"

"In my boat."

"You had not noticed it before?"

"No."

"Yet you had looked in the boat?"

"Yes."

"And from the time the boat was returned to you until you found the knife, that boat was where anyone could have approached and dropped this knife into it, or tossed it to the bottom of the boat?"

"Well, I guess so. Anyone could have if he'd been snooping around down there."

"And how much rental did this mysterious man give you for the boat?"

"That's objected to as incompetent, irrelevant, and immaterial and not proper cross-examination," Hamilton Burger said.

"Well," Mason said, smiling, "I'll get at it in another way. Do you have an established rental rate for that boat, Mr. Gilly?"

"Yes, sir."

"How much is it?"

"A dollar to a dollar and a half an hour."

"Now then, did this stranger pay you the regular rental rate for the boat?"

"We made a special deal."

"You got *more* than your regular rental rate?"

"Yes, sir."

"How much more?"

"Objected to as not proper cross-examination, calling for facts not in evidence, and incompetent, irrelevant, and immaterial," Hamilton Burger said.

"Overruled," Judge Hartley said.

"How much rental?" Mason asked.

"I can't recall offhand. I think it was fifty dollars," Gilly said, his eyes refusing to meet those of Mason.

"Was that the figure that you asked, or the figure that the man offered?"

"The figure that I asked."

"Are you sure it was fifty dollars?"

"I can't remember too well. He gave me a bonus. I can't recall how much it was."

"Was it more than fifty dollars?"

"It could have been. I didn't count it. I just took the bills he gave me and put them in the locked box where I keep my money."

"You keep your money in the form of cash?"

"Some of it."

"Did you ever count this bonus?"

"I can't remember doing so."

"It could have been more than fifty dollars?"

"I guess so. I don't know."

"Could it have been as much as a thousand dollars?"

"Oh, that's absurd!" Hamilton Burger protested to the Court.

"Overruled," Judge Hartley snapped.

"Was it?" Mason asked.

"I don't know."

"Did you enter it on your books?"

"I don't keep books."

"You don't know then how much cash is in this locked box where you keep your money?"

"Not to the penny."

"To the dollar?"

"No."

"To the hundred dollars?"

"No."

"Have you more than five hundred dollars in that box right now?"

"I don't know."

"More than five thousand dollars?"

"I can't tell."

"You may have?"

"Yes."

"Now, when were you convicted of perjury," Mason asked, "was that your first offense or the second?"

"The second."

Mason smiled. "That's all, Mr. Gilly."

Judge Hartley glanced at the clock. "It appears that it is now time for the noon adjournment. Court will recess until two o'clock. During this time the jurors will not form or express any opinion as to the merits of the case, but will wait until the case is finally submitted before doing so. Nor will the jurors discuss the case among themselves or permit it to be discussed in their presence. The defendant is remanded to custody. Court will recess until two o'clock."

Paul Drake and Della Street, who had been occupying seats which had been reserved for them in the front of the courtroom, came toward Perry Mason.

Mason caught Paul Drake's eye, motioned them back. He turned to his client. "By the way," Mason said, "where *were* you on the night of the fifth and the morning of the sixth of June?"

"In my apartment, in bed and asleep."

"Can you prove it?" Mason asked.

Jefferson said scornfully, "Don't be absurd! I am unmarried, Mr. Mason. I sleep alone. There was no occasion for me to try and show where I was at that time, and there is none now. No one is going to pay any attention to the word of a perjurer and a crook who never saw me in his life before. Who is this scum of the waterfront? This whole thing is preposterous!"

"I'd be inclined to think so, too," Mason told him, "if it wasn't for that air of quiet confidence on the part of the district attorney. Therefore, it becomes very important for me to know exactly where you were on the night of the fifth and the morning of the sixth."

"Well," Jefferson said, "on the night of the fifth . . . that is, on the evening of the fifth I— I see no reason to go into that. On the sixth . . . from midnight on the fifth until eight-thirty on the morning of the sixth I was in my apartment. By nine o'clock on the morning of the sixth I was in my office, and I can *prove* where I was from a little after seven on the morning of the sixth."

"By whom?"

"By my associate, Walter Irving. He joined me for breakfast at seven in my apartment, and after that we went to the office."

"What about that knife?" Mason asked.

"It's mine. It was stolen from a suitcase in my apartment."

"Where did you get it?"

"It was a gift."

"From whom?"

"That has nothing to do with the case, Mr. Mason."

"Who gave it to you?"

"It's none of your business."

"I *have* to know who gave it to you, Jefferson."

"I am conducting my own affairs, Mr. Mason."

"I'm conducting your case."

"Go right ahead. Just don't ask me questions about women, that's all. I don't discuss my female friends with anyone."

"Is there anything you're ashamed of in connection with that gift?"

"Certainly not."

"Then tell me who gave it to you."

"It would be embarrassing to discuss any woman with you, Mr. Mason. That might bring about a situation where you'd feel I was perjuring myself about my relationship with women . . . when I get on the stand and answer questions put by the district attorney."

Mason studied Jefferson's face carefully. "Look here," he said. "Lots of times a weak case on the part of the prosecution is bolstered because the defendant breaks down under cross-examination. Now, I hope this case is never going to reach a point where it will become necessary to put on any defense. But if it does, I've got to be *certain* you're not lying to me."

Jefferson looked at Mason coldly. "I *never* lie to *anyone*," he said, and then turning away from Mason signaled to the officer that he was ready to be taken back to jail.

Della Street and Paul Drake fell in step with Mason as the lawyer started down the aisle.

"What do you make of it?" Mason asked.

"There sure is something fishy about this whole thing," Drake said. "It stinks. It has all the earmarks of a frame-up. How can Burger think people of that sort can put across a deal like this on a man like Duane Jefferson?"

"That," Mason said, "is the thing we're going to have to find out. Anything new?"

"Walter Irving's back."

"The deuce he is! Where has he been?"

"No one knows. He showed up about ten-thirty this morning. He was in court."

"Where?"

"Sitting in a back row, taking everything in."

Mason said, "There's something here that is completely and thoroughly contradictory. The whole case is cock-eyed."

"The police have something up their sleeves," Drake said. "They have some terrific surprise. I can't find out what it is. Do you notice that Hamilton Burger seems to remain thoroughly elated?"

"That's the thing that gets me," Mason said. "Burger puts on these witnesses and acts as though he's just laying a preliminary foundation. He doesn't seem to take too much interest in their stories, or whether I attack their characters or their credibility. He's playing along for something big."

"What about Irving?" Drake asked. "Are you going to be in touch with him?"

"Irving and I aren't on friendly terms. The last time he walked out of my office he was mad as a bucking bronco. He cabled his company, trying to get me fired. You haven't found out anything about Marline Chaumont or her brother?"

"I haven't found out where they are," Drake said, "but I think I've found out how they gave me the slip."

"How?" Mason asked. "I'm interested in that."

"It's so damn simple that it makes me mad I didn't get onto it sooner."

"What?"

Drake said, "Marline Chaumont simply took her suitcases and had a porter deposit them in storage lockers. Then she took her brother out to an airport limousine, as though they were *incoming* passengers. She gave a porter the keys for two of the lockers, so two suitcases were brought out. She went in the limousine to a downtown hotel. She and her brother got out and completely vanished."

"Then, of course, she went back and got the other suitcases?" Mason asked.

"Presumably," Drake said, "she got a taxicab after she had her brother safely put away, went out to the airport, picked up the other two suitcases out of the storage lockers, and then rejoined her brother."

Mason said, "We've got to find her, Paul."

"I'm trying, Perry."

"Can't you check hotel registrations? Can't you—?"

"Look, Perry," Drake said, "I've checked every hotel registration that was made at about that time. I've checked with rental agencies for houses that were rented. I've checked with the utilities for connections that were put in at about that time. I've done everything I can think of. I've had girls telephoning the apartment houses to see if anyone made application for apartments. I've even checked the motels to see who registered on that date. I've done everything I can think of."

Mason paused thoughtfully. "Have you checked the car rental agencies, Paul?"

"What do you mean?"

"I mean the drive-yourself automobiles where a person rents an automobile, drives it himself, pays so much a day and so much a mile?"

The expression on Drake's face showed mixed emotions. "She wouldn't— Gosh, no! Good Lord, Perry! Maybe I overlooked a bet!"

Mason said, "Why couldn't she get a drive-yourself automobile, put her stuff in it, go to one of the outlying cities, rent a house there, then drive back with the automobile and—"

"I'd say it was one chance in ten thousand," Drake said, "but I'm not going to overlook it. It's all that's left."

"Okay," Mason said. "Try checking that idea for size, Paul."

15

PROMPTLY AT TWO O'CLOCK COURT RECONVENED AND Judge Hartley said, "Call your next witness, Mr. District Attorney."

Hamilton Burger hesitated a moment, then said, "I will call Mae Wallis Jordan."

Mae Jordan, quiet, demure, taking slow, steady steps, as though steeling herself to a task which she had long anticipated with extreme distaste, walked to the witness stand, was sworn, gave her name and address to the court reporter, and seated herself.

Hamilton Burger's voice fairly dripped sympathy. "You are acquainted with the defendant, Duane Jefferson, Miss Jordan?" he asked.

"Yes, sir."

"When did you first get acquainted with him?"

"Do you mean, when did I first see him?"

"When did you first get in touch with him," Hamilton Burger asked, "and how?"

"I first saw him after he came to the city here, but I have been corresponding with him for some time."

"When was the date that you first *saw* him? Do you know?"

"I know very well. He arrived by train. I was there to meet the train."

"On what date?"

"May seventeenth."

"Of this year?"

"Yes, sir."

"Now then, you had had some previous correspondence with the defendant?"

"Yes."

"How had that correspondence started?"

"It started as a . . . as a joke. As a gag."

"In what way?"

"I am interested in photography. In a photographic magazine there was an offer to exchange colored stereo photographs of Africa for stereo photographs of the southwestern desert. I was interested and wrote to the box number in question."

"In South Africa?"

"Well, it was in care of the magazine, but it turned out that the magazine forwarded the mail to the person who had placed the ad in the magazine. That person was—"

"Just a moment," Mason interrupted. "We object to the witness testifying as to her conclusion. *She* doesn't know who put the ad in the magazine. Only the records of the magazine can show that."

"We will show them," Hamilton Burger said cheerfully. "However, Miss Jordan, we'll just skip that at the moment. What happened?"

"Well, I entered into correspondence with the defendant."

"What was the nature of that correspondence generally?" Hamilton Burger asked. And then, turning to Mason, said, "Of course, I can understand that this may be objected to as not being the best evidence, but I am trying to expedite matters."

Mason, smiling, said, "I am always suspicious of one

who tries to expedite matters by introducing secondary evidence. The letters themselves would be the best evidence."

"I only want to show the *general* nature of the correspondence," Hamilton Burger said.

"Objected to as not being the best evidence," Mason said, "and that the question calls for a conclusion of the witness."

"Sustained," Judge Hartley said.

"You received letters from South Africa?" Hamilton Burger asked, his voice showing a slight amount of irritation.

"Yes."

"Those letters were signed how?"

"Well . . . in various ways."

"What's that?" Hamilton Burger asked, startled. "I thought that—"

"Never mind what the district attorney thought," Mason said. "Let's have the *facts.*"

"How were those letters signed?" Hamilton Burger asked.

"Some of them were signed with the name of the defendant, the first ones were."

"And where are those letters now?"

"They are gone."

"Where?"

"I destroyed them."

"Describe the contents of those letters," Hamilton Burger said unctuously. "Having proved, Your Honor, that the best evidence is no longer available, I am seeking to show by secondary evidence—"

"There are no objections," Judge Hartley said.

"I was going to state," Mason said, "that I would like to ask some questions on cross-examination as to the nature and contents of the letters and the time and manner of their destruction, in order to see whether I wished to object."

"Make your objection first, and then you may ask the questions," Judge Hartley said.

"I object, Your Honor, on the ground that no proper foundation for the introduction of secondary testimony has been laid and on the further ground that it now appears that at least some of these letters did not even bear the name of the defendant. In connection with that objection, I would like to ask a few questions."

"Go ahead," Hamilton Burger invited, smiling slightly.

Mason said, "You said that those letters were signed in various ways. What did you mean by that?"

"Well—" she said, and hesitated.

"Go on," Mason said.

"Well," she said, "some of the letters were signed with various . . . well, gag names."

"Such as what?" Mason asked.

"Daddy Longlegs was one," she said.

There was a ripple of mirth in the courtroom, which subsided as Judge Hartley frowned.

"And others?"

"Various names. You see we . . . we exchanged photographs . . . gag pictures."

"What do you mean by gag pictures?" Mason asked.

"Well, I am a camera fan, and the defendant is, too, and . . . we started corresponding formally at first, and then the correspondence became more personal. I . . . he asked me for a picture, and I . . . for a joke I—"

"Go ahead," Mason said. "What did you do?"

"I had taken a photograph of a very trim spinster who was no longer young, a rather interesting face, however, because it showed a great deal of character. I had a photograph of myself in a bathing suit and I . . . I made a trick enlargement, so that the face of the trim spinster was put on my body, and I sent it to him. I thought that if he was simply being flirtatious, that would stop him."

"Was it a joke, or was it intended to deceive him?" Mason asked.

She flushed and said, "That first picture was intended to deceive him. It was done so cunningly that it would be impossible for him to know that it was a composite picture—at least, I thought it would be impossible."

"And you asked him to send you a picture in return?"

"I did."

"And did you receive a picture?"

"Yes."

"What was it?"

"It was the face of a giraffe wearing glasses, grafted on the photograph of a huge figure of a heavily muscled man. Evidently, the figure of a wrestler or a weight-lifter."

"And in that way," Mason asked, "you knew that he had realized your picture was a composite?"

"Yes."

"And what happened after that?"

"We exchanged various gag pictures. Each one trying to be a little more extreme than the other."

"And the letters?" Mason asked.

"The letters were signed with various names which would sort of fit in with the type of photograph."

"You so signed your letters to him?"

"Yes."

"And he so signed his letters to you?"

"Yes."

Mason made his voice elaborately casual. "He would sign letters to you, I suppose, as 'Your Prince,' or 'Sir Galahad,' or something like that?"

"Yes."

"Prince Charming?"

She gave a quick start. "Yes," she said. "As a matter of fact, at the last he signed *all* of his letters 'Prince Charming.' "

"Where are those letters now?" Mason asked.

"I destroyed his letters."

"And where are the letters that you wrote to him, if you know?"

"I . . . I destroyed them."

Hamilton Burger grinned. "Go right ahead, Mr. Mason. You're doing fine."

"How did you get ahold of them?" Mason asked.

"I . . . I went to his office."

"While he was there?" Mason asked.

"I— When I got the letters, he was there, yes."

Mason smiled at the district attorney. "Oh, I think, Your Honor, I have pursued this line of inquiry far enough. I will relinquish the right to any further questioning on the subject of the letters. I insist upon my objection, however. The witness can't swear that these letters ever came from this defendant. They were signed 'Prince Charming' and other names she said were gag names. That's her conclusion."

Judge Hartley turned toward the witness. "These letters were in response to letters mailed by you?"

"Yes, Your Honor."

"And how did you address the letters you mailed?"

"To 'Duane Jefferson, care of the South African Gem Importing and Exploration Company.' "

"At its South African address?"

"Yes, Your Honor."

"You deposited those letters in regular mail channels?"

"Yes, Your Honor."

"And received these letters in reply?"

"Yes, Your Honor."

"The letters showed they were in reply to those mailed by you?"

"Yes, Your Honor."

"And you burned them?"

"Yes, Your Honor."

"The objection is overruled," Judge Hartley said. "You may introduce secondary evidence of their contents, Mr. District Attorney."

Hamilton Burger bowed slightly, turned to the witness. "Tell us what was in those letters which were destroyed," he said.

"Well, the defendant adopted the position that he was lonely and far from the people he knew, that he didn't have any girl friends, and . . . oh, it was all a gag. It's *so* difficult to explain."

"Go ahead; do the best you can," Hamilton Burger said.

"We adopted the attitude of . . . well, we pretended it was a lonely hearts correspondence. He would write and tell me how very wealthy and virtuous he was and what a good husband he would make, and I would write and tell him how beautiful I was and how— Oh, it's just simply out of the question to try and explain it in cold blood this way!"

"Out of context, so to speak?" Hamilton Burger asked.

"Yes," she said. "That's just it. You have to understand the mood and the background, otherwise you wouldn't be able to get the picture at all. The letters, standing by themselves, would appear to be hopelessly foolish, utterly asinine. That was why I felt I had to have them back in my possession."

"Go ahead," Hamilton Burger said. "What did you do?"

"Well, finally Duane Jefferson wrote me one serious letter. He told me that his company had decided to open a branch office in the United States, that it was to be located here, and that he was to be in charge of it and that he was looking forward to seeing me."

"And what did you do?"

"All of a sudden I was in a terrific panic. It was one thing to carry on a joking correspondence with a man who was thousands of miles away and quite another thing suddenly to meet that man face to face. I was flustered and embarrassed."

"Go on. What did you do?"

"Well, of course, when he arrived—he wired me what train he was coming on, and I was there to meet him and —that was when things began to go wrong."

"In what way?"

"He gave me a sort of brush-off, and *he* wasn't the type of person *I* had anticipated. Of course," she went on hastily, "I know what a little fool I was to get a preconceived notion of a man I'd never seen, but I had built up a very great regard for him. I considered him as a friend and I was terribly disappointed."

"Then what?" Hamilton Burger asked.

"Then I called two or three times on the telephone and talked with him, and I went out with him one night."

"And what happened?"

She all but shuddered. "The man was utterly impossible," she said, glaring down at the defendant. "He was patronizing in a cheap, tawdry way. His manner showed that he had completely mistaken the tone of my correspondence. He regarded me as . . . he treated me as if I were a . . . he showed no respect, no consideration. He had none of the finer feelings."

"And what did *you* do?"

"I told him I wanted my letters back."

"And what did he do?"

She glared at Duane Jefferson. "He told me I could *buy* them back."

"So what did you do?"

"I determined to get those letters back. They were mine, anyway."

"So what did you do?"

"On June fourteenth I went to the office at a time when I knew neither the defendant nor Mr. Irving would normally be there."

"And what did you do?" Hamilton Burger asked.

"I entered the office."

"For what purpose?"

"For the sole purpose of finding the letters I had written."

"You had reason to believe those letters were in the office?"

"Yes. He told me they were in his desk and that I could come and get them at any time after I had complied with his terms."

"What happened?"

"I couldn't find the letters. I looked and I looked, and I pulled open the drawers of the desk and then—"

"Go on," Hamilton Burger said.

"And the door opened," she said.

"And who was in the doorway?"

"The defendant, Duane Jefferson."

"Alone?"

"No. His associate, Walter Irving, was with him."

"What happened?"

"The defendant used vile language. He called me names that I have never been called before."

"And then what?"

"He made a grab for me and—"

"And what did you do?"

"I backed up and tipped over a chair and fell over. Then Mr. Irving grabbed my ankles and held me. The defendant accused me of snooping and I told him I was there only to get my letters."

"Then what?"

"Then he stood for a moment looking at me in apparent surprise, and then said to Mr. Irving, 'Damned if I don't believe she's right!'"

"Then what?"

"Then the phone rang and Irving picked up the receiver, listened for a minute and said, 'Good God! The police!'"

"Go on," Hamilton Burger said.

"So the defendant ran over to a filing cabinet, jerked it open, pulled out a whole package of my letters tied up with string and said, 'Here, you little fool! Here are your letters. Take them and get out! The police are looking for you. Someone saw you break into the place, and the police have been notified. Now, see what a damn fool you are!' "

"What happened?"

"He started pushing me toward the door. Then Mr. Irving pushed something into my hand and said, 'Here, take these. They'll be a reward for keeping your big mouth shut.' "

"And what did you do?"

"As soon as they pushed me out of the door, I made a dash for the women's restroom."

"Go on," Hamilton Burger said.

"And just as I opened the door of the restroom, I saw the defendant and Walter Irving run out of their office and dash to the men's room."

"Then what?"

"I didn't wait to see any more. I dashed into the restroom and unfastened the string on the package of letters I had been given, looked through the contents to see that they were mine, and destroyed them."

"*How* did you destroy them?"

"I put them in the wastepaper receptacle with the used towels, where they would be picked up and incinerated."

"And then what did you do?"

"Then," she said, "I was trapped. I knew the police were coming. I—"

"Go ahead," Hamilton Burger said.

"I had to do something to get out of there."

"And *what* did you do?" Hamilton Burger said, a smile on his face.

"I felt that perhaps the exits might be watched, that I must have been seen by someone who had given the police a good description, so I . . . I looked around for someplace to go, and I saw a door which had the sign on it saying, 'Perry Mason, Attorney at Law, Enter.' I'd heard of Perry Mason, of course, and I thought perhaps I could hand him a line, telling him I wanted a divorce or something of that sort, or that I'd been in an automobile accident . . . just make up a good story, anything to hold his interest. That would enable me to be in his office when the police arrived. I felt I could hold his interest long enough to avoid the police. I wanted to stay there just long enough so I could get out after the police had given up the search. I realize now that it was a crazy idea, but it was the only available avenue of escape. As it happened, Fate played into my hands."

"In what way?"

"It seemed Mr. Mason's secretaries were expecting a typist. They'd telephoned some agency and a typist was supposed to be on her way up. I stood, hesitating, in the doorway for a moment, and the receptionist took me for the typist. She asked me if I was the typist, so of course I told her yes and went to work."

"And," Hamilton Burger said smugly, "you worked in the office of Perry Mason that afternoon?"

"I worked there for some little time, yes."

"And then what?"

"When the coast was clear I made my escape."

"When was that?"

"Well, I was working on a document. I was afraid that if it was finished, Mr. Mason would ring up the secretarial agency to find out what the bill was. I just didn't know what to do. So when there was a good break, I slipped down to the restroom, then to the elevator and went home."

"You have mentioned something that was pushed into your hand. Do you know what that consisted of?"

"Yes."

"What?"

"Diamonds. Two diamonds."

"When did you find out about them?"

"After I'd been working for a few minutes. I'd slipped

what had been given me into my handbag. So when I had a good chance I looked. I found two small packets of tissue paper. I removed the paper and found two diamonds.

"I got in a panic. I suddenly realized that if these men should claim the intruder had stolen diamonds from their office, I'd be framed. I wouldn't have any possible defense anyone would believe. So I just had to get rid of these diamonds. I realized right away I'd walked into a trap."

"What did you do?"

"I stuck the diamonds to the underside of the desk, where I was working in Mr. Mason's office."

"How did you stick them to this desk?"

"With chewing gum."

"How much chewing gum?"

"A perfectly terrific amount. I had about twelve sticks in my purse, and I chewed them all up and got a big wad of gum. Then I put the diamonds in the gum and pushed them up against the underside of the desk."

"Where are those diamonds now?"

"As far as *I* know, they're still there."

"Your Honor," Hamilton Burger said, "if the Court please, I suggest that an officer of this court be dispatched to the office of Perry Mason, with instructions to look at the place described by this witness and bring back the wad of chewing gum containing those two diamonds."

Judge Hartley looked at Mason questioningly.

Mason smiled at the judge. "*I* certainly would have no objection, Your Honor."

"Very well," Judge Hartley ruled. "It will be the order of the Court that an officer of this court proceed to take those diamonds and impound them."

"And may they be sent for *immediately*, Your Honor," Hamilton Burger asked, "before . . . well, before something happens to them?"

"And what would happen to them?" Judge Hartley asked.

"Well, now that it is known," Hamilton Burger said, "now that the testimony has come out . . . I . . . well, I would dislike to have anything happen to the evidence."

"So would I," Mason said heartily. "I join the prosecutor's request. I suggest that one of the deputy district attorneys instruct an officer to proceed at once to my office."

"Can you designate the desk that was used by this young lady?" Hamilton Burger asked.

"The desk in question was one that was placed in the law library. It can be found there."

"Very well," the judge ruled. "You may take care of that matter, Mr. District Attorney. Now, go on with your questioning."

Hamilton Burger walked over to the clerk's desk, picked up the knife which had been marked for identification. "I show you a dagger with an eight-inch blade, one side of the hilt being engraved with the word 'Duane,' the other side with the initials 'M.J.' I will ask you if you are familiar with that knife."

"I am. It is a knife which I sent the defendant at his South African address as a Christmas present last Christmas. I told him he could use it to protect . . . protect my honor."

The witness began to cry.

"I think," Hamilton Burger said suavely, "that those are all of the questions I have of this witness. You may cross-examine, Mr. Mason."

Mason waited patiently until Mae Jordan had dried her eyes and looked up at him. "You are, I believe, a very fast and accurate typist?"

"I try to be competent."

"And you worked in my office on the afternoon in question?"

"Yes."

"Do you know anything about gems?"

"Not particularly."

"Do you know the difference between a real diamond and an imitation diamond?"

"It didn't take an expert to tell those stones. Those were very high-grade stones. I recognized what they were as soon as I saw them."

"Had you bought those stones from the defendant?" Mason asked.

"What do you mean, had I bought those stones?"

"Did you pay him anything? Give him any consideration?"

"Certainly not," she snapped.

"Did you pay Mr. Irving for those stones?"

"No."

"Then you knew those stones did not belong to you?" Mason asked.

"They were given to me."

"Oh, then you thought they were yours?"

"I felt certain I'd walked into a trap. I felt those men would say I'd gone to their office and stolen those diamonds. It would be my word against theirs. I knew they hadn't given me two very valuable diamonds just to keep quiet about having exchanged letters."

"You say *they* gave you the diamonds. Did you receive them from Jefferson or from Irving?"

"From Mr. Irving."

Mason studied the defiant witness for a moment. "You started corresponding with the defendant while he was in South Africa?"

"Yes."

"And wrote him love letters?"

"They were not love letters."

"Did they contain matters which you wouldn't want this jury to see?"

"They were foolish letters, Mr. Mason. Please don't try to put anything in them that wasn't in them."

"I am asking you," Mason said, "as to the nature of the letters."

"They were *very foolish* letters."

"Would you say they were indiscreet?"

"I would say they were indiscreet."

"You wanted them back?"

"I felt . . . well . . . foolish about the whole thing."

"So you wanted the letters back?"

"Yes, very badly."

"And, in order to get them back, you were willing to commit a crime?"

"I wanted the letters back."

"Please answer the question. You were willing to commit a crime in order to get the letters back?"

"I don't know that it's a crime to enter an office to get things that belong to me."

"Did you believe it was illegal to use a skeleton key to enter property belonging to another person, so that you could take certain things?"

"I was trying to get possession of property that belonged to me."

"Did you believe that it was illegal to use a skeleton key to open that door?"

"I . . . I didn't consult a lawyer to find out about my rights."

"Where did you get the key which opened the door?"

"I haven't said I had a key."

"You've admitted you entered the office at a time when you knew both Jefferson and Irving would not be there."

"What if I did? I went to get my own property."

"If you had a key which opened the door of that office, where did you get it?"

"Where does one ordinarily get keys?"

"From a locksmith?"

"Perhaps."

"Did you get a key to that office from a locksmith?"

"I will answer no questions about keys."

"And suppose the Court should instruct you that you had to answer such questions?"

"I would refuse on the grounds that any testimony from me relating to the manner in which I entered that office would tend to incriminate me, and therefore I would not have to answer the question."

"I see," Mason said. "But you have already admitted that you entered the office illegally. Therefore, an attempt to exercise your constitutional prerogative would be too late."

"Now, if the Court please," Hamilton Burger said, "I would like to be heard on this point. I have given this question very careful thought. The Court will note that the witness simply stated that she entered the office at a time when the defendant and his associate were absent. She has not stated *how* she entered the office. As far as her testimony is concerned, the door could well have been unlocked; and, inasmuch as this is a public office, where it is expected the public will enter in order to transact business, there would have been nothing illegal about an entrance made in the event the door had been unlocked. Therefore, the witness is in a position, if she so desires, to refuse to testify as to the manner in which she entered that office, on the ground that it might tend to incriminate her."

Judge Hartley frowned. "That's rather an unusual position for a witness called on behalf of the prosecution, Mr. District Attorney."

"It's an unusual case, Your Honor."

"Do you wish to be heard on that point, Mr. Mason?" Judge Hartley asked.

Mason smiled and said, "I would like to ask the witness a few more questions."

"I object to any more cross-examination on this point," Hamilton Burger said, his voice showing exasperation and a trace of apprehension. "The witness has made her position plain. Counsel doesn't dare to cross-examine her about the pertinent facts in the case, so he continually harps upon the one point where this young woman, yielding to her emotions, has put herself in an embarrassing position. He keeps prolonging this moment, as a cat plays with a mouse, hoping thereby to prejudice the jury against this witness. The witness has made her position plain. She refuses to answer questions on this phase of the matter."

Mason smiled. "I have been accused of prolonging this phase of the examination in an attempt to prejudice the jury. I don't want to prejudice the jury. I'd like to get information which the jurors want.

"When the district attorney was prolonging the examination of Mr. Gilly in an attempt to prejudice the jury against the defendant, you didn't hear me screaming. What's sauce for the goose should be sauce for the gander."

Judge Hartley smiled. "The objection is overruled. Go ahead with your questions."

"Will you tell us the name of the person who furnished you with the key that enabled you to get into the office of the South African Gem Importing and Exploration Company?"

"No."

"Why not?"

"Because, if I answered that question, it would tend to incriminate me, and therefore I shall refuse to answer."

"You have discussed this phase of your testimony with the district attorney?"

"Oh, Your Honor," Hamilton Burger said, "this is the same old gambit so frequently pursued by defense attorneys. I will stipulate that this witness has discussed her testimony with me. I would not have put her on the stand unless I knew that her testimony would be pertinent and relevant. The only way I could know what it was, was to talk with her."

Mason kept his eyes on the witness. "You have discussed this phase of your testimony with the district attorney?"

"Yes."

"And have discussed with him what would happen in case you were asked a question concerning the name of the person who furnished you the keys?"

"Yes."

"And told him you would refuse to testify on the ground that it would incriminate you?"

"Yes."

"Did you make that statement to the district attorney, or did he suggest to you that you could refuse to answer the question on that ground?"

"Well, I . . . I . . . of course I know my rights."

"But you have just stated," Mason said, "that you didn't know that it was a crime for you to enter an office to get property that belonged to you."

"Well, I . . . I think there's a nice legal point there. As I now understand it, a public office . . . that is, a place that is intended to be open to the public is different from a private residence. And where property belongs to me—"

Mason smiled. "Then you are *now* taking the position, Miss Jordan, that it was no crime for you to enter that office?"

"No."

"Oh, you are *now* taking the position that it *was* a crime for you to enter that office?"

"I now understand that under the circumstances it— I refuse to answer that question on the ground that the answer may incriminate me."

"In other words, the district attorney suggested to you that you should consider it was a crime, and therefore you could refuse to answer certain questions when I asked them?"

"We discussed it."

"And the suggestion came from the district attorney that it would be well under the circumstances for you to refuse to answer certain questions which I might ask on cross-examination. Is that right?"

"There were certain questions I told him I wouldn't answer."

"And he suggested that you could avoid answering them by claiming immunity on the ground that you couldn't be forced to incriminate yourself?"

"Well, in a way, yes."

"Now then," Mason said, "you had two diamonds with you when you left that office?"

"Yes."

"They didn't belong to you?"

"They were given to me."

"By whom?"

"By Mr. Irving, who told me to take them."

"Did he say *why* you were to take them?"

"He said to take them and keep my big mouth shut."

"And you took them?"

"Yes."

"And you kept your mouth shut?"

"I don't know what you mean by that."

"You didn't tell anyone about the diamonds?"

"Not at that time."

"You knew they were valuable?"

"I'm not simple, Mr. Mason."

"Exactly," Mason said. "You knew they were diamonds and you knew they were valuable?"

"Certainly."

"And you took them?"

"Yes."

"And what did you do with them?"

"I've told you what I did with them. I fastened them to the underside of the desk in your office."

"Why?" Mason asked.

"Because I wanted a place to keep them."

"You could have put them in your purse. You could have put them in your pocket," Mason said.

134

"I . . . I didn't want to. I didn't want to have to explain how I came by the diamonds."

"To whom?"

"To anybody who might question me."

"To the police?"

"To *anyone* who might question me, Mr. Mason. I felt I had walked into a trap and that I was going to be accused of having stolen two diamonds."

"But you had been given those diamonds?"

"Yes, but I didn't think anyone would believe me when I told them so."

"Then you don't expect the jury to believe your story now?"

"Objected to," Hamilton Burger snapped. "Argumentative."

"Sustained," Judge Hartley said.

"Isn't it a fact," Mason asked, "that someone who gave you a key to the office which you entered illegally and unlawfully, also gave you a package of diamonds which you were to plant in that office in a place where they would subsequently be found by the police?"

"No!"

"Isn't it a fact that you carried those diamonds into the building wrapped up in tissue paper, that you put those diamonds in a package and concealed them in the office, that you were forced to leave hurriedly because you learned the police had been tipped off, and after you got in my office and started to work, you checked through your purse in order to make certain that you had disposed of all of the diamonds and to your horror found that two of the diamonds you were supposed to have planted in that office had been left in your purse, and that, therefore, in a panic, you tried to get rid of those diamonds by the means you have described?"

"Just a moment!" Hamilton Burger shouted. "I object to this on the ground that it assumes facts not in evidence,

135

that it is not proper cross-examination, that there is no foundation for the assumption that—"

"The objection is overruled," Judge Hartley snapped.

"Isn't it a fact," Mason asked, "that you did what I have just outlined?"

"Absolutely not. I took no diamonds with me when I went to that office. I had no diamonds in my possession when I went in."

"But you don't dare to tell us who gave you a key to that office?"

"I refuse to answer questions about that."

"Thank you," Mason said. "I have no further questions."

Mae Jordan left the stand. The jurors watched her with some skepticism.

Hamilton Burger called other witnesses who established technical background—the exact position of the cruise ship in the harbor when Baxter jumped overboard, passengers who had seen Baxter jump and the owner of a launch which had been cruising in the vicinity. He also introduced police experts who had examined the bloodstains on Gilly's boat and bloodstains on the knife and pronounced them to be human blood.

Mason had no cross-examination except for the expert who had examined the bloodstains.

"*When* did you make your examination?" Mason asked.

"June nineteenth."

"At a time when the bloodstains were at least ten days to two weeks old?"

"So I should judge."

"On the boat?"

"Yes."

"On the knife?"

"Yes."

"They could have been older?"

"Yes."

"They could have been a month old?"

"Well, they could have been."

"The only way you have of knowing when those blood-stains got on the boat was from a statement made to you by Jack Gilly?"

"Yes."

"And did you know Jack Gilly had previously been convicted of perjury?"

The witness squirmed.

"Objected to as incompetent, irrelevant, and immaterial and not proper cross-examination," Hamilton Burger said.

"Sustained," Judge Hartley snapped. "Counsel can confine his cross-examination to the bloodstains, the nature of the tests, and the professional competency of the witness."

"That's all," Mason said. "I have no more questions."

Max Dutton, Hamilton Burger's last witness of the afternoon, was distinctly a surprise witness. Dutton testified that he lived in Brussels; he had come by airplane to testify at the request of the district attorney. He was, he testified, an expert on gems. He used a system of making models of gems so that it would be possible to identify any particular stone of sufficient value to make it worth-while. He made microscopic measurements of the dimensions, of the angles, of the facets, and of the locations of any flaws. The witness testified he maintained permanent records of his identifications, which facilitated appraisals, insurance recoveries and the identification of stolen stones.

He had, he said, been employed by Munroe Baxter during his lifetime; Munroe Baxter had given him some gems and asked him to arrange for the identification of the larger stones, so that they could be readily identified if necessary.

The witness tried to state what Munroe Baxter had told him—the manner in which he had received the stones—but on objection by Perry Mason the objection was sustained by the Court. However, Hamilton Burger was able to show that the stones came to the witness in a box bearing the imprint of the Paris office of the South African Gem Importing and Exploration Company.

The witness testified that he had selected the larger stones and had made complete charts of those stones, so that they could be identified. He further stated that he had examined a package of stones which had been given him by the police and which he understood had been recovered from the desk of the defendant, and that ten of those stones had proved to be identical to the stones he had so carefully charted.

"Cross-examine," Hamilton Burger said.

"This system that you have worked out for identifying stones takes into consideration every possible identifying mark on the stones?" Mason asked.

"It does."

"It would, therefore, enable anyone to duplicate those stones, would it not?"

"No, sir, it would not. You might cut a stone to size; you might get the angle of the facets exactly the same. But the flaws in the stone would not be in the proper position with relation to the facets."

"It would, however, be possible to make a duplication in the event you could find a stone that had certain flaws?"

"That is very much like asking whether it would be possible to duplicate fingerprints, provided you could find a person who had exactly identical ridges and whorls," the witness said.

"Do you then wish to testify under oath that your system of identifying stones is as accurate as the identification of individuals through the science of fingerprinting?" Mason asked.

The witness hesitated a moment, then said, "Not quite."

"That's all," Mason announced, smiling. "No further questions."

The court took its evening adjournment.

As Mason gathered his papers together Walter Irving

pushed his way through the crowd that was leaving the courtroom. He came up to Mason's table. His grin was somewhat sheepish.

"I guess perhaps I owe you an apology," he said.

"You don't owe me anything," Mason told him. "And make no mistake about it, I don't owe you anything."

"You don't owe me anything," Irving said, "but I'm going to make an apology anyway. And I'm further going to tell you that that Jordan girl is a brazen-faced liar. I *think* she broke into that office to plant those diamonds; but regardless of her purpose in getting into the office, there was never any scene such as she testified to. We didn't get back from lunch until after she had done what she wanted to do in that office and had skipped out. We can prove that, and that one fact makes that Jordan girl a damn liar.

"And what's more, I didn't give that Jordan girl any diamonds," Irving said. "I didn't tell her to keep her mouth shut. Now that I've seen her, I remember having seen her at the train. She met Duane and tried to force herself on him. As far as I know, that's the only time in my life I've ever set eyes on her. That girl is playing some deep game, and she's not playing it for herself, Mr. Mason. There's something behind it, something very sinister and something being engineered by powerful interests that have made a dupe of your district attorney."

"I hope so," Mason said. "Where have you been, incidentally?"

"I've been in Mexico. I admit, I underestimated your abilities, but I was trying to give you an opportunity to direct suspicion to me in case you wanted to."

"Well, I haven't wanted to," Mason said, and then added significantly, "yet."

Irving grinned at him. "That's the spirit, Counselor. You can always make a pass at me and confuse the issues as far as the jury is concerned, even if you don't want to be friendly with me. Remember that I'm available as a suspect."

Mason looked into his eyes. "Don't think I'll ever forget it."

Irving's grin was one of pure delight. His reddish-brown eyes met the cold, hard gaze of the lawyer with steady affability. "Now you're cooking with gas! Any time you want me, I'll be available, and I can, of course, give Duane a complete alibi for the morning of the sixth. We had breakfast together a little after seven, got to the office shortly before nine, and he was with me all morning."

"How about the evening of the fifth?" Mason asked.

Irving's eyes shifted.

"Well?" Mason asked.

"Duane was out somewhere."

"Where?"

"With some woman."

"Who?"

Irving shrugged his shoulders.

Mason said, "You can see what's happening here. If the district attorney makes enough of a case so that I have to put the defendant on the stand, there is every possibility that Duane Jefferson's manner, his aloofness, his refusal to answer certain questions, will prejudice his case with the jury."

"I know," Irving said. "I know exactly what you're up against. Before you ever put him on the stand, Mr. Mason, let me talk with him and I'll hammer some sense into his head, even if it does result in his undying enmity forever afterwards. In short, I want you to know that you can count on me all the way through."

"Yes," Mason said, "I understand you sent a most cooperative cablegram to your company in South Africa?"

Irving kept grinning and his eyes remained steady. "That's right," he said. "I asked the company to fire you. I'm sending another one tonight, which will be a lot different. You haven't found Marline Chaumont yet, have you?"

"No," Mason admitted.

Irving lost his grin. "I told you you wouldn't. That's where you loused the case up, Mason. Aside from that, you're doing fine."

And, as though completely assured of Mason's goodwill, Walter Irving turned and sauntered out of the courtroom.

16

■

BACK IN HIS OFFICE THAT EVENING, MASON PACED THE floor. "Hang it, Paul!" he said to the detective. "Why is Hamilton Burger so completely confident?"

"Well, you jarred him a couple of times this afternoon," Drake said. "He was so mad he was quivering like a bowl of jelly."

"I know he was mad, Paul. He was angry, he was irritated, he was annoyed, but he was still sure of himself.

"Hamilton Burger hates me. He'd love to get me out on a limb over a very deep pool and then saw off the limb. He wouldn't even mind if he got slightly wet from the resulting splash. Now, there's something in this case that we don't know about."

"Well," Drake said, "as far as this case is concerned, what does he have, Perry?"

"So far he doesn't have anything," Mason said. "That's what worries me. Why should he have that much assurance over a case which means nothing. He has a woman adventuress and a smuggler; he has a man who concededly planned to fake a suicide. The man was a strong swimmer.

He had an air tank under his clothes. He did exactly what he had planned he was going to do, to wit, jump over the side of the ship and disappear, so that people would think he was dead.

"Then Hamilton Burger brings on the scum of the earth, the sweepings of the waterfront. He uses a man who deliberately rented a boat to be used in an illegal activity, a man who has been twice convicted of felony. His last conviction was for perjury. The jury isn't going to believe that man."

"And what about the girl?" Della Street asked.

"That's different," Mason said. "That girl made a good impression on the jury. Apparently, she was hired to take those gems to the office and plant them. The jury doesn't know that. Those jurors are taking her at face value."

"Figure value," Paul Drake corrected. "Why did you let her off so easy, Perry?"

"Because every time she answered a question she was getting closer to the jury. Those jurors like her, Paul. I'm going to ask to recall her for further cross-examination. When I do that, I want to have the lowdown on her. You're going to put out operatives who will dig up the dirt on her. I want to know everything about her, all about her past, her friends, and before I question her again, I want to know where she got that key which opened the office."

Drake merely nodded.

"Well," Mason said impatiently, "aren't you going to get busy, Paul?"

The detective sat grinning. "I am busy, Perry. I've been busy. This is once I read your mind. I knew what you'd want. The minute that girl got off the stand, I started a whole bunch of men working. I left this unlisted number of yours with my confidential secretary. She may call any minute with some hot stuff."

Mason smiled. "Give yourself a merit badge, Paul. Hang it, there's nothing that gets a lawyer down worse than having to cross-examine a demure girl who has hypnotized the jury. I can't keep shooting blind, Paul. The next time I start sniping at her, I've got to have ammunition that will score dead-center hits.

"Now, here's something else you'll have to do."

"What's that, Perry?"

"Find Munroe Baxter."

"You don't think he's dead?"

"I'm beginning to think Walter Irving was right. I think the supposedly half-witted brother of Marline Chaumont may well be Baxter, despite those hospital records. In a deal of this magnitude we may find a big loophole. If this fellow in the mental hospital was so much of a zombie, what was to prevent Marline Chaumont from identifying him as her brother, getting him out, then farming him out and substituting Munroe Baxter? What are we doing about finding her, Paul?"

"Well, we're making headway, thanks to you," Drake said. "I'm kicking myself for being a stupid fool. You were right about those car rentals, and I sure overlooked a bet there. Two of those car rentals have agencies right there at the airport. In order to rent a car, you have to show your driving license. That means you have to give your right name."

"You mean Marline Chaumont rented a car under her own name?"

"That's right. Showed her driving license, rented the automobile and took it out."

"Her brother was with her?"

"Not at that time. She left the airport by limousine as an incoming passenger, went uptown with her brother and two suitcases, then came back, rented a car, picked up the other two suitcases, drove out, picked up her brother, and then went someplace."

"Where?" Mason asked.

"Now, that's something I wish I knew. However, we stand a chance of finding out. The car rental is predicated on the mileage driven, as well as on a per diem charge.

The mileage indicator on the car when Marline Chaumont brought it back showed it had been driven sixty-two miles."

Mason thought a moment, then snapped his fingers.

"What now?" Drake asked.

"She went out to one of the suburban cities," Mason said. "She's rented a place in one of those suburbs. Now then, she'll want to rent another car, and again she'll have to use her driving license. She was afraid to keep that car she had rented at the airport because she thought we might be checking there."

"We would have been checking within a matter of hours if I'd been on my toes," Drake said ruefully.

"All right," Mason said, "she rented a car there. She was afraid we might trace her, get the license number of the car, have it posted as a hot car and pick her up. So she got rid of that car just as soon as she could. Then she went to one of the outlying towns where they have a car rental agency and signed up for another car. She's had to do it under her own name because of the license angle. Get your men busy, Paul, and cover *all* of the car rental agencies in those outlying towns."

Paul Drake wormed his way out of the chair to stand erect, stretch, say, "Gosh, I'm all in myself. I don't see how you stand a pace like this, Perry."

He went over, picked up the unlisted telephone, said, "Let me call my office and get people started on some of this."

Drake dialed the number, said, "Hello. This is Paul. I want a bunch of men put out to cover all of the outlying towns. I want to check every car rental agency for a car rented by Marline Chaumont. . . . That's right. Everything.

"Now you can— How's that? . . . Wait a minute now," Drake said. "Give that to me slow. I want to make some notes. Who made the report? . . . All right, bring it down here at once. I'm in Mason's office—and get those men started."

Drake hung up the telephone and said, "We've got something, Perry."

"What?"

"We've found out the ace that Hamilton Burger is holding up his sleeve."

"You're sure?"

"Dead sure. One of the detectives who worked on the case knows the angle. He tipped a newspaper reporter off to come and see you get torn to ribbons tomorrow, and the reporter pumped him enough to find out what it was. That reporter is very friendly with one of my men, and we got a tip-off."

"What is it?" Mason asked.

"We'll have all the dope in a minute. They're bringing the report down here," Drake said. "It concerns the woman that Duane Jefferson is trying to protect."

Mason said, "Now, we're getting somewhere, Paul. If I know that information, I don't care what Hamilton Burger thinks he's going to do with it. I'll out-general him somehow."

They waited anxiously until knuckles tapped on the door. Drake opened the door, took an envelope from his secretary, said, "You're getting operatives out checking those car rentals?"

"That's already being done, Mr. Drake. I put Davis in charge of it, and he's on the telephone right now."

"Fine," Drake said. "Let's take a look. I'll give you the dope, Perry."

Drake opened the envelope, pulled out the sheets of flimsy, looked through them hastily, then whistled.

"All right," Mason said, "give."

Drake said, "The night of June fifth Jefferson was down at a nightspot with a woman. It was the woman's car. The parking attendant parked the car and some customer scratched a fender. The attendant got records of license numbers and all that. The woman got in a panic, gave the parking attendant twenty bucks, and told him to forget the whole thing.

"Naturally, the attendant had the answer as soon as that happened. She was a married woman. There's no doubt the guy with her was Duane Jefferson."

"Who was she?" Mason asked.

"A woman by the name of Nan Ormsby."

"Okay," Mason said. "Perhaps I can use this. It'll depend on how far the affair has gone."

Drake, who had continued reading the report, suddenly gave another whistle.

"What now?" Mason asked.

"Hold everything," Drake said. "You have as juror number eleven Alonzo Martin Liggett?"

"What about him?" Mason asked.

"He's a close friend of Dan Ormsby. Ormsby is in partnership with his wife. They have a place called 'Nan and Dan, Realtors.' Nan Ormsby has been having trouble with her husband. She wants a settlement. He doesn't want the kind of a settlement she wants. He hasn't been able to get anything on her yet.

"Now, with a juror who is friendly to Dan Ormsby, you can see what'll happen."

"Good Lord!" Mason said. "If Hamilton Burger uses that lever—"

"Remember, this tip comes straight from Hamilton Burger's office," Drake said.

Mason sat in frowning concentration.

"How bad is it?" Drake asked.

"It's a perfect setup for a D.A.," Mason said. "If he can force me to put my client on the stand, he can go to town. The jury isn't going to like Duane Jefferson's pseudo-British manner, his snobbishness. You know how they feel about people who get tied up with the British and then become more English than the English, and that's what Jefferson has done. He's cultivated all those mannerisms. So Hamilton Burger will start boring into him—he was breaking up a home, he was out with a married woman—and there's Dan Ormsby's friend sitting on the jury."

"Any way you can beat that, Perry?" Drake asked.

"Two ways," Mason said, "and I don't like either one. I can either base all of my fight on trying to prove that there's been no *corpus delicti,* and keep the case from going to the jury, or, if the judge doesn't agree with me on that, I'll put the defendant on the stand, but confine my direct examination to where he was at five o'clock on the morning of the sixth and roar like the devil if the district attorney tries to examine him as to the night of the fifth. Since I wouldn't have asked him anything about the night of the fifth—only the morning of the sixth—I can claim the D.A can't examine him as to anything on the night of the fifth."

"He'll have to make a general denial that he committed the crime?" Drake asked.

Mason nodded.

"Won't that open up the question of where he was on the night of the fifth when the boat was being rented?"

"The prosecution's case shows that the defendant wasn't seen until the morning of the sixth, after the boat had been rented—that is, that's the prosecution's case so far. We have the testimony of Jack Gilly to that effect."

"Well," Drake said, "I'll go down to my office and start things going. I'll have my men on the job working all night. You'd better get some sleep, Perry."

Mason's nod showed his preoccupation with other thoughts. "I've got to get this thing straight, Paul. I have a sixth sense that's warning me. I guess it's the way Hamilton Burger has been acting. This is one case where I've got to watch every time I put my foot down that I'm not stepping right in the middle of a trap."

"Well," Drake said, "you pace the floor and I'll cover the country, Perry. Between us, we may be in a better position tomorrow morning."

Mason said, "I should have known. Burger has been

triumphant, yet his case is a matter of patchwork. It wasn't the strength of his own case that made him triumphant, but the weakness of my case."

"And now that you know, can you detour the pitfalls?" Drake asked.

"I can try," Mason said grimly.

17

JUDGE HARTLEY CALLED COURT TO ORDER PROMPTLY AT ten.

Hamilton Burger said, "I have a couple more questions to ask Mr. Max Dutton, the gem expert."

"Just a moment," Mason said. "If the Court please, I wish to make a motion. I feel that perhaps this motion should be made without the presence of the jury."

Judge Hartley frowned. "I am expecting a motion at the conclusion of the prosecution's case," he said. "Can you not let your motion wait until that time, Mr. Mason? I would like to proceed with the case as rapidly as possible."

"One of my motions can wait," Mason said. "The other one, I think, can properly be made in the presence of the jury. That is a motion to exclude all of the evidence of Mae Jordan on the ground that there is nothing in her testimony which in any way connects the defendant with any crime."

"If the Court please," Hamilton Burger said, "the witness, Dutton, will testify that one of the diamonds which was found on the underside of the desk in Perry Mason's office was one of the identical diamonds which was in the Munroe Baxter collection."

Mason said, "That doesn't connect the defendant, Duane Jefferson, with anything. Jefferson didn't give her those diamonds. Even if we are to take her testimony at face value, even if we are to concede for the sake of this motion that she took those diamonds out of the office instead of going to the office to plant diamonds, the prosecution can't bind the defendant by anything that Walter Irving did."

"It was done in his presence," Hamilton Burger said, "and as a part of a joint enterprise."

"You haven't proven either one of those points," Mason said.

Judge Hartley stroked his chin. "I am inclined to think this motion may be well taken, Mr. District Attorney. The Court has been giving this matter a great deal of thought."

"If the Court please," Hamilton Burger pleaded desperately, "I have a good case here. I have shown that these diamonds were in the possession of Munroe Baxter when he left the ship. These diamonds next show up in the possession of the defendant—"

"Not in the possession of the defendant," Mason corrected.

"In an office to which he had a key," Hamilton Burger snapped.

"The janitor had a key. The scrubwoman had a key. Walter Irving had a key."

"Exactly," Judge Hartley said. "You have to show some act of domination over those diamonds by the defendant before he can be connected with the case. That's a fundamental part of the case."

"But, Your Honor, we *have* shown that act of domination. Two of those diamonds were given to the witness Jordan to compensate her for keeping silent about her letters. We have shown that Munroe Baxter came up and took hold of that towing line which was attached to the heavy fishing rod; that the defendant stabbed him, took the belt containing the diamonds, weighted the body, then

149

towed it away to a point where it could be dropped to the bottom."

Judge Hartley shook his head. "That is a different matter from the motion as to the testimony of Mae Jordan. However, if we are to give every credence to all of the prosecution's testimony and all inferences therefrom, as we must do in considering such a motion, there is probably an inference which will be sufficient to defeat the motion. I'll let the motion be made at this time, and reserve a ruling. Go ahead with your case, Mr. District Attorney."

Hamilton Burger put Max Dutton back on the stand. Dutton testified that one of the gems which had been recovered from the blob of chewing gum that had been found fastened to the underside of Mason's desk was a part of the Baxter collection.

"No questions," Mason said when Hamilton Burger turned Dutton over for cross-examination.

"That," Hamilton Burger announced dramatically and unexpectedly, "finishes the People's case."

Mason said, "At this time, Your Honor, I would like to make a motion without the presence of the jury."

"The jurors will be excused for fifteen minutes," Judge Hartley said, "during which time you will remember the previous admonition of the Court."

When the jurors had filed out of court the judge nodded to Perry Mason. "Proceed with your motion."

"I move that the Court direct and instruct the jury to return a verdict of acquittal," Mason said, "on the ground that no case has been made out which would sustain a conviction, on the ground that there is no evidence tending to show a homicide, no evidence of the *corpus delicti,* and no evidence connecting the defendant with the case."

Judge Hartley said, "I am going to rule against the defense in this case, Mr. Mason. I don't want to preclude you from argument, but the Court has given this matter very careful consideration. Knowing that such a motion would be made, I want to point out to you that while, as a usual thing, proof of the *corpus delicti* includes finding the body, under the law of California that is not necessary. *Corpus delicti* means the body of the crime, not the body of the victim.

"Proof of *corpus delicti* only shows that a crime has been committed. After the crime has been committed, then it is possible to connect the defendant with that crime by proper proof.

"The *corpus delicti,* or the crime itself, like any other fact to be established in court, can be proved by circumstantial as well as direct evidence. There can be reasonable inferences deduced from the factual evidence presented.

"Now then, we have evidence which, I admit, is not very robust, which shows that Munroe Baxter, the purported victim, was carrying certain diamonds in his possession. Presumably he would not have parted from those diamonds without a struggle. Those diamonds were subsequently found under circumstances which at least support an inference that they were under the domination and in the possession of the defendant.

"One of the strongest pieces of evidence in this case is the finding of the bloodstained knife in the boat. I am free to admit that if I were a juror I would not be greatly impressed by the testimony of the witness Gilly, and yet a man who has been convicted of a felony, a man who has been convicted of perjury may well tell the truth.

"We have in this state the case of *People* v. *Cullen,* 37 California 2nd, 614, 234 Pacific 2nd, 1, holding that it is not essential that the body of the victim actually be found in order to support a homicide conviction.

"One of the most interesting cases ever to come before the bar of any country is the case of *Rex* v. *James Camb.* That was, of course, a British case, decided on Monday, April twenty-sixth, nineteen hundred and forty-eight, before the Lord Chief Justice of England.

"That is the famous *Durban Castle* case in which James Camb, a steward aboard the ship, went to the cabin of a young woman passenger. He was recognized in that cabin. The young woman disappeared and was never seen again. There was no evidence, other than circumstantial evidence, of the *corpus delicti,* save the testimony of the defendant himself admitting that he had pushed the body through the porthole but claiming that the woman was dead at the time, that she had died from natural causes and he had merely disposed of the body in that way.

"In this case we have, of course, no admission of that sort. But we do have a showing that the defendant sat in a boat, that some huge body, too big in the normal course of things to be a fish, attached itself to the heavy fishing tackle which the defendant was dangling overboard; that the defendant or the defendant's companion thereupon reached down and stabbed with a knife. A knife was subsequently found in the boat and the knife was smeared with human blood. It was the defendant's knife. I think, under the circumstances, there is enough of a case here to force the defense to meet the charge, and I think that if the jury should convict upon this evidence, the conviction would stand up."

Hamilton Burger smiled and said, "I think that if the Court will bear with us, the Court will presently see that a case of murder has been abundantly proved."

Judge Hartley looked almost suspiciously at the district attorney for a moment, then tightened his lips and said, "Very well. Call the jury."

Mason turned to his client. "This is it, Jefferson," he said. "You're going to have to go on the stand. You have not seen fit to confide in me as your lawyer. You have left me in a position where I have had to undertake the defense of your case with very little assistance from you.

"I think I can prove the witness Mae Jordan lied when she said that you came into the office while she was still there. I have the girl at the cigar counter who will testify that you men did not come in until *after* the manager of the building was standing down at the elevators. I think once we can prove that she lied in one thing, we can prove that she is to be distrusted in her entire testimony. But that young woman has made a very favorable impression on the jury."

Jefferson merely bowed in a coldly formal way. "Very well," he said.

"You have a few seconds now," Mason said. "Do you want to tell me the things that I should know?"

"Certainly," Jefferson said. "I am innocent. That is all you need to know."

"Why the devil won't you confide in me?" Mason asked.

"Because there are certain things that I am not going to tell anyone."

"In case you are interested," Mason said, "I know where you were on the night of June fifth, and furthermore, the district attorney knows it, too."

For a moment Duane Jefferson stiffened, then he turned his face away and said indifferently, "I will answer no questions about the night of June fifth."

"You won't," Mason said, "because I'm not going to ask them on direct examination. Now just remember this one thing: I'm going to ask you where you were during the early morning hours of June sixth. You be *damn* careful that your answer doesn't ever get back of the time limit I am setting. Otherwise, the District Attorney is going to rip you to shreds. Your examination is going to be very, very brief."

"I understand."

"It will be in the nature of a gesture."

"Yes, sir, I understand."

The jury filed into court and took their seats.

"Are you prepared to go on with your case, Mr. Mason?" Judge Hartley asked.

Mason said, "Yes, Your Honor. I won't even bother the Court and the jury by wasting time with an opening statement. I am going to rip this tissue of lies and insinuations wide open. My first witness will be Ann Riddle."

Ann Riddle, the tall, blonde girl who operated the cigar stand, came forward.

"Do you remember the occasion of the fourteenth of June of this year?"

"Yes, sir."

"Where were you at that time?"

"I was at the cigar stand in the building where you have your offices."

"Where the South African Gem Importing and Exploration Company also has its offices?"

"Yes, sir."

"You operate the cigar stand in that building?"

"Yes, sir."

"Do you remember an occasion when the manager of the building came down to stand at the elevator with a young woman?"

"Yes, sir."

"Did you see the defendant at that time?"

"Yes, sir. The defendant and Mr. Irving, his associate, were returning from lunch. They——"

"Now just a minute," Mason said. "You don't *know* they were returning from lunch."

"No, sir."

"All right, please confine your statements to what happened."

"Well, they were entering the building. The manager was standing there. One of the men—I think it was Mr. Irving, but I can't remember for sure—started to walk over to the manager of the building, then saw that he was intent upon something else, so he turned away. The two men entered the elevator."

"This was after the alarm had been given about the burglary?" Mason asked.

"Yes, sir."

"You may inquire," Mason said to Hamilton Burger.

Hamilton Burger smiled. "I have no questions."

"I will call the defendant, Duane Jefferson, to the stand," Mason said.

Duane Jefferson, cool and calm, got up and walked slowly to the witness stand. For a moment he didn't look at the jury, then when he did deign to glance at them, it was with an air of superiority bordering on contempt. "The damn fool!" Mason whispered under his breath.

Hamilton Burger tilted back in his swivel chair, he interlaced his fingers back of his head, winked at one of his deputies, and a broad smile suffused his face.

"Did you kill Munroe Baxter?" Mason asked.

"No, sir."

"Did you know that those diamonds were in your office?"

"No, sir."

"Where were you on the morning of the sixth of June? I'll put it this way, where were you from 2:00 A.M. on the sixth of June to noon of that day?"

"During the times mentioned I was in my apartment, sleeping, until a little after seven. Then I had breakfast with my associate, Walter Irving. After breakfast we went to the office."

"Cross-examine," Mason snapped viciously at Hamilton Burger.

Hamilton Burger said, "I will be very brief. I have only a couple of questions, Mr. Jefferson. Have *you* ever been convicted of a felony?"

"I—" Suddenly Jefferson seemed to collapse in the witness chair.

"Have you?" Hamilton Burger thundered.

"I made one mistake in my life," Jefferson said. "I have tried to live it down. I thought I had."

"Did you, indeed?" Hamilton Burger said scornfully. "Where were you convicted, Mr. Jefferson?"

"In New York."

"You served time in Sing Sing?"

"Yes."

"Under the name of Duane Jefferson?"

"No, sir."

"Under what name?"

"Under the name of James Kincaid."

"Exactly," Hamilton Burger said. "You were convicted of larceny by trick and device."

"Yes."

"You posed as an English heir, did you not? And you told—"

"Objected to," Mason said. "Counsel has no right to amplify the admission."

"Sustained."

"Were you, at one time, known as 'Gentleman Jim,' a nickname of the underworld?"

"Objected to," Mason said.

"Sustained."

Hamilton Burger said scornfully, "I will ask no further questions."

As one in a daze, the defendant stumbled from the stand.

Mason said, his lips a hard, white line, "Mr. Walter Irving take the stand."

The bailiff called, "Walter Irving."

When there was no response, the call was taken up in the corridors.

Paul Drake came forward, beckoned to Mason. "He's skipped, Perry. He was sitting near the door. He took it on the lam the minute Burger asked Jefferson about his record. Good Lord! What a mess! What a lousy mess!"

Judge Hartley said not unkindly, "Mr. Irving doesn't seem to be present, Mr. Mason. Was he under subpoena?"

"Yes, Your Honor."

"Do you wish the Court to issue a bench warrant?"

"No, Your Honor," Mason said. "Perhaps Mr. Irving had his reasons for leaving."

"I daresay he did," Hamilton Burger said sarcastically.

"That's the defendant's case," Mason said. "We rest."

It was impossible for Hamilton Burger to keep the gloating triumph out of his voice. "I will," he said, "call only three witnesses on rebuttal. The first is Mrs. Agnes Elmer."

Mrs. Agnes Elmer gave her name and address. She was, she explained, the manager of the apartment house where the defendant, Duane Jefferson, had rented an apartment shortly after his arrival in the city.

"Directing your attention to the early morning of June sixth," Hamilton Burger said, "do you know whether Duane Jefferson was in his apartment?"

"I do."

"Was he in that apartment?"

"He was not."

"Was his bed slept in that night?"

"It was not."

"Cross-examine," Hamilton Burger said.

Mason, recognizing that the short, direct examination was intended to bait a trap into which he must walk on cross-examination, flexed his arms slowly, as though stretching with weariness, said, "How do you fix the date, Mrs. Elmer?"

"A party rang up shortly before midnight on the fifth," Mrs. Elmer said. "It was a woman's voice. She told me it was absolutely imperative that she get in touch with Mr. Jefferson. She said Mr. Jefferson had got her in—"

"Just a minute," Mason interrupted. "I object, Your Honor, to this witness relating any conversations which occurred outside of the presence of the defendant."

"Oh, Your Honor," Hamilton Burger said. "This is plainly admissible. Counsel asked this question himself. He asked her how she fixed the date. She's telling him."

Judge Hartley said, "There may be some technical merit to your contention, Mr. District Attorney, but this is a court of justice, not a place for a legal sparring match. The whole nature of your examination shows you had carefully baited this as a trap for the cross-examiner. I'm going to sustain the objection. You can make your own case by your own witness.

"Now, the Court is going to ask the witness if there is any other way you can fix the date, any way, that is, depending on your own actions."

"Well," the witness said, "I know it was the sixth because that was the day I went to the dentist. I had a terrific toothache that night and couldn't sleep."

"And how do you fix the date that you went to the dentist?" Mason asked.

"From the dentist's appointment book."

"So you don't know of your own knowledge what date you went to the dentist, only the date that is shown in the dentist's book?"

"That's right."

"And the entry of that date in the dentist's book was not made in your own handwriting. In other words, you have used a conversation with the dentist to refresh your memory."

"Well, I asked him what date I came in, and he consulted his records and told me."

"Exactly," Mason said. "But you don't know of your own knowledge how he kept his records."

"Well, he's supposed to keep them—"

Mason smiled. "But *you* have no independent recollection of anything except that it was the night that you had the toothache, is that right?"

"Well, if you'd had that toothache—"

"I'm asking you if that's the only way you can fix the date, that it was the night you had the toothache?"

"Yes."

"And then, at the request of the district attorney, you tried to verify the date?"

"Yes."

"When did the district attorney request that you do that?"

"I don't know. It was late in the month sometime."

"And did you go to the dentist's office, or did you telephone him?"

"I telephoned him."

"And asked him the date when you had your appointment?"

"Yes."

"Aside from that, you wouldn't have been able to tell whether it had been the sixth, the seventh, or the eighth?"

"I suppose not."

"So you have refreshed your recollection by taking the word of someone else. In other words, the testimony you are now giving as to the date is purely hearsay evidence?"

"Oh, Your Honor," Hamilton Burger said, "I think this witness has the right to refresh her recollection by—"

Judge Hartley shook his head. "The witness has testified that she can't remember the date except by fixing it in connection with other circumstances, and those other circumstances which she is using to refresh her recollection depend upon the unsworn testimony of another. Quite plainly hearsay testimony, Mr. District Attorney."

Hamilton Burger bowed. "Very well, Your Honor."

"That's all," Mason said.

"Call Josephine Carter," Burger said.

Josephine Carter was sworn, testified she was a switchboard operator at the apartment house where the defendant had his apartment, that she worked from 10:00 P.M. on the night of the fifth of June until 6:00 A.M. on the morning of June sixth.

"Did you ring the defendant's phone that night?"

"Yes."

"When?"

"Shortly before midnight. I was told it was an emergency and I—"

"Never mind what you were *told*. What did you *do*?"

"I rang the phone."

"Did you get an answer?"

"No. The party who was calling left a message and asked me to keep calling to see that Mr. Jefferson got that message as soon as he came in."

"How often did you continue to ring?"

"Every hour."

"Until when?"

"When I went off duty at six in the morning."

"Did you ever get an answer?"

"No."

"From your desk at the switchboard can you watch the corridor to the elevator, and did you thereafter watch to see if the defendant came in?"

"Yes. I kept watch so as to call to him when he came in."

"He didn't come in while you were on duty?"

"No."

"You're certain?"

"Positive."

"Cross-examine," Burger snapped at Mason.

"How did you know the phone was ringing?" Mason asked smilingly.

"Why I depressed the key."

"Phones get out of order occasionally?"

"Yes."

"Is there any check signal on the board by which you can tell if the phone is ringing?"

"You get a peculiar sound when the phone rings, sort of a hum."

"And if the phone doesn't ring, do you get that hum?"

"I . . . we haven't been troubled that way."

"Do you know of your own knowledge that you fail to get that hum when the phone is not ringing?"

"That's the way the board is supposed to work."

"I'm asking you if you know of your own knowledge?"

"Well, Mr. Mason, I have never been in an apartment where the phone was not ringing and at the same time been downstairs at the switchboard trying to ring that telephone."

"Exactly," Mason said. "That's the point I was trying to make, Miss Carter. That's all."

"Just a moment," Hamilton Burger said. "I have one question on redirect. Did you keep an eye on the persons who went in and out, to see if Mr. Jefferson came in?"

"I did."

"Is your desk so located that you could have seen him when he came in?"

"Yes. Everyone who enters the apartment has to walk down a corridor, and I can see through a glass door into that corridor."

"That's all," Burger said, smiling.

"I have one or two questions on recross-examination," Mason said. "I'll only bother you for a moment, Miss Carter. You have now stated that you kept looking up whenever anyone came in, to see if the defendant came in."

"Yes, sir."

"And you could have seen him if he had come in?"

"Yes, sir. Very easily. From my station at the switchboard I can watch people who come down the corridor."

"So you want the Court and the jury to understand that you are certain the defendant didn't come in during the time you were on duty?"

"Well, he didn't come in from the time I first rang his telephone until I quit ringing it at six o'clock, when I went off duty."

"And what time did you first ring his telephone?"

"It was before midnight, perhaps eleven o'clock, perhaps a little after eleven."

"And then what?"

"Then I rang two or three times between the time of the first call and one o'clock, and then after 1:00 A.M. I made it a point to ring every hour on the hour."

"Just short rings or—"

"No, I rang several long rings each time."

"And after your first ring around midnight you were satisfied the defendant was not in his apartment?"

"Yes, sir."

"And because you were watching the corridor you were satisfied that he couldn't have entered the house and gone to his apartment without your seeing him?"

"Yes, sir."

"Then why," Mason asked, "if you *knew* he wasn't in his apartment and *knew* that he hadn't come in, did you keep on ringing the telephone at hourly intervals?"

The witness looked at Mason, started to say something, stopped, blinked her eyes, said, "Why, I . . . I . . . I don't know. I just did it."

"In other words," Mason said, "you *thought* there was a possibility he might have come in without your seeing him?"

"Well, of course, that *could* have happened."

"Then when you just now told the district attorney that it would have been impossible for the defendant to have come in without your seeing him, you were mistaken?"

"I . . . well, I . . . I had talked it over with the district attorney and . . . well, I thought that's what I was supposed to say."

"Exactly," Mason said, smiling. "Thank you."

Josephine Carter looked at Hamilton Burger to see if there were any more questions, but Hamilton Burger was making a great show of pawing through some papers. "That's all," he snapped gruffly.

Josephine Carter left the witness stand.

"I will now call Ruth Dickey," Hamilton Burger said.

Ruth Dickey came forward, was sworn, and testified that she was and had been on the fourteenth of June an elevator operator in the building where the South African Gem Importing and Exploration Company had its offices.

"Did you see Duane Jefferson, the defendant in this case, on the fourteenth of June a little after noon?"

"Yes, sir."

"When?"

"Well, he and Mr. Irving, his associate, rode down in the elevator with me about ten minutes past twelve. The defendant said he was going to lunch."

"When did they come back?"

"They came back about five minutes to one and rode up in the elevator with me."

"Did anything unusual happen on that day?"

"Yes, sir."

"What?"

"The manager of the building and one of the stenographers got into the elevator with me, and the manager asked me to run right down to the street floor because it was an emergency."

"Was this before or after the defendant and Irving had gone up with you?"

"After."

"You're certain?"

"Yes."

"About how long after?"

"At least five minutes."

"How well do you know the defendant?" Hamilton Burger asked.

"I have talked with him off and on."

"Have you ever been out with him socially?"

She lowered her eyes. "Yes."

"Now, did the defendant make any statements to you with reference to his relationship with Ann Riddle, the young woman who operates the cigar stand?"

"Yes. He said that he and his partner had set her up in business, that she was a lookout for them, but that no one else knew the connection. He said if I'd be nice to him, he could do something for me, too."

"You may cross-examine," Hamilton Burger said.

"You have had other young men take you out from time to time?" Mason asked.

163

"Well, yes."

"And quite frequently you have had them make rather wild promises about what they could do about setting you up in business if you would only be nice to them?"

She laughed. "I'll say," she said. "You'd be surprised about what some of them say."

"I dare say I would," Mason said. "That's all. Thank you, Miss Dickey."

"That's all our rebuttal," Hamilton Burger said.

Judge Hartley's voice was sympathetic. "I know that it is customary to have a recess before arguments start, but I would like very much to get this case finished today. I think that we can at least start the argument, unless there is some reason for making a motion for a continuance."

Mason, tight-lipped, shook his head. "Let's go ahead with it," he said.

"Very well, Mr. District Attorney, you may make your opening argument."

18

■

HAMILTON BURGER'S ARGUMENT TO THE JURY WAS REL-atively short. It was completed within an hour after court reconvened following the noon recess. It was a master-piece of forensic eloquence, of savage triumph, of a bit-ter, vindictive attack on the defendant and by implication on his attorney.

Mason's argument, which followed, stressed the point that while perjurers and waterfront scum had made an at-tack on his client, no one had yet shown that Munroe Baxter was murdered. Munroe Baxter, Mason insisted, could show up alive and well at any time, without having contradicted the testimony of any witness.

Hamilton Burger's closing argument was directed to the fact that the Court would instruct the jury that *corpus delicti* could be shown by circumstantial evidence, as well as by direct evidence. It was an argument which took only fifteen minutes.

The Court read instructions to the jurors, who retired to the jury room for their deliberations.

Mason, in the courtroom, his face a cold, hard mask, thoughtfully paced the floor.

Della Street, sitting at the counsel table, gave him her silent sympathy. Paul Drake, who had for once been too depressed even to try to eat, sat with his head in his hands.

Mason glanced at the clock, sighed wearily, ceased his pacing and dropped into a chair.

"Any chance, Perry?" Paul Drake asked.

Mason shook his head. "Not with the evidence in this shape. My client is a dead duck. Any luck with this car rental?"

"No luck at all, Perry. We've covered every car rental agency here and in outlying towns where they have branches."

Mason was thoughtful for a moment. "What about Walter Irving?"

"Irving has flown the coop," Drake said. "He left the courtroom, climbed into a taxicab and vanished. This time my men knew what he was going to try to do, and they were harder to shake. But within an hour he had ditched the shadows. It was a hectic hour."

"How did he do it?"

"It was very simple," Drake said. "Evidently it was part of a prearranged scheme. He had chartered a helicopter that was waiting for him at one of the outlying airports. He drove out there, got in the helicopter and took off."

"Can't you find out what happened? Don't they have to file some sort of a flight plan or—"

"Oh, we know what happened well enough," Drake said. "He chartered the helicopter to take him to the International Airport. Halfway there, he changed his mind and talked the helicopter into landing at the Santa Monica Airport. A rented car was waiting there."

"He's gone?"

"Gone slick and clean. We'll probably pick up his trail later on, but it isn't going to be easy, and by that time it won't do any good."

Mason thought for a moment. Suddenly he sat bolt upright. "Paul," he said, "we've overlooked a bet!"

"What?"

"A person renting a car has to show his driving license?"

"That's right."

"You've been looking for car rentals in the name of Marline Chaumont?"

"That's right."

"All right," Mason said. "Start your men looking for car rentals in the name of Walter Irving. Call your men on the phone. Start a network of them making a search. I want that information, and I want it now."

Drake, seemingly glad to be able to leave the depressing atmosphere of the courtroom, said, "Okay, I'll start right away, Perry."

Shortly before five o'clock a buzzer announced that the jury had reached its verdict. The jury was brought into court and the verdict was read by the foreman.

"We, the jury impaneled to try the above-entitled case, find the defendant guilty of murder in the first degree."

There was no recommendation for life imprisonment or leniency.

Judge Hartley's eyes were sympathetic as he looked at Perry Mason. "Can we agree upon having the Court fix a time for pronouncing sentence?" he asked.

"I would like an early date for hearing a motion for a new trial," Mason said. "I will stipulate that Friday will be satisfactory for presenting a motion for new trial and fixing sentence. We will waive the question of time."

"How about the district attorney's office?" Judge Hartley asked. "Will Friday be satisfactory?"

The deputy district attorney, who sat at the counsel table, said, "Well, Your Honor, I think it will be all right. Mr. Burger is in conference with the press at the moment. He——"

"He asked you to represent the district attorney's office?" Judge Hartley asked.

"Yes, Your Honor."

"Represent it then," Judge Hartley said shortly. "Is Friday satisfactory?"

"Yes, Your Honor."

"Friday morning at ten o'clock," Judge Hartley said. "Court is adjourned. The defendant is remanded to custody."

Reporters, who usually swarmed about Perry Mason asking for a statement, were now closeted with Hamilton Burger. The few spectators who had been interested enough to await the verdict got up and went home. Mason picked up his brief case. Della Street tucked her hand through his arm, gave him a reassuring squeeze. "You warned him, Chief," she said. "Not once, but a dozen times. He had it coming."

Mason merely nodded. Paul Drake, hurrying down the corridor, said, "I've got something, Perry."

"Did you hear the verdict?" Mason asked.

Paul Drake's eyes refused to meet Mason's. "I heard it."

"What have you got?" Mason asked.

"Walter Irving rented an automobile the day that Marline Chaumont disappeared from the airport. Last night he rented another one."

"I thought so," Mason said. "Has he turned back the first automobile?"

"No."

"He keeps the rental paid?"

"Yes."

"We can't get him on the ground of embezzling the

automobile, so we can have police looking for it as a 'hot' car?"

"Apparently not."

Mason turned to Della Street. "Della, you have a short-hand book in your purse?"

She nodded.

"All right," Mason said to Paul Drake, "let's go, Paul."

"Where?" Drake asked.

"To see Ann Riddle, the girl who bought the cigar counter in our building," Mason said. "We may be able to get to her before she, too, flies the coop. Hamilton Burger is too busy with the press, decorating himself with floral wreaths, to do much thinking now."

Drake his voice sympathetic, said, "Gosh, Perry, it's ... I can imagine how you feel ... having a client convicted of first-degree murder. It's the first time you've ever had a client convicted in a murder case."

Mason turned to Paul Drake, his eyes were cold and hard. "My client," he said, "hasn't been convicted of anything."

For a moment Drake acted as if his ears had betrayed him, then, at something he saw in Mason's face, he refrained from asking questions.

"Get the address of that girl who bought the cigar stand," Mason said, "and let's go."

19

∎

MASON, HIS FACE IMPLACABLY DETERMINED, SCORNED the chair offered him by the frightened blonde.

"You can talk now," he said, "or you can talk later.

Whichever you want. If you talk now it may do you some good. If you talk later you're going to be convicted as an accessory in a murder case. Make up your mind."

"I've nothing to say."

Mason said, "Irving and Jefferson went into the building *before* the excitement. When they entered their office, Mae Jordan was there. They caught her. The phone rang. They were warned that the police had been notified that a girl was breaking into the office and that the police were coming up; that the girl who had seen the woman breaking in and the manager of the building were waiting at the elevators. There was only one person who could have given them that information. That was you."

"You have no right to say that."

"I've said it," Mason said, "and I'm saying it again. The next time I say it, it's going to be in open court.

"By tomorrow morning at ten o'clock we'll have torn into your past and will have found out all about the connection between you and Irving. By that time it'll be too late for you to do anything. You've committed perjury. We're putting a tail on you. Now start talking."

Under the impact of Mason's gaze she at first averted her eyes, then restlessly shifted her position in the chair.

"Start talking," Mason said.

"I don't have to answer to you. You're not the police. You—"

"Start talking."

"All right," she said. "I was paid to keep a watch on things, to telephone them if anything suspicious happened. There's nothing unlawful about that."

"It goes deeper than that," Mason said. "You were in on the whole thing. It was their money that put you in the cigar store. What's your connection with this thing?"

"You can't prove any of that. That's a false and slanderous statement. Duane Jefferson never told that little tramp anything like that. If he did, it was false."

"Start talking," Mason said.

She hesitated, then stubbornly shook her head.

Mason motioned to Della Street. "Go over to the telephone, Della. Ring up Homicide Squad. Get Lieutenant Tragg on the line. Tell him I want to talk with him."

Della Street started for the telephone.

"Now wait a minute," the blonde said hurriedly. "You can't—"

"Can't what?" Mason asked as her voice trailed into silence.

"Can't make anything stick on me. You haven't got any proof."

"I'm getting it," Mason told her. "Paul Drake here is an expert detective. He has men on the job right now, men who are concentrating on what you and Irving were doing."

"All right. Suppose my gentleman friend *did* loan me the money to buy a cigar stand. There's nothing wrong with that. I'm over the age of consent. I can do what I damn please."

Mason said, "This is your last chance. Walter Irving is putting out a lot of false clues, shaking off any possible pursuit. Then he'll go to Marline Chaumont. She's in one of the outlying towns. When she and Irving get together, something's going to happen. He must have given you an address where you could reach him in case of any emergency. That will be Marline's hide-out. Where is it?"

She shook her head.

Mason nodded to Della Street. Della Street started putting through the call.

Abruptly the blonde began to cry.

"I want Homicide Department, please," Della Street said into the phone.

The blonde said, "It's in Santa Ana."

"Where?" Mason asked.

She fumbled with her purse, took out an address, handed it to Mason. Mason nodded, and Della Street hung up the telephone.

"Come on," Mason said.

"What do you mean, come on?" the girl said.

"You heard me," Mason told her. "We're not leaving you behind to make any telephone calls. This is too critical for us to botch it up now."

"You can't *make* me go!"

"I can't make you go with *me,* but I can damn sure see that you're locked up in the police station. The only bad thing is that will cost about fifteen minutes. Which do you want?"

She said, "Stop looking at me like that. You frighten me. You—"

"I'm putting it to you cold turkey," Mason said. "Do you want to take a murder rap or not?"

"I—" She hesitated.

"Get your things on," Mason said.

Ann Riddle moved toward the closet.

"Watch her, Della," Mason said. "We don't want her to pick up any weapons."

Ann Riddle put on a light coat, picked up her purse. Paul Drake looked in the purse and made sure there was no weapon in it.

The four of them went down in the elevator, wordlessly got in Mason's car. Mason tooled the car out to the freeway, gathered speed.

20

■

THE HOUSE WAS IN A QUIET RESIDENTIAL DISTRICT. A light was on in the living room. A car was parked in the garage. A wet strip on the sidewalk showed that the lawn had recently been sprinkled.

Mason parked the car, jerked open the door, strode up the steps to the porch. Della Street hurried along behind him. Paul Drake kept a hand on the arm of Ann Riddle.

Mason rang the bell.

The door opened half an inch. "Who is it?" a woman's voice asked.

Mason pushed his weight against the door so suddenly that the door was pushed inward.

Marline Chaumont, staggering back, regarded Mason with frightened eyes. "You!" she said.

"We came to get your brother," Mason said.

"My brother is—how you call it?—sick in the upstairs. He has flies in his belfry. He cannot be disturbed. He is asleep."

"Wake him up," Mason said.

"But you cannot do this. My brother he— You are not the law, *non?*"

"No," Mason said. "But we'll have the law here in about five minutes."

Marline Chaumont's face contorted into a spasm of anger. "You!" she spat at the blonde. "You had to pull a double cross!"

"I didn't," Ann Riddle said. "I only—"

"I know what you did, you double-crosser!" Marline Chaumont said. "I spit on you. You stool squab!"

"Never mind that," Mason said. "Where's the man you claim is your brother?"

"But he *is* my brother!"

"Phooey," Mason told her.

"He was taken from the hospital—"

"The man who was taken from the state hospital," Mason said, "isn't related to you any more than I am. You used him only as a prop. I don't know what you've done with him. Put him in a private institution somewhere, I suppose. I want the man who's taken his place, and I want him now."

"You are crazy in the head yourself," Marline Chaumont said. "You have no right to—"

"Take care of her, Paul," Mason said, and started marching down the hall toward the back of the house.

"You'll be killed!" she screamed. "You cannot do this. You—"

Mason tried the doors one at a time. The third door opened into a bedroom. A man, thin and emaciated, was lying on the bed, his hands handcuffed at the wrists.

A big, burly individual who had been reading a magazine got slowly to his feet. "What the hell!" he thundered.

Mason sized him up. "You look like an ex-cop to me," he said.

"What's it to you?" the man asked.

"Probably retired," Mason said. "Hung out your shingle as a private detective. Didn't do so well. Then this job came along."

"Say, what're you talking about?"

"I don't know what story they told *you*," Mason said, "and I don't know whether you're in on it or not, but whatever they told you, the jig's up. I'm Perry Mason, the lawyer."

The man who was handcuffed on the bed turned to Perry Mason. His eyes, dulled with sedatives, seemed to be having some difficulty getting in focus.

"Who are you?" he asked in the thick voice of a sleep talker.

Mason said, "I've come to take you out of here."

The bodyguard said, "This man's a mental case. He's inclined to be violent. He can't be released and he has delusions—"

"I know," Mason said. "His real name is Pierre Chaumont. He keeps thinking he's someone else. He has a delusion that his real name is—"

"Say, how do you know all this?" the bodyguard asked.

Mason said, "They gave you a steady job. A woman handed you a lot of soft soap, and you probably think she's one of the sweetest, most wonderful women on earth. It's time you woke up. As for this man on the bed, he's going with me right now. First we're going to the best doctor we can find, and then . . . well, then we'll get ready to keep a date on Friday morning at ten o'clock.

"You can either be in jail at that time or a free man. Make your choice now. We're separating the men from the boys. If you're in on this thing all the way, you're in a murder case. If you were just hired to act as a guard for a man who is supposed to be a mental case, that's something else. You have your opportunity to make your decision right now. There's a detective downstairs and police are on their way out. They'll be here within a matter of minutes. They'll want to know where you stand. I'm giving you your chance right now, and it's your *last* chance."

The big guard blinked his eyes slowly. "You say this man *isn't* a mental case?"

"Of course he isn't."

"I've seen the papers. He was taken from a state hospital."

"Some other guy was taken from a state hospital," Mason said, "and then they switched patients. This isn't a debating society. Make up your mind."

"You're Perry Mason, the lawyer?"

"That's right."

"Got any identification on you?"

Mason handed the man his card, showed him his driving license.

The guard sighed. "Okay," he said. "You win."

21

■

THE BAILIFF CALLED COURT TO ORDER.

Hamilton Burger, his face wearing a look of smug satisfaction, beamed about the courtroom.

Judge Hartley said, "This is the time fixed for hearing a motion for new trial and for pronouncing judgment in the case of *People* v. *Duane Jefferson.* Do you wish to be heard, Mr. Mason?"

"Yes, Your Honor," Perry Mason said. "I move for a new trial of the case on the ground that the trial took place in the absence of the defendant."

"What?" Hamilton Burger shouted. "The defendant was present in court every minute of the time! The records so show."

"Will you stand up, Mr. Duane Jefferson?" Mason asked.

The man beside Mason stood up. Another man seated near the middle of the courtroom also stood up. Judge Hartley looked at the man in the courtroom.

"Come forward," Mason said.

"Just a minute," Judge Hartley said. "What's the meaning of this, Mr. Mason?"

"I asked Mr. Jefferson to stand up."

"He's standing up," Hamilton Burger said.

"Exactly," Mason said.

"Who's this other man?" the Court asked. "Is he a witness?"

"He's Duane Jefferson," Mason said.

"Now, just a minute, just a minute," Hamilton Burger said. "What's all this about, what kind of a flim-flam is counsel trying to work here? Let's get this thing straight. Here's the defendant standing here within the bar."

"And here's Duane Jefferson coming foward," Mason said. "I am moving for a new trial on the ground that the entire trial of Duane Jefferson for first-degree murder took place in his absence."

"Now just a moment, just a moment!" Hamilton Burger shouted. "I might have known there would be something like this. Counsel can't confuse the issues. It doesn't make any difference now whether this man is Duane Jefferson or whether he's John Doe. He's the man who committed the murder. He's the man who was seen committing the murder. He's the man who was tried for the murder. If he went under the name of Duane Jefferson, that isn't going to stop him from being sentenced for the murder."

"But," Mason said, "some of your evidence was directed against my client, Duane Jefferson."

"*Your* client?" Hamilton Burger said. "That's your client standing next to you."

Mason smiled and shook his head. "*This* is my client," he said, beckoning to the man standing at the gate of the bar to come forward once more. "This is Duane Jefferson. He's the one I was retained to represent by the South African Gem Importing and Exploration Company."

"Well, he's not the one you defended," Hamilton Burger said. "You can't get out of the mess this way."

Mason smiled and said, "I'm defending him now."

"Go ahead and defend him. He isn't accused of anything!"

"And I'm moving for a new trial on the ground that the trial took place in the absence of the defendant."

"This is the defendant standing right here!" Hamilton Burger insisted. "The trial took place in *his* presence. *He's* the one who was convicted. I don't care what you do with this other man, regardless of what his name is."

"Oh, but you introduced evidence consisting of articles

belonging to the real Duane Jefferson," Mason said. "That dagger, for instance. The contents of the letters."

"What do you mean?"

"Mae W. Jordan told all about the letters she had received from Duane Jefferson, about the contents of those letters. I moved to strike out her testimony. The motion was denied. The testimony went to the jury about the Daddy Longlegs letters, about the Prince Charming letters, about the gag photographs, about the getting acquainted, and about the dagger."

"Now, just a moment," Judge Hartley said. "The Court will bear with you for a moment in this matter, Mr. Mason, but the Court is going to resort to stern measures if it appears this is some dramatic presentation of a technicality which you are using to dramatize the issues."

"I'm trying to clarify the issues," Mason said. "What happened is very simple. Duane Jefferson, who is standing there by the mahogany swinging gate which leads to the interior of the bar, is a trusted employee of the South African Gem Importing and Exploration Company. He was sent to this country in the company of Walter Irving of the Paris office to open a branch office. They were to receive half a million dollars' worth of diamonds in the mail.

"Walter Irving, who had been gambling heavily, was deeply involved and knew that very shortly after he had left Paris there would be an audit of the books and his defalcations would be discovered.

"This man, James Kincaid, was groomed to take the place of Duane Jefferson. After the shipment of gems was received, James Kincaid would take the gems and disappear. Walter Irving would duly report an embezzlement by Jefferson and thereafter Jefferson's body would be discovered under such circumstances that it would appear he had committed suicide.

"The trouble was that they couldn't let well enough alone. They knew that Munroe Baxter was smuggling diamonds into the country, and they decided to kill Baxter and get the gems. Actually, Walter Irving had been working with Baxter in connection with the smuggling and for a fee had arranged for the stones to be delivered to Baxter under such circumstances that they could be smuggled into this country.

"The spurious Duane Jefferson didn't need to be clever about it, because he intended to have the shipment of stones in his possession and the real Duane Jefferson's body found, long before the police could make an investigation. However, because of a tax situation, the shipment of gems was delayed, and naturally they couldn't afford to have the spurious Jefferson disappear until the shipment had been received, so that Walter Irving could then report the defalcation to the company. Therefore, the real Duane Jefferson had to be kept alive."

"Your Honor, Your Honor!" Hamilton Burger shouted. "This is simply another one of those wild-eyed, dramatic grandstands for which counsel is so noted. This time his client has been convicted of first-degree murder, and I intend to see to it personally that his client pays the supreme penalty."

Mason pointed to the man standing in the aisle. "This is my client," he said. "This is the man I was retained to represent. I intend to show that his trial took place in his absence. Come forward and be sworn, Mr. Jefferson."

"Your Honor, I object!" Hamilton Burger shouted. "I object to any such procedure. I insist that this defendant is the only defendant before the Court."

Judge Hartley said, "Now, just a moment. I want to get to the bottom of this thing, and I want to find out exactly what counsel's contention is before I start making any rulings. Court will take an adjournment for fifteen minutes while we try to get at the bottom of this thing. I will ask counsel for both sides to meet me in chambers. The defendant, in the meantime, is in custody. He will remain in custody."

Mason grinned.

The tall, gaunt man standing in the aisle turned back toward the audience. Mae Jordan moved toward him. "Hello, Prince Charming," she ventured somewhat dubiously. Jefferson's eyes lit up.

"Hello, Lady Guinevere," he said in a low voice. "I was told you'd be here."

"Prince . . . Prince Charming!"

Mason said, "I'll leave him in your custody, Miss Jordan." Then Mason marched into the judge's chambers.

22

■

"WELL?" JUDGE HARTLEY SAID.

"It was quite a plot," Mason explained. "Actually, it was hatched in Paris as soon as Walter Irving knew he was going to be sent over to assist Duane Jefferson in opening the new office. A girl named Marline Chaumont, who had been a Paris party girl for the company and who knew her way around, was in on it. James Kincaid was in on it. They would have gotten away with the whole scheme, if it hadn't been for the fact that they were too eager. They knew that Baxter was planning to smuggle in three hundred thousand dollars' worth of diamonds. Gilly was to have taken the fishing boat out and made the delivery. They persuaded Gilly that Baxter had changed his mind at the last minute because of Gilly's record. He wanted these other men to take the boat out. Gilly was lying when he testified about his rental for the boat. He received twenty-five hundred dollars. That was the agreed price. Marline Chaumont has given me a sworn statement."

"Now just a minute," Judge Hartley said. "Are you

now making this statement about the client you're representing in court?"

"I'm not representing him in court," Mason said. "I'm representing the real Duane Jefferson. That's the one I was retained to represent. I would suggest, however, that the Court give this other man an opportunity to get counsel of his own, or appoint counsel to represent him. He, too, is entitled to a new trial."

"He can't get a new trial," Hamilton Burger roared, "even if what you say is true. You defended him and you lost the case."

Mason smiled coldly at Hamilton Burger. "You might have made that stick," he said, "if it hadn't been for the testimony of Mae Jordan about all of her correspondence with Duane Jefferson. That correspondence was with the real Duane Jefferson, not with the man you are trying for murder. You can't convict Duane Jefferson of anything, because he wasn't present during his trial. You can't make the present conviction stick against the defendant now in court, because you used evidence that related to the real Duane Jefferson, not to him.

"What you should have done was to have checked your identification of the man you had under arrest. You were so damned anxious to get something on me that when you found from his fingerprints that he had a record, you let your enthusiasm run away with you.

"You let Mae Jordan testify to a lot of things that had happened between her and the real Duane Jefferson. It never occurred to you to make certain that the man she sent the knife to was the same man you were trying for murder.

"The spurious Jefferson and Irving drugged the real Jefferson shortly after they left Chicago on the train. They stole all of his papers, stole the Jordan letters, stole the knife. It will be up to you to prove that at the next trial—and I'm not going to help you. You can go get the evidence yourself. However, I have Marline Chaumont in

180

my office and I have a sworn statement made by her, which I now hand to the Court, with a copy for the district attorney.

"Just one suggestion, though. If you ever want to tie this case up, you'd better find out who that man was who was in the boat with Kincaid, because it certainly wasn't Irving.

"And now may I ask the Court to relieve me of any responsibility in the matter of the defendant, James Kincaid, who is out there in the courtroom. He tricked me into appearing in court for him by artifice, fraud, and by misrepresenting his identity. My only client is Duane Jefferson."

"I think," Judge Hartley said, "I want to talk with this Duane Jefferson. I suppose you can establish his identity beyond any question, Mr. Mason?"

"His fingerprints were taken in connection with his military service," Mason said.

"That should be good enough evidence," Judge Hartley agreed, smiling. "I'd like to have a talk with him now."

Mason got up, walked to the door of chambers, looked out at the courtroom, and turned back to smile at the judge. "I guess I'll have to interrupt him," Mason said. "He and the witness Mae Jordan are jabbering away like a house afire. There seems to be a sort of common understanding between them. I guess it's because they're both interested in photography."

Judge Hartley's smile had broadened. "Perhaps, Mr. Mason," he suggested tentatively, "Miss Jordan is telling Mr. Jefferson where she got that key."

The Case of
the Gilded Lily

FOREWORD

MY FRIEND DR. WALTER CAMP IS AN OUTSTANDING FIG-
ure in the field of legal medicine.

One of his greatest attributes is the calm detached manner with which he approaches any scientific problem. It
is impossible to think of Dr. Camp ever being "stam-
peded" so that he would lose his intellectual integrity on
the one hand, or on the other hand let any personal or
financial considerations color his judgment.

Dr. Camp is both an M.D. and a Ph.D., yet despite
his intellectual and scientific achievements, and a brain
which functions as unemotionally (and as accurately) as
an adding machine, he remains a warm, friendly human
being.

Dr. Camp is one of the country's leading toxicologists.
He is a Professor of Toxicology and Pharmacology at the
University of Illinois and is Coroner's Toxicologist for
Cook County, which includes the seething metropolis of
Chicago.

For the past couple of years he has been Secretary of
the American Academy of Forensic Sciences, and heaven
knows how much time, energy and time-consuming effort
he and his personal secretary, Polly Cline, have poured
into that organization.

Dr. Camp is no prima donna with a temperament, although his achievements and record would entitle him to
develop all the idiosyncrasies of temperament; on the
contrary, he loves to work with others, to become a member of a "team," and then to minimize his own part in
that team's achievement.

Such men, who have the ability to get things done, who
have the executive qualities necessary to co-ordinate the

work of others, and the stability necessary to work with others, are rare.

This year, the annual meeting of the Academy of Forensic Sciences was held under the guidance of Dr. Camp, Secretary; Fred Inbau (Professor of Criminal Law at Northwestern University), President; and Dr. Richard Ford (head of the Department of Legal Medicine at Harvard University), Program Chairman. Those of us who attended found it one of the most inspirational and informative academy sessions ever to be held in an organization covering such a complex field. This was due mainly to the fact that these three men worked together as a team with such perfect co-ordination, such smooth co-operation, and such clockwork efficiency that many of us failed to realize the untold hours of planning, working, and almost constant consultation which made the extraordinary results possible.

Dr. Camp has worked on many a spectacular case where anyone less cool, less objective in his approach, would have been swept off his scientific feet. There was for instance the famous Ragen case where a man on the receiving end of a shotgun blast was later claimed to have died because of mercuric poisoning. There was another famous case: that of a gangster awaiting execution in the electric chair who beat the executioner to the punch, reportedly with the aid of a lethal dose of strychnine.

Dr. Camp, as a referee in these cases, handled himself in a manner which was a credit to the best traditions of forensic science. He refused to be influenced by rumors, the pressures of interested parties, or popular excitement. He approached the problems as a scientist, and he solved them as a scientist.

And so I dedicate this book to my friend:

WALTER J. R. CAMP, M.D., PH.D.

—Erle Stanley Gardner

CAST OF CHARACTERS

11 murders by the cream of crime writers $1.

Gardner

1. The Case of the Postponed Murder by Erle Stanley Gardner. The brand new Perry Mason finds Perry defending a woman who was "caught in the act" of murder. (Publ. Ed. $5.95)

2. The Case of the Fenced-In Woman by Erle Stanley Gardner. A marriage on the rocks and a house divided by a barbed wire fence add up to the strangest Mason mystery ever. (Publ. Ed. $5.95)

Christie

3. Nemesis by Agatha Christie. Miss Marple gets a letter from a dead man—asking her to investigate a forgotten crime. (Publ. Ed. $5.95)

4. Hallowe'en Party by Agatha Christie. A child drowns after boasting of seeing a murder. And a town explodes under Hercule Poirot's probing. (Publ. Ed. $5.95)

Queen

5. A Fine and Private Place by Ellery Queen. The clues point to the victim's young wife, or do they? (Publ. Ed. $5.95)

Foley

6. The First Mrs. Winston by Rae Foley. Was she shot by the virginal farm-girl who had just become the second Mrs. Winston? (Publ. Ed. $4.95)

Marric

7. Gideon's Press by J. J. Marric. Gideon of Scotland Yard against fanatics who are trying to overthrow the government by assorted acts of violence—such as drowning shiploads of immigrants at sea. (Publ. Ed. $4.95)

Creasey

8. Inspector West At Home by John Creasey. Who framed "Handsome" West on a dope rap, got him suspended from Scotland Yard, and started all the gossip about his faithful wife? (Publ. Ed. $5.95)

MacDonald

9. A Deadly Shade of Gold by John D. MacDonald. A friend's suspicious death and a missing golden idol launch Travis McGee on another breathtaking international caper. (Publ. Ed. $7.50)

Eberhart

10. Danger Money by Mignon G. Eberhart. Half in love with her boss, the heroine is in danger when his wife is murdered. 49th and latest thriller by the "Queen" of suspense. (Publ. Ed. $5.95)

Simenon

11. Maigret and the Millionaires by Georges Simenon. Murder in a bathtub leads Maigret from his usual underworld haunts to the unfamiliar territory of swank Paris hotels and their VIP clientele. (Publ. Ed. $5.95)

The Detective Book Club, Roslyn, New York 11576

11 mysteries for $1, including 4 by Gardner and Christie, plus the latest Eberhart and MacDonald thrillers.

For $1, you get 4 thrillers by the "King and Queen" of mystery: Erle Stanley Gardner and Agatha Christie. Plus the latest adventures of Travis McGee and Inspector Maigret. Plus 5 more, including a brand-new Mignon Eberhart whodunit.

These 11 mysteries in the publishers' original editions cost $65.00. But you get all 11, full-length and handsomely hardbound, for only $1, as long as the supply lasts.

What's the catch? You are. Only when you become a member, can we prove to you that The Detective Book Club gives more and asks less of you than any other club. Hence, the irresistible offer.

You pay no membership fee. There is no minimum number of books you must

J.J. Marric **GIDEON'S PRESS**

John Creasey **THE FIRST MRS. WINSTON** / **INSPECTOR WEST AT HOME**

Rae Foley **HALLOWEEN PARTY** / Agatha Christie

Ellery Queen **A FINE AND PRIVATE PLACE**

Erle Stanley Gardner **THE CASE OF THE POSTPONED MURDER**

Agatha Christie **NEMESIS**

Erle Stanley Gardner **THE CASE OF THE FENCED-IN WOMAN**

reject any volume before or after receiving it. And you may cancel at any time.

When you do accept a Club selection, you get three complete, uncondensed detective novels in one handsome, hardbound volume (like the one shown on this page) for only $3.89. That's less than you'd have to pay for any one of these novels in its trade edition.

The Club's editors select from more than 300 mystery books published each year. Their choices are so outstanding that many mystery writers are members, too. As a member, you'll be offered thrillers by top names like those featured above — plus Len Deighton, Dick Francis, Ngaio Marsh, Donald West-

■ 1 ■

STEWART G. BEDFORD ENTERED HIS PRIVATE OFFICE, hung up his hat, walked across to the huge walnut desk which had been a birthday present from his wife a year ago, and eased himself into the swivel chair.

His secretary, Elsa Griffin, with her never failing and characteristic efficiency, had left the morning paper on his desk, the pages neatly folded back so that Mrs. Bedford's photograph was smiling up at him from the printed page.

It was a good picture of Ann Roann Bedford, bringing out the little characteristic twinkle in her eyes, the sparkle and vitality of her personality.

Stewart Bedford was very, very proud of his wife. Mixed with that pride was the thrill of possession, the feeling that he, at fifty-two, had been able to marry a woman twenty years his junior and make her radiantly happy.

Bedford, with his wealth, his business contacts, his influential friends, had never paid attention to social life. His first wife had been dead for some twelve years. After her death the social circle of their friends would have liked to consider Stewart G. Bedford as the "most eligible bachelor," but Bedford wanted no part of it. He immersed himself in his business, continued to enhance his financial success, and took almost as much pride in the growing influence of his name in the business world as he would have taken in a son if he had had one.

Then he had met Ann Roann and his life suddenly slipped into a tailspin that caused a whirlwind courtship to culminate in a Nevada marriage.

Ann was as pleased with the social position she acquired through her marriage as a child with a new toy. Bedford still maintained his interest in his business, but it was no longer the dominant factor in his life. He wanted to get Ann Roann the things out of life which would make her happy, and Ann Roann had a long list of such things. However, her quick, enthusiastic response, her obvious gratitude, left Bedford constantly feeling like an indulgent parent on Christmas morning.

Bedford had settled himself at his desk and was reading the paper when Elsa Griffin glided in.

"Good morning, Elsa," he said. "Thanks for calling my attention to the account of Mrs. Bedford's party."

Her smile acknowledged his thanks. It was a nice smile.

To Stewart, Elsa Griffin was as comfortable as a smoking jacket and slippers. She had been with him for fifteen years; she knew his every want, his every whim, and had an uncanny ability to read his mind. He was very, very fond of her; in fact, there had been a romantic interlude after his first wife died. Elsa's quiet understanding had been one of the great things in his life. He had even considered marrying her—but that was before he had met Ann Roann.

Bedford knew he had made a fool of himself falling head over heels in love with Ann Roann, a woman who was just entering her thirties. He knew the hurt he was inflicting on Elsa Griffin, but he could no more control his actions than water rushing down a stream could stop on the brink of a precipice. He had plunged on into matrimony.

Elsa Griffin had offered her congratulations and wishes for every happiness and had promptly faded back into the position of the trusted private secretary. If she had suffered—and he was sure she had—there was no sign visible to the naked eye.

"There's a man waiting to see you," Elsa Griffin said.

"Who is he? What does he want?"

"His name is Denham. He said to tell you that Binney Denham wanted to see you and would wait."

"Benny Denham?" Bedford said. "I don't know any Benny Denham. How does it happen he wants to see me? Let him see one of the executives who—"

"It's not Benny. It's Binney," she said, "and he says it's a personal matter, that he'll wait until he can see you."

Bedford made a gesture of dismissal with his hand.

Elsa shook her head. "I don't think he'll leave. He really intends to see you."

Bedford scowled. "I can't be accessible to every Tom, Dick and Harry that comes in and says he wants to see me on a personal matter."

"I know," she said, "but Mr. Denham . . . there's something about him that's just a little . . . it's hard to describe . . . a persistence that's . . . well, it's a little frightening."

"Frightening!" Bedford said, bristling.

"Not in that way. It's just the fact that he has this terrible, deadly patience. You get the feeling that it would really be better to see him. He sits in the chair, quiet and motionless, and . . . and every time I look up he's looking at me with those peculiar eyes. I do wish you'd see him, S. G. I have a feeling you should."

"All right," Bedford said. "What the hell! Let's see what he wants and get rid of him. A personal matter. Not an old school friend that wants a touch?"

"No, no! Nothing like that. Something that . . . well, I have the feeling that it's important."

"All right," Bedford said, smiling. "I can always trust your intuition. We'll get him out of the way before we tackle the mail. Send him in."

Elsa left the office, and a few moments later Binney Denham was standing in the doorway bowing and smiling apologetically. Only his eyes were not apologetic. They were steady and appraising, as though his mission were a matter of life and death.

3

"I'm so glad you'll see me, Mr. Bedford," he said. "I was afraid perhaps I might have trouble. Delbert told me I *had* to see *you,* that I had to wait until I saw you, no matter how long it took, and Delbert is a hard man to cross."

Some inner bell rang a warning in Bedford's mind. He said, "Sit down. And who the devil is Delbert?"

"He's a sort of associate of mine."

"A partner?"

"No, no. I'm not a partner. I'm an associate."

"All right. Sit down. Tell me what it is you want. But you'll have to make it brief. I have some appointments this morning and there's some important mail here which has to be handled."

"Yes, sir. Thank you very much, sir."

Binney Denham moved over and sat on the extreme edge of the chair at the side of the desk. His hat was clutched over his stomach. He hadn't offered to shake hands.

"Well, what is it?" Bedford asked.

"It's about a business investment," Denham said. "It seems that Delbert needs money for financing this venture of his. It will only take twenty thousand dollars and he should be able to pay back the money within a few—"

"Say, what the devil *is* this?" Bedford said. "You told my secretary you wanted to see me about a personal matter. I don't know you. I don't know Delbert, and I'm not interested in financing any business venture to the tune of twenty thousand dollars. Now if that's all you—"

"Oh, but you don't understand, sir," the little man protested. "You see, it involves your wife."

Bedford stiffened with silent anger, but that inner bell which had sounded the note of warning before now gave such a strident signal that he became very cautious.

"And what about my wife?" he asked.

"Well, you see, sir, it's like this. Of course, you understand there's a market for these things now. These maga-

4

zines . . . I'm sure you don't like them any better than I do. I won't even read the things, and I'm quite certain you don't, sir. But you must know of their existence, and they're *very popular*."

"All right," Bedford said. "Get it out of your system. What are you talking about?"

"Well, of course, it . . . well, you almost have to know Delbert, Mr. Bedford, in order to understand the situation. Delbert is very insistent. When he wants something, he *really* wants it."

"All right, go on," Bedford snapped. "What about my wife? Why are you bringing her name into this?"

"Well, of course, I was only mentioning it because . . . well, you see, I know Delbert, and, while I don't condone his ideas, I—"

"What are his ideas?"

"He needs money."

"All right, he needs money. So what?"

"He thought you could furnish it."

"And my wife?" Bedford asked, restraining an impulse to throw the little man bodily out of the office.

"Well, of course your wife's record," Denham said.

"What do you mean, her record?"

"Her criminal record, fingerprints, et cetera," Denham said in that same quietly apologetic manner.

There was a moment of frozen silence. Bedford, too accustomed to playing poker in business to let Denham see the slightest flicker of expression on his face, was rapidly thinking back. After all, what did he know about Ann Roann? She had been the victim of an unhappy marriage she didn't like to discuss. There had been some sort of tragedy. Her husband's suicide had been his final confession of futility. There had been some insurance which had enabled the young widow to carry on during a period of readjustment. There had been two years of foreign travel and then she had met Stewart Bedford.

Bedford's own voice sounded strange to him. "Put your cards on the table. What is this? Blackmail?"

"Blackmail!" the man exclaimed with every evidence of horror. "Oh, my heavens, no, Mr. Bedford! Good heavens, no! Even Delbert wouldn't stoop to anything like that."

"Well, what *is* it?" Bedford asked.

"I'd like an opportunity to explain about the business investment. I think you'll agree it's a very sound investment and you could have the twenty thousand back within . . . well, Delbert says six months. I personally think it would be more like a year. Delbert's always optimistic."

"What about my wife's record?" Bedford's voice now definitely had a rasp to it.

"Well, of course, that's the point," Denham said apologetically. "You see, sir, Delbert simply *has* to have the money, and he thought you might loan it to him. Then, of course, he has this information and he knows that some of these magazines pay very high prices for tips. I've talked it over with him. I feel certain that they wouldn't pay anything like twenty thousand, but Delbert thinks they would if the information was fully authenticated and—"

"This information is authenticated?" Bedford asked.

"Oh, of course, sir, of course! I wouldn't even have mentioned it otherwise."

"How is it authenticated?"

"What the police call mug shots and fingerprints."

"Let me see."

"I'd much prefer to talk about the investment, Mr. Bedford. I didn't really intend to bring it up in this way. However, I could see you were rather impatient about—"

"What about the information?" Bedford asked.

The little man let go of the rim of his hat with his right hand. He fished in an inner pocket and brought out a plain Manila envelope.

"I'm sure I hadn't intended to tell you about it in this way," he said sorrowfully.

He extended the Manila envelope toward Bedford.

Bedford took the envelope, turned back the flap, and pulled out the papers that were on the inside.

It was either the damnedest clever job of fake photography he had ever seen or it was Ann Roann . . . Ann Roann's picture taken some years earlier. There was the same daring, don't-give-a-damn sparkle in her eyes, the lilt to her head, the twist of her lips, and down underneath was that damning serial number, below that a set of fingerprints and the sections of the penal code that had been violated.

Denham's voice droned on, filling in the gap in Bedford's thinking.

"Those sections of the penal code relate to insurance fraud, if you don't mind, Mr. Bedford. I know you're curious. I was too when I looked it up."

"What's she supposed to have done?" Bedford asked.

"She had some jewelry that was insured. She made the mistake of pawning the jewelry before she reported that it had been stolen. She collected on the insurance policy, and then they found where the jewelry had been pawned and . . . well, the police are very efficient in such matters."

"What was done with the charge?" Bedford asked. "Was she convicted, given probation? Was the charge dismissed, or what?"

"Heavens! I don't know," Denham said. "I'm not sure that even Delbert knows. These are the records that Delbert gave me. He said that he was going to take them to this magazine and that they'd pay him for the tip. I told him I thought he was being very, very foolish, that I didn't think the magazine would pay as much as he needed for his investment, and frankly, Mr. Bedford, I don't like such things. I don't like those magazines or this business of assassinating character, of digging up things out of a person's dead past. I just don't like it."

"I see," Bedford said grimly. He sat there holding in

front of him the photostatic copy of the circular describing his wife—age, height, weight, eye color, fingerprint classification.

So this was blackmail. He'd heard about it. Now he was up against it. This little man sitting there on the edge of the chair, holding his hat across his stomach, his hands clutching the rim, his manner apologetic, was a blackmailer and Bedford was being given the works.

Bedford knew all about what he was supposed to do under such circumstances. He was supposed to throw the little bastard out of his office, beat him up, turn him over to the police. He was supposed to tell him, "Go ahead. Do your damnedest! I won't pay a dime for blackmail!" Or he was supposed to string the man along, ring up the police department, explain the matter to the officer in charge of such things, a man who would promise to handle it discreetly and keep it very, very confidential.

He knew how such things were handled. They would arrange for him to turn over marked money. Then they would arrest Binney Denham and the case would be kept very hush-hush.

But would it?

There was this mysterious Delbert in the background . . . Delbert, who apparently was the ringleader of the whole thing . . . Delbert, who wanted to sell his information to one of those magazines that were springing up like mushrooms, magazines which depended for their living on exploiting sensational facts about people in the public eye.

Either these were police records or they weren't.

If they were police records, Bedford was trapped. There was no escape. If they weren't police records, it was a matter of forgery.

"I'd want some time to look into this," he said.

"How much time?" Binney Denham asked, and for the first time there was a certain hard note in his voice that caused Bedford to look up sharply, but his eyes saw only a little man sitting timidly on the very edge of the chair, holding his hat on his stomach.

"Well, for one thing, I'd want to verify the facts."

"Oh, you mean in the business deal?" Denham asked, his voice quick with hope.

"The business deal be damned!" Bedford said. "You know what this is and I know what it is. Now get the hell out of here and let me think."

"Oh, but I wanted to tell you about the business deal," Denham said. "Delbert is certain you'll have every penny of your money back. It's just a question of raising some operating capital, Mr. Bedford, and—"

"I know. I know," Bedford interrupted. "Give me time to think this over."

Binney Denham got to his feet at once. "I'm sorry I intruded on you without an appointment, Mr. Bedford. I know how busy you are. I realize I must have taken up a lot of your time. I'll go now."

"Wait a minute," Bedford said. "How do I get in touch with you?"

Binney Denham turned in the doorway. "Oh, *I'll* get in touch with *you,* sir, if you don't mind, sir. And of course I'll have to talk with Delbert. Good day, sir!" and the little man opened the door a crack and slipped away.

■ 2 ■

DINNER THAT NIGHT WAS A TETE-A-TETE AFFAIR WITH Ann Roann Bedford serving the cocktails herself on a silver tray which had been one of the wedding presents.

Stewart Bedford felt thoroughly despicable as he slid

the tray face down under the davenport while Ann Roann was momentarily in the serving pantry.

Later on, after a dinner during which he tried in vain to conceal the tension he was laboring under, he got the tray up to his study, attached it to a board with adhesive tape around the edges so that any latent fingerprints on the bottom would not be disfigured, and then fitted it in a pasteboard box in which he had recently received some shirts.

Ann Roann commented on the box the next day when her husband left for work carrying it under his arm. He told her in what he hoped was a casual manner that the color of the shirts hadn't been satisfactory and he was going to exchange them. He said he'd get Elsa Griffin to wrap and mail the package.

For a moment Bedford thought that there was a fleeting mistrust in his wife's slate gray eyes, but she said nothing and her good-by kiss was a clinging pledge of the happiness that had come to mean so much to him.

Safely ensconced in his private office, Bedford went to work on a problem that he knew absolutely nothing about. He had stopped at the art store downstairs to buy some drawing charcoal and a camel's-hair brush. He rubbed the edge of the stick of drawing charcoal into fine dust and dusted this over the bottom of the tray. He was pleased to find that he had developed several perfectly legible latent fingerprints.

It now remained to compare those fingerprints with the fingerprints on the criminal record which had been left him by the apologetic little man who needed the "loan" of twenty thousand dollars.

So engrossed was Stewart Bedford in what he was doing that he didn't hear Elsa Griffin enter the office.

She was standing by his side at the desk, looking over his shoulder, before he glanced up with a start.

"I didn't want to be disturbed," he said irritably.

10

"I know," she said in that voice of quiet understanding. "I thought perhaps I could be of help."

"Well, you can't."

She said, "The technique used by detectives is to take a piece of transparent cellophane tape and place it over the latent fingerprints. Then when you remove the Scotch tape the dust adheres to the tape and you can put the print on a card and study it at leisure without damaging the latent print."

Stewart Bedford whirled around in his chair. "Look here," he said. "Just how much do you know and what are you talking about?"

She said, "Perhaps you didn't remember, but you left the intercommunicating system open to my desk when you were talking with Mr. Denham yesterday."

"The devil I did!"

She nodded.

"I wasn't conscious of it. I'm almost sure I shut it off."

She shook her head. "You didn't."

"All right," he said. "Go get me some cellophane tape. We'll try it."

"I have some here," she said. "Also a pair of scissors."

Her long, skillful fingers deftly snipped pieces of the transparent tape, laid them over the back of the silver tray, smoothed them into position, and then removed the tape so they could study the fingerprints, line for line, whorl for whorl.

"You seem to know something about this," Bedford said.

She laughed. "Believe it or not, I once took a correspondence course in how to be a detective."

"Why?"

"I'm darned if I know," she admitted cheerfully. "I just wanted something to do and I've always been fascinated with problems of detection. I thought it might sharpen my powers of observation."

Bedford patted her affectionately. "Well, if you're so

darn good at it, draw up a chair and sit down. Take this magnifying glass and let's see what we can find out."

Elsa Griffin had, as it turned out, a considerable talent for matching fingerprints. She knew what to look for and how to find the different points of similarity. In a matter of fifteen minutes Stewart Bedford came to the sickening realization that there could be no doubt about it. The fingerprints on the police record were an identical match for the four perfect latents which had been lifted from the silver tray.

"Well," Bedford said, "since you know all about it, what suggestions do you have, Elsa?"

She shook her head. "This is a problem you have to solve for yourself, S. G. If you once start paying, there's no end to it."

"And if I don't?" he asked.

She shrugged her shoulders.

Bedford looked down at the silver tray which reflected a distorted image of his own harassed features. He knew what it would mean to Ann Roann to have something of this sort come out.

She was so full of life, vivacity, happiness. Bedford could visualize what would happen if one of these magazines that were becoming so popular should come out with the story of Ann Roann's past; the story of an adventurous girl who had sought to finance her venture into the matrimonial market by defrauding an insurance company.

No matter what the alternative, he couldn't let that happen.

There would, he knew, be frigid expressions of sympathy, the formal denunciation of "those horrible scandal sheets." There would be an attempt on the part of some to be "charitable" to Ann Roann. Others would cut her at once, deliberately and coldly.

Gradually the circle would tighten. Ann Roann would have to plead a nervous breakdown . . . a foreign cruise

12

somewhere. She would never come back—not the way Ann Roann would want to come back.

Elsa Griffin seemed to be reading his mind.

"You might," she said, "play along with him for a while; stall for time as much as possible, but try to find out something about who this man is. After all, he must have his own weaknesses.

"I remember reading a story one time where a man was faced with a somewhat similar problem and—"

"Yes?" Bedford said as she paused.

"Of course, it was just a story."

"Go ahead."

"The man couldn't afford to deny their blackmail claims. He didn't dare to have the thing they were holding over him become public, but he . . . well, he was clever and . . . of course, it was just a story. There were two of them just as there are here."

"Go on! What did he do?"

"He killed one of the blackmailers and made the evidence indicate the other blackmailer had committed the murder. The frantic blackmailer tried to tell the true story to the jury, but the jury just laughed at him and sent him to the electric chair."

"That's farfetched," Bedford said. "It could only work in a story."

"I know," she said. "It was just a story, but it was so convincingly told that it . . . well, it just seemed terribly plausible. I remembered it. It stuck in my mind."

Bedford looked at her in amazement, seeing a new phase of her character which he had never dreamed existed.

"I never knew you were so bloodthirsty, Elsa."

"It was only a story."

"But you stored it in your mind. How did you become interested in this detective business?"

"Through reading the magazines which feature true crime stories."

"You like them?"

"I love them."

Again he looked at her.

"They keep your mind busy," she explained.

"I guess I'm learning a lot about people very fast," he said, still studying her.

"A girl has to have *something* to occupy her mind when she's left all alone," she said defensively but not defiantly.

He hastily looked back at the tray, then gently put it back in the shirt box. "We'll just have to wait it out now, Elsa. Whenever Denham calls on the telephone or tries to get in touch with me, stall him off if you can. But when he gets insistent, put the call through. I'll talk with him."

"What about these?" she asked, indicating the lifted fingerprints on the Scotch tape.

"Destroy them," Bedford said. "Get rid of them. And don't just put them in a wastebasket. Cut them into small pieces with scissors and burn them."

She nodded and quietly left the office.

There was no word from Binney Denham all that day. It got so his very failure to try to communicate got on Bedford's nerves. Twice during the afternoon he called Elsa in.

"Anything from Denham?"

She shook her head.

"Never mind trying to stall him," Bedford said. "When he calls, put the call through. If he comes to see me, let him come in. I can't stand the strain of this suspense. Let's find out what we're up against as soon as we can."

"Do you want a firm of private detectives?" she asked. "Would you like to have them shadow him when he leaves the office and—"

"Hell, no!" Bedford said. "How do I know that I could trust the private detectives? They might shadow him and find out all about what he knows. Then I'd be paying blackmail to two people instead of one. Let's keep this on

14

a basis where we're handling it ourselves . . . and, of course, there *is* a possibility that the guy is right. It may be just a loan. It may be that this partner—this Delbert he refers to—is really a screwball who needs some capital and is taking this way of raising it. He may really be hesitating between selling his information to a magazine and letting me advance the loan. Elsa, if Denham telephones, put through the call immediately. I want to get these fellows tied up before there's any possibility they'll peddle that stuff to a magazine. It would be dynamite!"

"All right," she promised. "I'll put him through the minute he calls."

But Binney Denham didn't call, and Bedford went home that evening feeling like a condemned criminal whose application for a commutation of sentence is in the hands of the governor. Every minute became sixty seconds of agonizing suspense.

Ann Roann was wearing a hostess gown which plunged daringly to a low *V* in front and was fastened with an embroidered frog. She had been to the beauty parlor, and her hair glinted with soft high lights.

Stewart Bedford found himself hoping that they would have another tête-à-tête dinner, with candlelight and cocktails, but she reminded him that a few friends were coming in and that he had to change to a dinner coat and black tie.

Bedford lugged the cardboard box up to his room, opened it, tore off the strips of adhesive tape which held the silver cocktail tray to the board, and managed to get the tray down to the serving pantry without being noticed.

The little dinner was a distinct success. Ann Roann was at her best, and Bedford noted with satisfaction the glances that came his way from men who had for years taken him for granted. Now they were looking at him as though appraising some new hidden quality which they had overlooked. There was a combination of envy and

15

admiration in their expressions that made him feel a lot younger than his years. He found himself squaring his shoulders, bringing in his stomach, holding his head erect.

After all, it was a pretty good world. Nothing was so bad that it couldn't be cured somehow. Things were never as bad as they seemed.

Then came the call to the telephone. The butler said that a Mr. D. said the call was quite important, and he was certain that Mr. Bedford would want to be advised.

Bedford made a great show of firmness. "Tell him that I'm not receiving any calls at the moment," he said. "Tell him he can call me at the office tomorrow, or leave me a number where I can call him back in an hour or two."

The butler nodded and vanished, and for a moment Bedford felt as though he had won a point. After all, he'd show these damn blackmailers that he wasn't going to jump every time they snapped their fingers. Then the butler was back.

"Beg your pardon, sir," he said, "but Mr. D. said the message is *most* important, that I was to tell you his associate is getting entirely out of control. He said he'd call you back in twenty minutes, that that was the best he could do."

"Very well," Bedford said, trying to keep up the external semblance of poise, but filled with sudden panic. "I'll talk with him when he calls."

He didn't realize how frequently he was consulting his wrist watch during the next interminable quarter of an hour, until he saw Ann Roann watching him speculatively; then he cursed himself for letting his tension show. He should have gone to the telephone immediately.

None of the guests seemed to notice anything unusual. Only Ann Roann's deep slate eyes followed him with that peculiarly withdrawn look which she had at times when she was thinking something out.

It was exactly twenty minutes from the time of the first call that the butler came to the door. He caught Bedford's eye and nodded. This time Bedford, moving in a manner which he tried to make elaborately casual, started toward the door, said, "All right, Harvey. I'll take the call in my upstairs office. Hang up the downstairs phone as soon as I get on the line."

"Very good, sir," the butler said.

Bedford excused himself to his guests, climbed the stairs hurriedly to his den, closed the door tightly, picked up the receiver, said, "Yes, hello. This is Bedford speaking." He heard Denham's voice filled with apologies.

"I'm terribly sorry I had to disturb you tonight, sir, but I thought you'd like to know. You see, Delbert talked with someone who knows the people who run this magazine and it seems he wouldn't have any difficulty at all getting—"

"Whom did he talk with?" Bedford asked.

"I don't know, sir. I'm sure I don't know. It was just someone who knew about the magazine. It seems that they do pay a lot of money for some of the things they publish and—"

"Bosh and nonsense!" Bedford interrupted. "No scandal sheet is going to pay that sort of money for a tip of that sort. Besides, if they publish I'll sue them for libel."

"Yes, sir. I know. I wish you could talk with Delbert. I think you could convince him. But the point is *I* couldn't convince him. He's going to go to the magazine first thing in the morning. I daresay that when they learn what he has, they'll offer him a very paltry sum, but I thought you'd like to know, sir."

"Now look," Bedford said. "Let's be sensible about this thing. Delbert doesn't want to deal with that magazine. You tell Delbert to get in touch with *me*."

"Oh, Delbert wouldn't do *that,* sir! He's terribly afraid of you, sir."

"Afraid of me?"

"Yes, of course, sir. That's why I . . . well, I thought you'd understand. *I* thought we should tell *you*. I thought we owed you that much out of respect for your position. It was all *my* idea coming to you. Delbert, you see, just wanted to make an outright sale. He says there're certain disadvantages doing business this way, that you might trap him in something. He's . . . well, he doesn't want to do it this way at all. He wants to give the magazine a piece of legitimate news and take whatever they give him as legitimate compensation. He tried to keep me from going to you. He says there's every possibility you could trap us in some way."

"Now look," Bedford said. "This man Delbert is a fool. I am not going to be told what to do and what not to do."

"Yes, sir."

"I'm not going to be terrified by anybody."

"Yes, sir."

"I also know this information is phony. I know there's something cockeyed about it somewhere."

"Oh, I'm sorry to hear you say that, sir, because Delbert—"

"Now, wait a minute," Bedford interrupted. "Just hold your horses. I've told you where *I* stand, but I've also made up my mind that rather than have any trouble about it, I'm willing to go ahead and do what you people want. Now is that clear?"

"Oh, yes, sir. That's very clear! If I can tell Delbert that, it will make him feel *very* much different—that is, I hope it does. Of course, he's afraid that you're too smart for us. He's afraid that you'll lay a trap."

"Trap, nothing!" Bedford said. "Now, let's get this straight. When I do business, I do business on a basis of good faith. My word is good. I'm not setting any traps. Now, you tell Delbert to keep in line, and you call at my office tomorrow and we'll arrange to fix things up."

"I'm afraid it has to be done tonight, sir."

"Tonight! That's impossible!"

"Well, that's all right then," Denham said. "If you feel that way, that's—"

"Wait a minute! Wait a minute!" Bedford shouted. "Don't hang up. I'm just telling you it's impossible to get things lined up for tonight."

"Well, I don't know whether I can hold Delbert in line or not."

"I'll give you a check," Bedford said.

"Oh, good heavens, no, sir! Not a check! Delbert wouldn't ever hear of that, sir. He'd feel certain that was an attempt to trap him. The money would have to be in cash, if you know what I mean, sir. It would have to be money . . . well . . . money that couldn't be traced. Delbert is very suspicious, Mr. Bedford, and he thinks you're a very smart businessman."

"Let's quit playing cops and robbers," Bedford said. "Let's get down to a business basis on this thing. I'll go to the bank tomorrow morning and get some money, and you can—"

"Just a moment, please," Denham's voice said. "Delbert said never mind. Just let the matter drop."

"Let's quit playing cops and robbers," Bedford said. Bedford could hear voices at the other end of the line. He could hear the sound of Denham's pleading, and once or twice he fancied he could hear a gruff voice, then Denham would cut in in that same apologetic drone. He couldn't hear the words, just the tone of voice.

Then Denham was back on the phone again.

"I'll tell you what you do, Mr. Bedford. This is probably the best way of handling it. Now, tomorrow morning just as soon as your bank opens you go to your bank and get twenty thousand dollars in traveler's checks. The checks are to be one hundred dollars each. You get those checks and go to your office and then I'll get in touch with you at your office. I'm awfully sorry I bothered you tonight, Mr. Bedford. I knew we shouldn't have done it. I told Delbert that it was an imposition. But Delbert gets terribly impatient and he *is* suspicious. You see, this deal means a lot to him, and . . . well, you'd have to know him to understand.

"I'm just trying to do the best I can, Mr. Bedford, and it puts *me* in a terribly embarrassing position. I'm terribly sorry I called you."

"Not at all," Bedford heard himself saying. "Now you look here, Denham. You keep this Delbert person, whoever he is, in line. I'll see that you get the money tomorrow. Now don't let him get out of line. You stay with him."

"Yes, sir."

"Can you be with him all the time tonight? Don't let him out of your sight. I don't want him to get any foolish ideas."

"Well, I'll try."

"All right. You do that," Bedford said. "I'll see you tomorrow. Good-by."

He heard Binney Denham hang up, and reached for his handkerchief to wipe the cold sweat on his forehead before dropping the receiver into place. It was then he heard the second unmistakable click on the line.

In an agony of apprehension he tried to remember if he had heard the sound of the butler hanging up the receiver on the lower phone after he came on the line. He had no recollection of the sound.

Was it possible the lower phone had been open during the conversation? Had someone been listening?

Who?

How long had they had this damned butler anyway? Ann Roann had hired him. What did she know about him? Was it possible this whole thing was an inside job?

Who was this damned Delbert? How the devil did he know that there actually was any Delbert at all? How did he know that he wasn't dealing with Denham, and with Denham alone?

Filled with a savage determination, Bedford opened the drawer of his dresser, took out the snub-nosed blued steel .38 caliber gun and shoved it in his brief case. Damn it, if these blackmailers wanted to play tough, he'd be just as tough as they were.

He opened the door from the den, descended the stairs quietly, and then at the foot of the stairs came to a sudden pause as he saw Ann Roann in the butler's pantry. She had found the silver serving tray and was holding it so that the light shone on the back.

The silver tray hadn't been washed and there remained a very faint impression of charcoal-dusted fingerprints, of places where the strips of adhesive tape had left marks on the polished silver.

■ 3 ■

STEWART G. BEDFORD FELT UNREASONABLY ANGRY AS HE signed his name two hundred times to twenty thousand dollars' worth of checks.

The banker, who had tried to make conversation, didn't help matters any.

"Pleasure or business trip, Mr. Bedford?"

"Neither."

"No?"

"No."

Bedford signed his name in savage silence; then, realizing that his manner had only served to arouse curiosity, added, "I like to have some cash reserves on hand these days, something you can convert to cash in a minute."

"Oh, I see," the banker said, and thereafter said nothing.

Bedford folded the checks and left the bank. Why the

devil couldn't they have taken the money in tens and twenties the way they did with kidnap ransom in the movies. Served him right for getting mixed up with a damn bunch of blackmailers.

Bedford entered his private office and found Elsa Griffin sitting there waiting for him.

Bedford raised his eyebrows.

"Mr. Denham and a girl are waiting for you," she said.

"A girl?"

She nodded.

"What sort of a girl?"

"A babe."

"A moll?"

"It's hard to tell. She's really something for looks."

"Describe her."

"Blonde, nice complexion, beautiful legs, plenty of curves, big limpid eyes, a dumb look, a little perfume, and that's all."

"You mean that's really all?"

"That's all there is."

"Well, let's have them in," Bedford said, "and I'll leave the intercom on so you can listen."

"Do you want me to . . . to do anything?"

He shook his head. "There's nothing we can do except give them the money."

Elsa Griffin went out and Binney Denham came in with the blonde.

"Good morning, Mr. Bedford, good morning. I want to introduce you to Geraldine Corning."

The blonde batted her big eyes at him and said in a throaty, seductive voice, "Gerry, for short."

"Now it's like this," Binney Denham said. "You're going out with Gerry."

"What do you mean, going out with her?"

"Going out with me," Gerry said.

"Now look here," Bedford began angrily. "I'm willing to—"

22

He was stopped by the peculiar look in Binney Denham's eyes.

"This is the way Delbert says it has to be," Denham said. "He has it all figured out, Mr. Bedford. I've been having a lot of trouble with Delbert . . . a whole lot of trouble. I don't think I could explain things to him if there were to be any variation."

"All right," Bedford said angrily. "Let's get it over with."

"You have the checks?"

"I have the checks here in my brief case."

"Well, that's fine! That's just dandy! I told Delbert I knew we could count on you But he's frightened, and when a man gets frightened he does unreasonable things. Don't you think so, Mr Bedford?"

"I wouldn't know," Bedford said grimly.

"That's right You wouldn't, would you?" Binney said. "I'm sorry I asked you the question in that way, Mr. Bedford. I was talking about Delbert. He's a peculiar mixture, and you can say that again."

Gerry's eyes smiled at Bedford. "I think we'd better start."

"Where are we going?" Bedford asked.

"Gerry will tell you. I'll ride down in the elevator with you if you don't mind. Mr. Bedford, and then I'll leave you two. I'm quite certain it will be all right."

Bedford hesitated.

"Of course," Denham said, "I'm terribly sorry it had to work out in this way. I know that you've been inconvenienced enough as it is, and I just want you to know that I've been against it all along, Mr. Bedford. I know that your word is good, and I'd like to deal with you on that basis, but you just can't understand Delbert unless you've had dealings with him. Delbert is terribly suspicious. You see, he's afraid. He feels that you're a smart businessman and that you may have been in touch with somebody who would make trouble. Delbert just wants to go right ahead and make a sale to the magazine. He says that that's perfectly legitimate and no one can—"

"Oh, for heaven's sake!" Bedford exploded. "Let's cut out this comedy. I'm going to pay. I've got the money. You want the money. Now let's go!"

Gerry moved close to him, linked her arm through his, holding it familiarly.

"You heard what he said, Binney. He wants to go."

Bedford made for the door that led to the outer office.

"Not that way," Binney said apologetically. "We're supposed to go out through the exit door directly to the elevator."

"I have to let my secretary know I'm going out," Bedford said, making a last stand. "She *has* to know I'm going out."

Binney coughed. "I'm sorry, sir. Delbert was most insistent on that point."

"Now look here—" Bedford began, then stopped.

"It's better this way, Mr. Bedford. This is the way Delbert wanted it."

Bedford permitted Geraldine Corning to lead him toward the door. Binney Denham held it open and the three of them went out in the corridor, took the express elevator to the ground floor.

"This way," Binney said and escorted them to a new-looking, yellow car which was parked at the curb directly in front of the building.

"Are you worried about women drivers?" Geraldine asked him.

"How good are you?" Bedford asked.

"At driving?"

"Yes."

"Not too good."

"I'll drive."

"Okay by me."

"How about Denham?"

24

"Oh, Binney's not coming. Binney's all finished. He'll follow for a ways, that's all."

Bedford got in behind the wheel.

The blonde slid gracefully in beside him. She was, Bedford conceded to himself, quite a package—curves in the right places; eyes, complexion, legs, clothes—and yet he couldn't be sure whether she was stupid or putting on an act.

"Bye, Binney," she said.

The little man bowed and smiled and bowed and smiled again. "Have a nice trip," he said as Bedford gunned the engine into life.

"Which way?" he asked.

"Straight ahead," the blonde said.

For one swift moment Bedford had a glimpse of Elsa Griffin on the sidewalk. Thanks to the intercom she had learned their plans in time to get to the sidewalk before they had left the office.

He saw that she was holding a pencil and notebook, He knew she had the license number of the car he was driving.

He managed to keep from looking directly at Elsa and eased the car out into traffic.

"Now, look," Bedford said. "I want to know something about what I'm getting into."

"You aren't afraid of me, are you?"

"I want to know what I'm getting into."

"You do as you're told," she instructed him, "and there won't be any trouble."

"I don't do business that way."

"Then drive back to your office," she said, "and forget the whole business."

Bedford thought that over, then kept driving straight ahead.

The blonde squirmed around sideways on the seat and drew up her knees, making no attempt to conceal her legs. "Look, big boy," she said. "You and I might just as well get along. It'll be easier that way."

Bedford said nothing.

She made a little grimace at his silence and said, "I like to be sociable."

Then after a moment she straightened in the seat, pulled her skirt back down over her knees and said, "Okay, be grumpy if you want to. Turn left at the next corner, grouch-face."

He turned left at the next corner.

"Turn right on the freeway and go north," she instructed.

Bedford eased his way into the freeway traffic, instinctively looked at the gasoline gauge. It was full. He settled down for a long drive.

"Turn right again and leave the freeway up here at the next crossroads," she said.

Bedford followed instructions. Again the blonde doubled her knees up on the seat and rested one hand lightly on his shoulder.

Bedford realized then that she was carefully regarding the traffic behind them through the rear window of the car.

Bedford raised his eyes to the rearview mirror.

A single car followed them off the freeway, maintaining a respectable distance behind.

"Turn right," Geraldine said.

Bedford had a glimpse of the driver of that other car. It was Binney Denham.

From that point on Geraldine, seated beside him, gave a series of directions which sent him twisting and turning through traffic.

Always behind them was that single car, sometimes close, sometimes dropping far behind, until finally, apparently satisfied that no one was following them, the car disappeared and Geraldine Corning said, "All right, now we drive straight ahead. I'll tell you where to stop."

They followed the stream of traffic out Wilshire. At length, following her directions, he turned north.

"Slow down," she said.

Bedford slowed the car.

"Look for a good motel," she told him. "This is far enough."

As she spoke, they passed a motel on the left, but it was so shabby Bedford drove on without pausing. There was another motel half a mile ahead. It was named The Staylonger.

"How's this?" Bedford asked.

"I guess this will do. Turn in here. We get a motel unit and wait."

"How do I register?" Bedford asked.

She shrugged her shoulders. "I'm to keep you occupied until the thing is all over. Binney thought you'd be less nervous if you had me for company."

"Look here," Bedford said. "I'm a married man. I'm not going to get into any damned trap over this thing."

"Have it your way," she said. "We just wait here, that's all. There isn't any trap. Let your conscience be your guide."

Bedford entered the place. The manager smiled at him, showing gold teeth. He asked no questions.

Bedford signed the name, "S. G. Wilfred," and gave a San Diego address. At the same time he gave the story that he had hurriedly thought up. "We're to be joined by some friends who are driving in from San Diego. We got here early. Do you have a double cabin?"

"Sure we do," the manager said. "In fact, we have anything you want."

"I want a double."

"If you register for a double, you'll have to pay for both cabins. If you take a single, I'll reserve the other cabin until six o'clock and then your friends can register and pay."

"No, I'll pay for the whole business," Bedford said.

27

"That'll be twenty-eight dollars."

Bedford started to protest at the price; then, looking out at the young blonde sitting in the car, realized that it would be better to say nothing. He put twenty-eight dollars on the counter and received two keys.

"They're the two cabins down at the end with the double garage in between—numbers fifteen and sixteen. There's a connecting door," the manager said.

Bedford thanked him, went back to the car, drove it down, parked it in the garage and said, "Now what?"

"I guess we wait," Gerry told him.

Bedford unlocked one of the cabins and held the door open. She walked in. Bedford followed her.

It was a nice motel—a double bed, a little kitchenette, a refrigerator, and a connecting door between that and another unit that was exactly the same. There was also a toilet and tiled shower in each unit.

"Expecting company?" Geraldine asked.

"That's your room," Bedford said. "This one is mine."

She looked at him almost scornfully, then said, "Got the traveler's checks?"

Bedford nodded. She indicated the table and said, "You'd better start signing."

Bedford zipped open his brief case and was reaching for the traveler's checks when he saw the gun. He had forgotten about that. He hurriedly turned the brief case so she couldn't see in it and took out the books of traveler's checks.

He sat at the table and started signing the checks.

She slipped out of her jacket, looked at herself appraisingly in the mirror, studied her legs, straightened her stockings, glanced over her shoulder at Bedford and said, "I think I'll freshen up a bit."

She went through the connecting door into the other unit. Bedford heard the sound of running water. He heard a door close, a drawer open and close, then the outer door opened.

Suddenly suspicious, Bedford put down his pen, walked through the door and into the other room.

Geraldine was standing in her bra, panties and stockings in front of an open suitcase.

She turned casually and raised her eyebrows. "All signed so soon?" she asked.

"No," Bedford said angrily. "I heard a door open and close. I was wondering if you were taking a powder."

She laughed. "Just getting my suitcase out of the trunk compartment of the car," she said. "I'm not leaving you. You'd better go on with your signing. They'll want the checks pretty quick."

There was neither invitation nor embarrassment in her manner. She stood there watching him speculatively, and Bedford, annoyed at finding himself not only aware but warmly appreciative of her figure, turned back to his own unit in the motel and gave himself over to signing checks. For the second time that day he signed his name two hundred times, then went to the half-opened connecting door. "Everybody decent?" he asked.

"Oh, don't be so stuffy. Come on in," she said.

He entered the room to find Geraldine attired in a neat-fitting gabardine skirt which snugly outlined the curves of her hips, a soft pink sweater which clung to her ample breasts, and an expensive wide contour belt around her tiny waist.

"You have them?" she asked.

Bedford handed her the checks.

She took the books, carefully looked through each check to make sure that it was properly signed, glanced at her wrist watch and said, "I'm going out to the car for a minute. You stay here."

She went out, locking the door from the outside, leaving Bedford alone in the motel. Bedford whipped out a notebook, wrote the telephone number of his unlisted line, which connected directly with Elsa Griffin's desk. He wrote, "Call this number and say I am at The Staylonger Motel." He pulled a twenty-dollar bill from his billfold, doubled it over, with the leaf from his notebook inside, then folded the twenty-dollar bill again and thrust it in his vest pocket. He went to her suitcase, tried to learn something of her identity from an inspection of the contents.

The suitcase and the overnight bag beside it were brand new. The initials G. C. were stamped in gold on the leather. There were no other distinguishing marks.

He heard her step on the wooden stair outside the door and quietly withdrew from the vicinity of the baggage.

A moment later the girl opened the door. "I've got a bottle," she said. "How about a highball?"

"Too early in the day for me."

She lit a cigarette, stretched languidly, moved over to the bed and sat down. "We're going to have to wait quite a while," she said by way of explanation.

"For what?"

"To make sure everything clears, silly. You're not to go out—except with me. We stay here."

"When can I get back to my business?"

"Whenever everything's cleared. Don't be so impatient."

Bedford marched back into the other unit of the motel and sat down in a chair that was only fairly comfortable. Minutes seemed to drag into hours. At length he got up and walked back to the other unit. Geraldine was stretched out in the overstuffed chair. She had drawn up another chair to use as a footrest and the short skirt had slid back to show very attractive legs.

"I just can't sit here all day doing nothing," he said angrily.

"You want this thing to go through, don't you?"

"Of course I want it to go through; otherwise I wouldn't have gone this far. But after all, there are certain things that I don't intend to put up with."

"Come on, grumpy," she said. "Why not be human?

We're going to be here a while. Know anything about cards?"

"A little."

"How about gin rummy?"

"Okay," he said. "What do we play for?"

"Anything you want."

Bedford hesitated a moment, then made it a cent a point.

At the end of an hour he had lost twenty-seven dollars. He paused in his deal and said, "For heaven's sake, let's cut out this beating around the bush. *When* do I get out of here?"

"Sometime this afternoon, after the banks close."

"Now wait a minute!" he said. "That's going too damned far."

"Forget it," she told him. "Why don't you loosen up and be yourself? After all, I'm as human as you are. I get bored the same as you do. You're already parted with your money. You have everything to lose and nothing to gain by trying to crab the deal now. Sit down and relax. Take your coat off. Take your shoes off. Why don't you have a drink?"

She went over to the refrigerator, opened the door of the freezing compartment and took out a tray of ice cubes.

"Okay," Bedford surrendered. "What do you have?"

"Scotch on the rocks, or Scotch and water."

"Scotch on the rocks," he said.

"That's better," she told him. "I could like you if you weren't so grouchy. Lots of people would like to spend time here with me. We could have fun if you'd quit grinding your teeth. Know any funny stories?"

"They don't seem funny now," he said.

She opened a new fifth of Scotch, poured out generous drinks, looked at him over the brim of the glass, said, "Here's looking at you, big boy."

"Here's to crime!" Bedford said.

"That's better," she told him.

Bedford decided to try a new conversational gambit.

"You know," he told her, "you're quite an attractive girl. You certainly have a figure."

"I noticed you looking it over."

"You didn't seem very much concerned at the . . . at the lack of . . . of your costume."

"I've been looked at before."

"What do you do?" Bedford asked. "I mean, how do you make a living?"

"Mostly," she said, smiling, "I follow instructions."

"Who gives the instructions?"

"That," she said, "depends."

"Do you know this man they call Delbert?"

"Just by name."

"What kind of a man is he?"

"All I know is what Binney tells me. I guess he's a screwball . . . but smart. He's nervous—you know, jumpy."

"And you know Binney?"

"Oh, sure."

"What about Binney?"

"He's nice, in a mild sort of way."

"Well," he said, "let's get on some ground we can talk about. What did you do before you met that character?"

"Corespondent," she said.

"You mean, a professional corespondent?"

"That's right. Go to a hotel with a man, take my clothes off, wait for the raiding party."

"I didn't know they did that any more."

"It wasn't in this state."

"Where was it?"

"Some place else."

"You're not very communicative."

"Why not talk about you?" she said. "Tell me about your business."

"It's rather complicated," he explained.

32

She yawned. "You're determinedly virtuous, aren't you?"

"I'm married."

"Let's play some more cards."

They played cards until Geraldine decided she wanted to take a nap. She was pulling a zipper on her skirt as Bedford started for the connecting door.

"That's not nice," she said. "I have to be sure you don't go out."

"Are you going to lock the door?"

"It's locked."

"It is?"

"Sure," she said nonchalantly. "I have the keys. I locked it from the outside while I was out at the car. You didn't think I was dumb, did you?"

"I didn't know."

"Don't you ever take a nap?"

"Not in the daytime."

"Okay. I guess we'll have to suffer it out then. More cards or more Scotch—or both?"

"Don't you have a magazine?"

"You've got me. They didn't think you needed anything else to keep you entertained. After all, there are some details they couldn't have anticipated," she laughed.

Bedford went into his room and sat down. She followed him. After a while Bedford became drowsy with the sheer monotony of doing nothing. He stretched out on the bed. Then he dozed lightly, slept for a few minutes.

He wakened with the smell of seductive perfume in his nostrils. The blonde, wearing a loose-flowing, semi-transparent creation, was standing beside him, looking down at him, holding a small slip of paper.

Bedford wakened with a start. "What is it?" he asked.

"A message," she said. "There's been a hitch. We're going to be delayed."

"How long?"

"They didn't say."

"We have to eat," Bedford said.

"They've thought of that. We can go out and eat. I pick the place. You stay with me—all the time. No phones. If you want to powder your nose, do it before we start. If there's any double cross, you've just lost your money and Delbert goes to the magazine. I'm to tell you that. You're to do as I say.

"They want you to be contented and not be nervous. They thought I could keep you amused. I told them you don't amuse very easy, so they said I could take you out—but no phones."

"How did you communicate with them?" he asked.

She grinned. "Carrier pigeons. I have them in my bra. Didn't you see them?"

"All right. Let's ride around a while," he said. "Let's eat."

He was surprised to find himself experiencing a feeling of companionship as she slid in the car beside him. She twisted around to draw up her knees so that her right knee was resting across the edge of his leg. Her hands with fingers interlaced were on his shoulder.

"Hello, good-looking," she said.

"Hello, blonde," he told her.

Bedford drove down to the beach highway, drove slowly along, keeping to the outside of the road.

"Well," he said at length, "I suppose you're getting hungry."

"Thanks," she said.

He raised his eyebrows in silent interrogation.

"You're thinking of me as a human being," she explained. "After all, I am, you know."

"How did you get in this work?" he asked abruptly.

"It depends on what you mean by 'this work,'" she said.

There was a moment's silence. Bedford thought of two or three possible explanations which would elaborate on his remark, and decided against all of them.

After a moment she said, "I guess you just drift into things in life. Once you start drifting the current keeps moving more and more swiftly, until you just can't find the opportunity to turn and row against it. Now, I suppose that's being philosophical, and you don't expect that from me."

"I don't know what I am supposed to expect from you."

"Expect anything you want," she said. "They can't arrest you for expecting."

Bedford was thoughtful. "Why start drifting in the first place?" he asked.

"Because you don't realize there's any current, and even when you do, you like it better than sitting still. Damn it, I'm not going to give you a lot of philosophy on an empty stomach."

"There's a place here where they have wonderful steaks," Bedford said, starting to pull in and then suddenly changing his mind.

He looked up to see her eyes mildly amused, partially contemptuous, studying his features. "You're known there, eh?" she asked.

"I've been there."

"One look at me and your reputation is ruined, is that it?"

"No, that's *not* it," he said savagely. "And you should know that's not it. But under the circumstances, I'm not anxious to leave a broad back trail. I don't know who I'm playing with or what I'm playing with."

"You're sure not playing with me," she said. "And remember, I'm to pick the eating place. You pay the check."

He drove up the road for a couple of miles. "Try this one," she said abruptly, indicating a tavern.

They found a booth in a dining room that was built out over the water. The air was balmy, the sun warm, the ocean had a salty tang, and they ate thick filet mignon steaks with French-fried onions, Guinness stout, and garlic bread.

They had dessert, a brandy and Benedictine, and Bedford paid the check. "And this is for you," he told the waiter, handing him the folded twenty with the message inside.

He scraped back his chair, careful to have Geraldine on her way to the door before the waiter unfolded the bill. He knew he was being foolish, jeopardizing the twenty thousand dollar investment he had made in a blackmail payoff, but he had the feeling he was outwitting his enemies.

Only afterward, when they had again started driving up the coast road, did he regret his action. After all, it could do no good and it might do harm, might, in fact, wreck everything.

Yet his reason told him they weren't going to any scandal magazine, not when they had a bonanza that could be clipped for twenty thousand dollars at a crack.

And the more he thought of it, the more he felt certain Delbert was only a fictitious figment. Binney Denham and the blonde were all there were in the "gang."

Was it perhaps possible that this acquiescent blonde was the brains of the gang? Yet now, somehow, he accepted her as a fellow human being. He preferred to regard her as a good scout who had somehow come under the power of Binney, a sinister individual beneath his apologetic mask.

The silence between Bedford and the girl was warm and intimate.

"You're a good guy," she told him, "when a girl gets to know you. You're a shock to a girl's vanity at first. I guess some married men are like that and are all wrapped up in their wives."

"Thanks," he told her. "You're a good scout yourself, when a fellow gets to know you."

"How long you been married?"

"Nearly two years."

"Happy?"

"Uh-huh."

"This deal you're mixed up in involves her, doesn't it?"

"If it's all the same with you, I'd rather not talk about her."

"Okay by me. We probably should be getting back."

"They'll let you know when everything is clear?"

"Uh-huh. It takes a little time to negotiate two hundred traveler's checks, you know, and do it right."

"And you're supposed to keep me out of circulation until it's done right, is that it?"

Her eyes flickered over him slowly. "Something like that," she said.

"Why didn't Binney do the job?"

"They thought you might get impatient with him."

"They?" he asked.

"Me and my big mouth," she told him. "Let's talk about politics or sex or business statistics, or something that I can agree with you on."

"You think you could agree with me on politics?"

"Sure, I'm broad-minded. You know something?"

"What?"

"I'd like a drink."

"We can stop in one of these roadhouses," Bedford suggested.

She shook her head. "They might not like that. Let's go back to the motel. I'm not to let you out of my sight, and I'm going to have to powder my nose. How'd you happen to get mixed up in a mess of this sort?"

"Let's not talk about it," he said.

"Okay. Drive back. I guess you just drifted into it the same way I did. They start telling you what to do, and you give in. After the first time it's harder to resist. I know it was with me. But you have to turn against the current sometime. I guess the best time is when you first feel the current.

"I'm spilling to you. I shouldn't. It's not in the job.

They wouldn't like it. I guess it's because you're so damned decent. I guess you've always been a square shooter.

"You take me, I've always gone along the easy way. I guess I haven't guts enough to stand up and face things."

They drove in silence for a while. At length she said, "There's only one way out."

"For whom?"

"For both of us. I'd forgotten how damned decent a decent guy could be."

"What's the way out?" he asked.

She shook her head, became suddenly silent.

She cuddled a little closer to him. Bedford's mind, which had been working furiously, began to relax. After all, he had been a fool, putting himself in the power of Binney Denham and the mysterious individual whom he knew only as Delbert. They had his money. They wouldn't want any publicity now. Probably they'd play fair with him because they'd want to put the bite on him again—and again and again.

Bedford knew he was going to have to do something about that, but there would be a respite now, a period of time during which he'd have an opportunity to plan some sort of attack.

Bedford turned in at the motel. The manager looked out of the door to see who it was, apparently recognized the car, waved a salutation, and turned back from the window.

Bedford drove into the garage. Geraldine Corning, who had both keys, unlocked the door and entered his cabin with him. She got the bottle of Scotch, took the deck of cards, suddenly laughed and threw the cards in the wastebasket. "Let's try getting along without these things. I was never so bored in my life. That's a hell of a way to make money."

She went to the refrigerator, got out ice cubes, put them

in the glasses, poured him a drink, then poured herself one.

She went to the kitchenette, added a little water to each drink, came back with a spoon and stirred them. She touched the rim of her glass to his and said, "Here's to crime!"

They sat sipping their drinks.

Geraldine kicked her shoes off, ran the tips of her fingers up her stockings, looked at her leg, quite plainly admiring it, stretched, yawned, sipped the drink again and said, "I feel sleepy."

She stretched out a stockinged foot, hooked it under the rung of one of the straight-backed chairs, dragged it toward her, propped her feet up and tilted back in the overstuffed chair.

"You know," she said, "there are times in a girl's life when she comes to a fork in the road, and it all happens so easily and naturally that she doesn't realize she's coming to a crisis."

"Meaning what?" Bedford asked.

"What do they call you?" she asked. "Your friends . . ."

"My first name's Stewart."

"That's a helluva name," she said. "Do they call you Stu?"

"Uh-huh."

"All right, I'll call you Stu. Look Stu, you've shown me something."

"What?"

"You've shown me that you can't get anywhere drifting. I'm either going to turn back or head for shore," she said. "I'm damned sick and tired of letting people run my life. Tell me something about your wife."

Bedford stretched out on the bed and dropped both pillows behind his head. "Let's not talk about her."

"You mean you don't want to discuss her with *me?*"

"Not exactly."

"What I wanted to know," Geraldine said somewhat

wistfully, "was what kind of a woman it is who can make a man love her the way you do."

"She's a very wonderful girl," Bedford said.

"Hell! I know *that*. Don't waste time telling me about that. I want to know how she reacts toward life and . . . and somehow I'd like to know what it is that Binney has on her."

"Why?"

"Damned if I know," she said. "I thought I might be able to help her." She put back her head and sucked in air in a prodigious yawn. "Cripes! but I'm sleepy!"

For some time there was silence. Bedford put his head back against the pillows and found himself thinking about Ann Roann. He felt somehow that he should tell Geraldine something about her, something about her vitality, her personality, her knack of saying witty things that were never unkind.

Bedford heard a gentle sigh and looked over to see that Geraldine had fallen asleep. He himself felt strangely drowsy. He began to relax in a way that was most unusual considering the circumstances. The nervous tension drained out of him. His eyes closed, then opened, and for a moment he saw double. It took him a conscious effort to fuse the two images into one.

He sat up and was suddenly dizzy, then dropped back against the pillows. He knew then that the drink had been drugged. By that time it was too late to do anything about it. He made a halfhearted effort to get up off the bed, but lacked the energy to do it. He surrendered to the warm feeling of drowsiness that was sweeping over him.

He thought he heard voices. Someone was saying something in whispers, something that concerned him. He thought he heard the rustle of paper. He knew that this had something to do with some responsibility of his in the waking world. He tried to arouse himself to cope with that responsibility, but the drug was too strong within him and the warm silence enveloped him.

He heard the sound of a motor, and then the motor backfired and again he tried to arouse from a lethargy. He was unable to do so.

What seemed like an eternity later Bedford began to regain consciousness. He was, he knew, stretched out on a bed in a motel. He should get up. There was a girl in the room. She had drugged his drink. He thought that over with his eyes closed for what seemed like ten or fifteen minutes, thinking for a moment, then dozing, then waking to think again. *His* drink had been drugged, but the *girl's* drink must have also been drugged. They had been out somewhere. She had left the bottle in the room. Someone must have entered the room and drugged the bottle of whisky while they were out. She was a nice girl. He had hated her at first, but she had a lot of good in her after all. She liked him. She wouldn't have resented his making a pass at her. In fact, she resented it because he hadn't. It had been a blow to her vanity. Then it had started her thinking, started her thinking about his wife. She had wanted to know about Ann Roann.

The thought of Ann Roann snapped his eyes open.

There was no light in the room except that which came through the adjoining door from the other unit in the motel unit hurt his eyes momentarily. He started to get up and became conscious of a piece of paper pinned to his left coat sleeve. He turned the paper so that the light struck it. He read: "Everything has cleared. You can go now. Love, Gerry."

Bedford struggled to a sitting position.

He walked toward the lighted door of the adjoining unit of the motel, his eyes rapidly becoming accustomed to the brighter light from the interior of the room. He started to call out, "Everybody decent?" and then thought better of it. After all, Geraldine would have left the door closed if she had cared. There was a friendly warmth about her, and, thinking of her, Bedford felt suddenly very kindly. He remembered when he had gone through that door earlier and had found her standing there practically nude. She really had an unusually beautiful figure. He had kept staring at her and she had merely stared back with an expression of amused tolerance. She had made no attempt to reach for her robe or turn her back. She had just stood there.

Bedford stepped into the room.

The first thing he saw was the figure lying on its side on the floor, the red pool which had spread out onto the carpet, the surface glazed over and reflecting the light from the reading lamp in a reddish splotch against the wall.

The figure was that of Binney Denham, and the little man was quite dead. Even in death he seemed to be apologetic. It was as though he was protesting against the necessity of staining the faded rug with the pool of red which had flowed from his chest.

■ 4 ■

FOR A MOMENT PANIC GRIPPED STEWART BEDFORD. HE hurried back to the other room, found his hat and his brief case. He opened the brief case, looked for his gun. The gun was gone.

He put on his hat, held the brief case in his hand, closed the door into the adjoining unit, and by so doing shut out all of the light except a flickering red illumination which came and went at regular intervals.

Bedford pulled aside the curtain, looked out and saw that this light came from a large red sign which flashed on and off the words *The Staylonger Motel,* and down below that a crimson sign which glowed steadily, reading *Vacancy*.

Bedford tried the door of the motel, shuddering at the thought that perhaps Geraldine had left the door locked from the outside. However, the door was unlocked, the knob turned readily, and the door swung open.

Bedford looked out into the lighted courtyard. The units of the motel were arranged in the shape of a big *U*. There were lights on over each doorway and each garage, giving the motel an appearance of great depth.

Bedford looked in the garage between the two units which he and Geraldine had been occupying. The garage was empty. The yellow car was gone.

Faced with the problem of getting out where he could find a taxicab, Stewart Bedford realized that he simply lacked the courage to walk down the length of that lighted central yard. The office was at the far end, right next to the street. The manager would be almost certain to see him walking out and might ask questions.

Bedford closed the door of unit fifteen, walked rapidly around the side of the building until he came to the end of the motel lot. There was a barbed wire fence here, and Bedford slid his brief case through to the other side, then tried to ease himself between the wires. These barbed wires were tightly strung; Bedford was nervous, and just as he thought he was safely through, he caught the knee of the trousers and felt the cloth rip slightly.

Then he was free and walking across the uneven surface of a field. The light from the motel sign behind him gave him enough illumination so he could avoid the pitfalls.

He found himself on a side road which led toward the main highway, along which there was a steady stream of automobiles coming and going in both directions.

Bedford walked rapidly along this road.

A car coming along the main highway slowed, then suddenly turned down the side road. Bedford found himself caught in the glare of the headlights. For a moment he was gripped with panic and wanted to resort to flight. Then he realized that his would be a suspicious circumstance which might well be communicated to the police and result in a prowl car exploring the territory. He elevated his chin, squared his shoulders, and walked steadily along the side of the road toward the headlights, trying to walk purposefully as though going on some mission—a businessman with a brief case walking to keep some appointment at a neighboring establishment.

The headlights grew brighter. The car swerved and came to a stop abreast of Bedford. He heard the door open.

"Stu! Oh, Stu!" Elsa Griffin's voice called.

She was, he saw, half-hysterical with apprehension, and in the flood of relief which came over him at the sound of her voice he didn't notice that it was the first time in over five years she had called him by his familiar nickname.

"Get in, get in," she said, and Stewart Bedford slid into the car.

"What happened?" she asked.

"I don't know," Bedford said. "All sorts of things. I'm afraid we're in trouble. How did *you* get here?"

"Your telephone message," she said. "Someone who said he was a waiter telephoned that a man had left a message and a twenty-dollar—"

"Yes, yes," he interrupted. "What did you do?"

She said, "I went down to the motel and rented a unit. I used an assumed name and a fictitious address. I juggled the figures on my license, and the manager never noticed. I spotted that yellow car—I'd already checked the license. It was a rented car from one of the drive-yourself agencies."

"So what did you do?" he asked.

"I sat and watched and watched and watched," she said. "Of course I couldn't sit right in the doorway and keep my eye on the cabin, but I sat back and had my door open so that if anyone came or went from that cabin I would see it, and if the car drove out I could be all ready to follow."

"Go on," he said. "What happened?"

"Well," she said, "about an hour and a half ago the car backed out and turned."

"What did you do?"

"I jumped in my car and followed. Of course, not too close, but I was close enough so that after the car got on the highway I could easily keep behind it. I had gone a couple of miles before I dared draw close enough to see that this blonde girl was alone in my car. I turned around and came back and parked my car. And believe me, I've had the devil of an hour. I didn't know whether you were all right or not. I wanted to go over there, and yet I was afraid to. I found that by standing in the bathroom, with the window open, I could look out and see the garage door and the door of the two units down there at the end. So I stood there in the bathroom watching. And then I saw you come out and go around the back of the house. I thought perhaps you were coming around toward the street by the back of the houses. When you didn't show up, I realized you must have gone through the fence, so I jumped in my car and drove around, and when I came to this cross street I turned down it and there you were."

"Things are in quite a mess, Elsa," he said. "There's somebody dead in that cabin."

"Who?"

"Binney Denham."

"How did it happen?"

"I'm afraid he was shot," he said. "And we may be in trouble. I put my gun in my brief case when I got that phone call last night. I had it with me."

"Oh, I was afraid," she said. "I was afraid something like that might happen."

"Now wait a minute," Bedford said. "*I* didn't kill him. I don't know anything about it. I was asleep. The girl gave me a drugged drink—I don't think it was her fault. I think someone got into the cabin and drugged the whole bottle of whisky. She poured drinks out of that."

"Well," Elsa Griffin said, "I have Perry Mason, the lawyer, waiting in his office."

"The devil you have!" he exclaimed in surprise.

She nodded.

"How come you did that?"

She said, "I just had a feeling in my bones. I knew there was something wrong. I rang Mr. Mason shortly after you left the office and told him that you were in trouble, that I couldn't discuss it, but I wanted to know where I could reach him at any hour of the day or night. Of course, he's done enough work for you so he feels you're a regular client and . . . well, he gave me a number and I called it about an hour ago, right after I returned from chasing that blonde. I had a feeling something was wrong. I told him to wait at his office until he heard from me. I told him that it would be all right to send you a bill for whatever it was worth, but I wanted him there."

Stewart Bedford reached out and patted her shoulder. "The perfect secretary!" he said. "Let's go."

■ 5 ■

IT WAS AFTER TEN O'CLOCK. PERRY MASON, THE FAMOUS trial lawyer, sat in his office. Della Street, his trusted confidential secretary, occupied the easy chair on the other side of the desk.

Mason looked at his watch and said, "We'll give them until eleven and then go home."

"You talked with Stewart G. Bedford's secretary?"

"That's right."

"I take it it's terribly important?"

"She said money was no object, that Mr. Bedford had to see me tonight, but that she would have to get hold of him before she could bring him up here."

"That sounds strange."

"Uh-huh."

"He married about two years ago, didn't he?"

"I believe so."

"Do you know his secretary?"

"I've met her three or four times. Quite a girl. Loyal, quiet, reserved, efficient. Wait a minute, Della, here's someone now."

Knuckles tapped gently at the heavy corridor door from the private office.

Della Street opened it.

Elsa Griffin and Stewart Bedford entered the office.

"Thank heaven you're still here!" Elsa Griffin said. "We got here as fast as we could."

"What's the trouble, Bedford?" Mason asked, shaking hands. "I guess both of you know my secretary, Della Street. What's it all about?"

"I don't think it's anything to worry about," Bedford said, making an obvious effort to be cheerful.

"I do," Elsa Griffin said. "They can trace S. G. through the traveler's checks."

Mason indicated chairs. "Suppose you sit down and tell me about it from the beginning."

Bedford said, "I had a business deal with a man whom I know as Binney Denham. That may not be his name. He seems to have got himself murdered down in a motel this evening."

"Do the police know about it?"

"Not yet."

"Murdered?"

"Yes."

"How do you know?"

"He saw the body," Elsa Griffin said.

"Notify anyone?" Mason asked.

Bedford shook his head.

"We thought we'd better see you," Elsa Briffin said.

"What was the business deal?" Mason asked.

"A private matter," Bedford explained.

"What was the business deal?" Mason repeated.

"I tell you it's just a private matter. Now that Denham is dead there's no reason for anyone to—"

"What was the business deal?" Mason asked.

"Blackmail," Elsa Griffin said.

"I thought so," Mason said grimly. "Let's have the story. Don't hold anything back. I want it all."

"Tell him, S. G.," Elsa Griffin said, "or I will."

Bedford frowned, thought for a moment, then told the story from the beginning. He even took out the police photograph of his wife and her description and finger-prints. "They left this with me," he explained, giving it to Mason.

Mason studied the card. "That's your wife?"

Bedford nodded.

"Of course you know it's her picture, but you can't tell about the fingerprints," Mason said. "After all, it may be a fake."

"No, they're her prints all right," Bedford said.

"How do you know?"

Bedford told him about the silver cocktail tray, the lifted fingerprints.

"You'll have to report the murder," Mason said.

"What happens if I don't?"

"Serious trouble," Mason said. "Miss Griffin, you go down to a pay station, call the police department, don't give them your name. Tell them there's a body down in unit sixteen at The Staylonger Motel."

"I'd better do it," Bedford said.

Mason shook his head. "I want a girl's voice to make the report."

"Why?"

"Because they'll find out a girl was in there."

"Then what do we do?" Bedford asked.

Mason looked at his watch, said, "I now have the job of getting Paul Drake of the Drake Detective Agency out of bed and on the job, and I can't put it on the line with him because I don't dare to let him know what he's investigating.

"What's the license number of that automobile?"

"It's a rented automobile from one of the drive-yourself agencies and—"

"What's the number?" Mason asked.

Elsa Griffin gave it to him. "License number CXY 221."

Mason called Paul Drake of the Drake Detective Agency at his unlisted number. After he heard Drake's sleepy voice on the line, he said, "Paul, here's a job that will require your personal attention."

"Good lord!" Drake protested. "Don't you *ever* sleep?"

Mason said, "Police are discovering a body at The Staylonger Motel, down by the beach. I want to know everything there is to know about the case."

"What do you mean, they are *discovering* a body?"

"Present participle," Mason said.

"Because minutes are precious," Mason told him. "Here's a car license number. It's probably a drive-yourself number. I want you to find out just where that car is, who rented it, and if it's been returned I want to know the exact time of its return. Now then, here's something else. I want you to get some operative who is really above suspicion, someone who can put on a front of being entirely, utterly innocent, preferably a woman. I want that woman to rent that car just as soon as it is available."

"What does she do with it after she rents it?"

49

"She drives it to some place where my criminalist can go over it with a vacuum sweeper, testing it for hairs, fibers, bloodstains, weapons, fingerprints."

"Then what?"

"Then," Mason said, "I want this woman to go up somewhere in the mountains first thing in the morning and get some topsoil for her garden, fill the car full of pasteboard boxes containing leaf mold, and pick up some frozen meat to take home to her locker."

"In other words," Drake said, "you want her to contaminate the hell out of any evidence that's left."

"Oh, nothing like that!" Mason said. "I wouldn't *think* of doing anything like that, Paul! After all, there wouldn't be anything left to contaminate. We'd have a criminalist pick up all of the evidence that was in it."

Drake thought that over. "Isn't it a crime to juggle evidence around?"

"Suppose the criminalist removed every bit of evidence *first?*"

"Then what do we do with the criminalist?"

"Let him report to the police if he wants," Mason said. "In that way we know what he knows first. Otherwise, the police know what's in the car, and we don't find out until the district attorney puts his expert on the stand as a witness."

"Then why all the leaf mold and frozen meat and stuff?" Drake asked.

"So some criminalist doesn't come up with soil samples, bloodstains and hairs, make a wild guess as to where they came from and testify to it as an expert," Mason told him.

Drake groaned. "Okay," he said wearily. "Here we go again. What criminalist do you want?"

"Try Dr. Leroy Shelby if you get hold of the car."

"Is he supposed to know what it's all about?"

"He's supposed to find every bit of evidence that's in that car," Mason said.

"Okay," Drake told him wearily. "I'll get busy."

"Now get this," Mason said. "We're one jump ahead of the police, perhaps just half a jump. They may have the license number of that automobile by morning. Get Dr. Shelby out of bed if you have to. I want all the evidence that's in that car carefully impounded."

"They'll ask Shelby who hired him."

"Sure they will. That's where you come in."

"Then they'll come down on me like a thousand bricks."

"What if they do?" Mason asked.

"Then what do I tell them?"

"Tell them I hired you."

There was relief in Drake's voice. "I can do that?"

"You can do that," Mason told him, "but get busy."

Mason hung up the phone, said to Bedford, "Your next job is to get home and try to convince your wife that you've been at a directors' meeting or a business conference, and make it sound convincing. Think you can do that?"

"If she's already gone to bed, perhaps I can," Bedford said. "She isn't as inquisitive when she's sleepy."

"You're to be congratulated," Mason told him drily. "Be available where I can call you in the morning. If anybody asks you any questions about anything at all, refer them to me. Now, probably someone will want to know about those traveler's checks. You tell them it was a business deal and that it's too confidential to be discussed with anyone. Refer them to me."

Bedford nodded.

"Think you can do that?" Mason asked.

"I can do it all right," Bedford said, and then added, "Whether I can get away with it or not is another question."

Bedford left the office. Elsa Griffin started to go with him, but Mason stopped her. "Give him a few minutes' head start," he said.

"What do I do after I have called the police?"

51

"For the moment," Mason told her, "you get out of circulation and keep out of circulation."

"Could I come back here?"

"Why?"

"I'm anxious to know what's going on. I would like to be on the firing line. You're going to wait here, aren't you?"

Mason nodded.

"I wouldn't be in the way and perhaps I could help you with telephone calls and things."

"Okay," Mason told her. "You know what to tell the police?"

"Just about the body."

"That's right."

"Then, of course, they'll want to know who's talking."

"Never mind what they want to know," Mason said. "Tell them about the body. If they interrupt you to ask you a question, don't let them pull that gag and get away with it. Keep right on talking. They'll listen when you start telling them about the body. As soon as you've told them that, hang up."

"Isn't that against the law?"

"What law?"

"Suppressing evidence?"

"What evidence?"

"Well, when a person finds a body . . . just to go away and say nothing about . . . about who you are—"

"Is your identity going to help them find the body?" Mason asked. "You can tell them where it is. That's what they're interested in. The body. But don't tell them who you are. You make a note of the time of the call."

"But how about withholding my name?"

"That," Mason told her, "is information which might tend to incriminate you. You don't have to give that to anyone, not even on the witness stand."

"Okay," she said. "I'll follow your instructions."

"Do that," Mason told her.

She closed the door behind her as she eased out into the corridor.

Della Street looked at Mason. "I presume we'll want some coffee?"

"Coffee, doughnuts, cheeseburgers, and potato chips," Mason said and then shuddered. "What an awful mess to put in your stomach this time of night."

Della Street smiled. "Now we know how Paul Drake feels. This time the situation is reversed. We're usually out eating steaks while Drake is in his office eating hamburgers."

"And sodium bicarb," Mason said.

"*And* sodium bicarb." She smiled. "I'll telephone the order for the food down to the lunch counter."

Mason said, "Get the Thermos jug out of the law library, Della. Have them fill that with coffee. We may be up all night."

■ 6 ■

AT ONE O'CLOCK IN THE MORNING PAUL DRAKE TAPPED his code knock on the hall door of Mason's private office.

Della Street let him in.

Paul Drake walked over to the client's big, overstuffed chair, slid into his favorite position with his knees over the arms and said, "I'm going to be in the office from now on, Perry. I've got men out working on all the angles. I thought you'd like to get the dope."

"Shoot," Mason said.

"First on the victim. His name is Binney Denham. No one seems to know what he does. He had a safe-deposit box in an all-night-and-day bank. The safe-deposit box was in joint tenancy with a fellow by the name of Harry Elston. At nine forty-five last night Elston showed up at the bank and went to the box. He was carrying a brief case with him. Nobody knows whether he put in or took out. Police have now sealed up the box. An inheritance tax appraiser is going to be on hand first thing in the morning and they'll open it up. Bet it'll be empty."

Mason nodded.

"Aside from that, you can't find out a thing. Denham has no bank account, left no trail in the financial world, yet he lived well, spent a reasonable amount of money, all in cash.

"Police are going to check and see if he made income-tax returns as soon as things open up in the morning.

"Now, in regard to that car. It was a drive-yourself car. I tried to get it, but police already had the license number. They telephoned in and the car is impounded."

"Who rented it, Paul?"

"A nondescript person with an Oklahoma driving license. The driving license data was on the rental contract. The police have checked and it doesn't mean a damned thing. Fictitious name. Fictitious address."

"Man or woman?"

"Mousy little man. No one seems to remember much about him."

"What else?"

"Down at the motor court, police have some pretty good description stuff. It seems that the two units were occupied by a man and a babe. The man claimed he was expecting another couple. They got a double unit, connecting door. The man registered; the girl sat in the car. The manager didn't get a very good look, but had the impression she was a blonde, with good skin, swell figure, and that indefinable something that marks the babe, the chick, the moll. The man looked just a little bit frightened. Businessman type. Got a good description of him."

"Shoot," Mason said.

"Fifty to fifty-four. Gray suit. Height five feet nine. Weight about a hundred and ninety or a hundred and ninety-five. Gray eyes. Rather long, straight nose. Mouth rather wide and determined. Wore a gray hat, but seemed to have plenty of hair, which wasn't white except a very slight bit of gray at the temples."

Elsa Griffin flashed Mason a startled glance at the accuracy of the description.

Mason's poker face warned her to silence.

"Anything else, Paul?" the lawyer asked.

"Yes. A girl showed up and rented unit number twelve—rather an attractive girl, dark, slender, quiet, thirty to thirty-five."

"Go ahead," Mason said.

"She registered; was in and out, is now out and hasn't returned as yet."

"How does she enter into the picture?" Mason asked.

"She's okay," Drake said. "But the manager says he caught a woman prowling her place—a woman about thirty, thirty-one, thirty-two. A swell-looker, striking figure, one of the long-legged, queenly sort; dark hair, gray eyes. She was prowling this unit twelve. The manager caught her coming out. She wasn't registered at the place and he wanted to know what she was doing. She told him she was supposed to meet her friend there, that the friend wasn't in; the door was unlocked, so she had gone in, sat down and waited for nearly an hour."

"Have any car?" Mason asked.

"That's the suspicious part of it. She must have parked her car a block or two away and walked back. She was on foot, but there's no bus line nearer than half a mile to the place, and this gal was all dolled up—high heels and everything."

"And she was prowling unit number twelve?"

"Yes, that's the only suspicious thing the manager noticed. It was around eight o'clock. The woman in unit twelve had just checked in two hours or so earlier, then had driven out.

"The manager took this other woman—the prowler—at face value; didn't think anything more about it. But when the police asked him to recall anything at all that was out of the ordinary, he recalled her.

"Police don't attach any significance to her . . . as yet anyway.

"The manager remembered seeing the yellow car go out somewhere around eight o'clock, he thinks it was, and, while he can't be positive, it's his impression the blonde girl was driving the car and no one else was in the car with her. That gave the police an idea that she *might* have left before the shooting took place. They can't be certain about the time of the shooting."

"It was a shooting?" Mason asked.

"That's right. One shot from a .38 caliber revolver. The guy was shot in the back. The bullet went through the heart and he died almost instantly."

"How do they know it was fired from the back?" Mason asked. "They haven't had an autopsy yet."

"They found the bullet," Drake said. "It went entirely through the body and failed to penetrate the front of the coat. The bullet rolled out when they moved the body. That happens a lot more frequently than you'd suppose. The powder charge in a .38 caliber cartridge is just about sufficient to take the bullet through a body, and if the clothes furnish resistance the bullet will be trapped."

"Then they have the fatal bullet?"

"That's right."

"What sort of shape is it in, do you know, Paul? Is it flattened out pretty bad, or is it—"

"No, it's in pretty good shape, as I understand it. The police are confident that there are enough individual markings so they can identify the gun if and when they find it.

"Now, let me go on, Perry. They got the idea that if the blonde took out alone it might have been because this man Denham showed up and he was having an argument with her boy friend. He used the name of S. G. Wilfred when he registered and gave a San Diego address. The address is phony and the name seems to be fictitious."

"Okay, go ahead. What happened?"

"Well, the police got the idea that if this man, whom we'll call Wilfred, had popped Denham in a fight over the gal and then was left without a car there at the motel, he might have tried to sneak out the back way. So they started looking for tracks, and sure enough, they found where he had gone through a barbed wire fence and evidently snagged his clothes. The police got a few clothing fibers from the barbed wire where he went through—that was clever work. Your friend, Lieutenant Tragg, was on the job, and as soon as he saw the tracks going through the barbed wire he started using a magnifying glass. Sure enough, he caught some fibers on the barbed wire."

"What about the tracks?" Mason asked.

"They've having a moulage made of the footprints. They followed the tracks through the wire, across a field and out to a side road. They have an idea the man probably walked down to the main highway and hitchhiked his way into town. The police will be broadcasting an appeal in the newspapers, asking for anyone who noticed a hitchhiker to give a description."

"I see," Mason said thoughtfully. "What else, Paul?"

"Well, that car was returned to the rental agency. A young woman put the car in the agency parking lot, started toward the office and then seems to have disappeared. Of course, you know how these things go. The person who rents the car puts up a fifty-dollar deposit, and the car rental people don't worry about cars that are brought in. Its up to the renter to check in at the office in order to get the deposit back. The rental and mileage on a daily basis don't ordinarily run up to fifty bucks."

"The police have taken charge of the car?"

"That's right. They've had a fingerprint man on it, and

I understand there are some pretty good fingerprints. Of course, they're fingerprinting units fifteen and sixteen down there at the motel."

"Well," Mason said, "they'll probably have something pretty definite then."

"Hell! They've got something pretty definite right now," Drake said. "The only thing they *haven't* got is the man who matches the fingerprints. But don't overlook any bets on that. They'll have him, Perry."

"When?"

Drake lowered his eyes in thoughtful contemplation of the problem. "Even money they have him by ten o'clock in the morning," he said, "and I'd give you big odds they have him by five o'clock in the afternoon."

"What are you going to do now?" Mason asked.

"I have a couch in one of the offices. I'm going to get a little shut-eye. I've got operatives crawling all over the place, picking up all the leads they can."

"Okay," Mason said. "If anything happens, get in touch with me."

"Where will you be?"

"Right here."

Drake said, "You must have one hell of an important client in this case."

"Don't do any speculating," Mason told him. "Just keep information coming in."

"Thanks for the tip," Drake told him and walked out.

Mason turned to Elsa Griffin. "Apparently," he said, "no one has attached the slightest suspicion to you."

"That was a very good description of the occupant of unit twelve," she said.

"Want to go back?" Mason asked.

There was a sudden, swift alarm in her face.

"Go back? What for?"

Mason said, "As you know, Bedford told me about your help in getting the fingerprints off that silver platter. How would you like to go back down to the motel, drive in to your place at unit twelve. The manager will probably come over to see if you're all right. You can give him a song and dance, then take a fingerprint outfit and go to work on the doorknobs, on the drawers in the dresser, any place where someone would be apt to have left fingerprints. Lift those fingerprints with tape and bring them back to me."

"But suppose . . . suppose the manager is suspicious. Suppose he rechecks my license number. I juggled the figures when I gave him the license number of the car when I registered."

"That," Mason said, "is a chance we'll have to take."

She shook her head. "That wouldn't be fair to Mr. Bedford. If anybody identified me, the trail would lead directly to him."

"There are too damn many trails leading directly to him the way it is," Mason told her. "Paul Drake was right. It's even money they'll have him by ten o'clock in the morning. In any event, they'll have him by five o'clock in the afternoon. He left two hundred traveler's checks scattered around, and Binney Denham was getting the money on those checks. Police will start backtracking Denham during the day. They'll find out where some of those checks were cashed. Then the trail will lead directly to Bedford. They'll match his fingerprints."

"And then what?" she asked.

"Then," Mason told her, "we have a murder case to try. Then we go to court."

"And then what?"

"Then they have to prove him guilty beyond all reasonable doubt. Do you think he killed Denham?"

"No!" she said with sudden vehemence.

"All right," Mason said, "he has his story. He has the note that was pinned to his sleeve, the note he found when he woke up saying he could leave."

"But what reason does he give for not reporting the body?"

"He did report the body," Mason said. "You reported it. *He* told you to telephone the police. He did everything he could to start the police on their investigation, but he just tried to keep his name out of it. It was an ill-advised attempt to avoid publicity because he was dealing with a blackmailer."

She thought it over for a while and said, "Mr. Bedford isn't going to like that."

"What isn't he going to like about it?"

"Having to explain to the police why he was down there."

"He doesn't have to explain anything," Mason said. "He can keep silent. *I'll* do the talking."

"I'm afraid he won't like that either."

Mason said impatiently, "There's going to be a lot about this he won't like before he gets done. Persons who are accused of murder seldom like the things the police do in connection with developing the case."

"He'll be accused of murder?"

"Can you think of any good reason why he won't?"

"You think I can do some real good by going down and looking for fingerprints?"

Mason said, "It's a gamble. From what Drake tells me, you're apparently not involved in any way. The manager of the motel won't want to have his guests annoyed. He'll keep the trouble centralized in cabins fifteen and sixteen as far as possible. You have a cocktail and spill a little on a scarf you'll have around your neck so it will be obvious you've been drinking. Go into the motel just as though nothing had happened. If the manager comes over to you about a prowler in your cabin, tell him the woman was perfectly all right, that she was a friend of yours who was coming to visit you, that you told her to go in and wait in case you weren't there, that you got tied up on a date with someone you liked very much and had to stand her up.

"I'd like to have the fingerprints of whoever it was

that was in that cabin, but what I'd mainly like is to have *you* remove all of *your* fingerprints. After you get done developing latent prints and lifting any that you find, take some soap and warm water and scrub the place all to pieces. Get rid of anything incriminating."

"Why?" she asked.

"Because," Mason said, "if later on the police get the idea that there's something funny about the occupant of unit number twelve and start looking for fingerprints, they won't find yours.

"Don't you see the thing that's going to attract suspicion to you above all else is *not* going back there tonight? If your cabin isn't occupied, the manager will report that as another suspicious circumstance to the police."

"Okay," she said. "I'm on my way. Where do I get the fingerprint outfit?"

Mason grinned. "We keep one here for emergencies. You know how to lift fingerprints all right. Bedford said you did it from that cocktail tray."

"I know how," she said. "Believe it or not, I took a correspondence course as a detective. I'm on my way."

"If anything happens," Mason warned, "anything at all, call Paul Drake's agency. I'll be in constant touch with Paul Drake. If anyone should start questioning you, dry up like a clam."

"On my way," she told him.

SEVEN O'CLOCK FOUND PAUL DRAKE BACK IN PERRY MA-
son's office.

"What do you know about this Binney Denham, Perry?" the detective asked.

"What do *you* know about him?" Mason countered.

"Only what the police know. But it's beginning to pile
up into something."

"Go on."

"Well, he had the lock box in joint tenancy with Harry
Elston. Elston went to the lock box, and now police can't
find him. That's to have been expected. Police found
where Binney Denham was living. It was a pretty swank
apartment for one man who was supposedly living by
himself."

"Why do you say supposedly?"

"Police think it was rather a convivial arrangement."

"What did they find?"

"Forty thousand dollars in cash neatly hidden under
the carpet. Hundred dollar bills. A section of the carpet
had been pulled up so many times that it was a dead
giveaway. The floor underneath it was pretty well paved
with hundred dollar bills."

"Income tax?" Mason asked.

"They haven't got at that yet. They'll enlist the aid of
the income-tax boys this morning."

"Makes it nice," Mason said.

"Doesn't it," Paul Drake observed.

"What else do you know?"

"Police are acting on the theory that Binney Denham
may have been mixed up in a blackmail racket and that he

may have been killed by a victim. The man and the girl who occupied those two units could have been a pushover for a blackmailer.

"The police can't get a line on either one of them. They're referring to the man as Mr. X and the girl as Miss Y. Suppose Mr. X is a fairly well-known, affluent businessman and Miss Y is a week-end attraction, or perhaps someone who is scheduled to supplant Mrs. X as soon as a Reno divorce can be arranged. Suppose everything was all very hush-hush, and suppose Binney Denham found out about it. Binney drops in to pay his respects and make a little cash collection and gets a bullet in the back."

"Very interesting," Mason said. "How would Binney Denham have found out about it?"

Drake said, "Binney Denham had forty thousand bucks underneath the carpet on the floor of his apartment. You don't get donations like that in cash unless you have ways of finding out things."

"Interesting!" Mason said.

"You want to keep your nose clean on this thing," Drake warned.

"In what way?"

"You're representing somebody. I haven't asked you who it is, but I'm assuming that it could be Mr. X."

Mason said, "Don't waste your time assuming things, Paul."

"Well, if you're representing Mr. X," Drake said, "let's hope Mr. X didn't leave a back trail. This is the sort of thing that could be loaded with dynamite."

"I know," Mason said. "How about some of this coffee, Paul?"

"I'll try a little," Drake said.

Della Street poured the detective a cup of coffee. Drake tasted it and made a face.

"What's the matter?" Mason asked.

"Thermos coffee," Drake said. "I'll bet it was made around midnight."

"You're wrong," Della Street said. "I had it renewed a little after three this morning."

"Probably my stomach," Drake said apologetically. "I've got fuzz on my tongue and the inside of my stomach feels like a jar of sour library paste. Comes from spending too many nights living on coffee, hamburgers and bicarbonate of soda."

"Anybody hear the shot?" Mason asked.

"Too many," Drake said. "Some people think there was a shot about eight-fifteen; some others at eight forty-five; some at nine-thirty. Police may be able to tell more about the time of death after the autopsy.

"The trouble is this Staylonger joint is on the main highway and there's a little grade and a curve there right before you get to turn-in for the motel. Trucks slack up on the throttle when they come to this curve and grade, and quite a few of them backfire. People don't pay much attention to sounds like that. There are too many of them."

Drake finished the coffee. "I'm going down and get some ham and eggs. Want to go?"

Mason shook his head. "Sticking around a while, Paul."

"Jeepers!" Drake said. "Mr. X must be a millionaire."

"Just talking, or asking for information?" Mason asked.

"Just talking," Drake said and heaved himself out of the chair.

Twenty minutes after he had left, Elsa Griffin tapped on the door of Mason's private office, and when Della Street opened the door, slid into the room with a furtive air.

Mason said, "You look like the beautiful spy who has just vamped the gullible general out of the secret of our newest atomic weapon."

"I did a job," she said enthusiastically.

"Good!" Mason told her. "What happened?"

"When I got there everything had quieted down. There was a police car in the garage and apparently a couple of men were inside units fifteen and sixteen, probably going over everything for fingerprints."

"What did you do?"

"I drove in to unit twelve, parked my car, went in and turned on the lights. I waited for a little while, just to see if anyone was going to show up. I didn't want to be dusting the place for fingerprints in case they did."

"What happened?"

"The manager came over and knocked on the door. He was sizing me up pretty much—I guess he thought perhaps I had a wild streak under my quiet exterior."

"What did you do?"

"I put him right on that. I told him that I was a member of a sorority and that we'd been having a reunion, that I came up to town for that and we'd had a pretty late party, that I was going to have to grab a few hours' shut-eye and be on my way in order to get back to my job."

"Did he say anything?"

"Not about the murder. He said there'd been a little trouble, without saying what it was, and then he said that some woman had been in my motel and asked if it was all right, and I told him, 'Heavens, yes,' that she was one of the sorority members who was to meet me and I'd told her that if I wasn't there to go in, make herself at home. I said I'd left the door unlocked purposely."

"Did he get suspicious?"

"Not a bit. He said there'd been some trouble and he'd been trying to check back on anything that had happened that was out of the ordinary; that he'd remembered this woman and he'd just wondered if it was all right."

"Tell you about what time it was?" Mason asked.

"Well, he didn't know the hour exactly, but as nearly as I can figure she must have been in there while I was out chasing that blonde. I had to follow her for quite a ways before I dared to swing alongside."

"And it *was* the blonde who was driving?"

65

"That's right, it was Geraldine Corning."

"What about fingerprints?" Mason asked.

She said, "I got a flock of them. I'm afraid most of them are mine, but some of them probably aren't. I have twenty-five or so that are good enough to use. I've put numbers on each of the cards that have the lifted prints and then I have a master list in my notebook which tells where each number came from."

"Clean up the place when you left?" Mason asked.

"I took a washrag, used soap and gave everything a complete scrubbing, then I made a good job by polishing it with a dry towel."

Mason said, "You'd better leave your fingerprints on a card so I can have Drake's men check these lifted prints and eliminate yours. Let's hope that we've got some prints of that prowler. Do you have any idea who she might have been?"

"Not the least in the world. I just simply can't understand it. I don't know why in the world anyone should have been interested in the cabin *I* was occupying."

"It may have been just a mistake," Mason said.

"Mr. Mason, do you suppose that these . . . well, these blackmailers became suspicious when I showed up? Do you suppose they were keeping the place under surveillance? They'd know me if they saw me."

Mason said, "I'm not making any suppositions until I get more evidence. Go down to Drake's office, put your fingerprints on a card, leave the bunch of lifted fingerprints there, tell Paul Drake to have his experts sort out all of the latents that are yours and discard them, and bring any other fingerprints to me."

"Then what do I do?"

Mason said, "It would be highly advisable for you to keep out of the office today."

"Oh, but Mr. Bedford will need me. Today will be the day when—"

"Today will be the day when police are going to come

to the office and start asking questions," Mason said. "Don't be too surprised if they should have the manager of The Staylonger Motel with them."

"What would that be for?"

"To make an identification. It would complicate matters if he found you sitting at your secretarial desk and then identified you as the occupant of unit twelve."

"I'll say!" she exclaimed in dismay.

"Ring up Mr. Bedford. Explain matters to him," Mason said. "Don't tell him about having gone back to cabin twelve and taken the fingerprints. Just tell him that you've been up most of the night, that I think it would be highly inadvisable for you to go to the office. Tell Mr. Bedford that he'll probably have official visitors before noon, that if they simply ask him questions about the traveler's checks to tell them it's a business transaction and he cares to make no comment. If they start checking up on him and it appears that they're making an identification of him by his fingerprints as the man who drove that rented car or as the man who was in the motel, or if they have the manager of the motel along with them, who makes an identification, tell Mr. Bedford to keep absolutely mum.

"Have him put on a substitute secretary. Have her call my office and call the office of the Drake Detective Agency the minute anyone who seems to have any connections with the police calls at the office. Think you can do that?"

She looked for a moment in Mason's eyes and said, "Mr. Mason, don't misunderstand me. I'd do anything . . . anything in the world in order to insure the happiness or the safety of the man I'm working for."

"I'm satisfied you would," Mason said, "and that's what makes it dangerous."

"What do you mean?"

"In case he was being blackmailed," Mason said, "it might occur to the police that your devotion to your boss would be such that *you'd* take steps to get rid of the blackmailer."

"Oh, I wouldn't have done anything like *that!*" she exclaimed hastily.

"Perhaps you wouldn't," Mason told her, "but we have the police to deal with, you know."

"Mr. Mason," she ventured, "don't you think this Denham was killed by his partner? He mentioned a man, whom he called Delbert. This Delbert was the insistent one."

"Could be," Mason said.

"I'm almost certain it was."

Mason looked at her in swift appraisal. "Why?"

"Well, you see, I've always had an interest in crime and detective work. I read a lot of these magazines that publish true crime stories. It was because of an ad in a magazine that I took my detective course by mail."

Mason flashed a glance at Della Street. "Go on."

"Well, it always seems that when a gang of crooks gets a big haul, they don't like to divide. If there are three, and one of them gets killed, then the loot only has to be split two ways. If there are two, and one of the men gets killed, the survivor keeps it all."

"Wait a minute," Mason said. "You didn't read that in the magazines that feature true crime stories.

"That gambit you're talking about now is radio, motion pictures and television. Some of the fiction writers get ideas about a murderer cutting down the numbers who share in the loot. The comic strips play that idea up in a big way. Where did you read this story?" Mason asked. "In what magazine?"

"I don't know," she admitted. "Come to think of it, I have the impression that this story I referred to was in a comic strip.

"You see, I like detective works. I read the crime magazines and see the crime movies—I suppose you can say I'm a crime fan."

"The point is," Mason said, "the authorities aren't going to charge any accomplice. They're going to charge Stewart Bedford. That is, I'm afraid they are."

"I see. I was just thinking, Mr. Mason. If a smart lawyer should get on the job and plant some evidence that would point to Denham's accomplice, Delbert, as the murderer, that would take the heat off Mr. Bedford, wouldn't it?"

"Smart lawyers don't plant evidence," Mason said.

"Oh, I see. I guess I read too much about crime, but the subject simply fascinates me. Well, I'll be getting along, Mr. Mason."

"Do that," Mason told her. "Go on home and make arrangements to be ill so that you can't come to the office. Don't forget to stop in at Paul Drake's office and leave your fingerprints."

"I won't," she promised.

When the door had closed Mason looked at Della Street. "That girl has ideas."

"Doesn't she!"

"And," Mason went on, "if *she* should plant some evidence against this Delbert . . . well, if she has any ideas of planting evidence against anyone, she'd better be damned careful. A good police officer has a nose for planted evidence. He can smell it a mile."

Della Street said, "The worst of it is that if she *did* try to plant evidence and the authorities found it had been planted, they'd naturally think *you* were the one who had planted it."

"That's a chance a lawyer always has to take," Mason said. "Let's go eat, Della."

■ 8 ■

BY THE TIME MASON AND DELLA STREET HAD RETURNED from breakfast, Sid Carson, Paul Drake's fingerprint expert, had finished with the lifted fingerprints that had been left him by Elsa Griffin and was in Mason's office, waiting to make a report.

"Nearly all of the prints," he said, "are those of Elsa Griffin, but there are four lifted latents here that aren't hers."

"Which are the four?" Mason asked.

"I have them in this envelope. Numbers fourteen, sixteen, nine, and twelve."

"Okay," Mason said, "I'll save them for future reference. The others are all Miss Griffin's?"

"That's right. She left a set of her fingerprints and we've matched them up. You can discard all of them except these four."

"Any ideas about these four?"

"Not much. They could have been left by some prior occupant of the motel. A little depends on climatic conditions and what sort of cleaning the place had, how long since it's been occupied and things of that sort. Moisture in the air has a great deal to do with the time a latent fingerprint will be preserved."

"How are these latents?" Mason asked. "Pretty good?"

"They're darn good. Very good indeed."

"Any notes about where they were found?"

"Yes, she did a good job. She lifted the prints, transferred them to cards, then wrote on the back of the cards where they were from. Two of these prints were from a mirror; two of them came from a glass knob on a closet door. She even made a little diagram of the knob, one of the sort of knobs that have a lot of facets so you can get hold of it and get a good grip for turning."

Mason nodded, said, "Thanks, Carson. I'll call on you again if we get any leads."

"Okay," Carson said and went out.

Mason contemplated the fingerprints under the cellophane tape.

"Well?" Della Street asked.

Mason said, "Della, I'm no fingerprint expert, but—" He adjusted a magnifying glass so as to get a clearer view.

"Well?" she asked.

"Hang it!" Mason said. "I've seen *this* fingerprint before."

"What do you mean, you've seen it before?"

"There's a peculiar effect here—" Mason's voice trailed away into silence.

Della Street came to look over his shoulder.

"Della!" Mason said. His voice was explosive.

She jumped at his tone. "What?"

"That card Bedford left with us, the card showing his wife and her fingerprints—get that card from the file, Della."

Della Street hurried to the filing case, came back with the card which Bedford had left with Mason, the card which the blackmailers had given him in order to show the authenticity of their information.

"Good heavens!" Della Street said. "Mrs. Bedford wouldn't have been there."

"How do you know?" Mason asked. "Remember what Bedford told us about getting the telephone call from Binney at his house while he was entertaining guests, that he wanted to talk in privacy, so he said he went up to his study and told the butler to hang up the phone as soon as he answered? Suppose Mrs. Bedford became suspicious. Suppose she sent the butler on an errand, tell-

71

ing him that she'd take over and hang up the phone. Suppose she listened in on the conversation and knew—"

"You mean . . . found out about—"

"Let's be realistic about this thing," Mason said. "When was this crime of defrauding the insurance company committed?"

"Several years ago, before her first marriage," Della Street said.

"Exactly," Mason told her. "Then she married, her husband committed suicide, she came into some money from insurance policies; then it was a couple of years before she married Bedford and a couple of years after the marriage before the blackmailers started to put the bite on Bedford.

"Yet, when the police went to Binney Denham's place, they found the floor carpeted with crisp new hundred dollar bills."

"You mean they'd been blackmailing her and—"

"Why wouldn't they?" Mason said. "Let's take a look at these fingerprints. If she knew Binney was starting to put the bite on her husband . . . a woman in that situation could become very, very desperate."

"But Mr. Bedford said they took such great precautions to see that they weren't followed. You remember what he told us about how the girl had him drive around and around and Binney followed in his car, and then Bedford picked the motel?"

"I know," Mason said, "but let's just take a look. I've seen this fingerprint before."

Mason took a magnifying glass, started examining the fingerprints on the card, then compared the two lifted fingerprints with the prints on the card.

He gave a low whistle.

"Struck pay dirt?" Della Street asked.

"Look here," Mason said.

"Heavens!" Della Street said, "I couldn't read a fingerprint in a year."

© Lorillard 1975

C'mon

Come for the filter.

You'll stay for the taste.

19 mg. "tar," 1.2 mg. nicotine av. per cigarette, FTC Report Apr. '75.

Warning: The Surgeon General Has Determined That Cigarette Smoking Is Dangerous to Your Health.

I'd heard enough to make me decide one of two things: quit or smoke True.

I smoke True.

**The low tar, low nicotine cigarette.
Think about it.**

King Regular: 11 mg. "tar", 0.6 mg. nicotine, King Menthol: 12 mg. "tar", 0.7 mg. nicotine, 100's Regular: 13 mg. "tar", 0.7 mg. nicotine, 100's Menthol: 13 mg. "tar", 0.8 mg. nicotine, av. per cigarette, FTC Report April '75.

Warning: The Surgeon General Has Determined That Cigarette Smoking Is Dangerous to Your Health.

"You can read these two," Mason said. "For instance, look at this fingerprint on the card. Now compare it with the fingerprint here. See that tented arch? Count the number of lines to that first distinctive branching, then look up here at this place where the lines make a—"

"Good heavens!" Della Street said. "They're identical!"

Mason nodded.

"Then Mrs. Stewart G. Bedford was following—"

"Following whom?" Mason asked.

"Her husband and a blonde."

Mason shook his head. "Not with the precautions that were taken by the girl in the rented car. Moreover, if she'd been following her husband and the girl, she'd have known the units of the motel where they were staying and she would have gone in there."

"Then who was she following?"

"Perhaps," Mason said, "she was following Binney Denham."

"You mean Denham went to the motel to collect the money?"

Mason nodded. "Possibly."

"Then why would she have gone into Elsa Griffin's motel? How would she have known Elsa Griffin was there?"

"That," Mason told her, "remains to be seen. Get Paul Drake's office for me, Della. Let's put a shadow on Mrs. Stewart G. Bedford and see where she goes this morning."

"And then?" Della Street asked.

Mason gave the matter a moment of frowning concentration. "If I'm going to talk with her, Della. I'd better do it before the police start asking questions of her husband."

THE WOMAN WHO EASED THE LOW-SLUNG, FOREIGN-MADE sports car into the service station was as sleek and graceful as the car she was driving. She smiled at the attendant and said, "Fill it up, please," then, opening the car door, swung long legs out to the cement, holding her skirt tightly against her legs as she moved out from under the steering wheel.

She gave her skirt a quick shake, said to the attendant, "And we might as well check the oil, water, and battery."

She turned and confronted the tall man whose slim-waisted, broad-shouldered figure and granite hard features caused her to take a second look.

"Good morning, Mrs. Bedford. I'm Perry Mason."

"The lawyer?"

He nodded.

"Well, how do you do, Mr. Mason. I've heard of you, of course. My husband has spoken of you. You seem to know me, but I don't recall ever having met you."

"You haven't," Mason said. "You're meeting me now. Would you like to talk with me for a moment?"

Her eyes instantly became cold and wary. "About what?"

"About five minutes," Mason said, with a warning glance in the direction of the service station attendant who, while looking at the nozzle on the gasoline hose, nevertheless held his head at a fixed angle of attention.

For a moment she hesitated, then said, "Very well," and led the way back over toward an open space where there were facilities for filling radiators and an air hose for tires.

"Now I'll ask you again. What do you wish to talk about, Mr. Mason?"

"About The Staylonger Motel and your visit there last night," Mason said.

The slate-gray eyes were just a little mocking. There was no sign to indicate that Mason's verbal shaft had scored.

"I wasn't visiting any motel last night, Mr. Mason, but I'll be glad to discuss the matter if you wish. The Staylonger Motel . . . it seems to me I've heard that name. Could you tell me where it is?"

"It's where you were last night," Mason said.

"I could become very annoyed with you for such insistence, Mr. Mason."

Mason took a card from his pocket, said, "This is the print of the ring finger on your right hand. It was found on the underside of the glass doorknob on the closet. Perhaps you'll remember that glass doorknob, Mrs. Bedford. It was rather ornamental—molded with facets that enable a person to get a good grip on the glass, but it certainly was a trap for fingerprints."

She regarded the lawyer thoughtfully. "And how do you know this is *my* fingerprint?"

"I've compared it."

"With what?"

"A police record."

She glanced away from him for a moment, then looked back at him.

"May I ask just what is your object, Mr. Mason? Is this some sort of a legal cat-and-mouse game? I am assuming that your reputation is such that you wouldn't be interested in the common, ordinary garden variety of blackmail."

Mason said, "The afternoon papers will announce the discovery of a murder at The Staylonger Motel. Police are naturally very much interested in anything out of the ordinary which happened there last night."

"And *your* interest?" she asked coolly.

"I happen to be representing a client, a client who prefers to remain anonymous for the time being."

"I see. And perhaps your client would like to involve me in the murder?"

"Perhaps."

"In which event I should talk with *my* lawyer instead of his—or hers."

"If you wish," Mason told her. "However, that probably wouldn't be the first conversation you'd have."

"With whom would I have the first conversation?"

"The police."

She said, "The attendant is finishing with my car. There's a hotel a few blocks down the street. It has a mezzanine floor, with a writing room and reasonable privacy. I'll drive there. You may follow me, if you wish."

"Very well," Mason told her. "However, please don't try any stunts with that powerful sports car of yours. You might be able to lose me in traffic, and that might turn out to be a rather expensive maneuver as far as you're concerned."

She stared at him levelly. "When you get to know me better, Mr. Mason—if you ever do—you'll learn that I don't resort to cheap, petty tricks. When I fight, I fight fair. When I give my word, I stay with it. Of course, I'm assuming you can move through traffic at a reasonable rate of speed without having a motorcycle officer take your car by the fender and lead it across the intersections."

With that she turned, walked over to sign the sales slip that the gasoline attendant handed her, then guided the low-slung car out into traffic.

Mason followed her until she swung into a parking lot. He parked his own car, entered the lobby of the hotel, took the elevator to the mezzanine and followed her to a writing table at which there were two chairs.

Everything about her appearance seemed to emphasize long lines. She was, Mason noticed, wearing long earrings; the carved ivory cigarette holder in which she fitted a cigarette was long and emphasized the length of the tapering fingers of her left hand which held the cigarette.

Mason seated himself in the chair beside her.

She looked at Mason and smiled.

"All the way up here I tried my damnedest to think up some way that I could keep you from questioning me," she said, "and I couldn't do any good. I don't know whether you're bluffing about my fingerprints and the police record, but I can't afford to call your bluff, in case it is a bluff. Now then, what do you want?"

"I want to know about the jewels and the insurance company."

She took a deep drag from the cigarette, exhaled thoughtfully, then abruptly gave in.

"All right," she said. "I was Ann Duncan in those days. I have always had a hatred of anything mediocre. I wanted to be distinctive. I wanted to stand out. I had to go to work. I was untrained. Nothing was open except the sheerest kind of office drudgery. I tried it for a while. I couldn't make it. My appearance was striking enough so that the men I worked for didn't want to settle just for the mediocre office services, which were all they were willing to pay for.

"About all I inherited from my mother's estate was some jewelry. It was valuable antique jewelry and it was insured for a considerable amount.

"I needed a front. I needed some clothes. I needed an opportunity to circulate around where I'd be noticed. I was willing to take a gamble. I decided that if I could meet the right kind of people in the right way, life might hold a brighter future—a future different from the drab prospect of filing letters all day and having a surreptitious dinner date with the man I was working for after he'd telephoned his wife the old stall about being detained at the office."

"So what did you do?"

"I went about it in a very clumsy, amateurish way. Instead of going to a reputable firm and having the jewelry appraised and making the right sort of a business transaction, I went to a pawnshop."

"And then?"

"I felt that if I could get some money as a loan, later on I could repay the loan and redeem the jewelry. I felt that I could parlay the money I received into something worthwhile."

"Go on."

"I was living with a penurious aunt, a nosy busybody. I shouldn't say that about her. She's dead now. But anyhow I had to account for the loss of the jewelry, so I tried to make it look like a burglary, and then I pawned the jewelry."

"And your aunt reported the burglary to the police?"

"That was where the rub came in."

"You'd intended she would?"

"Heavens, no!"

"Then what?"

"I wasn't prepared for all the embarrassing questions. The jewelry was insured and my aunt insisted that I had to file a claim. She got a blank, made it out, gave it to me to sign. The police investigated. The insurance company investigated. Then the insurance company paid me the amount for which the jewelry was insured. It was money I didn't want, but I had to take it in order to keep my aunt from finding out what I had done. I didn't spend it. I kept it intact.

"Then I told my aunt a whopping fib about going to visit some friends. I took the money I'd received from the pawnbroker, got myself some glad rags, and went to Phoenix, Arizona. I registered at one of the winter resort hotels where I felt I stood a chance of meeting the sort of people I was interested in."

"And what happened then?" Mason asked.

"Then," she said, "the police found the jewelry in the pawnshop. At first they thought they were just recovering stolen property. Then they got a description of the person who had pawned the jewels and began to put two and two together and . . . oh, it was hideous!"

"Go on," Mason told her. "What happened?"

"However," she said, "in the meantime I'd met a very estimable gentleman, an attorney at law, a widower. I don't know whether he would ever have been attracted to me if it hadn't been for the trouble I was in. He was a lawyer and I went to him for help. At first he was cold and skeptical, then when he heard my story he became sympathetic. He took an interest in me, helped straighten things out, saw that I met people.

"I had the most wonderful three months I'd ever had in my life. People liked me. I found that there is a great deal to the saying that clothes make the pirate.

"I met a man who fell for me hard. I didn't love him but he had money. He needed me. He was never sure of himself. He was always too damned cautious. I married him and tried to build his ego, to get him to face the world, to take a chance. I didn't do a very good job. He made a start, built up some degree of assurance, then got in a tight place, the old doubts came back and he killed himself. The pathetic part of it was that it turned out he had won the battle he was fighting. The news came an hour after he'd fired the shot that ended his life. I felt terrible. I should have been with him. I was at a beauty parlor at the time it happened. In a fit of despondency he pulled the trigger. He was like that. After his death his doctor told me he was what was known as a manic-depressive. The doctor said it was a typical case. He said I'd really prolonged his life by helping to give him stability. He said they had suicidal compulsions in their moments of deep depression and that some-times the fits came on them suddenly.

"My husband left me quite a bit of property and there was considerable insurance. I was moving in the right set then. I met Stewart Bedford.

"Stewart Bedford fascinated me. He's twenty years old-er than I am. I know what that means. There isn't a great deal of difference between thirty-two and fifty-two. There's a lot of difference between forty-two and sixty-two, and there's an absolutely tragic difference between fifty-two and seventy-two. You can figure it out mathematically, and you can't get any decent answer, no matter how you go at it. Stewart Bedford saw me and wanted me. He wanted me in the same way an art collector would want a painting which appealed to him and on which he had set his heart.

"I agreed to marry him. I found out that he wanted to show me off to his friends, and his friends move in the highest social circles.

"That was something I hadn't bargained on, but I tried to live up to my end of the agreement.

"And then this thing came up."

"What thing?"

"My record."

"How did it come up?"

"Binney Denham."

"He blackmailed you?"

"Of course he blackmailed me. It was hideous. I couldn't afford to have it appear that the wife Stewart Bedford was so proud of had been arrested for defraud-ing an insurance company."

"Then what?"

"Binney Denham is one of the most deceptive person-alities you ever met. I don't know what to do with the man. He pretends that he is working for someone who is obdurate and greedy. Actually, Binney is the whole show. There isn't anyone else except a few people whom

Binney hires to do his bidding, and they don't know what it's all about.

"A week ago I got tired of being bled white. I told Binney he could go to hell. I slapped his face. I told him that if he ever tried to get another cent out of me, I'd go to the police. And, believe me, I meant it. After all, I'm going to live my own life and not go skulking around in the corners and shadows because of Binney Denham."

"And did you tell your husband?" Mason asked.

"No. In order to understand this, Mr. Mason, you have to know a little more about backgrounds."

"What about them?"

"Before my husband married me he'd been having an affair with his secretary—a faithful, loyal girl named Elsa Griffin."

"He told you that?"

"Heavens, no!"

"How did you find out?"

"I sized up the situation before I committed myself. I wanted to make certain that it was all over."

"Was it?"

"Yes, as far as he was concerned."

"How about her?"

"She was going to have her heart broken anyway, win, lose or draw. I decided to go ahead and marry him."

"Did your husband know that you knew anything about this secretary?"

"Don't be silly. I played them close to my chest."

"So you'd been paying blackmail, and you got tired of it?" Mason said.

She nodded.

"And what did you decide to tell your husband about it?"

"Nothing, Mr. Mason. I felt that there was a good even-money gamble that Binney would leave me alone if he knew I was absolutely determined never to pay him another cent. After all, a blackmailer can't make any money publicizing what he knows."

"Nowadays he can," Mason said. "There are magazines which like to feature those things."

"I thought of that, but I told Binney Denham that if the thing ever became publicized I'd go all the way, that I'd tell about the blackmail I'd been paying to him and that I had enough evidence so I could convict him."

"And then what?"

She avoided his eyes for a moment and said, "I'm hoping that's all there is to it."

Mason shook his head.

"You mean, he . . . he went after Stewart?"

"What makes you ask that?"

"I . . . I don't know. There was a telephone call night before last. Stewart acted *very* strangely. He went up to take the call in his room. The butler was to hang up the phone after my husband picked up the receiver upstairs, but the butler was called away because of an emergency and the downstairs phone was off the hook; I happened to be going by and I saw the phone off the hook and could hear squawking noises. I picked up the telephone to hang it up and they stopped talking just as I hung up the telephone. Over the receiver I thought I heard that whining, apologetic voice of Binney Denham. I couldn't distinguish words, just the tone of voice. And then I made up my mind it was just my imagination. I thought of asking my husband about the call, then decided to do nothing."

Mason said, "I'm afraid you're in a jam, Mrs. Bedford."

"I've been in jams before," she said with cool calm. "Suppose you tell me what you're driving at."

"Very well, I will. You've had this secret hanging over your head. You paid out thousands of dollars in blackmail. Then all of a sudden you became bold and—"

"Let's say I became desperate."

"That," Mason said, "is what I'm getting at. For your

information, it was Binney Denham who was murdered last night at The Staylonger Motel down near the beach."

Again her eyes gleamed with an indefinable expression. Then her face was held rigidly expressionless.

"Do they know who did it?" she asked.

"Not yet."

"Any clues?"

Mason, looking her straight in the eyes, said. "The manager saw a woman down there last night at about the time the murder was being committed, a woman who came out of unit twelve. She had evidently been prowling. The description the manager gave fits you exactly."

She smiled. "I suppose lots of descriptions would apply to me. Descriptions are pretty generalized anyway."

Mason said, "There are certain distinctive mannerisms you have. The manager gave a pretty good description."

She shook her head.

"And," Mason said, "certain fingerprints that were lifted from cabin twelve were unmistakably yours."

"They couldn't be."

"They are. I just showed them to you."

"Do the police know that you have them?"

"No."

"I tell you I wasn't there, Mr. Mason."

Mason said nothing.

"You've done quite a bit of legal work for my husband?"

"Some."

"Isn't there some way of faking or forging fingerprints?"

"There may be. Fingerprint experts say there isn't."

"These prints you mentioned are in this cabin?"

"Not now. They were developed and lifted from the places they were found in the cabin."

"Then what happened?"

"The cabin was wiped free of all prints."

"Someone is lying to you, Mr. Mason. Those can't be my fingerprints. There's some mistake."

"Let's not have any misunderstanding," Mason said. "Didn't you follow Binney Denham down to that motel some time last night?"

"Mr. Mason, why on earth would I follow Binney Denham down to any motel?"

"Because your husband was at that motel paying twenty thousand dollars' blackmail to Binney Denham."

She tightened her lips. Her face was wooden.

"You didn't follow Binney down there, did you?"

"I'd rather be dead than have that slimy little blackmailer get his clutches on Stewart. Why I'd . . . I'd—"

Mason said, "That is exactly the reasoning the police will follow in trying to determine a motivation."

"A reason why I should murder Binney Denham?"

"Yes."

"I tell you I wasn't there! I was home last night waiting for Stewart and your information about him is erroneous. He never went near that motel. He was at some stuffy old directors' meeting and working on a deal so delicate he didn't dare to leave the room long enough to telephone me. You're sure Binney Denham is dead? There can't be any doubt about it?"

"No doubt whatever," Mason said.

She thought that over for a moment, then got to her feet. "I'd be a liar and a hypocrite, Mr. Mason, if I told you I was sorry. I'm not. However, his death is going to create a problem you're going to have to cope with.

"The police will start checking Binney's background. They'll find out he was a blackmailer. They'll try to get a list of his victims in order to find someone who had a compelling motive to kill him. As the lawyer who handles my husband's problems you're going to have to see the police learn nothing of Binney's hold on me. Stewart loves to take me out socially and . . . well, it's hard to explain. I suppose in a way it's the same feeling an owner has when he has a prize-winning dog. He likes to enter him in dog shows and see him carry off the blue ribbons. It's supposed to make other dog owners jealous or envious. Stewart loves to give me clothes, jewels, servants, background and then invite his friends to come in and look me over. They regard him as a very lucky husband, and Stewart likes that."

"And underneath you resent it?" Mason asked.

She turned again and looked him full in the eyes. "Make no mistake, Mr. Perry Mason. I love it. And as Stewart's lawyer you're going to have to find some way of saving him from a ruinous scandal. You'll have to find *some* way to keep from having my past brought to light."

"What do you think I am—a magician?" Mason asked.

"My husband does," she said. "And we're prepared to pay you a fee based on that assumption—and for proving those fingerprints are forgeries and that I wasn't anywhere near that motel last night."

With that she turned and walked away with long, steady steps, terminating the interview with dignity, finality, and in a way which left her complete mistress of the situation.

■ 10 ■

PERRY MASON TURNED HIS CAR INTO THE PARKING LOT by his building. The attendant, who usually saluted him with a wave of the hand, made frantic signals as he drove by.

Mason braked his car to a stop. The attendant came running toward him. "A message for you, Mr. Mason."

Mason took the sheet of paper. On it had been scribbled: "Police are looking for you. Della."

Mason hesitated a moment, thinking things over, then parked the car in the stall which was reserved for him and walked into the foyer of the office building.

A tall man seemed to appear from nowhere in particular. "If you don't mind, Mason, I'll ride up with you."

"Well, well, Lieutenant Tragg of Homicide," Mason said. "Can I be of some help to you, Lieutenant?"

"That depends," Tragg said.

"On what?" Mason asked.

"We'll talk it over in your office, if you don't mind."

They rode up in silence. Mason led the way down the corridor past the entrance door of his office, went to the door marked "Private," unlocked and opened the door.

Della Street's voice sharp with apprehension, said, "Chief, the police are looking for . . . oh!" she exclaimed as her eyes focused on Lieutenant Tragg.

Tragg's voice was gravely courteous as he said, "Good morning, Miss Street," but there was a certain annoyance manifest as he went on, "And how did you know the police were looking for Mr. Mason?"

"I just heard it somewhere. There isn't supposed to be anything secret about it, is there?" Della Street asked demurely.

"Apparently not," Tragg said, seating himself comfortably in the client's chair and waiting for Mason to adjust himself behind the office desk.

"Cigarette?" Mason asked, extending a package to Tragg.

"Thanks," Tragg said, taking one.

Mason snapped his lighter and held the flame out to Tragg.

"Service!" the police lieutenant said.

"With a smile," Mason told him, lighting his own cigarette.

Lieutenant Tragg, almost as tall as the lawyer, was

typical of the modern police officer who is schooled in his profession and follows the work because he enjoys it, just as his associate, Sergeant Holcomb, who made no secret of his enmity for Perry Mason, typified the old school of hard-boiled, belligerent cop. Between Mason and Tragg there was a genuine mutual respect and a personal liking.

"Staylonger Motel," Lieutenant Tragg said, looking at Mason.

Mason raised his eyebrows.

"Mean anything to you?"

"Nice name," Mason said.

"Ever been there?"

Mason shook his head.

"Some client of yours been there?"

"I'm sure I couldn't say. I have quite a few clients, you know, and I presume some of them stay at motels rather frequently. It's quite convenient when you're traveling by auto. You can get at your baggage when you want it and—"

"Never mind the window dressing," Tragg said. "We had a murder at The Staylonger Motel last night."

"Indeed?" Mason said. "Who was murdered?"

"A man by the name of Binney Denham. Rather an interesting character, too, as it turns out."

"Client of mine?" Mason asked.

"I hope not."

"But I take it there's *some* connection," Mason told him.

"I wouldn't be too surprised."

"Want to tell me about it?"

"I'll tell you some of the things we know," Tragg said. "Yesterday afternoon a man who looked the executive type, with dark hair, iron gray at the temples, trim figure, well-tailored clothes, and an air of success, showed up at The Staylonger Motel with a woman who was quite a bit younger. The man could have been fifty. The woman, who was blonde and seductive, could have been twenty-five."

"Tut-tut-tut!" Mason said.

Tragg grinned. "Yeah! I know. Almost unique in the annals of motel history, isn't it? Well, here's the funny part. The man insisted on a double cabin; said they were going to be joined by another couple. However, after getting two units with a connecting door, the man apparently parked the blonde in unit sixteen and established his domicile in unit fifteen.

"The man was driving a rented car. They had drinks, went out, came back, and that evening the blonde drove away—alone.

"At around eleven last night the police received a call from an unknown woman. The woman said she wanted to report a homicide at unit sixteen in The Staylonger Motel, and then the woman hung up."

"Just like that?" Mason asked.

"Just like that," Tragg said. "Interesting, isn't it?"

"In what way?"

"Oh, I don't know," Tragg said. "But when you stop to look at it, it has a peculiar pattern. Why should a woman call up to report a homicide?"

"Because she had knowledge that she thought the police should have," Mason said promptly.

"Then why didn't she state her name and address?"

"Because she didn't want to become involved personally."

"It's surprising the way you parallel my thinking," Tragg said. "Only I carry my thinking a step farther."

"How come?"

"Usually a woman who wants to keep out of a thing of that sort simply doesn't bother to report. Usually a woman who reports, if she's acting in good faith, will give her name and address. But if that woman had been advised by a smart lawyer who had told her, 'It's your duty to report the homicide to the police, but there's no law that says you have to stay on the phone long enough to give your name and address—' Well, you know how it is, Mason. It starts me thinking."

"It seems to be habit you have," Mason said.

"I'm trying to cultivate it," Tragg told him.

"I take it there's something more?" Mason asked.

"Oh, lots more. We made a routine check down at The Staylonger Motel. We get lots of false steers on these things, you know. This time it happened to be correct. This character was lying there in the middle of the floor with a bullet hole in his back. The executive-type businmessman and the curvaecous-type blonde and the rented car had completely disappeared.

"The blonde had driven away in the car. The man had gone through a barbed wire fence out the back way. He'd torn his clothes on the barbed wire. He evidently was in a hurry."

Mason nodded sympathetically. "Doesn't leave you much to work on, does it?"

"Oh, don't worry about a little thing like that," Tragg said. "We have *lots* to work on. You see we have the license number of the automobile. We traced it down. It was a rented automobile. We got hold of the automobile, and we've come up with some pretty good prints."

"I see," Mason said.

"Shortly after we phoned in the order to impound this automobile, we received a telephone call from the man who runs the car rental agency. He said that a woman came in to rent a car, inquired about cars that were available, wanted a car of a certain type, looked over the cars that he had, and then changed her mind. She had a slip of paper with license number on it. She seemed to be looking for some particular car."

"Did she say what car?" Mason asked.

"No, she didn't say."

Mason smiled. "The manager of the car rental agency may have a vivid imagination."

"Perhaps," Tragg said. "But the woman acted in a way that aroused the suspicions of the manager. He thought perhaps she might be trying to get hold of this particular car that had figured in a homicide. When she left, he followed her around the block. She got in a car that was driven by a man. The manager took down the license number of the automobile."

"Very clever," Mason said.

"The automobile was registered in the name of the Drake Detective Agency."

"You've talked with Drake?" Mason asked.

"Not yet," Tragg said. "I may talk with him later on. The Drake Detective Agency has offices here in the building on the same floor with you and does all of your work. You and Paul Drake are personal friends and close business associates."

"I see," Mason said, tapping ashes from the end of the cigarette.

"So I started making a few inquiries on my own," Tragg said. "Nothing particularly official, Mason. Just checking up."

"I see," Mason said.

"I notice that when Paul Drake is working on a particularly important case and stays up all night, he has hamburgers sent up from the lunch counter a couple of doors down the street. I probably shouldn't be telling you this, Mason, because it never pays for a magician to expose the manner in which he does his tricks. It has a tendency to destroy the effect.

"However, I dropped in to the lunch counter this morning, had a cup of coffee, chatted with the manager, told him I understood he'd been delivering quite a few hamburgers the night before, said I'd like to talk with the man who was on the night shift. Well, he'd gone home but hadn't gone to bed as yet, and the manager got him on the phone for me. I thought it would just be the same old seven and six of deliveries to Drake's office, but I hit unexpected pay dirt. I found that you and your secretary were up all night, and that you had hamburgers and coffee."

Mason said thoughtfully, "That's what comes of trying to get service. I should have gone down myself."

"Or sent Miss Street for them," Tragg said, smiling at Della Street.

"And so?" Mason said. "You put two and two together and made eighteen. Is that it?"

"I haven't put two and two together as yet," Tragg said. "I'm simply calling your attention to certain factors which I haven't tried to add up so far.

"Now, I'm going to tell you something, Mason. Binney Denham was a blackmailer. We haven't been able to get *all* the dope on him as yet. He kept his books in some sort of code. We haven't cracked that code. We do have fingerprints from that rented car. We have some cigarette stubs from the ash tray. We have a few other things we aren't talking about just yet.

"Now if you happen to have a client who was susceptible to blackmail, if Binney Denham happened to be bleeding that client white and the client decided to get out of it by just about the only way you can deal with a blackmailer of that type, the police would be as co-operative as is consistent with the circumstances—if we received a little co-operation in return.

"What we don't know is just where this curvaceous blonde entered into the picture. There are quite a few things we don't know. There are quite a few things we do know. There are quite few things we are finding out.

"Now, a good, smart lawyer who had a client in a jam of that sort might make a better deal with the police and perhaps with the D.A. by co-operating all the way along the line than by trying to hold out."

"Are you speaking for the D.A.?" Mason asked.

Tragg ground out his cigarette in the ash tray. "Now

there, of course, you've come to the weak point in my argument."

"Your district attorney is not particularly fond of the ground I walk on," Mason pointed out.

"I know," Tragg conceded.

"I think, under the circumstances," Mason said, "a smart lawyer would have to play them very close to his chest."

"Well, I thought I'd drop in,' Tragg said. "Just sort of a routine checkup. I take it you don't want to make any statement, Mason?"

Mason shook his head.

"Keep your own nose clean," Tragg warned. "There are people on the force who don't like you. I just thought I'd give you a friendly warning, that's all."

"Sergeant Holcomb going to be working on the case?" Mason asked.

"Sergeant Holcomb *is* working on the case."

"I see," Mason said.

Tragg got up, straightened his coat, reached for his hat, smiled at Della Street, and said, "At times you're rather obvious, Miss Street."

"I am?" Della Street asked.

Tragg nodded. "You keep looking at that private, unlisted telephone on the corner of Mason's desk. Doubtless you're planning to call Paul Drake as soon as I'm out of the door. I told you this was a *friendly* tip. For your information, I don't intend to stop in at Drake's office on the way out and I don't intend to talk with him *as yet*.

"I would like to be very certain that nothing happens to put your employer out of business as an attorney, because then he couldn't sign your pay checks, and personally it's a lot more fun for me to deal with brains than with the crooked type of criminal lawyer who has to get by by suborning perjury.

"I just thought I'd drop in for a social visit, that's all, and it might be a little easier for you to keep out of trouble if you knew that I'm going to have to report what I've found out down at the lunch counter about the consumption of sandwiches and coffee in the Mason office during the small hours of the morning.

"I don't suppose the persons who entered and signed the night register in the elevator would have been foolish enough to have signed their own names, but of course we'll be checking that and getting descriptions. I wouldn't be too surprised if the description of the man and the woman who went to your office last night didn't check with the description of the man and the woman who registered in units fifteen and sixteen at The Staylonger Motel. And, of course, we'll have a handwriting expert take a look at the man's signature on the register the elevator man keeps for after-hours visitors.

"Well, I'll be ambling along. I have a conference with my zealous assistant, Sergeant Holcomb. I'm not going to mention anything to him about having been here."

Tragg left the office.

"Hang it!" Mason said. "A man will think he's being smart and then overlook the perfectly obvious."

"Lieutenant Tragg?" Della Street asked.

"Tragg nothing!" Mason said. "I'm talking about myself. Having hamburgers sent up from that lunch counter is convenient for us and damned convenient for the police. We'll remember to keep out of *that* trap in the future."

"Thanks to Lieutenant Tragg," she said.

"Thanks to a very worthy adversary who is very shortly going to be raising hell with our client," Mason said.

MASON CAREFULLY CLOSED THE DOOR LEADING TO HIS private office, moved over close to Della Street, and lowered his voice. "You're going to have to take a coffee break, Della," he said.

"And then what?"

"Then while you're taking the coffee break, make certain that no one is in a position to see the number you're dialing. Call Stewart Bedford and tell him that under no circumstances is he to try to communicate with me, that I'll call him from time to time from a pay station; tell him that the police realize I'm interested in the case and may be watching my office."

Della Street nodded.

"Now," Mason said, "we're going to have to be very, very careful. Lieutenant Tragg knows that Paul Drake is working on the case. Tragg is a deadly combination of intelligence, ability, and persistence.

"They've got hold of that automobile from the drive-yourself agency and they've developed fingerprints. They don't have any way of picking up Stewart Bedford from those fingerprints because they don't know whose fingerprints they are, but if they ever get a line on Bedford they can then take his fingerprints and *prove* that he was in the automobile."

"What about Mrs. Bedford?" Della Street asked. "Aren't you obligated to tell Mr. Bedford about her?"

"Why?"

"You're representing him."

"As his attorney," Mason said, "I'm supposed to be looking out for his best interests."

"His wife is mixed in it. Shouldn't he know?"

"How is she mixed in it?"

"She was down there at the motel. She had all the motive in the world. Chief, you know as well as I do that she went down there because she thought Binney Denham was putting the bite on her husband and she didn't intend to stand for it. There was only one way she could have stopped it."

"You mean she killed him?"

"Why not?"

Mason pursed his lips.

"Well, why not?" Della Street insisted.

Mason said, "In a case of this kind we don't know what we're up against until all of the facts are in, and by that time it's frequently too late to protect our client. In this case I'm protecting my client."

"Just the one client?"

"Just the one client, Stewart G. Bedford."

"Then aren't you obligated to tell him about . . . about his wife?"

Mason shook his head. "I'm a lawyer. I have to take the responsibility of reaching certain decisions. Bedford is in love with his wife. It's quite probable that he's more in love with her than she is with him. Marriage for her may have been something of a business proposition. For him it represented a complete romantic investment in a new type of life."

"Well?" she asked.

"If I tell him about his wife's having been down there, about the fact that she may be suspect, Bedford will become heroic. He'll want to take all the blame in case he thinks there's any possibility she's guilty.

"I'm somewhat in the position of a physician who has to treat a patient. He doesn't tell the patient everything he knows. He prescribes treatment for the patient and does his best to see that the patient gets the right treatment."

Della Street thought that over for a moment, then said, "Will the police be able to locate Bedford today?"

"Probably," Mason said. "It's just a matter of time. Remember, Bedford is vulnerable on two or three fronts. For one thing, he bought a lot of traveler's checks, countersigned them and turned them over to the blackmailers. They cashed them. Somewhere along the line they've left a back trail that Tragg will pick up. Also remember that Bedford scribbled a note which he gave to the waiter at the cocktail lounge, asking him to call Elsa Griffin and give her the name of the motel. He didn't sign his name to the message, but after the newspapers begin to talk about the murder at The Staylonger Motel, the waiter will probably remember that that was the name of the motel he was to give Elsa Griffin over the telephone."

"Do you suppose the waiter saved the message?"

"He could have," Mason said. "There was twenty dollars in it for him, and that was bound to have registered in his mind. He could very well have saved the note.

"About all we can do is try to stall things along while Paul Drake gets information about Denham's background and see if we can locate that blonde."

"All right," Della Street said, "I'll take my coffee break and telephone Mr. Bedford."

"How are you feeling, Della?"

"As long as I can pour the coffee in, I can keep the eyes open."

"You'd better go home early this afternoon and try getting some sleep."

"How about you?"

"I'll be all right. I may break away this afternoon myself. Things are now where we have to wait for developments. I'm hoping Drake can come up with something before Tragg gets a line on our client. Get yourself some coffee and then go on home and turn in, Della. I'll phone you if anything comes up."

"I'll stick it out a while longer. I wish you'd get some rest and let *me* stay on the job and call *you*."

Mason looked at his watch. "Wait until noon, Della. If Drake hasn't turned up something by that time, we'll both check out. I'll leave word with Drake's office where they can call me."

"Okay," Della Street said. "I'll call Bedford right away."

■ 12 ■

MASON STOPPED IN AT PAUL DRAKE'S OFFICE.

"You don't look bad," Mason said to the detective.

"Why should I?"

"Up all night."

"We get used to it. *You* look like hell."

"*I'm* not accustomed to it. What are you finding out?"

"Not too much. The police are on the job and that makes things tough."

"This man Denham," Perry Mason said. "He had this blonde girl friend."

"So what?"

"I want her."

"Who doesn't? The police want her. The newspaper people want her."

"What's the description?" Mason asked.

"The description the police have is a girl about twenty-five to twenty-seven, five feet three, maybe a little on the hefty side, slim-waisted, plenty of hips, and lots of chest."

"What do they have from the rented car, Paul?"

"No one knows. The police keep that pretty much of a secret. They have *some* fingerprints."

"And from the units at the motel?"

"They have fingerprints there, too."

Mason said, "I'll give you a tip, Paul. The police are wise that you're working on the case."

"It would be a miracle if they weren't. You can't try to get information in a case of this sort without leaving a trail that the police can follow. I suppose that means they've connected me with you?"

Mason nodded.

"And you with your client?" Drake asked, watching Mason sharply.

"Not yet."

"Be careful. They will."

"It's just a matter of time," Mason conceded. "I want to find that blonde before they do."

"Then you'll have to give me some information that they haven't got," Drake said. "Otherwise, things being equal, there isn't a whisper of a chance, Perry. The police have the organization. They have the authority. They have all the police records. I have nothing."

"I can give you one tip," Mason said.

"What's that?"

"In this business names don't mean anything," Mason told him. "But initials do. My client tells me this girl gave the name of Geraldine Corning. She had a new overnight bag and suitcase with her initials stamped in gilt— *G.C.*"

"You don't think she gave her right name to this client of yours?"

"I doubt it," Mason said. "But I have a hunch her initials are probably the same. The last name won't mean much, but there aren't too many first names that begin with *G*. You might try Gloria or Grace, for a start."

"Blondes with first names of Gloria or Grace are a dime a dozen," Drake said. "The city's full of them."

"I know, but this was a girl who was hanging around with particular people."

"And you know what happens when you ask questions about girls who are hanging around with people like that?" Drake asked. "You run up against a wall of silence that is based on stark fear. You can open up any source of information and have things going good, and then you can casually mention, 'Do you know a girl by the name of Grace or Gloria Somebody-or-other who was playing around with this blackmailer Binney Denham?' Well, you know what happens. They clam up as though you'd pulled a zipper."

Mason thought that over. "I see your point, Paul. But a lot depends on this. We've simply *got* to get this girl located. She must have had a charge account some place that was paid by her sugar daddy or—"

"You know what would happen if we tried to get a line on all the blondes who have accounts that are paid by sugar daddies? We'd—"

"No, no, now wait a minute!" Mason said. "I'm just trying to narrow the thing down for you, Paul. She must have had an account at a beauty parlor. She must have had contacts, perhaps not with Binney Denham but perhaps with this Harry Elston who had the lock box with Binney. What can you find out about him?"

"Absolutely nothing," Drake said. "Elston visited the joint-tenancy lock box and faded from the picture. He's crawled into a hole and pulled the hole in after him."

"The police want him?"

"Very much."

Mason said, "Blackmailers and gamblers. Gamblers go to race tracks. Try covering the race tracks. See if you can get a line on this blonde. She had relatively new baggage. It may have been bought for this occasion.

"I'm going out to my apartment and get some shuteye. I'd like to have you stay on with this personally for another couple of hours if you can, Paul. Then you can turn it over to your operatives and get some sleep."

"Shucks! I'm good for another day and another night," Drake said.

Mason heaved himself out of his chair. "I'm not. Call me whenever you get a lead. I want to find that blonde and interview her before the police do, and I have an idea things are going to get pretty rugged this afternoon. I want to be able to think clearly when the going gets rough."

"Okay," Drake said. "I'll call you. But don't get to optimistic about that blonde. She's going to be hard to find, and in blackmailing circles the word will have gone out for everybody to clam up."

■ 13 ■

MASON TOOK A HOT SHOWER, CRAWLED INTO BED, AND sank instantly into restful oblivion only to be aroused, seconds later, it seemed to him, by the insistent ringing of the telephone.

He managed to get the receiver to his ear and muttered thickly into the telephone, "Hello!"

Paul Drake's voice, crisp and businesslike, said, "The fat's in the fire, Perry. Get going."

"What?" Mason asked.

"Police checking back on Denham's associates got on the trail of some traveler's checks. It seems a whole flock of traveler's checks were cashed. They bore the signatures of Stewart G. Bedford. Because of his prominence, the police were reluctant to start getting rough until they'd made a complete check.

"They got photographs of Bedford and took them out to Morrison Brems, the manager of The Staylonger Motel. Brems can't be certain, but he thinks from the photographs the police had that Bedford was the man who registered with the blonde.

"The police have—"

"Have they made an arrest?" Mason interposed.

"No."

"Brought him in for inquiry?"

"Not yet. They're going to his office to—"

Mason said, "I'm on my way."

Mason tumbled into his clothes, ran a comb through his hair, dashed out of the apartment, took the elevator down, jumped into his car and made time out to Bedford's office.

He was too late.

Sergeant Holcomb, a uniformed officer, and a plain-clothes detective were in Bedford's office when Mason arrived. A rather paunchy man with a gold-toothed smile stood patiently in the background.

"Hello," Mason said. "What's all the trouble?"

Sergeant Holcomb grinned at him. "You're too late," he said.

"What's the matter, Bedford?" Mason asked.

"These people seem to think I've been out at some motel with a blonde. They're asking me questions about blackmail and murder and—"

"And we asked you nicely to let us take your finger-prints," Sergeant Holcomb said, "and you refused to even give us the time of day. Now then, Mason, are you going to advise your client to give us his fingerprints or not?"

"He doesn't have to give you a damn thing," Mason said. "If you want to get his fingerprints, arrest him and book him."

"We can do that too, you know."

"And run up against a suit for false arrest," Mason

said. "I don't know anyone I'd rather recover damages from than you."

Sergeant Holcomb turned to the paunchy man. "Is this the guy?"

"I could tell better if I saw him with his hat on."

Sergeant Holcomb walked over to the hat closet, returned with a hat, slapped it down on Bedford's head. "Now take a look."

The man studied Bedford. "It looks like him."

Sergeant Holcomb said to the man in plain clothes, "Look the place over."

The man took a leather packet from his pocket, took out some various colored powders, a camel's-hair brush and started brushing an ash tray which he had picked up.

"You can't do that," Mason said.

"Try and stop him," Holcomb invited. "Just *try* and stop him. I don't know anyone I'd rather hang one on than you. We're collecting evidence. Try and stop us."

Holcomb turned to Bedford. "Now then, you got twenty thousand dollars in traveler's checks. Why did you want them?"

"Don't answer," Mason said, "until they can treat you with the dignity and respect due a man in your position. Don't even give them the time of day."

"All those checks were cashed within a period of less than twelve hours," Sergeant Holcomb went on. "What was the idea?"

Bedford sat tight-lipped.

"Perhaps," Holcomb said, "you were paying blackmail to a ring that was pretty smart. They didn't want you to be able to make a payoff with marked or numbered bills, so they worked out that method so they could cash the checks themselves."

"And thereby left a perfect trail?" Mason asked sarcastically.

"Don't be silly," Holcomb said. "The way those checks were cashed you couldn't tie them in with Binney

Denham in a hundred years. We'd never even have known about it if it hadn't been for the murder."

The plain-clothes officer studied several latent fingerprints which he had examined with a magnifying glass. Abruptly he looked up at Sergeant Holcomb and nodded.

"What have you got?" Holcomb asked.

"A perfect little fingerprint. It matches with the little fingerprint on the—"

"Don't tell him," Sergeant Holcomb interrupted. "That's good enough for me. Get your things, Bedford. You're in custody."

"On what charge?" Mason asked.

"Suspicion of murder," Holcomb said.

Mason said, "You can make any investigation you want to, or you can make an arrest and charge him with murder, but you're not going to hold him on suspicion."

"Maybe I won't hold him," Holcomb said, "but I'll sure as hell take him in. Want to make a bet?"

"Either charge him, or I'll get a habeas corpus and get him out."

Holcomb's grin was triumphant. "Go ahead, Counselor, get your habeas corpus. By the time you get it, I'll have him booked and have his fingerprints. If you think you can get a suit for malicious arrest on the strength of the evidence we have now, you're a bigger boob than I think you are.

"Come on, Bedford. Do you want to pay for a taxi, or shall we call the wagon?"

Bedford looked at Mason.

"Pay for the taxi," Mason said, "and make absolutely no statements except in the presence of your attorney."

"Fair enough!" Sergeant Holcomb said. "I don't need more than an hour to make my case bulletproof, and if you can get a habeas corpus in that time, you're a wonder!"

Stewart G. Bedford drew himself up to his full height. "Gentlemen," he said, "I desire to make a statement."

"Hold it!" Mason said. "You're not making any statements yet."

Bedford looked at him with cold, resolute eyes. "Mason," he said, "I have retained you to advise me as to my legal rights. No one has to advise me as to my moral rights."

"I tell you to hold it!" Mason said irritably.

Sergeant Holcomb said hopefully to Bedford, "This is *your* office. If you want him out, just say the word and we'll put him out."

"I don't want him out," Bedford said. "I simply want to state to you gentlemen that I *did* go to The Staylonger Motel yesterday."

"Now, that's better!" Sergeant Holcomb said, pulling out a chair and sitting down. "Go right ahead."

"Bedford," Mason said, "you may *think* you're doing the right thing, but——"

Sergeant Holcomb said, "Throw him out, boys, if he tries to interrupt. Go ahead, Bedford; you've got this on your chest and you'll feel better when you get rid of it."

"I was being blackmailed by this character Binney Denham," Bedford said. "There is something in my past that I hoped never would come out. Somehow Denham found out about it."

"What was it?" Holcomb asked.

Mason tried to say something, then checked himself.

"A hit-and-run," Bedford said simply. "It was six years ago. I had a few drinks. It was a dark, rainy night. It really wasn't my fault and I was perfectly sober. This elderly woman in dark clothes was crossing the street. I didn't see her until I was right on her. I hit her a solid smash. I knew the minute I had hit her there was nothing anyone could do for her. It threw her to the pavement with terrific force."

"Where was this?" Sergeant Holcomb asked.

"Out on Figueroa Street, six years ago. The woman's

name was Sara Biggs. You can find out all about her in the accident records.

"As I say, I'd had a few drinks, I know very well what I can do and I can't do when I'm drinking. I never drive a car if I'm sufficiently under the influence of liquor to have it affect my driving in the slightest. This accident wasn't due in any way to the few cocktails I'd had, but I knew that I *did* have liquor on my breath. There was nothing that could be done for the woman. The street was, at the moment, free of traffic. I just kept on going.

"I made it a point to check up on the accident in the papers. The woman had been killed instantly. I tell you, gentlemen, it was her own fault. She was crossing the street on a dark, rainy night in between intersections. Heaven knows what she was trying to do! She was out there in the street and that's all. As I learned afterwards, she was an elderly woman. She was dressed entirely in black. I didn't know *all* of these things at the time. All I knew was that I had been drinking and had hit someone and that it had been her fault. However, I'd had enough liquor so I knew I'd be the goat if I'd stopped."

"Okay," Sergeant Holcomb said. "So you beat it. You made a hit-and-run. This guy Denham found out about it. Is that right?"

"That's right."

"What did he do?"

"He waited for some time before he put the bite on me," Bedford said. "Then he showed up with a demand that I—"

"When?" Holcomb interrupted.

"Three days ago," Bedford said.

"You hadn't know him before that?"

"That was the first time in my life I ever met the slimy little rascal. He had this apologetic manner. He told me that he hated to do it, but he needed money and . . . well, he told me to get twenty thousand dollars in traveler's checks, and that was all there'd be to it.

"Then he told me he had to keep me out of circulation while the checks were being cashed. That was when he showed up yesterday morning. He had a blonde woman with him who gave the name of Geraldine Corning. She had a car parked in front of the building. I don't know how they'd secured that parking space, but the car was right in front of the door. Miss Corning drove me around until we were certain we weren't being followed; then she told me to pick out a good-looking motel and drive in."

"*You* picked out the motel, or *she* did?" Sergeant Holcomb asked.

"I did."

"All right. What happened?"

"We saw the sign of The Staylonger Motel. I suggested that we go in there. It was all right with her. I was already paying blackmail on one charge and I didn't propose to have them catch me on some kind of frame-up with a woman. I told the manager, Mr. Brems—the gentleman standing over there who has just identified me— that I expected another couple to join us and therefore wanted a double unit. He said I could do better by waiting until the other couple showed up and letting them pay for the second unit. I told him I'd pay the entire price and take both units."

"Then what?"

"I put Miss Corning in one unit. I stayed in the other. The door was open between the units. I tried to keep rigidly to myself, but it became too boring. We played cards. We had a drink. We went out for a drive. We stopped in a tavern. We had a very fine afternoon meal. We returned and had another drink. That drink was drugged. I went to sleep. I don't know what happened after that."

"Okay," Sergeant Holcomb said, "you're doing so good. Why not tell us about the gun?"

"I *will* tell you about the gun," Bedford said. "I had never been blackmailed in my life. It made me furious to think of doing business on that kind of a basis. I . . . I had a gun in my study. I took that gun and put it in my brief case."

"Go on," Holcomb said.

"I tell you the last drink I had was drugged."

"What time was that?"

"Sometime in the afternoon."

"Three o'clock? Four o'clock?"

"Probably four. I can't give you the exact hour. It was still daylight."

"How do you know it was drugged?"

"I could tell. I have never been able to sleep during the day. However, after I took this drink I couldn't focus my eyes. I saw double. I tried to get up and couldn't. I fell back on the bed and went to sleep."

"This blonde babe drugged the drink?" Sergeant Holcomb asked.

"I rather think that someone else had entered the motel during our absence and drugged the bottle from which the liquor was poured," Bedford said. "Miss Corning seemed to feel the effects before I did. She was sitting in a chair and she went to sleep while I was still awake. In fact, as I remember it, she went to sleep right in the middle of a conversation."

"They sometimes put on an act like that," Holcomb said. "It keeps the sucker from becoming suspicious. She dopes the drink, then pretends she's sleepy first. It's an old gag."

"Could be," Bedford said. "I'm just telling you what I know."

"Okay," Sergeant Holcomb said. "How did it happen you used this gun? I take it the guy showed up and—"

"I *didn't* use the gun," Bedford said positively. "I had the gun in my brief case. When I awakened, which was sometime at night, the gun was gone."

"So what did you do?" Holcomb asked skeptically.

"I became panic-stricken when I found the body of Binney Denham in that other unit in the motel. I took my brief case and my hat and went out through the back. I crawled through the barbed wire fence—"

"You tore your clothes?" Holcomb asked.

"I tore the knee of my pants, yes."

"And then what did you do?"

"I walked across the lot to the road."

"And then what?"

"Then I managed to get a ride," Bedford said. "I think, gentlemen, that covers the situation."

"He was killed with your gun?" Sergeant Holcomb asked.

"How do I know?" Bedford said. "I have told you my story, gentlemen. I am not accustomed to having my word questioned. I am not going to submit myself to a lot of browbeating cross-questioning. I have told you the absolute truth."

"What did you do with the gun?" Sergeant Holcomb said. "Come on, Bedford, you've told us so much you might as well make a clean breast of it. After all, the guy was a blackmailer. He was putting the bite on you. There's a lot to be said on your side. You knew that if you started paying you were going to have to keep on paying. You took the only way out, so you may as well tell us what you did with the gun."

"I have told you the truth," Bedford said.

"Nuts!" Sergeant Holcomb observed. "Don't expect us to believe a cock-and-bull story like that. Why did you take the gun in the first place if you didn't intend to use it?"

"I tell you I don't know. I presume I thought I might intimidate the man by telling him I had paid once, but that I wouldn't pay again. I probably had a rather nebulous idea that if I showed him the gun and told him I'd kill him if he ever tried to shake me down again, it might help get me off the hook as far as future payments were concerned. Frankly, gentlemen, I don't know. I never did make any really definite plan. I acted on impulse, some feeling of—"

"Yeah, I know," Sergeant Holcomb said. "I know all about it. Come on through with the truth now. What did you do with the gun after the shooting? Tell us that and then you'll have got it all off your chest."

Bedford shook his head. "I have told you all I know. Someone took my gun out of my brief case while I was sleeping."

Holcomb looked at the plain-clothes officer, said to Bedford, "Okay. We'll go talk with the D.A. You pay for the cab."

Holcomb turned to Mason. "You and your habeas corpus," he said. "This is one case that backfired on you. How do you like your client now, wise guy?"

Mason said, "Don't be silly. If Bedford had been going to shoot Denham, why didn't he do it *before* he paid the twenty thousand and save himself that much money?"

Sergeant Holcomb frowned for a moment, then said, "Because he didn't have the opportunity before he paid. Anyhow, he's smart. It would be worth twenty grand to him to give you that talking point in front of a jury.

"It's your question, Mason, and the D.A. will let you try to answer it yourself in front of the jury. I'll be there listening.

"Come on, Bedford. You're going places where even Perry Mason can't get you out. That statement of yours gives us all *we* need.

"Call the cab. We leave Mason here."

MASON, BONE TIRED, ENTERED THE OFFICES OF THE Drake Detective Agency.

"Drake gone home?" he asked the girl at the switchboard.

She shook her head and pointed to the gate leading to a long, narrow corridor. "He's still in. I think he's resting. He's in room seven. There's a couch in there."

"I'll take a peek inside," Mason said. "If he's asleep I won't disturb him. What's cooking? Anything?"

"He has a lot of operatives out and some reports are coming in, but nothing important. He's trying to locate this blonde young woman you were so anxious to find. He's left word to be called if we get anything on her."

"Thanks," Mason said. "I'll tiptoe down. If he's sleeping I won't disturb him."

Mason walked on down the corridor past a veritable rabbit warren of small-sized offices, gently opened the door of number seven.

This was a small office with a table, two straight-backed chairs, and a couch. Paul Drake lay on his back on the couch, snoring gently.

Mason stood for a moment in the doorway, regarding the sleeping figure, then eased out and closed the door.

Just as the door latched shut, the phone on the table shrilled noisily. Mason hesitated a moment, then gently opened the door.

Paul Drake came up to a sitting position on the couch. His eyes were still heavy with sleep as he groped for the telephone, got the receiver to his ear, said, "Hello . . . yes

. . . What is it? . . ." He sleep-sodden eyes looked up, saw Mason, and the detective nodded drowsily.

Mason saw Drake's expression suddenly change. The man galvanized into wakefulness as though he had been hit in the face with a stream of cold water. "Wait a minute," he said. "What's that address? . . . Okay, what's the name? . . . Okay . . . I've got it. I've got it."

Drake scribbled rapidly on a pad of paper, then said into the telephone, "Hold everything! Keep watch on the place. If she goes out, shadow her. I'll be out there right away—fifteen or twenty minutes. . . . Okay, good-by."

Drake banged the telephone, said, "We've got her, Perry."

"Who?"

"This Geraldine Corning babe."

"You're sure?"

"Her name's Grace Compton. I have the address here. You had a correct hunch on the initials on the baggage."

"How'd you locate her, Paul?"

"I'll tell you after we get started," Drake said, "Come on. Let's go."

Drake ran his fingers through his hair, grabbed a hat, started down the narrow corridor with Mason pounding along at his heels.

"Your car or mine?" Mason asked in the elevator.

"Makes no difference," Drake told him.

"We'll take mine," Mason said. "You do the talking while I'm driving."

Mason and the detective hurried across the parking lot, jumped into Mason's car. Drake was talking by the time the car was in motion.

"The location of the car rental agency gave us something to work on," Drake said. "We started combing the classified ad directory for stores in the neighborhood handling baggage. I've had five operatives on the job covering every place they could think of. One of them struck pay dirt. A fellow remembered having sold baggage to a blonde who answered the description and putting the initials *G.C.* on it. The blonde paid with a check signed 'Grace Compton,' and the man remembered the bank. After that it was easy. She's living in an apartment house, and apparently she's in at the moment."

"That's for us," Mason said. "Good work, Paul."

"Of course, it *could* be a false lead. After all, we're just working on a description and slender clues. There are lots of blonde babes who buy baggage."

"I know," Mason said, "but I have a hunch this is it."

Drake said, "Turn to the left at the next corner, Perry."

Mason swung the car around the corner, then, at Drake's direction, turned back to the right after three blocks.

"Find a parking place in here some place," Drake said.

Mason eased the car into a vacant place at the curb. He and Drake got out and walked up to the front of a rather ostentatious apartment house.

A man sitting in a parked car near the entrance to the apartment house struck a match, lit a cigarette. Drake said, "That's my man. Want to talk with him?"

"Do we need to?"

"No. Striking the match and lighting the cigarette means that she's still in there. That's his signal to us."

Mason walked up to the directory, studied the names, and saw that Grace Compton had apartment two-thirty-one.

"How about this door, Paul?" Mason asked, indicating the locked outer door. "Do we sound the buzzer in her apartment, or can you—?"

"That's easy," Drake said, looking at the lock on the outer door. He took a key from his pocket, inserted it in the lock. The door swung open.

"Let's walk," Mason said.

The climbed the stairs to the second floor, walked

back down the corridor and paused before the door bearing the number two-thirty-one.

"It's your show from here on," Drake said. "Of course, your hunch may be right and it may be wrong. All we have is a description."

"We'll take a chance," Mason said.

He pressed the bell button. A long, two shorts and a long.

They heard the quick thud of steps on the inside, then the door swung open. A blonde in lounging pajamas said, "My God! You—" She stopped abruptly at the sight of the two men.

"Miss Compton?" Mason asked.

Her eyes instantly became cautious. "What is it?" she asked.

"We just wanted to talk with you," Mason said.

"Who are you?"

"This is Paul Drake, a detective."

She said, "You can't pull that line of stuff with me. I—"

"I'm Perry Mason, a lawyer."

"Okay, so what?"

Mason said, "Know anything about The Staylonger Motel, Miss Compton?"

"Yes," she said breathlessly, "I was there. I was there with one of the big-name motion picture stars. He didn't want the affair revealed. He just swept me off my feet. Now I'm suing him for support of my unborn child. How did you know?"

Mason said, "Were you there with Mr. Stewart G. Bedford yesterday?"

Her eyes narrowed. "All right, if this is a pinch, get it off your chest. If it isn't, get out of here."

"It's not a pinch. I'm trying to get information *before* the police do."

"So you brought a detective along with you?"

"Private."

"Oh, I see. And you want to know just what I did yesterday. How perfectly delightful! Would you like to come in and sit down? I suppose you expect me to buy you a drink and—"

"You knew Binney Denham?"

"Denham? Denham?" she said and slowly shook her head. "The name means nothing to me. Am I supposed to know him?"

"If you're the one I think you are," Mason said, "you and Stewart Bedford occupied units fifteen and sixteen in The Staylonger Motel yesterday."

"Why, Mr. Mason, how you talk?" she said. "I never go to a motel without a chaperon . . . never!"

"And," Mason went on, "Binney Denham was found sprawled out stone dead in the unit you had been occupying. A .38 revolver had sent a bullet through his—"

She stepped back, her face white, her eyes wide and round. Her lips opened as though she might be going to scream. She pressed her knuckles up against her lips, hard.

Mason nodded to Paul Drake, calmly pushed his way into the apartment, closing the door behind him. He moved over to a chair, sat down, lit a cigarette, and said, "Sit down, Paul," acting as though he might have owned the apartment.

The girl looked at him for several long seconds, terror in her eyes.

At length she asked, "Is this . . . is this on the up and up?"

"Ring up the police," Mason said. "They'll tell you."

"What do *I* want with the police?"

"It's probably the other way around at that," Mason told her. "They'll be here any minute. Want to tell us what happened?"

She moved over to a chair, eased down to sit on the extreme edge.

"Any time," Mason said.

114

"What's *your* interest in it, Mr. Mason?"

"I'm representing Stewart Bedford. Police seem to think he might have had something to do with the murder."

"Gosh!" she said in a hushed voice. "He could have at that!"

"What happened?" Mason asked.

She said, "It was a shakedown. I don't know the details. Binney has hired me on several occasions to do jobs for him."

"What sort of jobs?"

"Keep the sucker out of circulation until Binney has the cash all in hand. Then Binney gives me a signal and I turn him loose."

"Why keep him out of circulation?" Mason asked.

"So he won't change this mind at the last minute and so we can be certain he isn't working with any firm of private detectives."

"What do you do?"

"I keep their minds on other things."

"Such as what?"

"Am I supposed to draw diagrams?"

"What did you do with Bedford?"

"I kept his mind on other things . . . and it was a job. He's in love with his wife. I tried to get him interested, and I might as well have been an ice cube on the drainboard of the kitchen sink. Then after a while we really did get friendly, and— Don't make any mistake about it. That's all it was. Just a good, decent friendship. I like the guy.

"I made up my mind then and there that that was to be my last play in the sucker racket. When I saw the way he felt about his wife, the way he . . . well, I'm young yet. There's still a chance. Maybe some man will feel that way about me some day if he meets me in the right way. He's never going to feel that way about me the way things are now."

"So what did you do?"

"That," she said, "is where somebody gave us both a double cross."

"What happened?"

"I went out. I left a bottle of liquor on the table. Somebody must have doped the liquor. We came back and had a drink. I didn't even know I was drugged until I woke up sometime after dark. Bedford was still sleeping. I'd given him about twice as much whisky as I took. I felt his pulse. It was strong and regular, so I figured there hadn't been any harm done. I thought for a while it might have been knockout drops, and those can be dangerous. I guess this was one of the barbiturates. It didn't seem to hurt anything."

"And then what?"

She said, "I took a shower and got dressed and put on some other clothes. I knew that it wouldn't be very long. The banks had closed and Binney should be showing up any minute."

"And he did?"

"He did."

"What did he tell you?"

"Told me that everything was clear and we could leave."

"Then what happened?"

"Then I accused him of drugging the drink, and he denied it. I got a little hot under the collar. I thought he didn't trust me any more. I was mad anyway. I told him that the next time he had a deal he could just get some other girl to do the job for him. One thing led to another. I told him Bedford was asleep. We tried to wake him up. We couldn't wake him. He'd get up—to a sitting position—and then lurch back to the pillows. He was limber-legged.

"Okay, there wasn't anything I could do about it. He was just going to have to sleep it off. I was mad at Binney, but that wasn't putting any starch in Bedford's legs.

"I wasn't going to stick around there. He had money. He could get a cab and get home. I pinned a note on his sleeve, saying things were all right, that he could leave any time. Then I went out to my car."

"Where was Binney Denham?"

"Denham was in his car."

"Then what did you do?"

"I drove back and turned the car in at the rental agency the way I was supposed to. On a deal of that sort I'm not supposed to try and get anything back on the deposit. I just park the car in the lot with the keys in it, walk toward the office as though I'm going to check in, and then just keep on going. They find the car parked, with the keys in it. There's a fifty-buck deposit on the thing and only eleven or twelve dollars due. They wait a while to see if anyone's coming back for the credit and then, after a while, some clerk clears the records, puts the surplus in his pocket and that's all there is to it."

"Did you leave Binney behind?"

"No, he pulled out about the same time I did."

"Then he must have turned around and gone back."

"I guess so. Was his car there?"

Mason shook his head. "Apparently not. What kind of a car?"

"A nondescript Chevy," she said. "He wants a car that nobody can describe, a car that looks so much like all the other cars on the road nobody pays any attention to it."

"Was there any reason for him to have gone back?"

"Not that I know of. He had the money."

"Was there anything he wanted to see Bedford about?"

"Not that I know. He had the dough. What else would he have wanted?"

Mason frowned. "It must have been something. He went back to see Bedford for some reason. He couldn't have

117

ing?"

"Not Binney."

"Do you know what the shakedown was?"

"Binney never tells me."

"What name did you give?"

"Geraldine Corning. That's my professional name."

"Planning on taking a trip?" Mason asked, indicating the new baggage by the closet door.

"I could be."

"Make enough out of this sort of stuff to pay?"

She said bitterly, "If I made a hundred times as much, it wouldn't pay. What's a person's self-respect worth?"

"Then you can't help Bedford at all?" Mason asked.

"I can't help him, and I can't hurt him. He paid, and paid up like a gentleman. It was quite a shakedown this time—twenty thousand bucks. All in traveler's checks."

"What did you do with them?"

"I got him to sign them and I put them out in the glove compartment of the rented car. That was what we had agreed to do. Binney was hanging around there some place where he could see.

"We'd made arrangements so that we were sure we were safe. We knew we couldn't be followed. We just cruised around until we were dead certain of that. I doubled and twisted and Binney followed until we knew no one was tailing us. Then I let Bedford pick whatever motel he wanted. That gave him confidence, relaxed him.

"I locked him in so he couldn't get out, went to the phone booth, called Binney, told him where I was and told him the mark had signed the traveler's checks."

"Then what?"

"Then I left them in the glove compartment of the rented car. That was the procedure we'd agreed on. Binney took the checks out and got them cashed."

"Do you have any idea how he went about doing it?"

She shook her head. "Probably he has a stand-in with

a banker friend somewhere. I don't know. I don't think he put them into circulation as regular checks. He just handled the deal his own way."

"How about Binney? Did he have an accomplice?"

She shook her head.

"He referred to a man he called Delbert."

She laughed. "Binney was the smooth one! Suckers would get so infuriated at this fictitious Delbert they could kill him with their bare hands, but they always had a certain sympathy for Binney. He was always *so* sweet and *so* apologetic."

"You were his only partner?"

"Don't be silly! I wasn't a partner. I was a paid employee. Sometimes he'd give me a couple of hundred extra, but not often. Binney was a one-way street on money. Getting dough out of that little double-crosser was—"

"Yes, go on," Mason prompted as her voice died down.

She shook her head.

"He double-crossed you?"

"Go get lost, will you? Why should I sit here and blab all I know. Me and my big mouth!"

Mason tried another line of approach.

"So you made up your mind it was your last case?"

"After talking with Bedford I did."

"How did that happen? What did Bedford say to you?"

"Damned if I know. I guess he really didn't say anything. It was the way he felt about his wife, the way he'd look right past me. He was so much in love with his wife he couldn't see any other woman. I got to wondering how a woman would go about getting the respect of a man like that . . . hell! I don't know what happened. Just put it down that I got religion, if you want to put a price tag on everything."

Mason said, "We only have your word for it. It was a sweet opportunity for a double cross. You yourself admit you had decided to quit the racket. You could have told Binney you were quitting. Binney might not have liked that. You admit you and Binney were in there working with Bedford, trying to get him to wake up. You had undoubtedly gone through Bedford's brief case and knew what was in it. When the party got rough you could have pumped a shot into Binney's back, gone through him to the tune of twenty thousand dollars, and simply driven away."

She said, "That's your nasty legal mind. You lawyers do think of the damnedest things."

"Anything wrong with the idea?"

"Everything's wrong with it."

"Such as what?"

"I told you I was quitting. I told you I'd got religion. Would I get moral and decide to quit a racket and then plan on bumping a guy off to get twenty grand? That'd be a hell of a way to get religion!"

"Perhaps you had to kill him," Mason said, watching her with narrow eyes. "Binney may not have liked the idea of your getting religion. He may have had ideas of his own. The party may have got rough."

She said, "You're bound to make me the fall guy, win, lose, or draw, aren't you? You're a lawyer. Your client has money, social position, political prestige. I have nothing. You'll throw me to the wolves to save your client. I'm a damn fool even to talk with you."

Mason said, "If you killed him in self-defense, I feel certain Mr. Bedford would see that you—"

"Get lost," she interrupted.

Mason got to his feet. "I just wanted to get your story."

"You've had it."

"If anything happened and you *did* have to act in self-defense, it would strengthen your case if you reported the facts to the police. You should also know that any evidence of flight can be construed as an admission of guilt."

She said sarcastically, "You've probably got a lot of things on your mind, Mr. Mason. I've got a lot of things on *my* mind now. I'm not going to detain you any longer and I'm not going to let you detain me."

She got up and walked to the door.

The two men walked slowly back down the stairs. "Have your operative keep her shadowed, Paul," Mason said. "I have a hunch she's planning on making a break for it."

"Want to try and stop her if she does?"

"Gosh no! I only want to find out where she goes."

"That might be difficult."

"See that your operative has money," Mason said. "Let him get on the same plane that she takes. Go wherever she goes."

"Okay," Drake said. "You go get in the car. I'll talk with my operative."

Mason walked over to his car. Drake walked past the parked automobile, jerked his head slightly, then walked on around the corner.

The man got out of the parked automobile, walked to the corner, overtook Drake, had a few minutes' brief conversation, then turned back to the car.

Drake came over to Mason and said, "He'll let us know anything that happens and he'll follow her wherever she goes; only the guy doesn't have a passport."

"That's all right," Mason said. "She won't have one either. Your man has enough money to cover expenses?"

"He has now," Drake said.

"We have to be certain she doesn't know she's being shadowed, Paul."

"This man's good. You want her to run, Perry?"

Mason said, somewhat musingly, "I wish she didn't give that impression of sincerity, Paul. Sure I want her to run. I'm representing a client who is accused of murder. According to her own story this girl had every reason to kill Binney Denham. Now if she resorts to flight I can accuse her of being the killer, *unless* the police find more evidence against Bedford. Therefore, I want her to have

121

lots of rope so she can hang herself . . . but somehow she bothers me. The story she tells arouses my sympathy."

"Don't start getting soft, Perry. She's a professional con woman. It's her business to make a sob-sister story sound reasonable. It's my guess she killed Denham. Don't shed any tears over her."

"I won't shed any tears," Mason said. "And if she dusts out of here in a hurry I've just about got a verdict of not guilty in the bag for Stewart G. Bedford."

■ 15 ■

MASON SAT IN THE ATTORNEY'S ROOM AT THE JAIL AND looked across at Bedford.

"I presume," he said, "you had that hit-and-run thing all figured out so you could save your wife's good name and were willing to sacrifice yourself in order to keep her from becoming involved."

Bedford nodded.

"Well, why the devil didn't you tell *me* what you were going to do?" Mason asked.

"I was afraid you'd disapprove."

"How did you get the details?" Mason asked.

"I took care of that all right," Bedford said. "As it happens, it was a case that I knew something about. This old woman was related to one of my employees. The doctors had decided she needed rather an expensive operation. My employee didn't approach me on it, but he *did* tell the whole story to Elsa Griffin. She relayed it to me. I told her to see that the man was able to get an advance which would cover the cost of the operation, and then told her to raise his wages in thirty days so that the raise would just about take care of payments on the advance. Two nights later the old woman started to cross the street, apparently in sort of a daze, and someone hit her and hit her hard. They never did find out who it was."

"Will your employee get suspicious?" Mason asked.

"I don't think so. The story was not told to me but to Elsa Griffin. Of course, that's one angle that I've got to take care of. Elsa will handle that for me."

"Well, you've stuck your neck in the noose now," Mason said.

"It's not so bad," Bedford told him. "As I understand it, a felony outlaws within three years, so they can't prosecute me on the hit-and-run charge because it's over three years ago. Don't you see, Mason? I simply *had* to have something that they could pin on me so there would be an excuse for me to be paying blackmail to Denham. Otherwise, the newspaper reporters would have started trying to find what it was that Denham had on me, and of course they'd have thought about my wife right away, started looking into her past, and then the whole ugly thing would have been out.

"In this way, I've covered my tracks in such a way that no one will ever think to investigate Mrs. Bedford."

"Let's hope so," Mason told him.

"Now look, Mason. I think I know who killed Denham."

"Who?"

"You remember that there was a woman prowling around the motel down there, a woman whose presence can't be accounted for.

"Now, I've got this thing figured out pretty well. Denham was a blackmailer. Someone decided that the only way out was to see that Denham was killed. The only way to kill him so that it wouldn't arouse suspicion and point directly to the person committing the murder was to wait until Denham was blackmailing someone else and then pull the job. In that way, it would be a perfect setup. It would look as though the other person had done the job."

"Go on," Mason said.

"So, as I figure it, this woman was either shadowing Denham or had some way of knowing when Denham was pulling a job. She knew that he was blackmailing me. She followed Denham down to the motel. When he got the payment from me, she killed him."

"With your gun?" Mason asked drily.

"No, no, now wait—I'm coming to that. I tell you I've got the whole thing all figured out."

"All right," Mason said. "How do you have it figured out?"

"Obviously she couldn't have followed Geraldine Corning and me down to the motel. In the first place, Geraldine took all sorts of precautions to keep from being followed, and in the second place, I was the one who picked the motel after she made up her mind that we weren't being followed. She said I could pick any motel I wanted, and I picked that one."

"Okay," Mason said. "You're making sense so far."

"All right. This woman knew, however, that Denham was getting ready to put the bite on another victim, so she started shadowing Denham. Denham drove down to the motel to pick up the money. She didn't have anything on him at that time. He went back and cashed the checks. That was where this woman *knew* that Denham was on another job.

"So when Denham came back to tell Geraldine that the coast was clear, Geraldine left and the woman had her chance. She had to be hiding down there in the motel. Naturally, she couldn't hide right on the grounds, so she tried the doors of the adjoining units. It just happened that Elsa had left the door of twelve unlocked because she didn't have anything valuable in there. The woman slipped into unit twelve and used it as her headquarters. Then she must have killed Denham with *her* gun.

"After that she cased the place and found that I was lying there asleep, apparently drugged. My brief case was on the floor. Naturally, she got to wondering who I was and how it happened I was asleep, and she went through the brief case. She saw the card giving my name and address in the brief case and she found my gun in there. What better than for her to take out the gun and conceal it where it would never be found. In that way I would be taking the rap for Denham's murder."

"Could be," Mason said noncommittally.

"Therefore, I want you to move heaven and earth to find that woman," Bedford said. "When we find her and get the *real* murder weapon, the ballistics experts can prove that it was the gun with which the murder was committed. Then we can find out what she did with my gun after the shooting.

"Can't you see the play, Mason? This woman prowler the manager saw in unit twelve is the key to the whole mystery.

"Now, I understand you sent Elsa back to the cabin to get fingerprints. Evidently our minds were working along the same lines. Elsa says she got some very good fingerprints of this woman, particularly a couple she got from a glass doorknob."

"Of course, a lot of the prints were Elsa's," Mason pointed out.

"I know. I know," Bedford said impatiently. "But some of them weren't. Elsa didn't even open that closet door. The two fingerprints on the knob simply *had* to be those of the woman.

"Now, this manager of the motel—whatever his name is—had a chance to talk with this woman. He saw her coming out of the motel, asked her what she was doing and all of that stuff. That makes him a valuable witness. I want you to have your men talk to him again and get the most minute description possible. Then you have these fingerprints to work on. Now damn it, Mason! Get busy on this thing and play it from that angle. It's a hunch I have."

"I see," Mason said.

Bedford said impatiently, "Mason, I've got money. I've got lots of money. The sky is the limit in this thing. You get all the detectives in the city if you need 'em, but you find that woman. She's the one we want."

"Suppose she did kill him with your gun?"

"She couldn't have. She shadowed Denham down there for one purpose, and only one purpose; she intended to kill him. She'd hardly intend to kill him with her bare hands."

Mason said, "Before we go all out on *that* theory, I'd like to be certain the murder wasn't committed with your gun. In order to prove that we need to have either the gun or some bullets that were fired from it. You don't know of any trees or stumps where you put up a target for practice, do you?"

"You mean so you can find some old bullets?"

"Yes."

"No. I don't think I ever fired the gun."

"How long have you had it?"

"Five or six years."

"You signed a firearms register when you bought it?"

"I can't remember. I guess I must have."

Mason said, "I have another lead. I want you to keep it confidential."

"What's that?"

"The blonde who was with you in the motel."

"What about her?"

"She had the opportunity and the motive," Mason pointed out. "She is the really logical suspect."

Bedford's face darkened. "Mason, what's the matter with you? That girl was a good kid. She probably had knocked around but she wasn't the type to commit a murder."

"How do you know?" Mason asked.

"Because I spent a day with her. She's a good kid. She was going to quit the racket."

"That makes her all the more suspect," Mason said. "Suppose she told Binney Denham she was going to quit and he started putting on pressure. That left her with only one out. Binney must have had enough on her to crack the whip if she tried to get free."

Bedford shook his head emphatically. "You're all wet, Mason. Get after this woman in number twelve."

"And," Mason went on, "we could convince a jury that the blonde would logically have taken the gun from your brief case and used it, whereas any woman who was shadowing Binney, intending to kill him, would have had her own gun."

"That's what I'm telling you."

"So then, if you try to play it your way," Mason went on, "and the murder weapon does turn out to have been your gun, you're hooked."

"You play it the way I'm telling you," Bedford instructed. "I have a hunch on this and I always play my hunches. After all, Mason, if I'm wrong it'll be my own funeral."

"You may mean that figuratively," Mason told him, getting up to go, "but that's one thing you've said that's *really* true."

■ 16 ■

MASON WAS YAWNING WITH WEARINESS AS HE FITTED A latchkey to the door of his private office and swung it open.

Della Street looked up from her secretarial desk, said, "Hello, Chief. How's it coming?"

"I thought I told you to go home and go to bed."

"I went home. I went to bed. I slept. I'm back and ready for another night session if necessary."

Mason shuddered. "Don't even think about it. One of those is enough to last me for quite a while."

"That's because you're under such a strain. You can't relax in-between times."

"Today," Mason told her, "there haven't been any in-between times."

"Paul Drake phoned while you were gone. He says he has something he thinks will prove interesting. He wants to come down and talk with you."

"Give him a ring," Mason said.

Della Street called Paul Drake, using the unlisted telephone, and not putting the call through the switchboard.

Mason tilted back in the swivel chair, closed his eyes, stretched his arms above his head and gave a prodigious yawn. "The trouble with a case of this sort," he said, "is that you have to keep one jump ahead of the police, and the police don't go to bed. They work in shifts."

Della Street nodded, heard Drake's tap on the panels of the door, and got up to open it for him.

"Hi, Paul," Mason said. "What's new?"

"You look all in," Drake told him.

"I had a hard day yesterday, and then things really started coming pretty fast last night. How are the police doing?"

"The police," Drake said, "are jubilant."

"How come?"

"They've found some bit of evidence that makes them feel good."

"What is it, Paul?"

"I can't find out, and neither can anyone else. They seem to think it's really something. However, that isn't what I wanted to see you about at the moment. I suppose you've heard that your client, Bedford, has made another statement."

Mason groaned. "I can't get back and forth fast enough to keep up with his statements. What's he said this time?"

"He told reporters he wants an *immediate* trial, and the district attorney says that if Bedford isn't bluffing, he'll give it to him, that there's a date on the calendar reserved for a case which has just been continued. Because Bedford is a businessman and insists that his name must be cleared and all that stuff, it looks as though the presiding judge might go along with them."

"Very nice," Mason said sarcastically. "Bedford never seems to think it's necessary to consult his lawyer before issuing these statements to the press.

"What about Harry Elston, Paul? Have you been able to get any line on him?"

"Not a thing, and the police haven't been able to," Drake said. "Elston opened that safe-deposit box about nine forty-five last night. He had a brief case with him, and, as I said, no one knows whether he put in or took out, but police are now inclined to think he took out and *then* put in."

"How come?"

"It was a joint lock box in both names. Now there isn't a thing in there in the name of Harry Elston, but the box is jammed full of papers belonging to Binney Denham.

They're papers that just aren't worth a hang, things that nobody would keep in a lock box."

"Some people keep strange things in lock boxes," Mason said.

"These are old letters, receipted statements, credit cards that have expired, automobile insurance that's expired, just a whole mess of junk that really isn't worth keeping, much less putting in a safe-deposit box."

Mason pursed his lips thoughtfully.

"The point is," Drake went on, "that the lock box is full—just so jam full you couldn't get another letter in it. The police feel that the idea of this was to keep them from thinking anything had been taken *out*. They're pretty well convinced the lock box was full of cash or negotiable securities, that Elston found out Denham was dead, cleaned out the box and put this stuff in it."

"How'd he find out Denham was dead?" Mason asked.

"Well, for a while the police were very much interested in the answer to that one. Now they're not concerned any more. They think that they have a dead open-and-shut case against Bedford. They think that any jury will convict him of first-degree murder. The D.A. says he hasn't decided whether he will ask for the death penalty as yet. He has stated that, while he will be ever mindful of the responsibilities of his office, he has never received any consideration from Bedford's counsel and sees no reason for extending any courtesies."

Mason grinned. "He wants to send my client to the gas chamber in order to get even with me. Is that it?"

"He didn't express it that way in so many words, but you don't have to look too far in between the lines to gather his thought."

"Nice guy!" Mason said. "Anything else, Paul?"

"Yes. This is what I really wanted to see you about. I got a telephone call just before I came in here. The operative who was shadowing Grace Compton only had time for a brief telephone call. He's at the airport. Our blonde friend is headed for Acapulco, Mexico. I guess she wants to do a little swimming. My operative is keeping her under surveillance. He has a seat on the same plane. He didn't have time to talk. He just gave me a flash."

"What did you tell him?"

"Told him to go to Acapulco."

"When are they leaving?"

"There's a plane for Mexico City leaving at eight-thirty."

Mason looked at his watch. "And she's down at the airport already?"

Drake nodded.

"What the devil is she doing waiting down there?"

"Darned if I know," Drake said.

"How has she disguised herself?" Mason asked.

"How did you know about the disguise?" Drake exclaimed. "I hadn't mentioned it."

"Figure it out for yourself, Paul. She knows that police have a pretty damn good description of her. She knows that they're looking for her. When the police are looking for someone, they're pretty apt to keep the airport under surveillance. Therefore, if Grace Compton was going to Acapulco, Mexico, the logical thing would be for her to stay in her apartment until the last minute, then dash out and make a run to get aboard the plane. Every minute that she's hanging around that airport makes it that much more dangerous for her. Therefore she must have resorted to some sort of disguise which she feels will be a complete protection."

"Well," Drake said, "you hit the nail right on the head that time, Perry. She's disguised so that no one's going to recognize her."

Mason raised his eyebrows. "How, Paul?"

Drake said, "I don't know the details. The only thing I know is that my man told me she was so disguised, that if he hadn't followed her and seen her go through the transformation, he wouldn't be able to recognize her. You see, he had time for a flash but no details. He says she's waiting to take the plane to Acapulco, and that's all I know."

"He'll call in again?" Mason asked.

"Whenever he gets a chance he phones in a report."

"He's one of your regular operatives?"

"Yes."

"Do you suppose he knows Della Street?"

"I think he does, Perry. He's been up and down in the elevator a thousand times."

Mason turned to Della Street. "Go on down to the airport, Della. Get a cab. Paul's operative will probably phone in before you get there. See if you can contact him. Describe him, Paul."

Drake said, "He's fifty-two. He used to have red hair. It's turning kind of a pink now and he's bald on top, but Della won't see that because he wears a gray hat with the brim pulled fairly well down. He's a slender man, about five foot seven, weight about a hundred and thirty-five pounds. He goes for gray, wears a gray suit, a gray tie, a gray hat. He has gray eyes, and he's the sort of guy you can look directly at and still not see."

"I'll find him," Della Street said.

"Not by looking for him," Drake said. "He's the most inconspicuous guy on earth."

"All right," Della said, laughing, "I'll be looking for the most inconspicuous guy on earth. What do I do after that, Chief?"

Mason said, "You get this girl spotted. Try to engage her in conversation. Don't be obvious about it. Let her make the first break if possible. Sit down beside her and start sobbing in a handkerchief. Be in trouble yourself. If she's frightened that may make her feel she has a bond in common with you."

"What am I going to be sobbing about?" Della Street asked.

Mason said, "Your boy friend was to have flown

down from San Francisco. He's stood you up. You're waiting, watching plane after plane."

"Okay," Della said. "I'm on my way."

"Got plenty of money for expenses?"

"I think so."

"Go to the safe and take out three hundred bucks," Mason said.

"Gosh! Am I supposed to go to Acapulco too?"

"I'm darned if I know," Mason told her. "If she gives you a tumble and starts confiding in you, stay with her as long as she's talking. If that means getting on a plane, get on a plane."

Della Street hurried to the emergency cash drawer in the safe, took out some money, pushed it down in her purse, grabbed her hat and coat, said, "On my way, Chief."

"Phone in if you get a chance," Mason said. "Use the unlisted telephone."

When she had gone, Mason turned to Paul Drake. "Now let's find out about this girl's apartment, Paul."

"What about it?"

"Did she give it up or simply close it and lock it?"

"Gosh! I don't know," Drake said.

"Find out, and when you find out let me know. If she's given up the apartment, and it's for rent, get a couple of good operatives whom you can trust, a man and woman. Have them pose as a married couple looking for an apartment. Pay a deposit to hold the place, or do anything necessary so they can get in there and dust for fingerprints."

"You want some of this girl's prints?"

Mason nodded.

"Why?"

"So I can show them to the police."

"The best way to get them," Drake said, "would be to give the police a tip on what's happening."

Mason shook his head.

"Why not?" Drake asked. "After all, they have her fingerprints. They have them from the car and from the motel and—"

"And they're building up a case against Stewart Bedford," Mason said. "They wouldn't do a thing to this girl now. They'd think she was a red herring I was drawing across the trail. For another thing I want the prints of someone else who must have been in that apartment. However, the main reason I don't want the police in on it is that I don't dare risk the legal status of what's happening."

"What's the legal status of what's happening?"

"A killer is resorting to flight," Mason said.

Drake frowned. "You got enough evidence to convict her of murder, Perry, even if you have evidence of flight?"

Mason said, "I don't want to *convict* her of murder, Paul. I want to acquit Stewart G. Bedford of murder. See what you can do about getting fingerprints and be sure to tell your man to watch out for Della Street. I have a feeling that we're beginning to get somewhere."

■ 17 ■

IT WAS SEVEN O'CLOCK WHEN DELLA STREET MADE HER report over the unlisted phone.

"I'm in a booth out here at the airport, Chief. I haven't been able to get to first base with her."

"Did you contact Drake's man?" Mason asked.

"Yes, that is, he contacted me. Paul certainly described him all right. I was looking all around for an inconspicuous man and not being able to find him, and then something kept rubbing against me, and it was the elbow of the man standing next to me at the newsstand. I moved away and then suddenly I looked at him and knew that was the man."

"And you picked out Grace Compton?" Mason asked.

"He did. She'd have fooled me."

"What's she done?" Mason asked.

"Well, she has on dark glasses, the biggest lensed, darkest dark glasses I've ever seen. Her hair is in strings. She's wearing a maternity outfit with—"

"A maternity outfit!" Mason exclaimed.

"That's right," Della Street said. "With a little padding and the proper kind of an outfit a girl with a good figure can do wonders."

"And you couldn't get anywhere with her?"

"Nowhere," Della Street said. "I've sobbed into my handkerchief. I've made every approach I could think of that wouldn't be recognized as an approach. I've got precisely nowhere."

"Anything else?" Mason asked.

"Yes. When she got slowly up and started for the restroom, I made a point of beating her to it. I knew where she was heading so I was in there first. I found out one reason why she's wearing those heavy dark glasses.

"That girl has had a beautiful beating. One eye is discolored so badly that the bruise would show below the edge of the dark glasses if she didn't keep it covered. She stood in front of a mirror and put flesh-colored grease paint on her cheek. I could see then that her mouth is swollen and—"

"And you're not getting anywhere?" Mason asked.

"Not with any build-up I can think of. No."

Mason said, "Go out and contact Drake's man, Della. Tell him that you'll take over the watching job while he calls me. Have him call me on this phone. Give him the unlisted number. Tell him to call at once. You keep your eye on the subject while he's doing it."

"Okay, I'll contact him right away, but I'd better not be seen talking to him. I'll scribble a note and slip it to him."

"That's fine," Mason said. "Be darn certain you're not caught at it. Remember, that's one bad thing about dark glasses. You can never tell where a person's eyes are looking."

"I'll handle it all right," she said, "and you can trust Drake's man. He can brush past you and pick up a note without anyone having the least idea of what's happened. He looks like a mild-mannered, shy, retiring, henpecked husband who's out for the first time without his wife, and is afraid of his own shadow."

"Okay," Mason said. "Get on the job. Now, Della, after this man telephones me and comes back out of the phone booth, grab a cab and come on back to the office."

"What a short-lived vacation!" she said. "I was thinking of a two-weeks' stay in Acapulco."

"You should have got her talking then. I can't pay out my client's money to have you sob your way down to Mexico unless you get results."

"My sobbing left her as cold and hard as a cement sidewalk," she said. "I should have tried a maternity outfit and the pregnancy approach. I can tell you one thing, Chief, that woman is scared stiff."

"She should be," Mason said. "Get Paul's man to phone, Della."

Some five minutes later Mason's unlisted phone rang. The lawyer picked up the receiver, said, "Hello," and a man's voice talking in a low, drab monotone, said, "This is Drake's man, Mr. Mason. You wanted me?"

"Yes. How did she work the disguise?"

"She came out of her apartment wearing a veil and heavy dark glasses. She got in a taxicab, went to the Siesta Arms Apartment House. She went inside. I couldn't see where she went, but I managed to butt my car into the rear end of the waiting taxi, got out and apologized profusely, got the guy in conversation, gave him five dollars to cover any damage that might have been sustained, which of course was jake with him because there wasn't any. He told me that he was waiting for a fare who had gone upstairs to pack up for her sister, that her sister was pregnant and was going to the airport to take a plane to San Francisco. This sister was to pick up the cab."

"Okay, then what happened?" Mason asked.

"Well, I waited there at the apartment house, right back of the cab. This woman didn't suspect a thing. When she came out, I would sure have been fooled if it wasn't for her shoes. She was wearing alligator skin shoes when she went in, and despite all the maternity disguise, she was wearing those same shoes when she came out. I let the cab driver take off, and I loafed along way, way behind, because I was pretty sure where they were going."

"They went to the airport?"

"That's right."

"And then what?"

"This woman got a tourist permit, bought a ticket to Acapulco, and checked the baggage. When she went down there she didn't have any more idea when the next plane was leaving than I did. She just sat down to wait for the next plane to Mexico City."

"She isn't suspicious?"

"Not a bit."

"Ride along on the same plane with her, just to make sure she doesn't try to disguise her appearance again. You'll be met in Mexico City by Paul Drake's correspondents there. You can work with them and they'll work with you. They know the ropes, speak the language, and have all the official pull they need. It will be better to handle it that way than for you to try and handle it alone."

"Okay, thanks."

"Now get this," Mason said. "This is important! You saw Paul Drake and me when we went up to call on Grace Compton?"

"That's right."

"You saw her when she came out?"

"Yes."

"She didn't come out and go anywhere between the time Drake and I left and the time she came out with the baggage and got the taxicab?"

"That's right."

"How much traffic was there in and out of that apartment building?"

"Quite a bit."

Mason said, "Some man went in. I'd like very much to spot him."

"Do you know what he looked like?"

"I haven't the faintest idea as yet," Mason said, "but I may have later. I'm wondering if you could recognize such a man if I dug him up. Could you?"

The expressionless voice, still in the same drab monotone, said, "Hell, no! I'm not a human adding machine. I was there to watch that blonde and see that she didn't give us the slip. Nobody told me to—"

"That's all right," Mason interrupted. "I was just trying to find out. That's all."

"If you'd told me, then I might have—"

"No, no, it's all right."

"Okay, anything else?"

"That's all," Mason said. "Have a good time."

For the first time there was expression in the man's voice. "Don't kid yourself, I won't!" he said.

When Della Street returned to the office, she found Perry Mason pacing the floor.

"What's the problem?" she asked.

Mason said, "I've got some cards. I've got to play them just right to be sure that each one of them takes a trick. I don't want to play into the hands of the prosecution so they can put trumps on my aces."

"Do they have that many trumps?" Della Sreet asked.

138

"In a criminal case," Mason said, "the prosecution has *all* the trumps."

Mason resumed his pacing of the floor, and had been pacing for some five minutes, when Drake's code knock sounded on the panel of the exit door.

Mason nodded to Della Street.

She opened the door. Drake came in and said, "Well, you had the right hunch, Perry. The babe's rent was up on the tenth. She told them there had been a change of plans because her sister expected to be confined in San Francisco and was having trouble. She said she had to leave for San Francisco almost immediately. She left money, for the cleaning charges and all that, and told the landlady how sorry she was."

"Wait a minute," Mason said. "Was this a face-to-face conversation or—?"

"No, she talked with the landlady on the telephone," Drake answered.

Mason said, "Some fellow gave her a working over. I'd sure like to find out who it was."

"Well," Drake said, "I put my operatives on the job and they tied up the apartment. They gave the landlady a fifty-dollar deposit, told her they wanted to stay in there and get the feel of the place for a while. She said to stay as long as they wanted.

"So they went all over the place for fingerprints and lifted everything they could find. Then they cleaned the place off so that no one could tell lifts had been made."

"How many lifts?" Mason asked.

Drake pulled an envelope out of his pocket. "They're all on these cards," he said. "Forty-eight of them."

Mason shuffled through the cards. "How are they identified, Paul?"

"Numbered lightly in pencil on the back."

"Pencil?"

"That's right. We ink the pencil in afterwards before we go to court. But just in case there are two or three prints you wouldn't want to use, you can change the numbers when they're written in pencil. In that way, when you get to court, your numbers are all in consecutive order. Otherwise, you might get into court and have prints from one to eight inclusive, then a gap of three or four prints, and then another set of consecutive numbers. That would be an invitation to opposing counsel to demand the missing fingerprints and raise hell generally."

"I see," Mason said.

"Well, that's it," Drake told him. "We've got our deposit up on the apartment. It won't be touched until the fifteenth. Now then, do you want the police to get a tip?"

"Not yet! Not yet!" Mason said.

"With that babe down in Acapulco, you may have trouble getting the evidence you want," Drake said.

Mason grinned. "I already have it, Paul."

Drake heaved himself up out of the chair. "Well, I hope you don't get another brain storm along about midnight tonight. See you tomorrow, Perry."

"Be seeing you," Mason said.

Della Street looked at Mason in puzzled perplexity. "You've got the expression of the cat that has just found the open jar of whipping cream," she said.

Mason said, "Go to the safe, Della. Get the fingerprints that Elsa Griffin got from that motel unit number twelve."

Della Street brought in the envelopes.

"Two sets," she said. "One of them the prints that were found to be those of Elsa Griffin, and the others are four that are prints of a stranger. These four are on numbered cards. The numbers are fourteen, sixteen, nine, and twelve respectively."

Mason nodded, busied himself with the cards Drake had handed him.

"All right, Della, make a note," he said.

"What is it?"

"Pencil number seven on Drake's list is being given an inked number fourteen. Number three on Drake's list given an inked number sixteen. Number nineteen on Drake's list given a number nine. Number thirty on Drake's list given the number twelve in ink. You got that?"

She nodded.

"All right," Mason said. "Take these cards and write the numbers in order on them—fourteen, sixteen, nine, and twelve. I want it in a woman's handwriting, and, while I wouldn't think of asking you to commit forgery, I'd certainly like to have the numbers as near a match for the numbers on these other cards as we can possibly make it."

"Why, Chief," Della Street said, "that's— Why those are the numbers of the significant lifted prints from unit twelve down there at the motel."

"Exactly," Mason said. "And as soon as you have these numbers copied on the cards, Della, you'll remember to produce them whenever I ask for latent prints on cards fourteen, sixteen, nine, and twelve."

"But, Chief, you can't do that!"

"Why not?"

"Why that's substituting evidence!"

"Evidence of what?"

"Why it's evidence of the person who was in that cottage. It's evidence that Mrs.—"

"Careful," Mason said. "No names."

"Well, it's evidence that that person was actually in that unit."

"How very interesting!" Mason said.

Della Street looked at him in startled consternation. "Chief, you can't do that! Don't you see what you're doing? You're just changing things all around. Why . . . Why—!"

"What am I doing?" Mason asked.

"Why you're numbering those cards fourteen, sixteen,

141

nine, and twelve and putting them in that envelope, and Elsa Griffin— Why she'll take the numbers on those cards, compare them with her notes and say that print number fourteen came from the glass doorknob and . . . well, in place of the person who was in there being there, it will mean that this blonde was in there instead."

Mason grinned. "And since the police have a whole flock of the blonde's fingerprints they'd have the devil of a time saying they didn't know who it was."

"But," Della Street protested, "then they would accuse Grace Compton of being the one who was in unit twelve when . . . when she wouldn't have been there at all."

"How do you know she wasn't there?" Mason asked.

"Well, her fingerprints weren't there."

Mason merely smiled.

"Chief, isn't . . . isn't there a law against that?"

"A law against what?"

"Destroying evidence."

"I haven't destroyed anything," Mason said.

"Well, switching things around. Isn't it against the law to show a witness a false—?"

"What's false about it?" Mason asked.

"It's a substitution. It's shuffling everything all around. It's—"

"There's nothing false about it," Mason said. "Each print is a true and correct fingerprint. I haven't altered the print any."

"But you've altered the numbers on the cards."

"Not at all," Mason said. "Drake told us that he put temporary pencil numbers on the cards so that it would be possible to ink in the numbers that we wanted."

Della Street said, "Well, you're practicing a deception on Elsa Griffin."

"I haven't said anything to Elsa Griffin."

"Well, you will if you show her these prints as being the ones that she took from that unit number twelve."

"If I don't *tell* her those were the prints that came

142

from unit number twelve, I wouldn't be practicing any deception. Furthermore, how the devil do we know that these prints are evidence?"

Della Street said, "Chief, *please* don't! You're getting way out on the end of a limb. In order to try and save Mrs. . . . well, you know who I mean if you don't want me to mention names. In order to save her, you're putting your neck in a noose and you're . . . you're *planting* evidence on that Compton girl."

Mason grinned. "Come on, Della, quit worrying about it. I'm the one that's taking the chances."

"I'll say you are."

"Get your hat," Mason told her. "I'll buy you a good steak dinner and then you can go home and get some sleep."

"What are *you* going to do?"

"Oh, I may as well go to bed myself. I think we're going to give Hamilton Burger a headache."

"But, Chief," Della said, "it's substituting evidence! Faking evidence! It's putting a false label on evidence! It's—"

"You forget," Mason said, "that we still have the original prints which were given us by Elsa Griffin. They still have the original numbers which she put on them. We've taken other prints and given them other numbers. That's our privilege. We can number those prints any way we want to. If by coincidence the numbers are the same, that's no crime. Come on. You're worrying too much."

JUDGE HARMON STROUSE LOOKED DOWN AT THE DEFENSE counsel table at Perry Mason, Mason's client, Stewart G. Bedford, seated beside him, and, immediately behind Bedford, a uniformed officer.

"The peremptory challenge is with the defense," Judge Strouse said.

"The defense passes," Mason said.

Judge Strouse glanced at Hamilton Burger, the barrel-chested, bull-necked district attorney whose vendetta with Perry Mason was well known.

"The prosecution is quite satisfied with the jury," Hamilton Burger snapped.

"Very well," Judge Strouse said. "The jurors will stand and be sworn to try the case."

Bedford leaned forward to whisper to Mason. "Well, now at least we'll know what they have against me," he said, "and what we have to fight. The evidence they presented before the grand jury was just barely sufficient to get an indictment, and that's all. They're purposely leaving me in the dark."

Mason nodded.

Hamilton Burger arose and said, "I am going to make a somewhat unprecedented move, Your Honor. This is an intelligent jury. It doesn't have to be told what I am going to try to do. I am waiving my opening statement. I will call as my first witness Thomas G. Farland."

Farland, being sworn, testified that he was a police officer, that on the sixth day of April he had been instructed to go to The Staylonger Motel, that he had met the manager there, a man named Morrison Brems, that he had exhibited his credentials, had stated that he wished to look in unit sixteen, that he had gone to unit sixteen and had there found a body lying on the floor. The body was that of a man who had apparently been shot, and the witness had promptly notified the Homicide Squad, which had in due time arrived with a deputy coroner, fingerprint experts, et cetera, that the witness had waited until the Homicide Squad arrived.

"Cross-examine!" Hamilton Burger snapped.

"How did you happen to go to the motel?" Mason asked.

"I was instructed."

"By whom?"

"By communications."

"In what way?"

"The call came over the radio."

"And what was said in the call?"

"Objected to as incompetent, irrelevant, and immaterial. Not proper cross-examination and hearsay," Hamilton Burger said.

Mason said, "The witness testified that he was 'instructed' to go to unit sixteen. Under the familiar rule that whenever a part of a conversation is brought out in direct examination the cross-examiner can show the entire conversation, I want to know what was said when the instructions were given to him."

"It's hearsay," Hamilton Burger said.

"It's a conversation," Mason said, smiling.

"The objection is overruled," Judge Strouse said. "The witness, having testified to part of the conversation, may relate it all on cross-examination."

"Well," Farland said, "it was just that I was to go to the motel, that's all."

"Anything said about what you might find there?"

"Yes."

"What?"

"A body."

"Anything said about how the announcer knew there was a body there?"

"He said it had been reported."

"Anything said about *how* it had been reported?"

"He said an anonymous telephone tip."

"Anything said about who gave the anonymous tip—whether it was a man's voice or a woman's voice?"

The witness hesitated.

"Yes or no?" Mason said.

"Yes," he said. "It was a woman's voice."

"Thank you," Mason said with exaggerated politeness. "That's all."

Hamilton Burger put a succession of routine witnesses on the stand, witnesses showing that the dead man had been identified as Binney Denham, that a .38 caliber bullet had fallen from the front of Denham's coat when the body was moved.

"Morrison Brems will be my next witness," Hamilton Burger said.

When Brems came forward and was sworn, Hamilton Burger nodded to Vincent Hadley, the assistant district attorney who sat on his left, and Hadley, a suave, polished courtroom strategist, examined the manager of the motel, bringing out the fact that on April sixth, sometime around eleven o'clock in the morning, the defendant, accompanied by a young woman, had stopped at his motel; that the defendant had told him he was to be joined by another couple from San Diego; that they wished two units; that the witness had suggested to the defendant it would be better to wait for the other couple to arrive and let them register, in which event they would be paying only for their half of the motel unit. However, the defendant had insisted on paying the whole charge and having immediate occupancy of the double.

"Under what name did the defendant register?" Vincent Hadley asked.

"Under the name of S. G. Wilfred."

"And wife?" Hadley asked.

"*And* wife."

"Then what happened?" Hadley asked.

"Well, I didn't pay too much attention to them after that. Of course, looking the situation over and the way it had been put up to me I thought—"

"Never mind what you thought," Hadley interrupted. "Just tell us what happened, what you observed, what you saw, what was said to you by the defendant, or by others in the presence of the defendant."

"Well, just where do you want me to begin?"

"Just answer the question. What happened next?"

"They were in there for a while, and then the girl—"

"Now, by the girl, are you referring to Mrs. Wilfred?"

"Well, of course she wasn't any Mrs. Wilfred."

"You don't *know* that," Hadley said. "She *registered* as Mrs. Wilfred, didn't she?"

"Well, the defendant here registered her as Mrs. Wilfred."

"All right. Call her Mrs. Wilfred then. What happened next?"

"Well, Mrs. Wilfred went out twice. The first time she went around to the outer door of unit fifteen and I thought she was going in that way, but—"

"Never mind what you thought. What did she *do?*"

"I know she locked him in, but I can't swear I saw the key turn in the lock, so I suppose you won't let me say a thing about that. Then after she'd done whatever it was she was doing, she went to the car and got out some baggage. She took that in to unit sixteen. Then a short time later she came out and went to the glove compartment of the car. I don't know how long she was there that time because I was called away and didn't get back for half an hour or so.

"Then quite a while later they both left the place, got in the car and drove away."

"Now just a minute," Hadley said. "Prior to the time

147

that you saw them drive away, had anyone else been near the car?"

"That I just can't swear to," Brems said.

"Then *don't* swear to it," Hadley said. "Just tell us what you know and what you saw."

"Well, I saw a beat-up sort of car parked down there by unit sixteen for a few minutes. I thought it was this other couple that had—"

"What did you *see?*"

"Well, I just saw this car parked there for a spell. After a while it drove away."

"Now the *car* didn't drive out. Someone must have driven it out."

"That's right."

"Do you know the person who was driving that car?"

"I didn't then. I do now."

"Who was it?"

"This here Mr. Denham—the man who was found dead."

"You saw his face?"

"Yes."

"Did he stop?"

"No, sir."

"He didn't stop when he drove his car out?"

"No, sir."

"Did he stop when he went in?"

"No, sir."

"All right. Now try to remember everything as you go along. What happened after that?"

"Well, of course I've got other things to do. I've got a whole motel to manage down there, and I can't just keep looking—"

"Just tell us what you saw, Mr. Brems. We don't expect you to tell us everything that happened. Only what *you saw.*"

"Well, the defendant and this girl—"

148

"You mean the one who had registered as Mrs. Wilfred?"

"Yes, that's the one."

"All right. What did they do?"

"They were out for quite a while. Then they came back in. I guess it was pretty late in the afternoon. I didn't look to get the exact time. They drove into the garage between the two units—"

"Now, just before that," Hadley interrupted. "While they were gone, did you have occasion to go down to the unit?"

"Well, yes, I did."

"What was the occasion?"

"I was checking up."

"Why?"

"Well . . . well, you see, when couples like that come in . . . well, we have three rates—our regular customer rate, our tourist rate, and our transient rate.

"Now, take a couple like this. We charge 'em about double the regular rates. Whenever they go out we check the units to see whether they're coming back or not.

"If they've left baggage, we look at it a bit if it's open. Sometimes if it isn't locked, we open it. Running a motel that way you have to cater to the temporary transients if you're going to stay in business, but you get high rates for doing it and usually a big turnover.

"Anyhow it isn't the sort of trade you like, and whenever the people go out, you go in and look around."

"And that's why you went in?"

"Yes, sir."

"And what did you do?"

"I tried the door of unit fifteen and it was locked. I tried the door of unit sixteen and *it* was locked."

"What did you do?"

"I opened the door with a passkey and went in."

"Which door?"

"Unit sixteen."

"What, if anything, did you find?"

"I found that the girl . . . that is, this Mrs. Wilfred . . . had a suitcase and a bag in unit sixteen and that the man had a brief case in unit fifteen."

"Did you look in the brief case?"

"I did."

"What did you see in it?"

"I saw a revolver."

"Did you look at the revolver?"

"Only in the brief case. I didn't want to touch it. I just saw it was a revolver and let it go at that, but I decided right then and there I'd better—"

"Never mind what you thought or what you decided. I'm asking you what you *did*, what you saw," Hadley said. "Now, let us get back to what happened after that."

"Yes, sir."

"Did you see the defendant again?"

"Yes, sir. He and this . . . this woman . . . this Mrs. Wilfred got back to the motel along late in the afternoon. They went inside and I didn't pay any more attention to them. I had some other things to do. Then I saw a car driving out somewhere around eight o'clock, I guess it was. Maybe a little after eight. I took a look at it and I saw it was this car the defendant had been driving, and this woman was in it. I didn't get a real good look at her, but somehow I didn't think anybody else was in that car with her."

"Had you heard anything unusual?"

"Personally, I didn't hear a thing. Some of the people in other parts of the motel did."

"Never mind that. I'm talking now about you personally. Did *you* hear anything unusual?"

"No, sir."

"And you so reported to the police when they questioned you?"

"That's right."

"When did you next have occasion to go to either unit fifteen or sixteen?"

"When this police officer came to me and said he wanted in."

"So what did you do then?"

"I got my passkey and went to the door of unit sixteen."

"Was the door locked?"

"No, sir. As a matter of fact, it wasn't."

"What happened?"

"I opened the door."

"And what did you see?"

"I saw the body of this man—the one they said was Binney Denham—lying sprawled there on the floor, with a pool of blood all around it."

"Did you look in unit fifteen?"

"Yes, sir."

"How did you get in there?"

"We went back out the door of unit sixteen and I tried the door of unit fifteen."

"Was it locked?"

"No, sir, it was unlocked."

"Was the defendant in there?"

"Not when we went in. He was gone."

"Was his brief case there?"

"No, sir."

"Did either the defendant or the woman who was registered by the defendant as his wife return to your motel later on?"

"No, sir."

"Did you subsequently accompany some of the authorities to the back of your lot?"

"Yes, sir. You could see his tracks going—"

"Now wait just a moment. I'm coming to that. What is in the back of your lot?"

"A barbed wire fence."

"What is the nature of the soil?"

"A soft, loam-type of soil when it's wet. It gets pretty hard in the summertime when the sun shines on it and it bakes dry. It's a regular California adobe."

"What was the condition of this soil on the night of April sixth?"

"Soft."

"Would it take the imprint of a man's foot?"

"Yes, sir, it sure would."

"Did you observe any such imprints when you took the authorities to the back of the lot?"

"Yes, sir."

"Are you acquainted with Lieutenant Tragg?"

"Yes, sir."

"Did you point out these tracks to Lieutenant Tragg?"

"I pointed out the route to him. *He* pointed out the tracks to *me*."

"And then what, if anything, did Lieutenant Tragg do?"

"Well, he went to the barbed wire fence right where the tracks showed somebody'd gone through the fence, and he found some threads. Some of the barbs on the barbed wire were pretty rusty and threads of cloth would stick easy."

"Now, from the time you saw Binney Denham, with his automobile which you have referred to as a rather beat-up car, near unit sixteen earlier in the day, did you see Mr. Denham again?"

"Not until I saw him lying there on the floor dead."

"Your motel is open to the public?"

"Sure. That's the idea of it."

"Mr. Denham could have come and gone without your seeing him?"

"Sure."

"You may cross-examine," Hadley said.

Mason said, "As far as you know, Denham could have gone into that unit sixteen right after the woman you have referred to as Mrs. Wilfred left, could he not?"

"Yes."

"Without your seeing him?"

"Yes."

"That's readily possible?"

"Sure it is. I look up when people drive in with automobiles and act like they're going to stop at the office, but I don't pay attention to people who come in and go direct to the cabins. I mean by that, if they drive right on by the office sign, I don't pay them any mind. I'm making a living renting units in a motel. I don't aim to pry into the lives of the people who rent those units."

"That's very commendable," Mason said. "Now, you rented other units in the motel during the day and evening, did you not?"

"Yes, sir."

"On the evening of April sixth and during the day of April seventh, did you assist the police in looking around for a gun?"

"Objected to as incompetent, irrelevant, and immaterial, not proper cross-examination," Hadley said, and then, getting to his feet, added, "If the Court please, we have asked this witness nothing of what he did on April seventh. We have only asked him about what took place on April sixth."

"I think, under the circumstances, the morning of April seventh would be too remote," Judge Strouse ruled. "The objection is sustained."

"Did you ever see that gun again?" Mason asked.

"I object to that as not proper cross-examination," Hadley said. "As far as the question is concerned, he may have seen it a week later. The direct examination of this witness was confined to April sixth."

"I'll sustain the objection," Judge Strouse ruled.

"Referring to the afternoon and evening of April sixth," Mason said, "did you notice anything else that was unusual?"

Brems shook his head. "No, sir."

153

Bedford leaned forward and whispered to Mason, "Pin him down. Make him tell about that prowler. Let's get a description. We've simply got to find who she is!"

"You noticed Binney Denham at the motel," Mason said.

"Yes, sir. That's right."

"And you knew that he wasn't registered in any unit?"

"Yes, sir."

"In other words, he was a stranger."

"Yes, sir. But you've got to remember, Mr. Mason, that I couldn't really tell for sure he wasn't in any unit. You see, this defendant here had taken two units and paid for them. He told me another couple from San Diego was coming up to join him. I had no way of knowing this here Denham wasn't the person he had had in mind."

"I understand," Mason said. "That accounts for the presence of Mr. Denham. Now, did you notice any *other* persons whom we might call unauthorized persons around the motel that day?"

"No, sir."

"Wasn't there someone in unit twelve?"

Brems thought for a minute, started to shake his head, then said, "Oh, wait a minute. Yes, I reported to the police—"

"Never mind what you reported to the police," Hadley interrupted. "Just listen to the questions and answer only the questions. Don't volunteer information."

"Well, there *was* a person I didn't place at the time, but it turned out to be all right later."

"Some person who was an unauthorized occupant of one of the motel units?"

"Objected to as calling for a conclusion of the witness and argumentative," Hadley said.

"This is cross-examination," Mason said.

"I think the word 'unauthorized' technically calls for the conclusion of the witness. However, I'm going to permit the question," Judge Strouse said. "The defense will be given the utmost latitude in the cross-examination of witnesses, particularly those witnesses whose direct examination covers persons who were present prior to the commission of this crime."

"Very well," Hadley said. "I'll withdraw the objection, Your Honor, just to keep the record straight. Answer the question, Mr. Brems."

"Well, I'll say this. A woman came out of unit twelve. She wasn't the woman who had rented the unit. I talked to her because I thought . . . well, I guess I'm not allowed to tell what I thought. But I talked to her."

"What did you talk to her about?" Mason asked.

"I questioned her."

"And what did she say?"

"Now there, Your Honor," Hadley said, "we are getting into something that is not only beyond the scope of cross-examination, but calls for hearsay evidence."

"The objection is sustained," Judge Strouse ruled.

"What did you ask her?" Mason asked.

"Same objection!" Hadley said.

"Same ruling."

Mason turned to Bedford and whispered, "You see, we're up against a whole series of technicalities there, Bedford. I can't question this witness about any conversation he had with her."

"But we've got to find out who she was. Keep after it. Don't let them run you up a blind alley, Mason. You're a resourceful lawyer. Fix your question so the judge has to let it in. We've *got* to know who she was."

"You say this woman who came out of unit twelve had not rented unit twelve?"

"That's right."

"And you stopped her?"

"Yes."

"And did you report this woman to the police?"

"Objected to. Not proper cross-examination. Incompetent, irrelevant, and immaterial," Hadley said.

155

"Sustained," Judge Strouse said.

"You have testified to a conversation you had with the police," Mason said.

"Well, of course, when things got coming to a head they wanted to know all about what had happened around the place. That was after they asked if they could look in unit sixteen to investigate a report they had had. I told them that they were welcome to go right ahead."

"All right," Mason said. "Now, as a part of that same conversation, did the police ask you if you had noticed any other prowlers during the afternoon or evening?"

"Objected to as incompetent, irrelevant, and immaterial, not proper cross-examination and hearsay," Hadley said.

Judge Strouse smiled. "Mr. Mason is now again invoking the rule that where part of a conversation has been brought out in direct examination, the entire conversation may be brought out on cross-examination. The witness may answer the question."

"Why, for the most part they kept asking me whether I'd heard any sound of a shot."

"I'm not talking about their primary interest," Mason said. "I'm asking if they inquired of you as to whether you had noticed any prowlers during the afternoon or evening."

"Yes, sir, they did."

"And did you then tell them, as a part of that conversation, about this woman whom you had seen in unit twelve?"

"Yes, sir."

"And what did you tell them?"

"Oh, Your Honor," Hadley said, "this is opening a door that is going to lead into matters which will confuse the issues. It has absolutely nothing to do with the case. We have no objection to Mr. Mason making Mr. Brems his own witness, if he wants to.

"He can then ask him any questions he wants, subject,

of course, to our objection that the evidence is incompetent, irrelevant, and immaterial."

"He doesn't have to make Mr. Brems his own witness," Judge Strouse ruled. "You have asked this witness on direct examination about a conversation he had with officers."

"Not a conversation. I simply asked him as to the effect of that conversation. Mr. Mason could have objected, if he had wanted to, on the ground that the question called for a conclusion of the witness."

"He didn't want to," Judge Strouse said, genially. "The legal effect is the same whether you ask the witness for his conclusion as to the conversation or whether you ask him to repeat the conversation word for word. The subject of the conversation came in on direct evidence. Mr. Mason can now have the entire conversation on cross-examination if he wants."

"But this isn't related to the subject that the police were interested in," Hadley objected. "It doesn't have anything to do with the crime."

"How do you know it doesn't?" Judge Strouse asked.

"Because we know what happened."

Judge Strouse said, "Mr. Mason may have *his* theory as to what happened. The Court is going to give the defendant the benefit of the widest latitude in all matters pertaining to cross-examination. The witness may answer to the question."

"Go on," Mason said. "What did you tell the officers about the woman in unit twelve?"

"I told them there'd been a prowler in the unit."

"Did you use the word 'prowler'?"

"I have the idea I did."

"And what else did you tell them?"

"I told them about talking with this woman."

"Did you tell them what the woman said?"

"Here again, Your Honor, I must object," Hadley said. "This is asking for hearsay evidence as to hearsay evidence. We are now getting into evidence of what some woman may have said to this witness and which conversation was in turn relayed to the officers. It is all very plainly hearsay."

"I will permit it on cross-examination," Judge Strouse ruled. "Answer the question."

"Yes, I said that this woman had told me she was a friend of the person who had rented that unit. She said she'd been told to go in and wait in case her friend wasn't at home."

"Can you describe that woman?" Mason asked.

"Objected to as incompetent, irrelevant, and immaterial. Not proper cross-examination," Hadley said.

"Sustained," Judge Strouse ruled.

Mason smiled. "Did you describe her to the officers at the time you had your conversation with them?"

"Yes, sir."

"How did you describe her to the officers?"

"Same objection," Hadley said.

Judge Strouse smiled. "The objection is overruled. It is now shown to be a part of the conversation which Mr. Mason is entitled to inquire into."

"I told the police this woman was maybe twenty-eight or thirty, that she was a brunette, she had darkish gray eyes, she was rather tall . . . I mean she was tall for a woman, with long legs. She had a way about her when she walked. Sort of like a queen. You could see—"

"Don't describe her," Hadley stormed at the witness. "Simply relate what you told the police."

"Yes, sir. That's what I'm telling—just what I told the police," Brems said, and then added gratuitously, "Of course, after that I found out it was all right."

"I ask that that last may go out as not being responsive to the question," Mason said, "as being a voluntary statement of the witness."

"It may go out," Judge Strouse ruled.

"That's all," Mason said.

Hadley, thoroughly angry, took the witness on redirect examination. "You told the police you thought this was a prowler?"

"Yes, sir."

"Subsequently you found out you were mistaken, didn't you?"

"Objected to," Mason said, "as leading and suggestive, not proper redirect examination. Incompetent, irrelevant, and immaterial."

"The objection is sustained," Judge Strouse said.

"But," shouted the exasperated assistant district attorney, "you subsequently *told* the police you *knew* it was all right, didn't you?"

"Objected to as not proper redirect examination," Mason said, "and as not being a part of the conversation that was testified to by the witness."

Judge Strouse hesitated, then looked down at the witness. *"When* did you tell them this?"

"The next day."

"The objection is sustained."

Hadley said, "You talked to the woman in unit twelve about it that same night, didn't you?"

"Objected to," Mason said, "as incompetent, irrelevant, and immaterial, calling for hearsay evidence, a conversation had without the presence or hearing of the defendant, not proper redirect examination."

"The objection is sustained," Judge Strouse ruled.

Hadley sat down in the chair, held a whispered conference with Hamilton Burger. The two men engaged in a vehement whispered argument; then Hadley tried another tack.

"Did you, the same night, as a part of that same conversation, state to the police that after you had talked with the woman you were satisfied she was all right and was telling the truth?"

"Yes, sir," the witness said.

"That's all," Hadley announced triumphantly.

"Just a moment," Mason said as Brems started to leave the stand. "One more question on re-cross-examination. Didn't you also at the same time and as a part of the same conversation describe the woman to the police as a prowler?"

"I believe I did. Yes, sir, at *that* time."

"That was the word you used—'a prowler'?"

"Yes, sir."

Mason smiled across at Hadley. "That's all my re-cross-examination," he said.

"That's all," Hadley said sullenly.

"Call your next witness," Judge Strouse observed.

Hadley called the manager of the drive-yourself car agency. He testified to the circumstances surrounding the renting of the car, the return of the car, the fact that the person returning it had not sought to cash in on the credit due on the deposit.

"No questions," Mason said.

Another employee of the drive-yourself agency testified to having seen the car driven onto the agency parking lot around ten o'clock on the evening of April sixth. The car was, he said, driven by a young woman, who got out of the car and started toward the office. He did not pay any attention to her after that.

"Cross-examine," Hadley said.

"Can you describe this woman?" Mason asked.

"She was a good-looking woman."

"Can you describe her any better than that?" Mason asked, as some of the jurors smiled broadly.

"Sure. She was in her twenties somewhere. She had . . . she was stacked!"

"What's that?" Judge Strouse asked.

"She had a good figure," the witness amended hastily.

"Did you see her hair?"

"She was blonde."

"Now then," Mason asked, "I want to ask you a question, and I want you to think carefully before you answer it. Did you, at any time, see any baggage being taken out of the car after she parked it in the lot?"

The man then shook his head. "No, sir, she didn't take out a thing except herself."

"You're certain?"

"I'm certain."

"You saw her get out of the car?"

"I'll say I did."

There was a ripple of laughter in the courtroom.

"That's all," Mason announced.

"No further questions," Hadley said.

Hadley called a fingerprint expert, who testified to examining units fifteen and sixteen of The Staylonger Motel for fingerprints on the night of April sixth and the early morning of April seventh. He produced several latent prints which he had developed and which he classified as being "significant."

"And why do you class these as being significant?" Hadley asked.

"Because," the witness said, "I was able to develop matching fingerprints in the automobile concerning which the witness has just testified."

Hadley's questions brought out that the witness had examined the rented automobile, had processed it for fingerprints, and had secured a number of prints matching those in units fifteen and sixteen of the motel where the body had been found, that *some* of these matching fingerprints were, beyond question, those of the defendant, Stewart G. Bedford.

"Cross-examine," Hadley announced.

"Who left the other '*matching*' prints that you found?" Mason asked the witness.

"I assume that they were made by the blonde young woman who drove the car back to the agency and—"

"You don't *know?*"

"No, sir, I do not. I do know that I secured and developed certain latent fingerprints in units fifteen and sixteen of the motel, that I secured certain latent prints from the automobile which has previously been described as having license number CXY 221, and that those prints in each instance were made by the same fingers that made the prints of Stewart G. Bedford on the police registration card when he was booked at police headquarters."

"And you found the prints which you have assumed were those left by the blonde young woman in both units fifteen and sixteen?"

"Yes, sir."

"Where?"

"In various places—on mirrors, on drinking glasses, on a doorknob."

"And those same fingerprints were on the automobile?"

"Yes, sir."

"In other words," Mason said, "as far as your own observations are concerned, those *other* fingerprints could have been left by the murderer of Binney Denham?"

"That's objected to," Hadley said. "It's argumentative. It calls for a conclusion."

"He's an expert witness," Mason said. "I'm asking him for his conclusion. I'm limiting the question as far as his own observations are concerned."

Judge Strouse hesitated, said, "I'm going to permit the witness to answer the question."

The expert said, "As far as *I* know or as far as my observations are concerned, either one of them could have been the murderer."

"Or the murder *could* have been committed by someone else?" Mason asked.

"That's right."

"Thank you," Mason told him. "That's all."

Hamilton Burger indicated that he planned to examine the next witness.

"Call Richard Judson," he said.

The bailiff called Richard Judson to the stand. Judson,

an erect man with good shoulders, slim waist, a deep voice, and cold blue eyes which regarded the world with an air of a banker appraising a real estate loan, proved to be a police officer who had gone out to the Bedford residence on the tenth of April.

"And what did you do at the Bedford residence?" Hamilton Burger asked.

"I looked around."

"Where?"

"Well, I looked around the grounds and the garage."

"Did you have a search warrant?"

"Yes, sir."

"Did you serve the search warrant on anyone?"

"There was no one home; no one was there to serve the warrant on."

"Where did you look first?"

"In the garage."

"Where in the garage?"

"All over the garage."

"Can you tell us a little more about the type of search you made?"

"Well, there was a car in the garage. We looked over that pretty well. There were some tires. We looked around them, some old inner tubes—"

"Now, you say 'we.' Who was with you?"

"My partner."

"A police officer?"

"Yes."

"Where else did you look?"

"We looked every place in the garage. We looked up in the rafters, where there were some old boxes. We made a good job of searching the place."

"And then," Hamilton Burger asked, "what did you do?"

"There was a drain in the center of the garage floor— a perforated drain so that the garage floor could be washed off with a hose. There was a perforated plate which covered the drain. We unscrewed this plate, and looked down inside."

"And what did you find?"

"We found a gun."

"What do you mean, a gun?"

"I mean a .38 caliber Colt revolver."

"Do you have the number of that gun?"

"I made a note of it, yes, sir."

"That was a memorandum you made at the time?"

"Yes, sir."

"That was made by you?"

"Yes, sir."

"Do you have it with you?"

"Yes, sir."

"What do your notes show?"

The witness opened his notebook. "The gun was blued steel .38 caliber Colt revolver. It had five loaded cartridges in the cylinder and one empty, or exploded, cartridge case. The manufacturer's number was 740818."

"What did you do with that revolver?"

"I turned it over to Arthur Merriam."

"Who is he?"

"He is one of the police experts on firearms and ballistics."

"You may cross-examine," Hamilton Burger said to Perry Mason.

"Now as I understand it, you had a search warrant, Mr. Judson?" Mason asked.

"Yes, sir."

"And what premises were included in the search warrant?"

"The house the grounds, the garage."

"There was no one home on whom you could serve this search warrant?"

"No, sir, not at the time we made the search."

"When was the search warrant dated?"

"I believe the eighth."

"You got it on the morning of the eighth?"

"I don't know the exact time of day."

"It was in the morning?"

"I think perhaps it was."

"And after you got the search warrant what did you do?"

"Put it in my pocket."

"And what did you do after that?"

"I was working on the case."

"What did you do while you were, as you say, working on the case and after putting the search warrant in your pocket?"

"I drove around looking things over."

"Actually, you drove out to the Bedford house, didn't you?"

"Well, we were working on the case, looking things over. We cruised around that vicinity."

"And then you *parked* your car, didn't you?"

"Yes, sir."

"From a spot where you could see the garage?"

"Well, yes."

"And you waited all that day, did you not?"

"The rest of the day, yes, sir."

"And the next day you were back on the job again?"

"Yes, sir."

"Same place?"

"Yes, sir."

"And you waited all that day?"

"Yes, sir."

"And the next day you were back on the job again, weren't you?"

"Yes, sir."

"Same place?"

"Yes, sir."

"And you waited during that day until when?"

"Oh, until about four o'clock in the afternoon."

"And then, from your surveillance, you knew that there was no one home, isn't that right?"

"Well, we saw Mrs. Bedford drive off."

"You then *knew* that there was no one home, didn't you?"

"Well, it's hard to *know* anything like that."

"You had been keeping the house under surveillance?"

"We had been, yes."

"For the purpose of finding a time when no one was home?"

"Well, we were just keeping the place under surveillance to see who came and who went."

"And at the first opportunity, when you thought there was no one home, you went and searched the garage?"

"Well . . . I guess that's about right. You can call it that if you want to."

"And you searched the garage but didn't search the house?"

"No, sir, we didn't search the house."

"You searched every inch of the garage, every nook and corner?"

"Yes, sir."

"You waited until you felt certain there was no one home, then you went out to make your search."

"We wanted to make a search of the garage. We didn't want to be interrupted and we didn't want to have anyone interfering with us."

Mason smiled frostily. "You have just said, Mr. Judson, that you wanted to make a search of the garage."

"Well, what's wrong with that? We had a warrant, didn't we?"

"You said of the *garage*."

"I meant of the whole place—the house—the whole business."

"You didn't *say* that. You said you wanted to search the *garage*."

"Well, we had a warrant for it."

166

"Isn't it true," Mason asked, "that the only place you really wanted to search was the garage, and you only wanted to search that because you had been given a tip that the gun would be found in the garage?"

"We were looking for the gun, all right."

"Isn't it a fact that you had a tip before you went out there that the gun would be found in the garage?"

"Objected to as incompetent, irrelevant, and immaterial, not proper cross-examination," Hamilton Burger said.

Judge Strouse thought for a moment. "The objection is overruled . . . if the witness knows."

"I don't know about any tip."

"Isn't it a fact you intended primarily to search the garage?"

"We searched there first."

"Was there some reason you searched there first?"

"That's where we started. We thought we might find a gun there."

"And what made you think that was where the gun was?"

"That was as good a place to hide it as any."

"You mean the police didn't have some anonymous telephone tip to guide you?"

"I mean we searched the garage, looking for a gun, and we found the gun in the garage. I don't know what tip the others had. I was told to go look for a gun."

"In the garage?"

"Well, yes."

"Thank you," Mason said. "That's all."

Arthur Merriam took the stand and testified to experiments he had performed with the gun which he had received from the last witness and which was introduced in evidence. He stated that he had fired test bullets from the gun, had examined them through a comparison microscope, comparing the test bullets with the fatal bullet. He had prepared photographs which showed the identity of striation marks on the two bullets while one was superimposed over the other. These photographs were introduced in evidence.

"You may cross-examine," Hamilton Burger said.

Mason seemed a little bored with the entire proceeding. "No questions," he said.

Hamilton Burger's next witness was a man who had charge of the sporting goods section of one of the large downtown department stores. This man produced records showing the gun in question had been sold to Stewart G. Bedford some five years earlier and that Bedford had signed the register of sales. The book of sales was offered in evidence; then, as a photostatic copy of the original was produced, the Court ordered that the original record might be withdrawn.

"Cross-examine," Hamilton Burger said.

"No questions," Mason announced, suppressing a yawn.

Judge Strouse looked at the clock, said, "It is now time for the afternoon adjournment. The Court admonishes the jurors not to discuss this case among yourselves, nor to permit anyone else to discuss it in your presence. You are not to form or express any opinion until the case is finally submitted to you.

"Court will take a recess until tomorrow morning at ten o'clock."

Bedford gripped Mason's arm. "Mason," he said, "someone planted that gun in my garage."

"Did you put it there?" Mason asked.

"Don't be silly! I tell you I never saw the gun after I went to sleep. That liquor was drugged and someone took the gun out of my brief case, killed Binney Denham, and then subsequently planted the gun in my garage."

"And," Mason pointed out, "telephoned a tip to the police so that the officers would be sure to find it there."

"Well, what does that mean?"

"It means that someone was very anxious that the officers would have plenty of evidence to connect you with the murder."

"And that gets back to this mysterious prowler who was in that motel where Elsa—"

"Just a minute," Mason cautioned. "No names."

"Well, that woman who was in there," Bedford said. "Hang it, Mason! I keep telling you she's important. She's the key to the whole business. Yet you don't seem to get the least bit excited about her, or try to find her."

"How am I going to go about finding her?" Mason asked impatiently. "You tell me there's a needle in a haystack and the needle is important. So what?"

The officer motioned for Bedford to accompany him.

"Hire fifty detectives," Bedford said, holding back momentarily. "Hire a hundred detectives. But *find that woman!*"

"See you tomorrow," Mason told him as the officer led Bedford through the passageway to the jail elevator.

◾ 19 ◾

PERRY MASON AND DELLA STREET HAD DINNER AT THEIR favorite restaurant, returned for a couple hours' work at the office, and found Elsa Griffin waiting for them in the foyer of the building.

"Hello," Mason said. "Do you want to see me?"

She nodded.

"Been here long?"

"About twenty minutes. I heard you were out to dinner but expected to return to the office this evening, so I waited."

Mason flashed a glance at Della Street. "Something important?"

"I think so."

"Come on up," Mason invited.

The three of them rode up in the elevator and walked down the corridor. Mason opened the door of the private office, went in and switched on the lights.

"Take off your coat and hat," Della Street said. "Sit down in that chair over there."

Elsa Griffin moved quietly, efficiently, as a woman moves who has a fixed purpose and has steeled herself to carry out her objectives in a series of definite steps.

"I had a chance to talk for a few minutes with Mr. Bedford," she said.

Mason nodded.

"A few words of *private* conversation."

"Go ahead," Mason told her.

She said, "Mr. Bedford feels that with all of the resources that he has placed at your command, you could do more about finding that woman who was in my unit there at the motel. Of course, when you come right down to it, *she* could have kept those two units, fifteen and sixteen, under surveillance from my cabin and then gone over and . . . well, at the proper moment she could have simply opened the door of sixteen and fired one shot and then made her escape."

"Yes," Mason said drily, "fired one shot with Bedford's gun."

"Yes," Elsa Griffin said thoughtfully, "I suppose she *would* have had to get into that other cabin and get possession of the gun first. . . . But she *could* have done that, Mr. Mason. She could have gone into the cabin after that blonde went out, and there she found Mr. Bedford asleep. She took the gun from his brief case."

Mason studied her carefully.

Abruptly she said, "Mr. Mason, don't you think it's bad publicity for Mrs. Bedford to wear those horribly heavy dark glasses and keep in the back of the courtroom? Shouldn't she be right up there in front, giving her husband moral support, and not looking as though—as though she were afraid to have people find out who she is?"

"Everyone knows who she is," Mason said. "From the time they started picking the jury, the newspaper people have been interviewing her."

"I know, but she'll never take off those horrid dark glasses. And they make her look terrible. They're great big lensed glasses that completely alter her appearance. She looks just like . . . well, not like herself at all."

"So what would you suggest that I do?" Mason asked.

"Couldn't you tell her to be more natural? Tell her to take her glasses off, to come up and sit as close to her husband as she can to give him a word of encouragement now and then."

"That's what Mr. Bedford wants?"

"I'm satisfied he does. I think that his wife's conduct has hurt him. He acts very differently from the way he normally does. He's . . . well, he's sort of crushed."

"I see," Mason said.

Elsa Griffin was silent for a few minutes, then said, "What have you been able to do with those fingerprints I got for you from the cabin, Mr. Mason?"

"Not very much, I'm afraid. You see, it's very difficult to identify a person unless you have a complete set of ten fingerprints, but as one who studied to be a detective, you know all about that."

"'Yes, I suppose so," she said dubiously. "I thought Mr. Brems gave a very good description of that prowler who was in my cabin."

Mason nodded.

"There's something about the way he describes her, something about her walk. I almost feel that I know her. It's the most peculiar feeling. It's like seeing a face that you can't place, yet which is very familiar to you.

You know it as well as you know your own, and yet somehow you can't get it fixed with the name. You just can't get the right connection. There's one link in the chain that's missing."

Again Mason nodded.

"I have a feeling that if I could only think of that, I'd have it. I feel that there's a solution to the whole business just almost at our finger tips, and yet it keeps eluding us like . . . like a Halloween apple."

Mason sat silent.

"Well," she said, getting to her feet, "I must be going. I wanted to tell you Mr. Bedford would like very much indeed to have you concentrate all of the resources at your command on finding that woman. Also, I'm satisfied he would like it a lot better if his wife wouldn't act as though she were afraid of being recognized. You know, really, she's a very beautiful woman and she has a wonderful carriage—"

Abruptly Elsa Griffin ceased speaking and looked at Mason with eyes that slowly widened with startled, incredulous surprise.

"What's the matter?" Mason asked. "What is it?"

"My God!" she exclaimed. "It *couldn't* be!"

"Come on," Mason said. "What is it?"

"Are you ill?" Della Street asked.

She kept looking at him with round, startled eyes.

"Good heavens, Mr. Mason! It's just hit me like a ton of bricks. Let me sit down."

She dropped down into a chair, moved her head slowly from side to side, looking around the office as though some mental shock had left her completely disoriented.

"Well," Mason asked, "what is it?"

"I was just mentioning Mrs. Bedford and thinking about her carriage and the way she walks and . . . Mr. Mason, it's just come to me. It's a terrible thing. It's just as though something had crashed into my mind."

"What is it?" Mason asked.

"Don't you see, Mr. Mason? That prowler who was in my unit at the motel. The description Mr. Brems gave fits her perfectly. Why, you couldn't ask for a better description of Mrs. Bedford than the one that Morrison Brems gave."

Mason sat silent, his eyes steadily studying Elsa Griffin's face. Abruptly she snapped her fingers.

"I have it, Mr. Mason! I have it! You've got her photograph on that police card—her photograph and her fingerprints. You could compare the latents I took there in my unit in the motel with her fingerprints on there, and ... and then we'd *know!*"

Mason nodded to Della Street. "Get the card with Mrs. Bedford's fingerprints, Della. Also, get the envelope with the unidentified latent prints. You'll remember we discarded Elsa Griffin's prints. We have four unidentified latents numbered fourteen, sixteen, nine, and twelve. I'd like to have those prints, please."

Della Street regarded Mason's expressionless face for a moment, then went to the locked filing case in which the lawyer kept matters to which he was referring in cases under trial, and returned with the articles Mason had requested.

Elsa Griffin eagerly reached for the envelope with the lifted fingerprints, took the cards from the envelope, examined them carefully, then grabbed the card containing Ann Roann Bedford's criminal record.

She swiftly compared the lifted latent prints with those on the card, looking intently from one to the other. Gradually her excitement became evident, then mounted to a fever pitch.

"Mr. Mason, these prints are hers!"

Mason took the card with Mrs. Bedford's criminal record. Elsa Griffin held onto the cards numbered fourteen, sixteen, nine, and twelve.

"They're hers, Mr. Mason! You can take my word for it. I've studied fingerpinting."

173

Mason said, "Let's hope you're mistaken. That would *really* put the fat in the fire. We simply couldn't have that."

Elsa Griffin picked up the envelope containing the lifted latents. "Mr. Mason," she said sternly, "you're representing Stewart G. Bedford. You *have* to represent his interests regardless of who gets hurt."

Mason held out his hand for the latent prints. She drew back slightly. "You can't be a traitor to his cause in order to protect . . . to protect the person who got him into all this trouble in the first place."

Mason said, "A lawyer has to protect his client's *best* interests. That doesn't mean he necessarily has to do what the client wants or what the client's friends may want. He must do what is best for the client."

"You mean you aren't going to tell Mr. Bedford that it was his own wife who, goaded to desperation by this blackmailer, finally decided to—"

"No," Mason interrupted, "I'm not going to tell him, and I don't want you to tell him."

She suddenly jumped from her chair, and raced for the exit door of the office.

"Come back here," Della Street cried, making a grab and missing Elsa Griffin's flying skirt by a matter of inches.

Before Della Street could get to the door, Elsa Griffin had wrenched it open.

Sergeant Holcomb was standing on the outer threshold. "Well, well, good evening, folks," he said, slipping an arm around Elsa Griffin's shoulders. "I gather there has been a little commotion in here. What's going on?"

"This young woman is trying to take some personal property which doesn't belong to her," Mason said.

"Well, well, well, isn't that interesting? Stealing from you, eh? Could you describe the property, Mason? Perhaps you'd like to go down to headquarters and swear out a complaint, charging her with larceny. What's your side of the story, Miss Griffin?"

Elsa Griffin pushed the lifted latents inside the front of her dress. "Will you," she asked Sergeant Holcomb, "kindly escort me home and then see that I am subpoenaed as a witness for the prosecution? I think it's time someone showed Mr. Perry Mason, the great criminal lawyer, that it's against the law to condone murder and conceal evidence from the police."

Sergeant Holcomb's face was wreathed in smiles. "Sister," he said, "you've made a *great* little speech. You just come along with me."

■ **20** ■

HAMILTON BURGER, HIS FACE PLAINLY INDICATING HIS feelings, rose to his feet when court was called to order the next morning and said, "Your Honor, I would like to call the Court's attention to Section 135 of the penal code, which reads as follows: 'Every person who, knowing that any book, paper, record, instrument in writing, or other matter or thing, is about to be produced in evidence upon any trial, inquiry, or investigation whatever, authorized by law, willfully destroys *or conceals* the same, with intent thereby to prevent it from being produced is guilty of a misdemeanor.' "

Judge Strouse, plainly puzzled, said, "The Court is, I think, familiar with the law, Mr. Burger."

"Yes, Your Honor," Hamilton Burger said. "I merely wished to call the section to Your Honor's attention. I know Your Honor is familiar with the law. I feel that perhaps some other persons are not, and now, Your Honor, I wish to call Miss Elsa Griffin to the stand."

Stewart Bedford looked at Mason with alarm. "What the devil's this?" he whispered. "I thought we were going to keep her out of the public view. We can't afford to have Brems recognize her as the one who was in unit twelve."

"She didn't like the way I was handling things," Mason said. "She decided to become a witness."

"When did that happen?"

"Late last night."

"You didn't tell me."

"I didn't want to worry you."

The outer door opened, and Elsa Griffin, her chin high, came marching into the courtroom. She raised her right hand, was sworn, and took the witness stand.

"What is your name?" Hamilton Burger asked.

"Elsa Griffin."

"Are you acquainted with the defendant in this case?"

"I am employed by him."

"Where were you on the sixth day of April of this year?"

"I was at The Staylonger Motel."

"What were you doing there?"

"I was there at the request of a certain person."

"Now then, if the Court please," Hamilton Burger said, addressing Judge Strouse, "a most unusual situation is about to develop. I may state that this witness, while wishing the authorities to take certain action, did nevertheless conspire with another person, whom I shall presently name, to conceal and suppress certain evidence which we consider highly pertinent.

"I had this witness placed under subpoena. She is here as an unwilling witness. That is, she is not only willing but anxious to testify to certain phases of the case. However, she is quite unwilling to testify as to other matters. As to these matters she has refused to make any statement, and I have no knowledge of how much or how little she knows as to this part of the case. She simply will not talk with me except upon one point.

"It is, therefore, necessary for me to approach this witness upon certain matters as a hostile witness."

"Perhaps," Judge Strouse said, "you had better first examine the witness upon the matters as to which she is willing to give her testimony, and then elicit information from her on the other points as a hostile witness, and under the rules pertaining to the examination of hostile witnesses."

"Very well, Your Honor."

Hamilton Burger turned to the witness.

"You are now and for several years have been employed by the defendant?"

"Yes."

"In what capacity?"

"I am his confidential secretary."

"Are you acquainted with Mr. Morrison Brems, the manager of The Staylonger Motel?"

"Yes."

"Did you have a conversation with Morrison Brems on April sixth of this year?"

"Yes."

"When?"

"Early in the evening."

"What was said at that conversation?"

"Objected to as incompetent, irrelevant, and immaterial," Mason said.

"Just a moment, Your Honor," Hamilton Burger countered. "We propose to show that this witness was at the time of this conversation the agent of the defendant, that she went to the motel in accordance with instructions issued by the defendant."

"You had better show that first then," Judge Strouse ruled.

"But that, Your Honor, is where we are having trouble, that is one of the points where the witness is hostile."

"There are some other matters on which the witness is not a hostile witness?" Judge Strouse asked.

"Yes."

"The Court has suggested that you proceed with those matters until the evidence which can be produced by this witness as a friendly witness is all before the Court. Then, if there are other matters on which the witness is hostile, and you request permission to deal with the witness as a hostile witness, the record will be straight as to what has been done and where, when and why it has been done."

"Very well, Your Honor."

Hamilton Burger turned again to the witness. "After this conversation did you return to The Staylonger Motel later on in the evening of April sixth?"

"Actually it was, I believe, early on the morning of April seventh."

"Who sent you to The Staylonger Motel?"

"Mr. Perry Mason."

"You mean that you received instructions from Mr. Mason while he was acting as attorney for Stewart G. Bedford, the defendant in this case?"

"Yes."

"What did Mr. Mason instruct you to do?"

"To get certain fingerprints from unit twelve, to take a fingerprint outfit and dust every place in the unit where I thought I could get a suitable latent fingerprint, to lift those fingerprints and then to obliterate every single remaining fingerprint which might be in unit twelve, after that to bring the lifted fingerprints to Mr. Mason."

"Did you understand the process of taking fingerprints and lifting them?"

"Yes."

"Had you made some study of that process?"

"Yes."

"Where?"

"I am a graduate of a correspondence school dealing with such matters."

"Where did you get the material necessary to lift latent fingerprints?"

"Mr. Mason furnished it."

"And what did you do after Mr. Mason gave you those materials?"

"I went to the motel and lifted certain fingerprints from unit twelve as I had been instructed."

"And then what?"

"I took those fingerprints to Mr. Mason so that the fingerprints which were mine could be discarded, and thereby, through a process of elimination, leave only the fingerprints of any person who had been prowling the cabin during my absence."

"Do you know if this was done?"

"It was done. I was so advised by Mr. Mason, who also told me that all the latent prints I had lifted were my prints, with the exception of those prints contained on four cards."

"Do you know what four cards these were?"

"Yes. As I lifted prints I put them on cards and numbered the cards. The cards containing the significant prints were numbered fourteen, sixteen, nine, and twelve.

"Fourteen and sixteen came from the glass doorknob of the closet door in the motel unit; nine and twelve came from the side of a mirror."

"Do you know where these four cards are now?"

"Yes."

"Where?"

"I have them."

"Where did you get them?"

"I snatched them from Perry Mason last night and ran to the police as Mr. Mason was trying to get them back."

"Did you give them to the police?"

"No."

"Why?"

"I didn't want anything to happen to them. You see by last night I knew whose prints they were. That is why I ran with them."

"Why did you feel that you had to run?" Burger asked.

Judge Strouse glanced down at Perry Mason expectantly. When the lawyer made no effort to object, Judge Strouse said to the witness, "Just a minute before you answer that question. Does the defense wish to object to this question, Mr. Mason?"

"No, Your Honor," Perry Mason said. "I feel that I am being on trial here and that therefore I should let the full facts come out."

Judge Strouse frowned. "You may feel that you are on trial, Mr. Mason. That is a matter of dispute. There can be no dispute that your client is on trial, and your primary duty is to protect the interests of that client regardless of the effect on your own private affairs."

"I understand that, Your Honor."

"This question seems to me to be argumentative and calls for a conclusion of the witness."

"There is no objection, Your Honor."

Judge Strouse hesitated and said, "I would like to point out to you, Mr. Mason, that the Court will take a hand if it appears that your interests in the case become adverse to your client and no objection is made to questions which are detrimental to your client's case."

"I think if the Court please," Mason said, "the opposite may be the case here. I feel that the answer of the witness may be strongly opposed to my personal interests but very much in favor of the defendant's case. You see that is the reason the witness is both a willing witness on some phases of the case and an unwilling witness on others. She feels that she should testify against me, but she is loyal to the interests of her employer."

"Very well," Judge Strouse said. "If you don't wish to object, the witness will answer the question."

"Answer the question," Hamilton Burger said. "Why did you feel that you had to run?"

"Because at that time I had identified those fingerprints."

"You had?"

"Yes, sir."

"You said that you had studied fingerprinting?"

"Yes."

"And you were able at that time to identify these fingerprints?"

"Yes, sir."

"You compared them with originals?"

"Well, enough to know whose they were."

Hamilton Burger turned to the Court and said, "I confess, Your Honor, that on some of these matters I am feeling my way because of the peculiar situation which exists. The witness promised to give her testimony on the stand but would not tell me——"

"There is no objection," Judge Strouse interrupted. "There is, therefore, nothing before the Court. You will kindly refrain from making any argument or comments as to the testimony of this witness until it comes time to argue the matter to the jury. Simply proceed with your question and answer, Mr. District Attorney."

"Yes, Your Honor," Hamilton Burger said.

Judge Strouse looked down at Mason. His expression was thoughtfully dubious.

"You yourself were able to identify those prints?" Hamilton Burger asked.

"Yes, sir."

"Whose prints did you think they were?"

"Now just a minute," Judge Strouse said. "Apparently counsel is not going to object that no proper foundation has been laid and that this calls for an opinion of the witness. Miss Griffin?"

"Yes, Your Honor?"

"You state that you studied fingerprinting?"

"Yes, I did, Your Honor."

"How?"

"By correspondence."

"Over what period of time?"

"I took a complete course. I graduated. I learned to distinguish the different characteristics of fingerprints. I learned how to take fingerprints and compare them and how to classify them."

"Is there any objection from defense counsel?" Judge Strouse asked.

"None whatever," Mason said.

"Very well, whose prints were they?" Burger asked.

"Now just a minute," Mason said. "If the Court please I feel that that question is improper."

"I feel the objection is in order," Judge Strouse ruled.

"However," Mason went on, "I am not interposing the objection which perhaps Your Honor has in mind. I feel that this witness, while she may have qualified as an expert on fingerpinting, has qualified as a limited expert. She is what might be called an amateur expert. I feel that, therefore, the question should not be as to whose fingerprints these were, but in her opinion, for what it may be worth, what points of similarity there are between these prints and known standards."

Judge Strouse said, "The objection is sustained."

Hamilton Burger, his face darkening with annoyance, asked, "In your opinion, for what it may be worth, what points of similarity are there between these latents and the known prints of any person with which you may have made a comparison?"

Elsa Griffin raised her head. Her defiant eyes glared at the defendant, then at Mason, and then turned to the jury. In a firm voice she said, "In my opinion, for what it may be worth, these prints have so many points of similarity I can say they were made by the fingers of Mrs. Stewart G. Bedford, the wife of the defendant in this case."

Hamilton Burger grinned. "Do you have those finger-prints with you?"

"I do."

"And how do you identify them?"

"The cards are numbered," she said. "The numbers are fourteen, sixteen, nine, and twelve respectively. Also I signed my name on the backs of these cards at a late hour last night so that there could be no possibility of substitution or mistake. I did that at the suggestion of the district attorney. He wanted me to leave these cards with him. When I refused he asked me to sign my name so there could be no possibility of trickery."

Hamilton Burger was grinning. "And then what did I do, if anything?"

"Then you signed your name beneath mine and put the date on the cards."

"I ask of the Court please that those prints be intro-duced in evidence," Hamilton Burger said, "as People's Exhibit under proper numbers."

"Now just a moment," Mason said. "At this point, Your Honor, I feel that I have a right to a *voir dire* ex-amination as to the authenticity of the exhibits."

"Go ahead," Hamilton Burger said. "In fact, handle your cross-examination on this phase of the case if you want, because from here on the witness becomes an un-willing witness."

"Counsel may proceed," Judge Strouse said.

"You made this positive identification of the latent prints last night, Miss Griffin?"

"Yes."

"In my office?"

"Yes."

"You were rather excited at the time?"

"Well . . . all right, I *was* a little excited, but I wasn't too excited to compare fingerprints."

"You checked all four of these fingerprints?"

"Yes."

"All four of them were the fingerprints of Mrs. Bedford?"

"Yes."

Bedford tugged at Mason's coat. "Look here, Mason," he whispered. "Don't let her—"

Mason brushed his client's hand to one side. "Keep quiet," he ordered."

Mason arose and approached the witness stand. "You are, I believe, skilled in classifying fingerprints?"

"I am."

"You know how to do it?"

"Very well."

Mason said, "I am going to give you a magnifying glass to assist you in looking at these prints."

Mason took a powerful pocket magnifying glass from his pocket, turned to the clerk, and said, "May I have some of the fingerprints which have been introduced in evidence? I don't care for the fingerprints of the defendant which were found in the car and in the motel, but I would like some of those other exhibits of the un-identified party, the ones that were found in the car and in the motel."

"Very well," the clerk said, thumbing through the ex-hibits. He handed Mason several of the cards.

"Now then," Mason said, "I call your attention to People's Exhibit number twenty-eight, which purports to be a lifted fingerprint. I will ask you to look at that and see if that fingerprint matches one on any of the cards num-bered fourteen, sixteen, nine, and twelve, which you have produced."

The witness made a show of studying the print with the magnifying glass, shook her head and said, "No!" and then added, "It can't. These prints are the prints of Mrs. Bedford. Those prints in the exhibits are the prints of an unidentified person."

"But isn't it true that this unidentified person, as far

as you know, might well have been Mrs. Bedford?" Mason asked.

"No, that person was a blonde. I saw her."

"But you don't know that it was the blonde who left the prints?"

"No, I don't *know* that."

"Then please examine this print closely."

Mason held the print out to Elsa Griffin, who looked at it with the magnifying glass in a perfunctory manner, then handed it back to Mason.

"Now," Mason said, "I call your attention to People's Exhibit number thirty-four, and ask you to compare this."

Again the witness made a perfunctory study with the magnifying glass and said, "No. None of these prints match."

"None of them?" Mason asked.

"None! I tell you, Mr. Mason, those are the prints of Mrs. Bedford, and you know it as well as I do."

Mason appeared to be somewhat rebuffed. He studied the prints, then looked at the cards in Elsa Griffin's hand.

"Perhaps," he said, "you can tell me just how you go about examining a fingerprint. Take this one, for instance, on the card numbered sixteen. That is one, I believe, that you secured from the under side of a glass doorknob in the cabin?"

"Yes."

"Now what is the first characteristic of that print which you noticed?"

"That is a tented arch."

"I see. A tented arch," Mason said thoughtfully. "Now would you mind pointing out just where that tented arch is? Oh, I see. Now this fingerprint which I hand you which has been numbered People's Exhibit number thirty-seven also has a tented arch, does it not?"

She looked at the print and said, "Yes."

"Now, using this print number sixteen which you say

you recovered from the closet doorknob, let us count from the tented arch through the ridges until we come to a branch in the ridges. There are, let's see, one, two, three, four, five, six, seven, eight ridges, and then we come to a branch."

"That is right," she said.

"Well, now let's see," Mason said. "We take this print which has been introduced by the prosecution as number thirty-seven and we count—let's see, why, yes, we count the same number of ridges and we come to the same peculiar branching, do we not?"

"Let me see," the witness said.

She studied the print through the magnifying glass. "Well, yes," she said, "that is what you would call *one* point of similarity. You need several to make a perfect identification."

"I see," Mason said. "One point of similarity could of course be a coincidence."

"Don't make any mistake, Mr. Mason," she said icily. "That *is* a coincidence."

"Very well, now, let's look at your print number sixteen again, the one which you got from underneath the closet doorknob, and see if you can find some other distinguishing mark."

"You have one here," she said. "On the tenth ridge."

"The tenth," Mason said. "Let me see . . . oh, yes."

"Well, now let's look at thirty-seven again, and see if you can find the same point of similarity there."

"There's no use looking," she said. "There won't be."

"Tut, tut!" Mason said. "Don't jump at conclusions, Miss Griffin. You're testifying as an expert, so let's just take a look now if you please. Count up these ridges and—"

The witness gasped.

"Do you find such a point of similarity?" Mason asked, seemingly as much surprised as the witness.

"I . . . I seem to. Somebody has been tampering with these fingerprints."

"Now, just a moment! Just a moment!" Hamilton Burger said. "This is a serious matter, Your Honor."

"Who's going to tamper with the fingerprints?" Mason asked. "The fingerprints that the witness has been testifying to were in her possession. She said that she had them in her possession all night. She wouldn't let them out of her possession for fear they might be tampered with. She signed her name on the back of each card. The district attorney signed his name and wrote the date. There are the signatures on the cards. These other cards are exhibits which the prosecution introduced in court. I have just taken those exhibits from the clerk. They bear the file number of the clerk and the exhibit number."

"Just the same," Hamilton Burger shouted, "there's some sort of a flimflam here. The witness knows it and I know it."

"Mr. Burger," Judge Strouse stated, "you will not make any such charges in this courtroom. Not unless they can be substantiated. Apparently there is no possibility of any substitution. Miss Griffin?"

"Yes, Your Honor?"

"Kindly look at the card numbered sixteen."

"Yes, Your Honor."

"You got that card last night?"

"I . . . I . . . yes, I must have."

"From the office of Perry Mason?"

"Yes."

"And you compared that card *at that time* with the fingerprints of Mrs. Stewart Bedford?"

"Yes, Your Honor."

"That card was in your possession and under your control at that time?"

"Yes, Your Honor."

"Now, speaking for the moment as to this one card,

exactly what did you do with that card *after* satisfying yourself the print was that of Mrs. Bedford? What did you do with it?"

"I put it in the front of my dress."

"And then what?"

"I was escorted by Sergeant Holcomb to the office of Hamilton Burger. Mr. Burger wanted to have me leave the prints with him. I refused to do so. At his suggestion, I signed my name on the back of each card. Then he signed his name and the date, so there could be no question of a substitution, so that I couldn't substitute them, and so that no one else could."

"And that's your signature and the date on the back of that card?"

"It seems to be but . . . I'm not certain. May I examine these prints for a moment?"

"Take all the time you want," Judge Strouse said.

Hamilton Burger said, "Your Honor, I feel that there should be some inquiry here. This is completely in accordance with the peculiar phenomena which always seem to occur in cases where Mr. Perry Mason is defense counsel."

"I resent that," Perry Mason said. "I am simply trying to cross-examine this expert, this so-called expert, I may add."

Elsa Griffin looked up from the fingerprint classification to flash him a glance of venomous hatred.

Judge Strouse said, "Counsel for both sides will return to their chairs at counsel tables. The witness will be given ample opportunity to make the comparison which she wishes."

Burger reluctantly lumbered back to his chair at the prosecution's table and dropped into it.

Mason walked back, sat down, locked his hands behind his head and, with elaborate unconcern, leaned back in the chair.

Stewart Bedford tried to whisper to him, but Mason waved him back into silence.

The witness proceeded to examine the cards, studying first one and then the other, counting ridges with a sharp-pointed pencil. The silence in the courtroom grew to a peak of tension.

Suddenly Elsa Griffin threw the magnifying glass directly at Perry Mason. The glass hit the mahogany table, bounced against the lawyer's chest. Elsa Griffin dropped all the fingerprint cards, put her hands to her eyes, and began to cry hysterically.

Mason got to his feet.

Judge Strouse said, "Just a moment. Counsel for both sides will remain seated. The Court wants to examine the witness. Miss Griffin, will you kindly regain your composure. The Court wishes to ask you certain questions."

She took her hands from her face, raised tearful eyes to the Court. "What is it?" she asked.

"Do you now conclude that your print number sixteen is the same as the print which has been introduced in evidence, prosecution's number thirty-seven—that both were made by the same finger?"

She said, "It is, Your Honor, but it *wasn't*. Last night it *was* the print of Mrs. Bedford. Somebody somewhere has mixed everything all up, and . . . and now I don't know what I'm doing, or what I'm talking about."

"Well, there's no reason to be hysterical about this, Miss Griffin," Judge Strouse said. "You're certain that this fingerprint number sixteen is the one that you took from the cottage?"

She nodded. "It has to be ... I ... I *know* that it's Mrs. Bedford's fingerprint!"

"There certainly can be no doubt about the authenticity of the Court Exhibit," Judge Strouse said. "Now apparently, according to the testimony of the prosecution's witness, the identity of these fingerprints simply means that the same woman who was in unit sixteen of the motel on April sixth was also in unit twelve of the motel on that same day, that this person also drove the rented automobile."

Elsa Griffin shook her head. "It isn't so, Your Honor. It simply can't be. It isn't—" Again she lapsed into a storm of tears.

Hamilton Burger said, "If the Court please, may I make a suggestion?"

"What is it?" Judge Strouse asked coldly.

Hamilton Burger said, "This witness seems to be emotionally upset. I suggest that she be withdrawn from the stand. I suggest that the four cards, each bearing her signature and the numbers fourteen, sixteen, nine, and twelve, be each stamped by the clerk for identification; that these cards then be given to the police fingerprint expert who is here in the witness room and who can very shortly give us an opinion as to the identity of those fingerprints. In the meantime, I wish to state to the Court that I am completely satisfied with the sincerity and integrity of this witness. I personally feel that there has been some trickery and substitution. I think that a deception and a fraud is being practiced on this court and in order to prove it I would ask to recall Morrison Brems, the manager of the motel, to the stand."

Judge Strouse stroked his chin. "The jury will disregard the comments of the district attorney," he said, "in regard to deception or fraud. This witness will be excused from the stand, the cards will be marked for identification by the clerk and then delivered to the fingerprint expert who has previously testified and who will be charged by the court with making a comparison and a report. Now in the meantime the witness Brems will come forward. You will be excused for the time being, Miss Griffin. Just leave the stand, if you will, and try to compose yourself."

The bailiff escorted the sobbing Elsa Griffin from the stand.

Morrison Brems was brought into court.

"I am now going to prove my point another way," Hamilton Burger said. "Mr. Brems, you have already been sworn in this case. You talked with this so-called prowler who emerged from unit number twelve?"

"Yes, sir."

"You saw that prowler leaving the cabin?"

"Yes, sir."

Hamilton Burger said, "I am going to ask Mrs. Stewart G. Bedford, who is in court, to stand up and take off the heavy dark glasses with which she has effectively kept her identity concealed. I am going to ask her to walk across the courtroom in front of this witness."

"Object," Bedford whispered frantically to Mason. "Object. Stop this! Don't let him get away with it!"

"Keep quiet," Mason warned. "If we object now we'll antagonize the jury. Let him go."

"Stand up, Mrs. Bedford," Judge Strouse ordered.

Mrs. Bedford got to her feet.

"Will you kindly remove your glasses?"

"This isn't the proper way of making an identification," Perry Mason said. "There should be a line-up, Your Honor, but we have no objection."

"Come inside the rail here, Mrs. Bedford, right through that gate," Judge Strouse directed. "Now just walk the length of the courtroom, if you will, turn your face to the witness, and—"

"That's the one. That's the one. That's the woman!" Morrison Brems shouted, excitedly.

Ann Roann Bedford stopped abruptly in her stride. She turned to face the witness. "You lie," she said, her voice cold with venom.

Judge Strouse banged his gavel. "There will be no comments except in response to questions asked by counsel," he said. "You may return to your seat, Mrs. Bedford, and you will please refrain from making any comment. Proceed, Mr. Burger."

A grinning Hamilton Burger turned to Perry Mason and made an exaggerated bow. "And now, Mr. Mason," he said, "you may cross-examine—to your heart's content."

"Now just a moment, Mr. District Attorney," Judge Strouse snapped. "That last comment was uncalled for; that is not proper conduct."

"I beg the Court's pardon," Hamilton Burger said, his face suffused with triumph. "I think, if the Court please, I can soon suggest to the Court what happened to the fingerprint evidence, but I'll be *very* glad to hear Mr. Mason cross-examine *this* witness and see what can be done with *his* testimony. However, I do beg the Court's pardon."

"Proceed with the cross-examination," Judge Strouse said to Perry Mason.

Perry Mason rose to his full height, faced Morrison Brems on the stand.

"Have you ever been convicted of a felony, Mr. Brems?"

The witness recoiled as though Mason had struck him.

Hamilton Burger, on his feet, was shouting, "Your Honor, Your Honor! Counsel can't *do* that! That's misconduct! Unless he has some grounds to believe—"

"You can always impeach a witness by showing he has been convicted of a felony," Mason said as Hamilton Burger hesitated, sputtering in his rage.

"Of course you can, of course you can," Hamilton Burger yelled. "But you can't ask questions like that where you haven't anything on which to base such a charge. That's misconduct! That's—"

"Suppose you let him answer the question," Mason said, "and then—"

"It's misconduct! That's unprofessional. That's—"

"I think," Judge Strouse said, "the objection will be overruled. The witness will answer the question."

"Remember," Mason warned, "you're under oath. I'm

asking you the direct question. Have you ever been convicted of a felony?"

The witness who had been so sure of himself as he had regarded Mason a few short seconds earlier seemed to shrivel inside his clothes. He shifted his position uncomfortably. The courtroom silence became oppressive.

"Have you?" Mason asked.

"Yes," Brems said.

"How many times?"

"Three."

"Did you ever use the alias of Harry Elston?"

The witness again hesitated. "You're under oath," Mason reminded him, "and a handwriting expert is going to check your handwriting, so be careful what you say."

"I refuse to answer," the witness said with a sudden desperate attempt at collecting himself. "I refuse to answer on the ground that to do so may incriminate me."

"And," Mason went on, "on the seventh day of April of this year you called on your accomplice Grace Compton who had occupied unit sixteen at The Staylonger Motel on April sixth under the name of Mrs. S. G. Wilfred, and beat her up because she had been talking with me, didn't you?

"Now just a minute, Mr. Brems. Before you answer that question, remember that I had a private detective shadowing Miss Compton, shadowing the apartment house where she lived, noticing the people who went in and out of the apartment, and that I am at the present time in touch with Grace Compton in Acapulco. Now answer the question, did you or didn't you?"

"I refuse to answer," the witness said, "on the ground that to do so might incriminate ne."

Mason turned to the judge, conscious of the open-mouthed jurors literally sitting on the edges of their chairs.

"And now, Your Honor, I suggest that the Court take a recess until we can have an opinion of the police fingerprint expert on these fingerprints and so the police will have some opportunity to reinvestigate the murder."

Mason sat down.

"In view of the situation," Judge Strouse said, "Court will take a recess until two o'clock this afternoon."

■ 21 ■

STEWART BEDFORD, DELLA STREET, PAUL DRAKE, AND Mason sat in Mason's office.

Bedford rubbed his hands over his eyes. "Those damn newspaper photographers," he said. "They've exploded so many flashbulbs in my face I'm completely blinded."

"You'll get over it in an hour or so," Mason told him. "But you'd better let Paul Drake drive you home."

"He won't need to," Bedford said. "My wife is on her way up here. Tell me, Mason, how the devil did *you* know what had happened?"

"I had a few leads to work on," Mason said. "Your story about the hit-and-run accident was of course something you thought up. Therefore, the blackmailers couldn't have anticipated that. But the blackmailers *did* know that you were at The Staylonger Motel because of blackmail which had been levied because of your wife. In order to get a perfect case against you, they wanted to bring your wife into it. Therefore, Morrison Brems, apparently as the thoroughly respectable manager of the motel, stated that he had seen a prowler emerging from unit twelve.

"When you and Grace Compton went out for lunch, Brems realized this was the logical time to drug the whisky, then kill Denham with your gun, loot the lock box which had been held in joint tenancy, and blame the crime on you with the motivation being your desire to stop a continuing blackmail of you and your wife.

"For that reason, Brems wanted to direct suspicion to your wife. Elsa Griffin hadn't fooled him any when she registered under an assumed name and juggled the figures of her license number. So Brems invented this mysterious prowler whom he said he had seen coming out of unit twelve. He gave an absolutely perfect and very detailed description of your wife, one that was so complete that almost anyone who knew her should have recognized her."

"But, look here, Mason, *I* picked that motel."

Mason grinned. "You thought you did. When you check back on the circumstances, you'll realize that at a certain point the blonde told you the coast was clear and to pick any motel. The first one you passed after that was a shabby, second-rate motel. You didn't want that and the blackmailers knew you wouldn't.

"The next one was The Staylonger and you picked that. If you hadn't, the blonde would have steered you in there anyway. You picked it the same way the man from the audience picks out a card from the deck handed him by the stage magician."

"But what about those fingerprints? How did Elsa Griffin get so badly fooled?"

"Elsa," Mason said, "was the first one to swallow the story of Morrison Brems. She fell for it, hook, line, and sinker. As soon as she heard the description of that woman, she became absolutely convinced that your wife had been down there at the motel. She felt certain that, if that had been the case, your wife must have been the one who killed Binney Denham. She wasn't going to say anything unless it appeared your safety was jeopardized.

"I sent her back down to unit twelve in order to get latent fingerprints. She was down there for hours. She had plenty of time not only to get the latent fingerprints, but to compare them as she took them. That is, she compared them with her own prints and when she did she found, to her chagrin, that she hadn't been able to lift a single fingerprint which hadn't been made by her. Yet she was absolutely certain in her own mind that your wife had been down there at the cabin. What she did was thoroughly logical under the circumstances. She was completely loyal to you. She had no loyalty and little affection for your wife. In spite of your instructions she had preserved those fingerprints which had been lifted from the back of the cocktail tray, so after she left the motel she drove to her apartment, got those prints, put numbers on the cards that fitted them in with the prints she was surrendering, and turned the whole batch in to me.

"She knew absolutely then that by the time her fingerprints had been eliminated there would be four prints of your wife left. She didn't intend to do anything about it unless the situation got desperate. Then she intended to use those prints to save you from being convicted.

"I will admit that there was a period when I myself was pretty much concerned about it. Elsa, of course, thought that your wife had worn gloves while she was in the cabin and so hadn't left any fingerprints. I thought that your wife was the one who had been in the cabin until I became fully convinced that she hadn't been."

"Then what did you do?"

"Then," Mason said, "it was very simple. I had fingerprints lifted from Grace Compton's apartment. I placed four of the best of those in my safe. I put the same numbers on the cards that Elsa had put on her cards."

Paul Drake shook his head. "You pulled a fast one there, Perry. They can sure get you for that."

"Get me for what?" Mason asked.

"Substituting evidence."

"I didn't substitute any evidence."

"There's a law on that," Drake said.

"Sure there is," Mason said, "but I didn't substitute any evidence. I told Della Street to get me fourteen, sixteen, twelve, and nine from the safe. That's what she did. Of course, I can't help it if there were two sets of cards with numbers on them, and if Della got the wrong set. That wasn't a substitution. Of course, if Elsa Griffin had asked me if those were the prints she had given me, then I would have had to acknowledge that they weren't, or else have been guilty of deceiving the witness and concealing evidence, but she didn't ask me that question. Neither did she really compare the prints. Since she *knew* these prints she had given me belonged to Mrs. Bedford she simply pretended to make a comparison, then she grabbed the prints and made for the door, where she had arranged to have Sergeant Holcomb waiting. Under the circumstances, I wasn't required to volunteer any information."

"But how the devil did you *know?*" Bedford asked.

Mason said, "It was quite simple. I knew that your wife hadn't left any fingerprints in the cabin because I knew she hadn't been there. Since the description given by Morrison Brems was so completely realistic down to the last detail and fitted your wife so exactly, I knew that Morrison Brems was lying. We all knew that Binney Denham had some hidden accomplice in the background. That is, we felt he did. After Grace Compton had been beaten up because she had talked with me, I knew there must be another accomplice. Who then could that accomplice be?

"The most logical person was Morrison Brems. Binney Denham wanted to pull his blackmailing stunts at a friendly motel where he was in partnership with the manager. You'll probably find that this motel was one of their big sources of income. Morrison Brems ran that motel. When people whose manner looked a little bit surreptitious registered there, Morrison Brems made it a point to check their baggage and their registration and find out who they were. Then the information was relayed to Binney Denham and that's where a lot of Denham's blackmail material came from.

"They made the mistake of trying to gild the lily. They were so anxious to see that your wife was brought into it that they described her as having been down there. The police hadn't connected up the description, but Brems certainly intended to see that they did before the case was over. Elsa Griffin connected it up as soon as she heard it, and kept pestering you to get after me to find the woman who had been down there. When I didn't move fast enough to suit her, she decided to bring in the fingerprints.

"Because she knew they were fingerprints that had been taken from the silver platter and not from the motel where she said she found them, she only went through the motions of comparing them. She was so certain whose prints they were that she just didn't bother to look for distinguishing charactertistics."

"But," Bedford asked, "how did you know they were gilding the lily, Mason? How did you know my wife hadn't been down there?"

Mason looked him in the eyes. "I asked her if she had been there," he said, "and she assured me she hadn't."

"And you did this whole thing, you staked your reputation and everything on her word?"

Mason, still looking at Bedford, said, "In this business, Bedford, you get to be a pretty damn good judge of character or else you don't last long."

"I still don't see how you knew that Brems had a criminal record."

Mason grinned. "I was simply relying on the law of averages and of character. It would have been as impossible for Morrison Brems to have lived as long as he has with the type of mind he has without having a criminal record as it would have been for your wife to have looked me in the eyes and lied about having gone to that cabin."

Knuckles tapped gently on the door of Mason's office.

"That'll be Ann Roann now," Bedford said, getting to his feet. "Mason, how the devil can I ever thank you enough for what you have done?"

Mason's answer was laconic. "Just write thanks underneath your signature when you make out the check."

HAVE YOU READ ALL THESE

MYSTERIES?
TWO COMPLETE NOVELS FOR
THE PRICE OF ONE

➤ AT YOUR BOOKSTORE OR USE THIS COUPON FOR ORDERING. ➤